Into the City of Elversult

Priests of Lath[illegible]
the city from hig[illegible]
spire underneath [illegible]

Corin has been [illegible]
enchanted sword. The former warrior spends his days drinking. . . .

Until he's given an opportunity for a new life by a young half elf named Llasha Moonsliver.

And Corin must set aside his self-pity and regret and focus on saving this young woman's life.

Until his thirst for vengeance gets in the way.

FORGOTTEN REALMS®

The Cities

Temple Hill
Drew Karpyshyn

The City of Ravens
Richard Baker

Other Novels by Drew Karpyshyn

Baldur's Gate II: Throne of Baal

FORGOTTEN REALMS®

The Cities

TEMPLE HILL

Drew Karpyshyn

Wizards of the Coast®

TEMPLE HILL

Distributed in the United States by Holtzbrinck Publishing. Distributed in Canada by Fenn Ltd.

Distributed to the hobby, toy, and comic trade in the United States and Canada by regional distributors.

Distributed worldwide by Wizards of the Coast, Inc. and regional distributors.

Made in the U.S.A.

Cover art by Bradley Williams
Map by Dennis Kauth
First Printing: September 2001
Library of Congress Catalog Card Number: 00-191029

9 8 7 6 5 4 3 2 1

UK ISBN: 0-7869-1947-7
US ISBN: 0-7869-1871-3
620-T21871

U.S., CANADA,
ASIA, PACIFIC, & LATIN AMERICA
Wizards of the Coast, Inc.
P.O. Box 707
Renton, WA 98057-0707
+1-800-324-6496

EUROPEAN HEADQUARTERS
Wizards of the Coast, Belgium
P.B. 2031
2600 Berchem
Belgium
+32-70-23-32-77

Visit our web site at **www.wizards.com/forgottenrealms**

Dedication

For my wife Jen.
You are my love, my world.

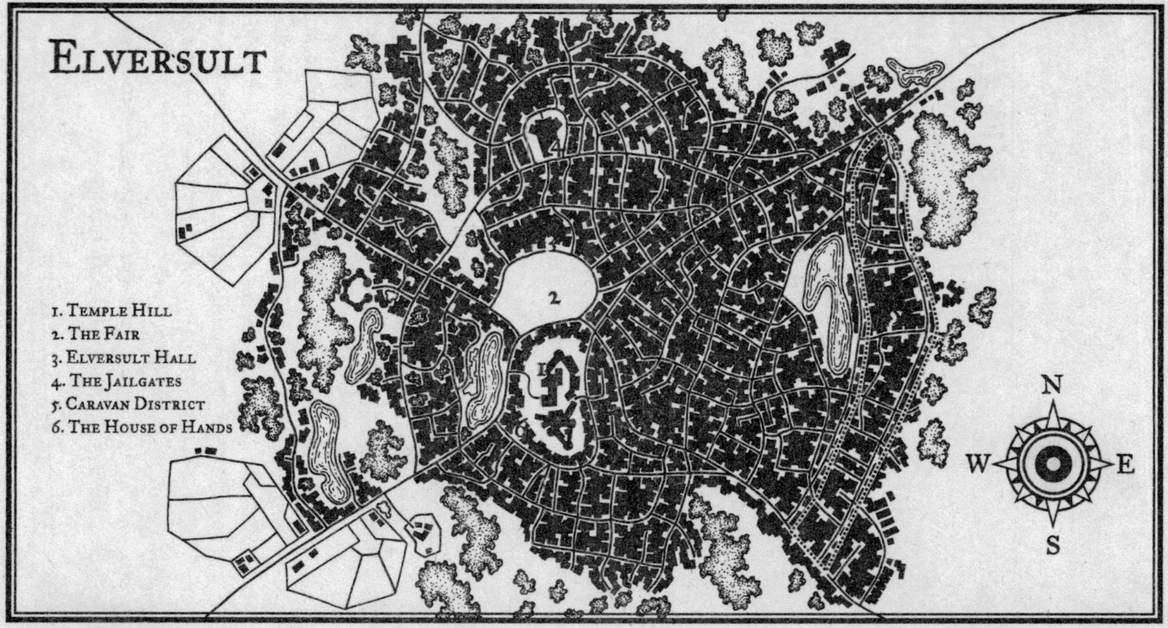
ELVERSULT
1. TEMPLE HILL
2. THE FAIR
3. ELVERSULT HALL
4. THE JAILGATES
5. CARAVAN DISTRICT
6. THE HOUSE OF HANDS
N
W
E
S

CHAPTER ONE

Alturiak, 1370 DR

Corin felt them before he saw them, felt them just as sure as he had felt the coming storm that had been raining down on them for the last hour. After a year of working for Igland's White Shields, escorting dozens upon dozens of caravans between Elversult and Iriabor, he had developed a sixth sense for these things.

Thunder broke overhead, and lightning illuminated the landscape for a brief second. Corin saw nothing out of the ordinary, but still he *knew*. He held up a clenched fist and pulled his mount up short. Behind him the other nine members of the White Shield Company did the same. Corin wasn't their official leader, but the others in the company respected him for his skill with a blade and his composure in the heat of battle. Despite his youth, they knew to trust his instincts; that was why Igland had him riding point.

The passenger coach that the Shields surrounded ground to a halt as well, and the door flew open. Fhazail's fat form rolled out from the carriage, a broad umbrella spread above to keep the downpour from ruining his fashionable courtier's clothes.

"What's going on here?" he wheezed to Igland, Captain of the White Shields.

"Something's not right," Igland answered. "Get back inside before the trouble hits."

Fhazail peered about, his beady eyes squinting through the storm. "I don't see anything except rain clouds. Are you telling me you're afraid of a little thunder and lightning?"

"Bandits," Corin said in a low voice. "Nearby. They'll hit us any minute."

"Impossible!" Fhazail sputtered, his jowls quivering. "How could you know that?" Turning from Corin, he addressed the captain, nervously twisting one of the heavy gold rings on his right hand, rotating the gemstone set into the face completely around his sausagelike finger. "You told me a small group of armed soldiers wouldn't attract attention, you promised we'd be safe if we went with your company!" His eyes narrowed even farther as he cast suspicious glances at the armed men surrounding him. "I could have hired fifty soldiers to protect Lord Harlaran's son, but you convinced me to use your small company instead!"

It was untrue, of course. Fhazail had chosen the White Shields because they were a fraction of the cost of hiring a full merchant escort. Corin suspected the steward had informed Lord Harlaran that he was hiring a virtual army to escort his son, then pocketed the difference. The gaudy jewelry on his right hand was matched by equally ostentatious, and expensive, rings on his right.

"Captain," Fhazail added in a softer voice, "did you betray me?"

Igland's reply was stiff and cold. "The White Shields are not traitors."

"Everyone's a traitor for the right price," Fhazail returned, rubbing his double chin and eyeing Corin in particular.

Igland ignored the insinuation. "There's always bandits

on the Trader Road, Corin just has a sixth sense for when they will attack."

Corin returned Fhazail's glare and said, "They probably don't even know who the boy's father is—kidnapping and ransom are likely the last things on their minds. They'd attack just for those bands of gold around your fingers, and the satisfaction of slitting our throats."

Fhazail was about to reply when a single arrow buried itself in the soft earth just inches from his feet. He stared down in surprise, then scampered back into the coach as several more shot into the wooden roof of the carriage. Suddenly the dark sky was filled with missiles launched from the hidden bandits' bows, falling down on Corin and the others like the rain that had drenched them for the past hour. The driver of the coach leaped down from his unprotected seat and squeezed his way inside the carriage over the protests of Fhazail. Rain was one thing, a storm of arrows was quite another.

Most of the arrows landed harmlessly on the ground. Some would have fallen on the men and their mounts as they closed ranks, but they threw up their painted broad shields, for which they were named, over their heads to catch the deadly projectiles. The few that made it past the soldiers' shield canopy bounced harmlessly off their mailed shirts.

Moments later a second volley landed with similar ineffective results. The bandits attacked, a ragtag collection of twenty or so humans on foot, with the odd orc and goblin thrown in for good measure. They appeared all at once, pouring out from behind the hillocks and mounds that lined the road, screaming with battle lust as they formed a disorganized horde in the middle of the Trader Road.

Corin knew the arrows had been merely a decoy, a chance for the robbers to close the distance between themselves and the caravan, negating the chance of a wizard wiping out the whole band with a single spell of mass destruction. However, there were no wizards in Igland's company. His men preferred the honest strength of forged steel and a well-trained sword arm.

As a single unit Igland's men charged forward through the downpour, lowering their heavy lances in unison. Their mounts splashed through the puddles in the road, churning up great clods of mud in their wake. Foolishly the bandits kept rushing head on, gathered in a tight little group in the center of the road as if they wanted to be ground under the heavy hooves of the war-horses.

Corin braced his lance in the stirrup and with his free hand wiped the rain from his forehead. He relished the coming slaughter—for slaughter it would be. Most of their foes would be trampled beneath the initial charge, the survivors would be run down by the riders even as they fled back into the hills. It was almost too simple.

Through the darkness of the storm and the torrential rains none of them ever saw the trip wires stretched across the road. The front runners went down, the horses flipping and twisting as the ropes entangled their legs, the riders tossed from their mounts to land with stunning force on the road before them, their heavy lances torn from their grasp and sent hurtling through the air. The second rank was too close behind them to pull up, and another set of snares sent them tumbling to the soaked earth in a chaotic mass of beasts and men sliding through the mud. The weight of their armor dragged the soldiers down, momentarily pinning them to the ground, unable to evade the final rank of riders, unhorsing them as well and spreading the carnage through all of Igland's company. The rhythmic thunder of charging hooves disintegrated into the cacophony of crashing armor, neighing horses, and screaming men.

Corin was thrown from his horse, miraculously landing uninjured in the soft mud. But even as he tried to roll to the side he was swept up in the chaos, carried along by the force of the charge, swallowed up by the rolling, crashing herd of dying men and animals. Limbs were crushed and skulls were trampled or kicked in by the iron shoes of the fallen horses; the mounts shrieked neighs of terror and pain as leg bones splintered and were ground to dust by the onslaught of their own mass and momentum.

The soldiers lay strewn about the road. Several bodies were mangled, limbs jutting out at unnatural angles, compound fractures protruding through skin or bulging obscenely beneath their mailed suits of armor. The horses lay beside their masters, kicking and thrashing in blind agony, as lethal to their owners now as they had been to their enemies in glorious battles of the past.

Corin crawled clear of the fallen men and writhing mounts and rose hastily to his feet. He had suffered no worse than bumps and bruises, though he had lost both his shield and lance in the fall. Somehow his sword was still in its scabbard, strapped to his side. Through the rain he noticed several other forms struggle to their feet, maybe half a dozen in all, to face the coming assault.

Corin didn't even have time to draw his weapon before the bandits fell on them. A goblin charged at him, waving a cruel looking short sword above his head. Corin lunged forward, colliding with his onrushing assailant and catching his attacker by surprise. On the wet ground footing was unsure, and the goblin bowled Corin over. As he fell Corin grabbed his attacker in a bear hug, dragging his startled adversary down with him. They struggled together, rolling through the muck as Corin tried to use his size and strength to gain the upper hand. The goblin stabbed with short, ineffective strokes, unable to put enough force into the blows to pierce Corin's armor in such close quarters.

A second goblin raced over to join in the fray, eager to strike a blow, looking for a clear shot at Corin. Corin made sure that shot never came, twisting and turning so that the first goblin's body was always between himself and this new opponent. The second goblin danced around the pair as they wrestled in the mud, slipping and sliding as he waited for an opening. Finally he gave up and began hacking indiscriminately at the tangled pair.

The first goblin screamed as his companion's blade bit deep into his back, severing the spinal cord. In one smooth motion Corin, still lying beneath the twitching body of his opponent, wrenched the short sword free from the now paralyzed hand of his first attacker and used it to slash at the unprotected leg of the second goblin hovering over them. The sword bit deep into the flesh, slicing through the tendon. With a howl the goblin collapsed on the ground, bringing his exposed throat within range of Corin's next blow. Corin did not miss.

He then rolled the paralyzed first goblin off him and dispatched his now helpless enemy with a single blow. He scrambled to his feet and pulled out his own long sword, quickly surveying the battle scene. Several figures were moving cautiously through the fallen bodies of the horses and soldiers. Orcs, likely, looking to finish off the wounded and steal some small trinket from the dead that they could keep hidden from the rest of the gang. Several more robbers had surrounded the carriage, preventing any chance of escape for the driver, Fhazail and the nobleman's young son.

Corin's brothers-in-arms, the four that were still standing, were on the defensive. They stood on the far side of the road, back to back in a small circle, swords weaving tight patterns in the air as they held their enemies momentarily at bay. Through the gloom of the storm Corin could make out several fallen bandits at the feet of his friends, and he recognized the distinctive armor of Igland among the four still standing. His companions faced overwhelming odds, completely surrounded by at least a dozen armed opponents who were only waiting for the reinforcements to finish their looting of Corin's fallen comrades before they moved in.

Corin sprinted across the road, his feet skidding across the wet earth, brandishing his blade above his head and screaming his battle lust to the broiling thunderclouds overhead. Several of the bandits spun to meet Corin's charge, turning their backs on the four soldiers in the middle of the pack. The soldiers acted instinctively, moving as one—the result of years of training and drills—attacking the suddenly exposed backs of their opponents.

Before the rest of the bandits could even react, four of their number lay dead or dying, and the soldiers had broken free of the confining circle. A second later Corin joined the battle, and the bandits found themselves being pressed on two fronts. With a single command from Igland the White Shields took the offensive.

Corin waded through the rabble of poorly equipped bandits, easily parrying the unskilled slashes and swipes of their rusty swords and returning them with lethally effective cuts and thrusts of his own finely wrought weapon. He carved a swath through his opponents, mowing them down like so much grain at the harvest, then turned for another pass.

In his peripheral vision he noticed his companions wreaking similar havoc on their incompetent foes. The bandits—disorganized, untrained cowards at heart—scattered beneath the fury of the White Shields' wrath. Corin took a step after them, but pulled up short when he heard Igland's voice shouting above the storm.

"Let them go, Corin! We have to protect the boy."

Corin turned his attention back to the carriage. The horses had been unhitched, leaving the carriage stranded in the road. The coach driver lay face down on the ground, motionless. Corin could make out the fleshy mountain of Fhazail through the carriage window, and another figure as well. It was too large to be Lord Harlaran's son, Corin assumed it was one of the robbers. He prayed the bandit was just tying Fhazail and the boy up, and not slitting their throats.

A half-dozen men stood near the coach, prepared for battle. From the way they held their weapons Corin could tell these were not the untrained fodder he had just dispatched with such ease, but experienced mercenaries. A second later the men were joined by four figures slinking in from the darkness—the orcs had finished their looting, and were now ready to fight.

"Ten against five," Igland muttered. "I like our chances."

There was no mad rush forward this time. Both parties knew a foolish mistake would mean certain death. The White Shields advanced slowly in a loose formation, the bandits spreading out as they approached. Igland barked a command, and Corin and one of the other soldiers slid back a step to guard against anyone trying to flank them.

For a brief second they faced each other—highway robbers and hired guards, buffeted by the howling wind and driving rain of the raging tempest.

From the carriage Fhazail's voice called out in a blubbery whine, "The leader tells me that if you throw down your weapons they'll let us all live. All they want is to ransom the boy. They don't want to hurt anyone."

Igland gave a contemptuous laugh. "Even you aren't gullible enough to believe that, are you Fhazail? The only one they care about is the boy. The rest of us are nothing but dragon meat to them. This ends in one of two ways, with their deaths or ours."

There was nothing more to say, the battle began. Igland's men pressed forward, maintaining their loose formation. The bandits held their ground, but Corin could already tell they weren't used to fighting as a unit. Though outnumbering their foes, the bandits weren't able to coordinate their efforts. They took turns engaging the soldiers, attacking, thrusting and parrying before falling back to allow another man to move in for a pass.

The strange, hypnotic rhythm of combat began to take hold of the bandits: advance, attack, parry, retreat, switch. They became predictable. After repelling only a few offensives Corin already knew all the moves of the two men facing him, knew how to counter their every blow. He picked up the rhythms of one of his foes—advance, attack, parry—but when the bandit tried to disengage, Corin was ready. Leaping forward he brought his sword in low and quick, forcing his opponent to take a hasty step back, throwing him off balance. Before he could recover Corin reversed the path of his sword with a flick of his wrist and a turn of his body and brought the blade in high. The bandit had to twist and lean back to avoid the blow causing him to stumble awkwardly on the slippery ground. Using both hands Corin slashed down in a diagonal arc. The bandit parried the blow, but the force nearly knocked the sword from his hand and deflected the bandit's own blade downward, leaving his chest exposed. Corin thrust forward, felt the point of his weapon penetrate the mail shirt, pierce the breastbone, and run deep into the chest cavity of his opponent. The entire sequence had taken less than a second.

Corin wrenched his sword free from his dying enemy to catch the wild stroke of his second foe. He had left himself vulnerable in finishing off the first bandit, but his remaining opponent had been too slow to capitalize on it—just as Corin knew he would. Corin kicked out with his boot, landing a sharp blow to the bandit's knee. The leg crumpled for a brief second, and as the bandit's weight slumped forward Corin brought the hilt of his sword crashing into the man's jaw, sending him reeling back, his arms pinwheeling to keep his balance as his weapon slipped from his grasp. Corin bounded after his foe. Somehow he managed to keep his footing through the muck and mire that used to be the road, his sword carving wide sweeping arcs through the air at belt level, each swipe a few inches closer to the madly retreating bandit than the one before. After three passes Corin made contact, slicing a shallow incision through both armor and skin. The fourth pass bit deep into the bandit's stomach, ripping a savage gash through his midriff. Corin spun to face the rest of the battle even as the dying man clutched at the intestines and blood pouring out of his ruptured stomach.

Two other bandits were down, orcs, both of them dispatched by Igland. The other soldiers were holding their own, and Corin could see it was only a matter of time before the victory was theirs. Before Corin could re-join the melee he noticed Igland on the far side of the battlefield gesturing frantically at the carriage.

A single orc had emerged from the coach—the figure Corin had noticed through the window. It was hitching the horses back up and getting ready to ride off with Fhazail and the boy while the others kept the White Shields occupied.

Corin and Igland raced toward the lone figure. Igland was closer, he reached the wagon just as the orc finished hitching the horses up. The orc turned to face him, drawing its sword. The blade glowed faintly in the darkness.

Corin was on the far side of the battle, he had to weave his way through the soldiers and bandits still locked in combat to reach his goal, floundering through the mud. He ducked to avoid a wild blow by one of the bandits as he raced by, but lost his balance and landed unceremoniously on his backside. Luckily his momentum carried him past the fray, sliding through the ooze like he used to do as a child after the spring rains turned the untilled fields into one giant mud pit.

He scrambled back to his feet and saw Igland writhing on the ground, his hands clutching at a stump that used to be his left leg. The orc towered over the fallen leader of the White Shields, relishing its opponent's suffering for a brief instant before raising its glowing blade above its head. No!" Corin screamed, too far to help but close enough to hear the sound of metal hacking through helmet and bone as the orc brought the killing blow down on Igland's skull.

The orc looked up from its victim to face its new opponent. Its shoulders were broad and powerful, its bare arms knotted by muscle and sinew. Its massive chest was covered with black chain armor, its legs were covered to the knee by a kilt of black iron links, and below the knee by heavy black boots. Its head was covered by a black iron skullcap, and its eyes glowed with hate and evil from below the helm. Corin was close enough now to pierce the gloom and stare directly into the hate filled gaze. *Up* into the hate filled gaze. The orc towered over Corin, by far the biggest he had ever seen.

"Orog," Corin whispered to himself.

A genetically superior race of orc, some said. A hideous cross breed of orc and ogre, others insisted. Corin had heard of these creatures, but had never faced one before. It brought its huge sword up with both hands—the blade was a foot longer than Corin's own and at least twice as thick—and stood poised in this position, boots sinking ever so slightly into the rain-softened ground.

Corin approached cautiously, sizing up his opponent. The stance was unorthodox, yet Corin sensed it was not a sign of inexperience. His opponent stood motionless as Corin moved in, its sword dripping with blood and rain, glowing faintly with its own eerie light. Corin didn't need to see the etchings on the blade to know it was a weapon of evil magic.

Corin lunged forward, a quick feint, then drew back. The orog brought the blade straight down, as if chopping wood. Corin easily avoided the blow, but before he could regain his balance on the slick earth and counter, the orog was already in the process of delivering another stroke. Corin gave ground and parried with his own blade. The heavy sword struck his own, sending shock waves of vibration through Corin's sword arm. A heavy boot caught him in the chest and knocked him onto his back, but he rolled to the side and avoided a lethal strike. He sprang to his feet, but the orog had already recovered and was launching a new assault. Corin slipped and staggered back, ducking and dodging the fierce blade as it ripped through the air. The fury of the orog's onslaught kept him off balance, leaving him completely on the defensive, unable to even attempt any type of counter attack.

Yet even as he was being all but overrun by his opponent, Corin knew he had the advantage. He continued to retreat, splashing through puddles and drawing the orog ever closer to the main battle, and farther and farther away from the prisoners and the coach he intended to use as an escape. Soon, Corin knew his friends would finish off the bandits and come to join him, overwhelming the orog with their coordinated efforts.

Suddenly the orog paused, an uncertain look on its repulsive, rain drenched face. It stared for a brief second at the figures engaged in combat over Corin's shoulder, watching as the last two bandits fell beneath the blades of three White Shields acting in concert. Then it cast a quick glance back at the carriage, seeming to realize the predicament it was in. Corin took the opportunity to lunge forward with his sword. At the last second the orog reacted to the thrust, turning to the side to avoid the blade and driving a burly shoulder into Corin's chest, sending him stumbling to the ground. But rather than finish Corin off and then face the three remaining soldiers, the orog turned and began a loping run back to the coach.

Corin followed, and heard the battle cries of his companions behind him as they rushed to catch up. The orog's size was a disadvantage now, its great boots sank into the mud with every step, slowing it down. Corin would catch up before they reached the coach. Then all he had to do was slow the monster down long enough for the others to join in.

Ten feet from the coach the creature turned to face him. Again it swung its massive weapon, this time in a sweeping overhand stroke. Corin dropped to one knee to absorb the force of the impact. He held his own blade out in front of him, parallel to the ground, braced to catch the blow. The orog's fierce weapon met with Corin's own, and its faint glow erupted in a blinding flash of magic. The weapon shattered Corin's own blade, its momentum barely even slowed as it continued on its arc, slicing through Corin's outstretched arm. The blade bit clean through Corin's sword arm just below the elbow, effortlessly carving armor, skin, sinew, and bone.

The force of the blow threw Corin onto his back, his severed hand dropped twitching to the ground beside him. The pain shooting up from the bloody stump that was once his hand nearly blinded Corin, but his warrior training forced his body to react instinctively. His legs pushed out hard against the ground, somersaulting him backward away from the killing blow.

The orog took a quick swipe at Corin as he rolled out of range, but the sight of the other White Shields quickly closing ground kept it from pursuing its crippled foe. Instead, it turned and took three huge strides, then leaped up into the driver's seat of the coach. Corin struggled to his knees, covered in slime and mud, still clutching his bloody stump and trying to staunch the flow of blood.

The orog stared down at him for a brief second, then in a thick growl shouted out above the fury of the storm, "When they ask who took your hand, human, tell them it was Graal!"

With that he whipped the horses once and the carriage lurched forward, rumbling off to disappear into the storm.

Two years later, Corin woke with a start, tipping his mug and spilling ale onto the tavern floor. The scream of rage and despair died in his throat as the nightmare faded away to be replaced by the dank surroundings of the Weeping Griffin, possibly the worst tavern in the whole of the Dragon Coast.

Instantly he knew where he was. He spent most afternoons there, huddled by himself at a table in the corner drinking until he passed out. Evenings and mornings, too. The ale was flat, stale, and bitter. More often than not roaches and other insects would be found drowned at the bottom of an empty flagon. The serving wenches were old and withered, their tongues sharp with age and made cruel by their own defeats. But the ale was cheap, and none of the other patrons here bothered him. They had problems of their own.

He rose unsteadily to his feet and fished a couple coppers from the pouch at his belt, then dropped them on the table. He staggered across the bar and out into the street, squinting against the brightness of the late afternoon sun. He wove his drunken way down the city street, staring at the ground; his left hand unconsciously rubbing the stump that was once the best sword arm in the now defunct White Shield Company of Elversult.

CHAPTER TWO

Two years later . . .

The brisk morning wind tugged softly at Lhasha's red silk scarf. Although it rarely fell below freezing in Elversult, the early mornings still held a little nip in the first tenday after the Midwinter Festival. The month of Alturiak wasn't called the Claws of Winter without reason.

By noon, Lhasha knew, the sun would be out and the light, long-sleeved orange blouse she wore would be more than adequate, but as she watched the faint fog of her own breath as it hit the cool morning air Lhasha regretted leaving her fur-lined cape back in her room. She pulled her arms in tight to her small body, grasping her elbows with tiny, graceful fingers. She felt a chill run down her neck and shivered. This time it was more than just the wind.

Lhasha could feel someone watching her. She glanced from side to side, but the shoppers in the Fair, Elversult's open air market, were all preoccupied with their own business.

Despite standing just a hair over five feet and weighing a shade less than a hundred pounds Lhasha was used to being noticed in a crowd. She was accustomed to the appreciative stares of men as they admired her silvery-blonde hair and her fine features, or the envious gazes of women as they mentally appraised the brightly colored silk outfits Lhasha always wore. She enjoyed being the center of attention.

This feeling was different. Threatening. Intimidating. Last night someone had followed her back to her room at the Wyvern's Pipe. Someone had crept in while she slept. And someone had left a dagger embedded in the pillow just inches from her head.

The warning hadn't been completely unexpected. Lhasha was one of the most successful, and last remaining, independent cat burglars in the city. She knew her stubborn refusal to join the Purple Masks, the local thieves' guild, was bound to have consequences. The telltale purple cloth wrapped around the dagger's handle left no doubt as to who was behind the visit.

She cast another quick glance over the crowd, looking for anything out of the ordinary. The Fair was busy. Not as busy as it would be after the Festival of Greengrass, but even during the final month of winter the Fair did a brisk business. Shopkeepers and merchants hawked their wares. Housewives, stable hands, tradesmen, mercenaries, and adventurers browsed the shops and booths. Humans, dwarves, gnomes, halflings, and even the odd elf gathered daily in the Fair to conduct their business and contribute to the trade that was the economic lifeblood of Elversult.

Lhasha noticed a patrol of city Maces watching over the crowds. Ever since Yanseldara had come to power, Elversult had been marked by a dramatic increase in the numbers of the city guard. Lhasha had yet to run across a party of Maces while ransacking the living room of a rich nobleman, so unlike many of Elversult's criminal element, she appreciated the order the constables brought to the once violent streets of the city.

The vigilant, visible presence of the Elversult authorities

calmed Lhasha's nerves and helped her put things in a more rational light. Her unease was simply unfounded paranoia, an understandable reaction to the dagger in her pillow. There was no reason for the Masks to be following her right now. They had made their point last night—join the guild, or get out of the business.

Lhasha was too independent to ever join the guild, and she was far too young to retire. That didn't leave her with a lot of options. A second visit from the Masks wouldn't end with just a warning. She could leave town, set up business somewhere else. But where could she go? All the major trade centers along the Dragon Coast had established thieves' guilds running the show. In Teziir the Astorians would be more likely to break your knees as a warning than leave a dagger behind. In Westgate the Night Masks wouldn't have given her any warning at all.

As for the cities beyond the Dragon Coast . . .well, Lhasha didn't know much about them at all. Rumors, tall tales and hearsay was the limit of her understanding of what lay beyond her homeland. Fendel might know something about them, she thought. The old gnome was her closest, dearest, wisest friend. Her only friend, to be truthful, but that didn't diminish his wisdom. If anyone could see a way out of Lhasha's dilemma it would be Fendel.

Lost in her thoughts, Lhasha wasn't paying close attention to where she was going. She hadn't noticed the drunken soldier staggering through the crowd, oblivious of everyone else in his inebriated state. The man outweighed her by at least a hundred pounds, and when they collided Lhasha was sent reeling to the ground. The soldier tottered, but managed to keep his balance despite the alcohol coursing through his veins. He didn't stop to help her up, didn't pause to apologize—just continued to bull his way heedlessly through the crowd.

A host of voices flooded in on her as several male hands eagerly helped her to her feet.

"Are you all right?"

"Did he hurt you?"

"The Maces should arrest the drunken lout!"

"I'm fine," Lhasha assured the shoppers who had jumped to her rescue. As she brushed herself off she added, "Don't call the Maces, its not worth it. Just let him go."

The half dozen men gathered around her slowly dispersed, casting hateful glares at the soldier's heedless back, muttering to themselves about the death of chivalry and lack of decent manners in today's society. Lhasha herself didn't stay to cast aspersions on the soldier, but slipped away into the crowd, the money purse of her rude assailant tucked away beneath the sleeve of her billowing blouse.

Picking his pocket had been pure instinct. When their bodies collided her hands had just reacted—bump and lift, a skill so basic to her profession it was virtually automatic. Now that the deed was done, Lhasha felt more than a little satisfaction at the small measure of revenge she had extracted from the drunken soldier's belt.

She let the small leather pouch slip from her sleeve into her palm. It felt light, almost empty. Strange, considering how well soldiers and mercenaries were paid in this city. She undid the drawstrings and peeked inside—three coppers. Not even enough to buy a decent meal. This was why she preferred burglary, the payoffs were almost always worth the effort.

Lhasha quickened her pace and doubled back through the throng of shoppers, curious to see what kind of a man came down to the Fair with so little money on him. Her quarry was easy to spot; he left a wake of upset shoppers and angry curses as he stumbled through the crowd.

He stood about six feet tall, with a solid build and dark hair. A scraggly, ill-kept beard covered his chin and cheeks. He wore chain armor, and a sword was strapped to his hip. But his armor was rusted and stained, his scabbard shabby and worn. Lhasha felt the first rumblings of guilt. With burglary she could chose her victims carefully, scouting them out before making her move. She never stole from those who couldn't afford it. Lhasha herself knew all too well what it was like to be poor, to go to bed hungry, or to sleep on the street because you couldn't afford a room. Still, it wasn't her fault the drunkard had bowled her over.

Lhasha was still debating her next move when she noticed the soldier's arm—or rather, the lack of it. Everything a few inches below his right elbow was missing. Lhasha had no ethical qualms about lifting trinkets and baubles from wealthy nobles, but she wasn't about to steal the last coppers from a destitute cripple.

She'd have to put the purse back. She quietly slipped through the crowd, edging ever closer to the one-armed man. Lhasha had never tried to "unpick" a pocket before, but how hard could it be, given the soldier's current condition? He kept his eyes straight ahead, completely ignoring the other people in the street. Even when he knocked into them he would simply bounce off and continue on his way without a second glance.

The weaving, uneven steps of her target made it difficult for Lhasha to time her move. She tried to anticipate whether the inebriated man would sway to the left or list to the right, but she continually guessed wrong. When the soldier bumped into a rather heavyset man in blue robes and staggered back against her, Lhasha seized the opportunity and jammed the purse back under his belt—only to see it fall to the ground after the soldier had taken a few more unsteady strides.

Cursing silently, Lhasha was forced to admit that unpicking a pocket was proving to be no simple task.

"What do you make of that, Captain?" Gareth had only been in the Maces a month, and despite his eagerness, he had sense enough to wait for orders from his superiors before taking action.

Kayla, Captain of Elversult's thirty-first watch unit, turned her attention in the direction the young man pointed. An attractive young blonde lady—barely old enough to be called a woman, Kayla thought—in finely tailored, brightly colored clothes was following very closely in the path of a drunk lurching down the street. She was hunched forward, hands reaching out toward the drunk as he shoved his way through the throng. Every few seconds the woman would lunge forward, several times appearing to slip her hand beneath the drunk's belt, or trying to, at least. Occasionally the girl would pause, pick something up from the ground, then resume her strange behavior. The man was completely oblivious to the bizarre charade.

"I think she's trying to pick his pocket," Kayla said at last, still not quite convinced. "But she must be the worst pickpocket the Dragon Coast has ever seen."

"Should we bring her in?" Gareth asked, already drawing the weapon for which the city soldiers were named.

Kayla held up a hand to stay the anxious rookie. "I don't think we'll need that to bring in one girl." Noticing the sword strapped to the drunken man's belt she added, "But be ready just in case."

On a single order from Kayla the five member unit began to move in on the unsuspecting woman, still hunched forward and completely absorbed in her work.

The crowd, recognizing the uniforms of the city constables, parted before the Maces. In less than a minute they had fallen into step behind their quarry, close enough to hear the young lady exclaim, "At last!" in an exasperated voice as she abruptly stopped, stood up straight, and cracked her back.

Kayla clamped a firm hand down upon the woman's shoulder, and the girl let out a shriek.

CHAPTER THREE

Corin staggered through the crowd, tuning out all the sounds of the Fair—snippets of conversations, the haggling of the customers, the merchants barking out their inventories, even the angry shouts of those foolish enough to get in his way. Protected by a fog of alcohol and apathy he managed to ignore it all. Yet when he heard a woman's scream right behind him his ingrained White Shield training to guard and protect took over.

Reacting to the sound, he spun on his heel and dropped into a fighting crouch, his left hand falling to the hilt of his blade. He may have been too drunk to walk a straight line, but a dozen years of drills and exercises still allowed his muscles to react to combat situations with military precision.

The scene behind him was not what he expected. A blonde girl was being accosted by a group of thugs. No, Corin realized, it wasn't a girl. Despite the waifish features and slight build, the blonde was definitely a woman—though her age was difficult to determine. She looked to be twenty, at most, but Corin thought he could detect a faint trace of elf heritage in her sharp features. If she had elf blood in her veins she might very well be over fifty, despite her appearance.

A much larger brunette woman in full scale armor had grabbed the small blonde by the shoulder. A few feet away four men stood ready, weapons drawn. Maces. The bitterness and anger perpetually simmering just beneath Corin's surface boiled over at the sight of the Elversult city guards.

"Release the girl, or I swear by Helm's Hands I'll crack your skull."

The armored woman's jaw dropped open, her expression one of horrified surprise. Behind her the other Maces recoiled at his words, as if the venom in Corin's voice had stung their cheeks.

Corin took an unsteady step forward, and half drew his sword. "I said . . . let . . . her . . . go."

The brunette woman flinched beneath his hate-filled gazed, but held her ground. "We just saved you from becoming the victim of a crime," she said slowly, as if speaking to a child too young to understand the situation. "The least you could do is thank us."

Corin had no intention of thanking anyone, least of all a patronizing member of the Elversult city guard. "Crime?" he asked the woman sarcastically. "I don't see any crime here."

One of the guards in the background, a young man, stepped up to stand beside his female partner. He pointed the butt of his mace at the blonde. "This woman just picked your pocket."

The blonde girl began to protest her innocence, but Corin ignored her, just as he had earlier ignored the sounds of the Fair. Keeping his eyes focused on the soldiers in front of him, Corin slid the stump of his right arm beneath his belt, working it through the loop of the drawstrings on his money purse. He held the leather pouch up as proof that the guard was lying. It dangled from his amputated limb.

"There's nothing so cowardly as making false accusations."

There was no reply. The Maces just stared at Corin's severed arm. Corin endured their gawking for a few seconds, then sheathed his sword and grabbed his purse with his left hand, stuffing it back under his belt.

"What else could I expect from the Maces, but incompetence?"

The young man tried to step forward and say something, rising to the bait, but the brunette woman—obviously the captain of the patrol—held out an arm to block his path.

"Let it go, Gareth," she said to him over her shoulder, cutting off his words. "We're here to keep the peace, not pick fights."

The young man refused to be cowed. "We keep these streets safe!" he shouted from his spot behind his captain, jabbing his finger in Corin's direction. "We deserve your respect!"

Corin spit on the ground. He could have been a Mace, had even applied to the city guard after the White Shields disbanded, but they had refused him because of the injury to his arm, hadn't even given him a chance.

"You think you're something special, just because you wear a uniform?" he shot back at the young man. "Even with one hand, I'm more soldier than you'll ever be."

From the corner of his eyes Corin noticed the blonde edging toward the crowd of curious onlookers that now gathered around the confrontation. The patrol captain noticed as well. She snapped out her hand, grabbing a fistful of the smaller woman's silk blouse to prevent her escape. "The only place you're going is the Jailgates, my pretty pickpocket."

Gareth, no longer held back by his captain, took a long stride that brought his face just inches away from Corin's own unshaven mug. He grimaced at the reek of alcohol and unwashed sweat cloaking the one-armed man, but didn't recoil.

"We've brought order and discipline to this city! Without us there'd be anarchy!"

He had more to say, but Corin ignored the tirade as he sized up his chances in a fight. One-on-one he was a match for any city constable, even with nearly a dozen ales in his gullet. But faced with overwhelming odds he wouldn't be able to let the rhythm of the battle develop, he wouldn't get a chance to pick up the subtle patterns of his opponents' thrusts and parries and exploit them. Outnumbered five to one Corin's only hope was blind rage and desperate fury, a clumsy, ineffective way to fight. Eventually they'd overpower him and haul him off to the Jailgates. The smart thing to do was walk away.

The young Mace, Gareth, was still shouting into Corin's face. "We protect those who can't protect themselves—like drunks and cripples!"

Corin's head-butt dropped Gareth to the street, smashing the young man's nose in an eruption of blood. Gasps of horror came from the crowd surrounding them, mingled with a few cheers. Caught off guard by Corin's violent outburst, the remaining members of the patrol hesitated a split second before reacting. Corin didn't.

He dropped another of the city guards with a kick to the knee, and by the time the pop of the dislocated joint reached his ears Corin had already drawn his sword and brought the flat of his blade down across the helm of the third man, stunning him. Corin, despite the dual fogs of alcohol and rage, still had enough self-control to keep from using his sword's lethal edge on an Elversult guard officer.

The fourth Mace had the sense to jump out of the reach of Corin's initial mad rush. He swung his weapon in a low arc, looking to sweep Corin's legs out from under him.

Corin parried the blow and retreated—right into range of the female captain's attack. Her weapon missed his temple by inches, but came crashing down across his right shoulder.

Corin's arm went numb and his knees buckled under the force of the blow, but he managed to keep his feet. He threw his elbow back and was rewarded with a painful grunt from the patrol captain as he caught her in the chest. The man still standing in front of him swung his mace in a downward arc, but Corin spun away to the side.

The crowd had formed a wide circle around the melee—safely out of range of the violence, but close enough to watch and egg the participants on. Violence in Elversult's street was officially discouraged since Yanseldara came to power, but a good street brawl could still get the general population fired up with bloodlust.

As Corin spun away from yet another of his opponent's attacks, he caught a glimpse of the blonde disappearing into the circle of enthusiastic spectators.

One of the Maces on the ground—the one with the dislocated knee—grabbed Corin by the ankle. Corin stomped down quickly with his free leg, leaving the pattern of his boot on the man's forehead as he kicked his opponent into unconsciousness.

While Corin was distracted by the man at his feet, the captain and the other Mace still standing tackled him, dragging the enraged warrior down to the ground, but they couldn't pin him. Punching, kicking, and twisting wildly he managed to work himself free and scramble away from his would-be captors—though he lost his sword in the struggle.

On his feet again, facing his opponents, Corin knew his chance had come and gone. The Mace Corin had dazed with the flat of his sword had risen to his feet. The young man with the broken nose was also up again, the front of his armor coated in blood. The two men now stood in formation with their captain and the fourth man who had survived Corin's initial assault. Reckless fury and the element of surprise had been Corin's only advantages, but his first mad rush had succeeded in incapacitating only one of his five opponents. Now with his sword out of reach on the ground Corin was weaponless, and confronting four armed and ready guards in battle formation.

The Maces advanced cautiously, spreading out into a wide semicircle. Corin could do little but wait for what he knew would be a coordinated attack he couldn't possibly hope to ward off.

The young one, Gareth, screamed and dropped his weapon. Hopping on one leg, he clutched at his other foot, the hilt of a tiny poniard protruding from the tongue of his boot. Blood from the deep stab wound was already soaking through the leather.

Gareth's unexpected scream attracted the attention of everyone; the Maces, the unruly spectators encircling the battle, even Corin. All eyes turning to the injured man noticed the small blonde figure scampering away on all fours, trying to disappear once again into the crowd after her successful sneak attack.

One of the Maces lunged after her, breaking formation. Corin threw himself at the captain, knocking her over. He didn't even break stride, but continued his rampage straight into the crowd, his momentum knocking several of those in the front ranks from their feet.

The crowd surged around him, grasping and grabbing at his clothes, trying to apprehend him—or at least push him back into the battle with the city guards. Others tackled the Maces who waded in after him, eager to strike an anonymous blow against Elversult's official guard. Mob mentality gripped the spectators, many of them still remembering the good old days when street brawls were the norm. Corin couldn't say how it started—an errant elbow, a careless boot tripping someone up—but a full-scale riot broke out within seconds.

Pandemonium swept the Fair. Those in the crowd trying to bring Corin down were attacked by others who wanted him to escape. The Maces disappeared under a wave of both foes and allies jumping into the fray, and Corin himself was buried beneath a press of bodies, indiscriminately punching and kicking at anything within range.

Corin lashed out without rhyme or reason, trying to clear enough space to get to his feet. Above the shouts and cries of the mob, Corin heard the shrill sound of the Maces' warning whistles. The three short blasts calling for help told Corin that reinforcements were only minutes away.

Fortunately, most of the crowd knew what the whistles meant as well. In accordance with Yanseldara's orders, violence in the streets was dealt with swiftly and harshly. The soon to be arriving Maces were liable to try and restore order by arresting everyone who happened to be at the scene of the crime. Most of Elversult's population, despite the increase in "legitimate" commerce, still had a few reasons to try to avoid being picked up in a general sweep by the authorities.

The chaos and confusion of several hundred people simultaneously trying to vacate the Fair worked to Corin's advantage. No longer the center of attention, he was able to get back to his feet. He stayed low . . . working his way with purpose and determination through the panicked masses toward one of the many side streets leading out of Elversult's open air market.

While crouching down, Corin spotted the blonde woman who had started the whole mess. She was also in a crouch, frantically signaling to him through the maze of running legs and falling bodies. Once she realized she had his attention she pointed down a narrow side lane. Corin couldn't hear her above the shouts and screams of the mob, or the shrieking whistles of the converging Mace patrols as they signaled to each other, but he could read her lips.

"This way. The alley is clear."

Staying low to avoid attracting the attention of the Maces, Corin pushed his way through the panicked crowd. The effects of his afternoon drinking binge still lingered in his system and several times he was knocked from his unsteady feet, but each time he would kick and claw his way from beneath the boots of the rabble. With a final lunge he burst from the crowd into the nearly deserted alley where the blonde girl was waiting for him.

In reality, the alley was nothing more than a narrow corridor between a pair of three story buildings. It was filled with refuse and waste, and when the stench hit Corin's nostrils it was all he could do to keep from expelling the contents of his stomach onto his boots.

The lane was half hidden in shadows, but as Corin's eyes adjusted he could see that the far end was sealed off with a twenty foot stone wall.

"It's a dead end!" he exclaimed accusingly. "We have to find another way out."

His guide shook her head emphatically.

"There is no other way out. By now the Maces will have set up road blocks and checkpoints along all the streets leading out of the Fair. And it won't be long until they organize themselves and start a systematic search for us through the crowd."

Corin snorted in disgust, almost retching as the foul air assailed his senses yet again.

"So we're just supposed to hide in here? Bury ourselves in the garbage and hope they eventually give up looking for us?"

The woman smiled, then began digging through the garbage along one of the walls. Corin shook his head in disbelief. She might have saved him from being beaten into submission, but cowering in a rotting back street wasn't his idea of an escape.

"Got it!" the woman exclaimed triumphantly, emerging from her digging with a tangled bundle of rope and wooden slats. Corin noticed two metal grappling hooks on the end.

"Help me untangle this ladder," she ordered.

Corin did his best, but between the alcohol and his amputation he proved to be more hindrance than help. Despite his ineffective efforts, the woman managed to unravel the ladder after only a few seconds. She dragged it over to the wall at the far end of the alley and—with a casual grace that spoke of years of practice—tossed the grappling hooks over the top of the wall. She pulled twice on the ladder to insure the anchors would hold, then began to climb.

Corin hesitated before following. He wasn't fond of heights at the best of times, and he definitely didn't relish the idea of being on top of the high wall while intoxicated.

Halfway up already, the woman glanced back down over her shoulder, obviously sensing his reluctance. "Once we're at the top, we'll just drop the ladder down the other side. It's our only way out." She paused for a second, her eyes shifting to focus on Corin's amputated stump. "I mean . . . it's a way out if you can manage the climb."

Corin glared up at her and grabbed one of the rungs with his left hand. "You just lead the way. I'll keep up."

It took less than a minute until Lhasha and her new companion were safely on the other side of the wall, standing in an alley very similar to the one they had just escaped from. Lhasha was impressed with how easily the one-handed man managed to climb up and down the ladder. Of course, she shouldn't have been surprised—not after seeing how he'd overpowered the Maces.

Beyond the wall the sounds of a full blown riot breaking out in the Fair could be heard. By the time the Maces restored order, Lhasha planned to be far, far away. She gave the ladder a firm snap, sending a rippling wave along its length. The grappling hooks on top came loose and fell at her feet with a loud clank.

"Thanks for rescuing me back there," she said as she rolled up the ladder. "They would have dragged me off to the Jailgates if you hadn't stepped in."

"I didn't do it for you," he replied gruffly. "I don't like the Maces."

Quite the understatement, Lhasha thought. "Whatever the reason, I appreciate it."

The man initially made no response. After several seconds of awkward silence he conceded in a grudging tone.

"I guess I should thank you for getting me out of that mob before the Maces found me. How did you know the ladder would be there, half-elf?"

Lhasha was momentarily taken aback. Few people noticed her mixed heritage. True, she was small and slight, but her features strongly favored her human father. People usually noticed her outlandish clothing, not the subtle characteristics—like the faint violet hue in her eyes, or the slight point of her ears—that betrayed her mixed heritage.

"My name is Lhasha, not Half-elf, and I put the ladder there long time ago. I used to work the Fair, in my younger days. I always wanted to have an emergency way out, in case something like this happened."

"You *are* a pickpocket!" he exclaimed, his good hand dropping to his belt to check on his purse. In a cold voice he added, "So you were trying to rob me."

Lhasha's back was to the wall they had just climbed. The man was between her and the alley's narrow exit to the main street. She noticed his sword was missing—he must have lost it in the fight. He was at least twice her size, and from his expressionless tone she had no idea what he was thinking. She chose her words very carefully.

"Actually, I wasn't trying to pick your pocket. I was trying to give your money back. It fell from your belt."

He grunted in reply, obviously not buying her story.

She decided to come clean. "All right, I admit I did steal your purse. But when I saw you only had one hand, I tried to give it back."

"I don't need your pity," he spat at her. "You should have kept it—I'm not a beggar."

"Could have fooled me," Lhasha shot back. "Not even enough coppers to buy a decent meal!" Instantly, she regretted her words.

Rage twisted the man's features into a grimace of primal fury, and he raised his good hand in a clenched fist above his head. But as quickly as the rage came, it vanished, replaced on his countenance by defeat and resignation. His hand dropped back to his side, his shoulders slumped.

"So this is what I've become, Corin the Pitiful." he muttered.

He turned from her and began to shuffle away down the alley. Lhasha caught up to him and placed a hand on his shoulder. She knew what it was like to be beaten down by life. She knew the value of a compassionate hand to help you up.

"Corin . . . wait. I have a friend, a priest. Maybe he can help you."

Corin turned back and smiled at her, but it was a bitter, hopeless smile. "No priest can help me. I spent everything I owned on clerics of the Morninglord, and all I have to show for it is an empty purse—as you know all too well."

"I've seen you with a sword," Lhasha said, trying to encourage him. "You don't have to live a life of poverty. You're good. Good enough to still be working as a mercenary."

Corin gave a caustic laugh. "You think I don't know that? But would you hire me with this?" He raised his stump for effect. "I'm not a stray dog, half-elf. You don't need to look after me."

Despite his rebuke, Lhasha still wanted to help him—she owed him for saving her from the Maces. But sometimes a compassionate helping hand was less effective than a swift boot in the breeches. When she spoke again her words were angry.

"Life gave you a tough . . . deal." She almost said "hand." "Now you're using that as an excuse to give up. You don't want my pity because you're too busy pitying yourself!"

Corin snorted in disgust. "You have all the answers, don't you? But it's not that simple. My life is . . . complicated."

Lhasha refused to be cowed. "Complicated? Really? Then explain it to me!"

"If you want a tale, go find a bard," he snarled, and turned his back on her again.

Lhasha could no longer hear the sounds of the unruly crowd coming from behind the alley wall.

"The Maces have things under control," she called out as he walked away, "soon they will be looking for us. I know somewhere we can go and be safe."

The man hesitated, then turned to face her.

"I'm not a charity case."

"Just paying you back for saving me in the Fair," she assured him. "Come with me," Lhasha urged, still convinced Fendel could do something about Corin's arm. "The fight with the Maces was as much my fault as yours. The least I can do is get you safely away from here."

"And where shall we go, half . . . Lhasha?"

"The friend I mentioned earlier. Fendel. He will help us."

"The cleric?"

"A cleric," Lhasha admitted, "but one unlike any you've ever met."

CHAPTER FOUR

The alley Corin and Lhasha used to make their escape was on the north side of the Fair. Corin didn't know where Lhasha planned to take him, but if her friend was a priest there was a good chance he'd be found at Temple Hill . . . on the south side of the Fair.

Lhasha led the way, winding through little-used streets and shadowy back lanes. The description the Maces would provide to their patrols might be sketchy, but Corin knew as a pair they were hard to miss. The half-elf would draw enough attention on her own—an attractive young blonde with long hair and fair skin was sure to draw the eye of every man they passed, and her garish clothing only made her stand out from the crowd even more. As for his own description, Corin knew there weren't too many one-armed men wandering around the city streets.

Corin's suspicions about their destination were eventually confirmed. Lhasha's course took them around Elversult's huge open-air market, to the shops and buildings built beneath, in the shadow of Temple Hill. Corin remained silent as bitter memories welled up in his mind, bubbling to the surface at the sight of the all too familiar surroundings. Through the tightly packed buildings on the narrow streets in the center of town, he caught glimpses of the foot trail snaking its way up to the top of the barren tor. Looking up, he could make out the silhouette of Lathander's Church in the late afternoon sun.

How many times had he made the trek up that hill, humbling himself before the priests of Lathander? Corin tried to ignore the foul taste welling up from his stomach, tried to block out the dark memories. But the fight in the Fair had sobered him up. The effects of his morning drinking binge were fading. As the veil of alcohol faded, he saw the past was still there waiting for him—just as it always was.

Without looking up again, Corin knew what he would see as Lhasha led them ever closer to the mount around which Elversult had been built. The gleaming spires and stained glass windows of the Dawnbringer's temple would reflect and refract the light of the sun, a shining beacon of hope atop the hill for all to see. False hope, for those foolish enough to believe. Corin had been one of them, once.

After the slaughter of his White Shield comrades, after the loss of his hand, Corin had turned to religion in search of help and healing. Out of the pantheon of churches within Elversult, Corin had chosen Lathander's—the god of the Morning Sun, the god of the New Day, the god of New Beginnings.

The priests had welcomed him into their temple—welcomed him and his gold. Corin had foolishly handed it over. Bit by bit, visit by visit, coin by coin. His entire life savings. Each time the priests would chant and pray, and spread perfumed incense on the air and speak about the glory of the Dawnbringer. Each time, they would end the day by telling Corin that Lathander had not seen fit to restore his hand at that time.

Only now could Corin see what a fool he'd been. How gullible. *At this time.* An implied hope for the future—hope Corin had invariably seized upon. He accepted their failures to help him without question, convinced the next day's pilgrimage up the winding, dusty path to the top of Temple Hill would end with him being made whole again. That hope was all he had—the hope that his hand could be restored. The priests of Lathander continually fed that hope with their false promises.

After a year of almost daily treks up the hill, Corin's money was all but spent. But the priests were not done stealing from him. If they had sent him on his way when the gold ran out, Corin might have been able to forgive them. He understood greed and theft—as a White Shield he had dealt with thieves every day.

There was still more he could give, the priests had explained, something more valuable than all the gold he'd donated. Corin could give himself, in every fiber of his being, over to the Dawnbringer. He could prove his devotion through service, in a way mere donations never could. This, the priests had assured him, was the way to salvation, redemption, and healing. To open his soul by serving Lathander.

Corin had served. Cleaning the church grounds, scrubbing the stones and statues of the temple's interior. Washing the stained glass windows. Polishing the spires and steeples of the edifice proclaiming Lathander's greatness. Toiling in the gardens within the walls. Preparing meals for the clerics, and cleaning up the dishes when they were done. Every menial, degrading task the servants of Lathander felt was beneath them, Corin did. He humbled himself in the eyes of the Dawnbringer, convinced such servitude would bring about a miracle.

After three months of toil, Corin had approached

Hathala Orndeir, the high priestess of Lathander. He went to her and begged her to help him, begged on his knees for her to implore her god to heal him.

Her reply was simple. "Those who serve only for their own gain are not true in their faith," she had said. "You are not yet ready to receive the miracle of Lathander's touch."

He should have attacked her, should have launched himself and snapped her fragile neck with his bare hands for her hypocrisy—or been blasted into oblivion by the power of Lathander when Hathala called down the wrath of her god to protect her, but Corin's spirit was no longer that of a White Shield, or even a warrior. He had given Lathander's church everything—his money, his service, his pride, his honor. All that remained was a hollow shell, incapable of action, and they still would not help him.

Corin left the church that night, quietly gathering his meager belongings. Hathala gave him a pittance of coins to take with him—wages for his months of service, she had explained. Corin was too bitter and broken to even refuse her charity.

Now, a year later—nearly two years after the loss of his hand—Corin found himself once again in the shadow of Temple Hill and the reviled church built atop it.

Corin spat on the ground to try and cleanse his mouth of the foul bile conjured up by the sight of the Tower of the Morn. Soon he could also discern the outline of the House of Coins . . . Waukeen's Temple, and the only other building on Temple Hill.

"Your friend, the cleric," Corin asked, breaking the silence, "is he a servant of the Dawnbringer? I've had enough of Lathander's kind."

Lhasha, her attention focused on watching the streets for possible pursuers, shook her head.

"Is he one of Waukeen's priests?" Corin asked. "A stubborn believer in a dead god?"

"No," Lhasha replied, "he worships Gond. He's a priest in the House of Hands."

Corin laughed softly, and rubbed his stump. "The House of Hands," he whispered to himself, "how fitting."

The church of Gond Wonderbringer wasn't actually on Temple Hill, but stood just at its foot on the western face of the mount. Corin had passed it many times on his repeated journeys up the hill, but had rarely given it a second thought. Compared to Lathander, and even Waukeen before she was slain in the Time of Troubles, Gond was a minor power. The god of inventors, blacksmiths and carpenters . . . hardly the deity Corin would have chosen to heal his grievous injury.

Lhasha never hesitated at the doors to Gond's church, but boldly walked right through. Corin paused. He was sick of churches, sick of getting his hopes up only to have them shattered by priests powerless to help him. But the half-elf's enthusiasm was a refreshing change from the despairing malaise that darkened his mind when he was by himself. He expected nothing, of course, but he had come this far . . . he might as well go all the way. At least I won't have to climb that damnable hill again, Corin thought as he followed Lhasha into the House of Hands.

A priest stepped forward to greet them, at least Corin assumed it was a priest. He wore a leather apron, and tools of every possible description hung from the belt around his waist. The only thing identifying him as a cleric was a picture of a cog wheel—Gond's holy symbol—emblazoned on the front of his smock.

"Lhasha, welcome as always," the man said by way of greeting. "I see you've brought a friend."

"Hello, Dergin," Lhasha replied with a smile. "This is

Corin." The priest nodded in acknowledgement, and Corin returned the gesture. "Is Fendel in?"

"Of course," Dergin said. "In his workshop, where else? Go on in."

To Corin he added, "Feel free to examine any of the many inventions you might come across in the church, it honors the Wonderbringer when we take an interest in his marvels."

"This way," Lhasha said, "in the back."

Corin still wasn't sure about Lhasha's faith in her friend, but he had to admit Gond's priests were unlike any he had met before. Even the church was something of an oddity. Instead of the sounds of chanting, bells, or gentle harps one might expect in a house of worship, the air was filled with the clang of hammer meeting anvil, the sawing of wood and the roaring of great fires that Corin assumed to be coming from furnaces in the back. The acrid smell of smoke and burning coal wafted through the halls, reminding Corin of the many smithies he had visited to have his weapons or armor repaired during his years as a White Shield.

Scattered about every room they passed through was an amazing collection of machines, gadgets, and inventions. The church was more a museum of technological innovation than a place of worship. Many of the larger rooms Lhasha led him through contained catapults, battering rams, or other machines of war, each uniquely—and often strangely—modified from the standard design. Other rooms had farming equipment and tools, each scythe or hoe improved upon in some way. Even the halls were lined with smaller devices and contraptions. Corin couldn't even begin to guess the purpose of most of them.

"It's all a little . . . overwhelming, isn't it?" Lhasha commented at one point. "Believe it or not, most of these things actually work."

They passed through the main building, and into the courtyard at the back. Half constructed frames of metal and wood littered the yard. The sounds of building—the pounding, sawing, grinding noises Corin could hear even in the main entrance of the temple—were much louder here, emanating from several large edifices haphazardly strewn about the grounds.

"The communal workshops," Lhasha explained, shouting to be heard above the din. "Ever since Fendel nearly blew up one of the kilns they've let him work in his own private building, out at the back. He hardly ever comes out. Built himself a little bedroom off the back, though half the time he falls asleep at his workbench."

Lhasha led the way to a small cottage nearly hidden behind the other buildings and knocked on the door.

From within the workshop an anxious voice called out, "I'm busy!"

"Fendel," Lhasha shouted, "it's me! Can I come in?"

Several seconds later the door swung open to reveal a grubby gnome. Like the priest at the entrance, he wore a leather smock bearing Gond's holy symbol. His clothes were stained with soot, and his face and balding crown were smudged with dark black stains Corin guessed to be grease. The tip of his rather large nose was similarly blackened, and the gray whiskers on his chin appeared singed. He smelled of forges and sawdust. Without a word, the gnome seized Lhasha's wrist in one hand and Corin's belt in the other, yanked them inside, and slammed the door behind them.

It took several seconds for Corin's eyes to adjust to the darkness of the room and reveal the carnage within. A table lay overturned in each corner of the room, all of them missing legs; one was even chopped right in two. Strewn about the floor were several chairs; dozens of hammers; and countless nails, knives, rulers, levels, writing quills, inkpots, sketches, drawings, and blueprints that had presumably been on the now upended tables. Corin's first thought was that a mage had conjured a minor demon and let it run rampage about the room. Then he noticed a strange looking contraption on wheels in the center of the workshop. It looked like a cylinder, six feet high, with dozens of farm implements—a scythe, a thresher, a hoe, a sickle—extending out from the center at various heights and angles.

"Fendel," Lhasha asked in amazement, "what happened?"

"Nothing to worry about, Lhasha-love. Just testing out a new invention . . . an automatic farmer. No more toiling away in the fields, no more spending sun up to sun down during the harvest season hurrying to bring the crop in. My little device does it all for you—and at the speed of twenty ordinary workers!"

Noticing their skeptical expressions Fendel added, "Of course, its not perfected yet. Still a few minor technical difficulties to work out. The thing tends to be a little . . . overzealous. Got away from me, you know."

As he spoke the gnome made a half-hearted attempt to gather up the papers scattered on the floor. He righted one of the tables, only to watch it immediately topple over again because of its two missing legs. With a sigh he righted a chair and set his hastily collected notes on the seat.

Lhasha started to help the clean up process, but the gnome waved his hand dismissively.

"Just leave it, Lhasha. Guests shouldn't have to clean up my mess. I'll get it later."

Lhasha shrugged, and let the few papers she had picked up slip from her hands and waft back down to the floor.

"Don't . . . ah . . . mention this little mishap, darling," Fendel added. "I've had a bad stretch with my work lately, and I'm already under some harsh restrictions from Artificer Daragath. If he hears about this, he might forbid me from working without some kind of . . . supervision."

"Of course, Fendel. We won't say a word. Isn't that right, Corin?"

Corin, who had stood in bemused silence since being ushered into the room, nodded in agreement.

The gnome clapped his grimy hands once and exclaimed, "Forgive me, I'm being rude!" He extended his arm as he said, "Fendel Burrohill. Pleased to meet you . . . what was it? Corin?"

Corin regarded the gnome's gesture with a stony stare, and made no move to reciprocate. Fendel hesitated, then glanced down at Corin's stump and quickly withdrew his own arm.

"Oh," the gnome said, "sorry."

Corin made no reply.

Lhasha interrupted, breaking the awkward silence that hung in the air between the two men. "Fendel, can you help us? We're in a bit of trouble with the Maces."

"Right," Fendel replied. "The riot in the Fair. When I heard they were looking for a pretty young woman in outlandish clothes I suspected you were involved."

"Outlandish!" Lhasha protested, but Corin's own deep voice drowned her out.

"How did you hear of the riot already, gnome?"

If Fendel took offense at Corin's demanding tone, he didn't show it. "I have my sources," he said cryptically. "Not much happens in this town that I don't know something about.

"Funny thing, though," he added after a brief pause. "None of the official reports mention your missing hand. Guess the Maces didn't want to admit they were whipped by a girl and a one-armed man. Might not be good for their reputation as peacekeepers in the city." Fendel's tone was light, and his craggy face was lit by a mischievous grin.

Despite himself, Corin couldn't be offended by the comments. Something about the gnome appealed to him. Or maybe he was just grateful to find someone who didn't treat his injury with pity or revulsion.

"Then they must not be too eager to have us found," Lhasha chimed in. "We were going to hide out here, but I guess that won't be necessary. But I still have a favor to ask."

"Find a chair with four legs and have a seat," Fendel urged, taking his own advice. "No need to stand while we discuss it. Another special item for your, uh . . . profession?"

Lhasha cast a quick glance at Corin as she found herself a chair. He ignored her and sought out a chair of his own. Despite his apparent indifference, Lhasha gave the warrior an explanation.

"Fendel sometimes makes special items for me, whenever I'm planning a job."

"You mean when you're going to steal something."

Fendel chuckled. "Your taciturn friend is blunt, Lhasha. Call it what you will, Corin, its a living. I'm sure Lhasha will tell you my rates are most reasonable and my creations most useful."

"Usually," Lhasha interjected.

"Yes, well . . . on occasion my inventions will go awry."

"So I see," Corin said, scanning the shambles that had once been a workshop.

"That's not why I'm here this time," Lhasha continued. "We—that is, Corin—has need of your clerical abilities. For healing."

"A little nicked up from the fight with the city guard, are we?"

"No," Corin replied softly, "this is . . . more serious."

"Ah, I see," Fendel said in a knowing voice. "Your hand. Or rather, your lack thereof. I can't promise anything. My powers aren't that great. I'm just a minor cog in the machinery of Gond's church. But let's take a look."

The gnome slid his chair over beside Corin's, and gently took his arm. "Hmmm . . . seems to be an old wound."

"Nearly two years ago," Corin replied, his voice devoid of emotion. "In the spring."

After several seconds of intense study, the gnome pushed his chair back. "I'm sorry, Corin. I don't have the power to heal anything like this. Lathander's temple up on the hill might be able to do something for you."

Corin snorted in disgust. "The Dawnbringer's priests proved just as useless as you." After a second he conceded, "At least you have the decency to admit your inability to help before leeching all the gold from my pocket."

"What about the High Artificer?" Lhasha asked.

The gnome rubbed his bald head, leaving dark smears across his wrinkled scalp. "If your friend's already been to see Lathander's people, I doubt there's much even the Artificer could do. Gond's focus isn't really on healing, you know. That's more Lathander's turf."

Corin had stubbornly ignored the faint flicker of hope Lhasha had kindled within him, but he couldn't ignore the darkness that enveloped his mind when the flicker was snuffed out. He knew only two reactions to the darkness: lashing out, or drinking until he didn't care. And there wasn't any ale handy.

Corin jumped up, kicked his chair over and shouted, "I knew this was a waste of time!"

Lhasha tried to say something, but Corin cut her off. "Consider your debt to me repaid, half-elf. You need not waste any more sympathy on me, and I won't waste any more time here!"

Fendel was quick to jump to Lhasha's defense, his voice calm and soothing.

"You've got a lot of anger inside of you, my scruffy-jawed friend. I see you like to take it out on other people. I'm beginning to understand how that riot broke out. Don't let your rage control you. Hasty decisions are often regrettable ones."

"My only regret is that I didn't die on that battlefield!"

Now it was Fendel's turn to snort.

"You've got to learn to look at the big picture, Corin. You're a lot better off than you realize. I may not be able to heal you, but if you give me a minute I might still be able to come up with a way to help you."

Part of Corin wanted to smash open the door and storm off, return to the Weeping Griffin, and spend his last few coppers on bitter ale, but something gave him pause. Fendel's words sounded confident, reassuring. There seemed to be some underlying wisdom in his voice, as if the gnome knew things Corin didn't. Things worth knowing.

"Very well," he said cautiously. "How can you help me?"

"Well, I'm not exactly sure it will work . . ."

"What?" Lhasha asked excitedly. "You've got that gleam in your eye, Fendel. What is it?"

"Corin, have you ever heard of something called a 'prosthetic'?"

The warrior shook his head.

"It's an artificial limb. A hand constructed from . . . well, metal, probably."

"A hook," Corin said incredulously. "I'm not a pirate!"

"Not a hook," Fendel explained patiently, "an artificial hand. Fingers, a thumb. If I do it right—and with some practice on your part—you could use it to pick things up, open doors, hold the reins of a horse. Probably even use a shield or wield a weapon."

Corin unconsciously began to rub his stump.

"This intrigues me, gnome . . . Fendel. Is such a thing really possible?"

"I've never actually seen one, but I've heard of such things. Even saw a sketch, once. It might be an interesting project, if you're willing to give it a try."

For several seconds Corin was silent, still rubbing his amputated arm as he considered the possibilities. At last he nodded. "If you truly think such a thing can be done, I am willing to try."

"Excellent!" Lhasha exclaimed. "I told you Fendel could help. I haven't had a problem yet that he couldn't solve!"

The gnome held up his grubby hand. "Hold on, Lhasha. This is no easy task. Not if it is to be done right. I can't use just any metal, of course. An iron hand wouldn't be much use. Something strong, but light . . . mithral, perhaps. Of course, it will occupy much of my time. I'd need some type of donation to Gond's temple to justify the expenditure of materials and effort to the High Artificer. It might be very expensive."

Corin's shoulders slumped. "I . . . I have nothing."

"I've got it!" Lhasha blurted out. "You can work for me! It's perfect—you can earn money to pay Fendel, and it'll solve my problem with the Purple Masks!"

Fendel and Corin stared at her as if she were insane, then both started talking at once.

"I'm no thief," Corin objected. "I'd be of no use to you."

"The Purple Masks?" Fendel scolded. "How are you mixed up with them?"

"This will work," Lhasha assured them both, quelling their protests. "Just listen to what I have to say. Fendel,

I was actually on my way to see you when I . . . uh . . . bumped into Corin. I'm in a bit of a professional bind, and I need some advice."

"The Masks still want you to join their guild, don't they?"

Lhasha nodded. "And they're done asking politely. I found a dagger in my pillow this morning when I woke up. A purple cloth was tied around the hilt."

The expression on the gnome's face changed to one of deep concern. "This isn't good, Lhasha. You won't get a second warning. And you can't join them—once they get their hooks in you, you'll never be free!"

Lhasha patted the old gnome gently on the arm. "I know, Fendel. But I didn't know what to do. You know I could never leave Elversult. Where else could I find such beautiful groves and woodlands right within the city limits?"

Fendel sighed. "That's your mother's side of the family talking. It's a shame you never knew her. You look mostly human, but I think your soul is closer to that of the elves."

"It doesn't matter now," Lhasha said happily. "I'll just hire Corin to be my bodyguard."

"But . . . you know almost nothing about me," Corin objected.

"I know you're good with a sword," Lhasha explained. "And I know you're basically a decent, honest person. Fendel would have said something if you were lying or a threat to me."

Fendel nodded. "That's true, Corin. I must confess I took a little peek into your character while I examined your hand. A minor spell granted by Gond to even the lowest of his clerics."

Corin was about to say something about the invasion of his privacy, but reconsidered. He couldn't fault such precautions. The White Shields had done the same type of magical screening to all their potential recruits. Elversult, despite the changes Yanseldara and the Maces had brought, was still a city founded by—and largely populated with—smugglers and brigands.

"So, Corin, what do you say? Will you serve as my bodyguard?"

Corin weighed the offer carefully. He was familiar with earning a living as a hired mercenary. That and being a White Shield were the only lives he'd ever really known. If he accepted, he'd be earning an honest living through his skill with the blade, proving wrong all those who doubted him because of his injury.

But as a White Shield his role had been to oppose bandits and raiders. Had he really fallen so low that he would now work for those he had opposed before?

Lhasha sensed his reluctance.

"Is something wrong?" she asked with genuine concern.

"You're a thief."

The half-elf flinched slightly at the venom in his voice before responding. "There are worse things, Corin. I may take a few choice items from my targets, but I've never taken a life. Everything I take can be replaced."

Corin didn't answer, so Lhasha continued to justify her chosen profession.

"Besides, as thieves go I'm not that bad. I never steal anything personal," she assured him. "No jewelry, no family heirlooms, nothing that could have any kind of sentimental attachment for the owner. Just coins, and only from those who can well afford to spare a few gold or silver pieces.

"Not as lucrative as stealing jewelry or rare works of art," Lhasha admitted, "but I make a comfortable living. It's amazing how much gold these people have just lying around. Obviously, they won't miss it much when it's gone.

"And besides," the young woman added, "most of my targets are politicians and nobles. Everything I steal was acquired dishonestly through a corrupt system that crushes the less fortunate beneath the polished boot heels of the upper class. You don't get rich in Elversult without getting your hands dirty somewhere along the way. Unlike them, I'm honest enough to admit what I am."

She was rationalizing, a blatant attempt to free her own conscience from the plague of guilt. Corin imagined she had been doing it for years.

Yet there was some merit to her arguments. Corin had worked for his fair share of unsavory clients over the years. Not thieves, exactly, but most merchants making a profit were operating somewhere beyond the acceptable limits of Elversult's commercial law.

Still, he resisted.

"I'm no thief. I wouldn't be of any use to you."

The half-elf shook her head. "I'm not looking for an accomplice, or an apprentice. When I go out on a job, I can look after myself. I'm careful, I'm professional. But being careful takes a lot out of me. After a job I need to relax, to unwind. What I really need is some protection for when I'm not on a job. I need someone to watch my back when I'm too busy enjoying life to watch out for myself. I'm not used to being a target. Eventually I'll get careless and leave myself vulnerable. When that happens, I'd like to have you around to cover for my mistake."

When Corin still didn't give an answer, Fendel chimed in.

"Lhasha, perhaps you should reconsider. The Purple Masks are a dangerous, powerful group. Being your bodyguard would put Corin's own life in danger on an almost daily basis. It might be too much for one man to handle."

“Don’t underestimate me,” Corin said sharply. He turned to face Lhasha, the steely confidence in his voice unfamiliar to his own ears; it had been nearly three years since he’d heard it last. “I can protect you better than any blade on the Dragon Coast, and unlike most of the other hired guards you can trust me . . . a White Shield’s loyalty never fails. If the Masks come after you again they’ll find me standing in their path.”

Fendel gave Corin a knowing smile.

“I figured you’d come around.”

CHAPTER FIVE

The salary negotiations were quick—Corin couldn't afford to be picky, and Lhasha's offer was generous. The warrior didn't even bother trying to haggle a few more coins per tenday out of her. The attractive half-elf almost seemed disappointed.

"We have to find a new place for you to stay," the warrior told his small employer as soon as the price was set. Now that he was responsible for Lhasha's safety, Corin wasn't about to let her stay another night in a room where someone had left a knife embedded in her pillow. "Pack everything up, and I'll carry it for you."

Fendel agreed. "The sooner you're out of that place, the better."

"What about your stuff?" Lhasha asked Corin. "Don't you need to go pack?"

The warrior shook his head, slapping the breast of his grimy mail shirt and tapping the rusted hilt of his sword. "This is all I need."

It didn't take long to gather Lhasha's stuff, the only thing she had in any measurable quantity was clothing. Lots and lots of clothing—closets full of exotic outfits tailored from bright silks and colorful fabrics. Corin had initially shuddered at the sight, imagining the hours it would take to carefully store such expensive garments for the trip across town, but Lhasha had packed everything with ruthless efficiency. As she packed, Corin rubbed the rough stubble on his chin, suddenly self-conscious about his own stained, torn clothes and his scraggly appearance.

"Where to?" she asked, once she had settled her bill at the front desk. The staff had seemed genuinely saddened to see her go.

Corin, with a large trunk full of Lhasha's wardrobe strapped to his back, didn't even need to think about his answer.

"We're heading to the Axe and Hammer."

Elversult was a bustling merchant city, with literally hundreds of places to stay. Some of them had the well earned reputation for being seedy establishments where the staff would steal anything not nailed down and betray anyone with a secret for a couple glittering coins waved beneath the nose. Other inns were renowned for the security of the rooms and the integrity—and tight lips—of the staff. By far the best of these was the dwarf run Axe and Hammer.

"Not on your life!" Lhasha exclaimed.

Corin pulled up short. Turning slowly so as not to overbalance the heavy load of clothes on his back, he gave her a questioning stare.

"I've been in there before," the half-elf explained. "It's nicknamed the Tomb for a reason, you know."

He knew. The entire staff was made up of dwarves, and they weren't there to make the guests feel good. In fact, most of them were there solely to keep order and insure none of the guests were bothered by anyone—including the other guests. The dour faces and gruff, military attitude of the staff permeated the very air of the Axe and Hammer. The sounds of laughter and conversation common to most taverns were virtually unheard of in their dining room.

"If I wanted to stay in a prison for my safety I'd go turn myself in at the Jailgates," Lhasha declared. Seeing the look on Corin's face, she added. "This isn't open for discussion, Corin."

The warrior took a deep breath and gathered his thoughts. There were other reputable inns in Elversult, though none was as safe as the Axe and Hammer.

"What about the Glowing Staff?" he finally suggested.

The Glowing Staff had been in business for nearly twenty years, run by an extended family of halflings. Like the Axe and Hammer, the employees there were honest and able to keep a secret. A security force of a dozen halflings armed with wooden clubs kept order in the tavern and responded quickly to any disturbances in the rooms on the upper floors of the three story building—not quite as intimidating as the dwarf warriors patrolling the Axe and Hammer's corridors, but an effective deterrent nonetheless.

The atmosphere at the Glowing Staff was one of cheer and warmth. One thing halflings were good at was making a guest feel welcome. The food was always appetizing and plentiful, drinks were refilled often, and laughter and singing from the tavern echoed through the halls.

"I've heard good things about it," Lhasha admitted. "Though I've never been there. They say that on most nights some of the kitchen staff bring out their lutes and flutes and provide tunes to amuse and entertain the guests."

Corin nodded. "They do."

"All right, we'll check it out. I could use some music to dance my troubles away."

The warrior made no effort to hide the disapproving

look on his face. "Don't do anything to draw attention to yourself," he warned.

Lhasha acted as if she hadn't even heard him.

Corin had wanted to rent the rooms himself—the less people who saw Lhasha checking in the better, as far as he was concerned. However, the half-elf would have none of it.

"You can't just shut me up and hide me away like some kind of stuck-up princess," she explained. "I always like to try and make friends with the staff when I stay someplace. They're more likely to watch out for me if they like me."

She did have a point, and Corin was already beginning to sense that he would win few arguments with the boisterous, headstrong young thief. He'd have to pick his battles.

"Top floor," Corin said to the halfling innkeeper once they arrived. "One room, two keys."

"Hold on," Lhasha interjected quickly. "I appreciate what you did for me in the Fair, Corin. But we just met, and the unshaved look doesn't really work for me—"

Corin cut her off. "I'm your bodyguard. I'll stand guard while you sleep."

"And what about you?" the half-elf had asked.

Not wishing to advertise Lhasha's profession to all within earshot, Corin dropped his voice to a low whisper. "I'll sleep whenever you're . . . uh . . . out gathering inventory. We only need the one room."

Lhasha shook her head. "No, that won't do. I won't sleep a wink with you hovering over my bed. It's creepy. Besides . . . what if I have company? You kind of wreck the mood, Corin. If you know what I mean."

"You wouldn't be my first client to bring someone back to their room. On those occasions I'll stand guard outside."

"Oh, I see . . ." Lhasha said sarcastically, "an armed guard outside my room. That won't look odd. Not at all. Way to keep a low profile. The Purp—" At the last second she caught herself. "My 'friends' don't know where I'm staying. The last thing we want to do is attract attention."

During their conversation the innkeeper had studiously been trying to occupy himself with other business—scratching his curly head, checking his fingernails for dirt, idly sorting the room keys. After all, the employees of the Golden Staff had a reputation for minding their own business. But sensing the argument was escalating, he stepped in to settle the issue.

"I assure you, sir," he said to Corin, "the lady is correct. You have no need to stand guard outside her door here. Our inn is the safest in all of Elversult. The doors are solid, the locks are sure, the windows are barred and we have guards who patrol the halls at regular intervals. Whoever her 'friends' are, they won't find the lady here."

"There," Lhasha said triumphantly, "it's settled. There's nothing to worry about. Two rooms please."

Corin knew they were wrong. Eventually the Purple Masks would figure out that Lhasha hadn't left the city, or gone into retirement. And when they did, barred windows, locked doors and random patrols wouldn't keep Lhasha safe. The best way to protect a client was unrelenting vigilance backed by cold steel—the White Shield way. But Corin knew this was another argument he couldn't win. Not right now, and she'd be safe enough for a little while. It would take some time until word of Lhasha resuming her activities reached the Purple Masks, and hopefully it would be well into the Month of the Sunsets before they managed to track her new location down.

"Two rooms," Corin finally consented, "but make sure they're adjacent."

They agreed to meet downstairs in the common room that first evening, just before supper. That would give them both time to clean up and get settled, and give Corin a chance to take care of any last minute details he hadn't been able to attend to while helping Lhasha relocate.

The pretty half-elf gave serious consideration to her choice of outfit for the evening. She needed to make a good first impression on the staff. She had to be dazzling, but not vain or conceited. A difficult trick to pull off, but she could manage.

She finally settled on a long flowing dress of shimmering violet hues, to bring out her eyes and compliment her silver-blonde hair. She glanced in the mirror, noting with satisfaction how the material shaped to her form when she stood still, and how it billowed and fluttered when she spun—a very important consideration. She planned to celebrate her new surroundings by dancing the night away to the music of the halfling minstrels for which the Glowing Staff was so famous.

Her difficulty in deciding on her wardrobe for the evening had put her a little behind schedule, and she arrived nearly fifteen minutes later than she and Corin had originally agreed on, but when every eye in the inn's dining hall turned to watch her descend the steps leading up to the guest rooms, Lhasha knew the time had been well spent.

She paused a few steps from the floor, partly to give everyone one final look before she took her seat, and partly to see if she could spot Corin. A handsome young man stepped up from a table in the corner and took a step toward her. Only then did Lhasha recognize her hired protector.

In the hours since getting Lhasha settled, Corin had undergone a remarkable transformation. The wild, scraggly beard was gone, and his unruly, tangled hair had been shaved down to the length of a Mace cadet's. He no longer wore his rusted armor, and his yellowish, stained shirt had been washed to a pristine white. The many small holes and rips had been skillfully mended. His trousers had been similarly washed and stitched. He still wore a belt, but the scabbard at his side was no longer shabby, and the hilt had been polished to a gleaming shine. Only the expression on his face remained unchanged: cold, dead eyes set in grim, unrelenting features.

As soon as he was close enough to speak without being overheard he whispered, "You're making a scene. Everyone's watching you."

"That's the point," she replied. "You clean up quite well, Corin. You look like a true gentleman."

It wasn't exactly the truth, of course. Few would mistake Corin's broad shoulders for a pampered nobleman's physique. Fewer still would confuse the aggressive strides with which he had crossed the floor for the gait of a wealthy man of leisure. But what harm could there be in a simple compliment?

The warrior winced at her words, obviously finding the term gentleman somewhat distasteful. Lhasha made a note to herself to avoid using it in the future.

"I found us a table in the corner. Out of the way."

Lhasha was about to protest, then thought better of it. She didn't want to spoil her grand entrance by appearing spoiled, or argumentative. If any of the staff got that impression, they'd never warm up to her.

She slipped her arm into the crook of Corin's elbow on his good limb, briefly startling him. He recovered quickly, and escorted her to the table, though his manner was overly stiff and formal. That wasn't a bad thing, Lhasha knew. It would be obvious to anyone watching that Corin was her bodyguard, and nothing more. She didn't want to scare off any of the many eligible looking young men already gathered in the hall.

A young serving girl came over, a halfling lass barely able to reach the center of the table even on her tiptoes.

"I love your dress, m'lady," she blurted out to Lhasha before taking their order, seemingly embarrassed at herself for having the audacity to make such a comment.

"Really? Why, thank you," Lhasha replied easily. She was used to such compliments. "If you want, I can give you the name of the merchant who sold me the fabric. I bet it would look wonderful on you—you've such a pretty face. And please, call me Lhasha."

Corin hissed and shook his head, anxious about his charge giving out her name. Lhasha ignored him.

The teenage waitress smiled shyly from beneath her curly brown hair. "That would be wonderful, m'lady . . . Lhasha. My birthday's coming, and I ever so much want a new dress for Greengrass."

The half-elf smiled back and patted the young server's hand. "Go see Jerril in the Fair," she said. "His prices are a bit high, but he's a sucker for a pretty face. You should be able to talk him down a fair bit. What's your name, dear?"

"Tebia," the halfling responded with a self-conscious laugh. "I'll go see this Jerril next tenday, if father will give me some time off. Now what can I get you folks this evening? Supper? A drink?"

"We'll just start with some wine for now, Tebia," Lhasha said.

"Water for me," Corin interjected.

"Are you sure, sir?" Tebia asked. "We have some of the finest ale in Elversult, if you're not partial to wine. Brewed right in our own cellars."

"Just water." Corin's voice was flat and cold, alienating.

The warm smile on the halfling's face faltered slightly.

"Don't mind him," Lhasha said reassuringly. "He's just had a long day."

Tebia nodded and gave Lhasha a thankful grin. "I'll be back in a jiff with your drinks."

As soon as she was gone, Corin leaned across the table to chide Lhasha in a harsh whisper. "Are you daft? You stride in her like a queen at a coronation, you chit chat with the first person you meet, and you start spreading your name around like the plague! We're supposed to be hiding out!"

Lhasha dismissed him with a wave of her hand. "Relax, Corin. If we skulk around here, giving everyone bitter looks and mistrusting glares we'll draw more attention to ourselves than my entrance ever did.

"As for being friendly with the staff, that's just good business. If they like us, they'll watch out for us. Would you rather have friendly faces making up my room and preparing my meals, or a bunch of disgruntled strangers?"

The warrior didn't answer right away.

Lhasha pressed her advantage. "Besides, you yourself said the staff here is discreet. I think you're just overreacting."

Lhasha doubted Corin had any valid responses to her argument, but she never got to find out for sure. At that moment Tebia returned with their drinks, setting them down on the table.

"Thank you, Tebia," Lhasha said sincerely. "I can already smell the wine's bouquet. It's quite lovely."

Corin mumbled a gruff thank you as well. Hardly the type of thing to endear him to the staff, but Lhasha chose to interpret his feeble effort as proof that Corin had assented to her opinions.

The meal was done, and the minstrels were in fine form. Lhasha, from the corner of her eye, was watching several young men who kept glancing over in her direction. They wanted to ask her to dance, she knew, but they were reluctant to approach with the grim-faced warrior perched only a few feet away.

She could feel the rhythm of the notes in her blood. At first she simply clapped her hands and tapped her feet in time to the music, laughing at the often bawdy lyrics shouted out by the fun loving, slightly inebriated crowd in the room, but the call of the music could not be denied for long.

"C'mon, Corin," she said on a sudden impulse, leaping up from her chair and seizing her companion by the wrist. "Come dance with me."

The warrior remained in his chair, oblivious to the tiny half-elf's efforts to pull him from his seat. "I'm on duty," he said flatly.

Lhasha stopped tugging on his arm, realizing from his tone that he wasn't simply being coy. Usually when a man told her he didn't want to dance, he really meant, "Ask again and I'll come." But Corin obviously wasn't interested in the playful games she was familiar with.

"Fine," she said. "Sit here like a lump. But don't expect me to keep you company."

Flashing her best smile, she made her way across the room to the eager crowd of potential partners. Leading one of the lucky young men out onto the floor, the half-elf cast a glance over her shoulder at Corin. The warrior had risen from his seat and was standing beside the table. His good hand rested lightly on the hilt of his sword. His eyes were burning, but Lhasha noted with some disappointment that they weren't burning with jealousy.

He was angry, she realized. Not because she was dancing with someone else, but simply because she was mingling with a crowd of strangers—all of whom were potential assassins in Corin's paranoid eyes. She sensed her bodyguard was uncertain whether to follow her onto the floor, or simply maintain a discreet vigil over her from his post near the table. She had put him in an awkward position, and he resented it.

Lhasha couldn't have cared less. Not while the music played with such wild abandon.

Lhasha danced for hours, only returning to the table to refresh herself with more wine. Corin never spoke during these brief interludes, he barely paid her any attention at all. But while she was spinning out on the dance floor, she felt his eyes constantly scanning the crowd around her, endlessly searching for an enemy that wasn't there. Fortunately, none of the other patrons seemed aware of his piercing gaze.

It was near midnight when the minstrels finally stopped to take a break, eliciting loud cheers and applause as they promised to return shortly. Laughing, Lhasha excused herself from her current partner, promising to add his name to the long list of repeat candidates once the musicians resumed their infectious strumming.

Alone, she came over and sat at the table. Corin hesitated, then took his own seat.

"A lot of good dancers here tonight," she said, not expecting a response. She didn't get one. "You can tell a lot about a man by the way he dances," she said absently, still trying to get a rise out of Corin. "A few of them are more than a little appealing."

"Don't worry," she added after a long pause, "I'll be careful not to invite any Mask assassins back up to my room."

"You remind me of Olear." Corin's answer was delivered in a voice completely devoid of emotion.

"Olear?" Lhasha said, curious. "Who was he? An old friend?"

"A client."

With an exaggerated sigh, Lhasha rose to the bait. "Tell me about Olear, Corin. I know you want to."

The warrior shrugged indifferently, but he did resume speaking.

"Before I joined the White Shields I did some mercenary work. On one job I was hired to guard the son of a merchant involved in a particularly nasty commerce war with a rival family."

"And Olear was his son?"

Corin nodded. "Flamboyant. Reckless. Had to be the center of attention. A lot like you."

Lhasha was about to give a light hearted protest to the not altogether inaccurate representation, but Corin never gave her the opportunity.

"He liked female company, even if he had to pay for it. And he hated having us stand guard outside his door while he was with his companions. Just like you.

"One night he sneaked away from us, determined to have a private evening with a very special lady of the night. She was a professional, but not the kind he imagined. We found him the next morning. What was left of him. Several pieces were missing and his body had been butchered and defiled with unholy magic, just to make sure he couldn't be raised."

Lhasha tried to laugh the tale off, but her guffaw sounded forced and artificial to her own ears. The story had been delivered with such emotionless simplicity, she couldn't help but believe it to be completely true.

"A trite morality tale, Corin," she said, putting up a bold front. "Save it for scaring children, instead of your clients."

She knew her voice lacked conviction. Despite her many outstanding promises of continued dances, and her more private intentions concerning the companionship of one handsome and charming young man in particular, when the band returned Lhasha went up to her room alone, except for the taciturn bodyguard who followed her up the stairs.

"Let me check your room," Corin said, once they reached Lhasha's door.

The half-elf sighed. "Corin, this isn't necessary right now. That dagger in my pillow was a message from the Purple Masks. Join them or leave town. When they find out I've moved out of my room at the Wyvern's Pipe, they'll just assume I've left Elversult for good. Until I pull a few jobs, they won't even be looking for me."

Lhasha knew she was right. There was no real danger, not this soon, but Corin persisted. "You need to get into the proper mindset," the warrior explained. "If you want to survive, we have to start forming good habits right now."

With a shrug, Lhasha handed the warrior her key—this wasn't worth fighting about. Corin opened the door cautiously, letting the light from the hall spill into the darkened room. Sword drawn, he peered in every corner and took a quick check under the bed.

Lhasha couldn't stop a soft giggle from escaping her throat. The warrior turned with a scowl, and Lhasha laughed again.

"I'm sorry Corin," she said after catching her breath. "You just look so funny peeking under my bed. Fendel used to do that when I was a little girl. Said he was looking for bed trolls. It always made me laugh."

Corin slowly got to his feet. "All clear," was all he said.

"Oh, I'm sure it is," Lhasha replied with a smile.

The warrior went over to the door that separated

their adjacent rooms. "Don't lock this," he said, undoing the latch.

"Can I at least keep it closed," Lhasha asked sarcastically, "So I don't have you staring in at me all night?"

"Close it if you must."

As soon as Corin stepped through to his own room, she did just that.

Lhasha slept late the next morning, Corin didn't hear her get up until almost noon. He himself had spent the night standing guard at the threshold of the door between their adjacent chambers.

He knew the chances of anything happening were low. It was still too soon. But he wanted to get used to staying up nights, and sleeping when it was light. Lhasha should be safe during the daylight hours, as long as she didn't stray beyond the relatively secure walls of the Golden Staff.

When he heard signs of life in the room beside him, he went over and knocked on the door.

"Just a minute," Lhasha called out. It was closer to five minutes when she finally opened the door. Corin wasn't thrilled to see she had again chosen a bright, eye catching outfit.

"Don't you have anything less conspicuous you could wear?"

"No," Lhasha said, "so don't even waste your breath asking again."

Before Corin could come up with a suitable reply, Lhasha asked him a question of her own.

"Didn't you get any sleep? You look terrible."

The warrior shook his head. "When you sleep, I stand guard. I'll get some sleep now, as long as you promise not to leave the inn without coming to get me first."

Resigning herself to the situation, Lhasha said, "I guess that's a sacrifice I have to make, isn't it? Well, at least I can go down to the tavern to pass the time."

Corin would have preferred her to stay upstairs, but he already knew his charge well enough to realize that wasn't an option.

"I'll meet you for supper," Corin said. "The same time as last night."

"Sleep tight," Lhasha said, closing the door between their rooms.

"Many of the young men are asking about you," Tebia, the halfling waitress, told Lhasha as she cleared away the supper plates. With a mischievous smile she added, "They want me to find out if you're going to be dancing with anyone in particular this evening."

"Not tonight," the half-elf answered. "I think I'll just turn in early." Seeing the sour, accusing look the young server shot Corin, Lhasha quickly added, "I'm just a little tired. I'll be back out on the dance floor tomorrow—I promise."

Seemingly satisfied, the halfling finished clearing the table. "Sleep well, Lhasha," she said as the half-elf went up the stairs to her room, Corin only a few steps behind.

"I'm glad to see you showing some restraint," the warrior said as they climbed the steps.

"Well, I've got to work sometime," Lhasha explained. "If I don't go out and earn some gold, we won't be able to stay here very long."

Corin waited until they had reached the rooms before responding to her comment. He followed Lhasha into her chambers and closed the door behind him before saying, "I don't think that's a good idea. You should keep a low profile for a while. Maybe the Masks will forget about you if you disappear for a month or two."

Lhasha shook her head with a rueful smile.

"We both know they won't forget, no matter how long I wait. And I need to earn some coin. Don't worry. I'll be careful."

The warrior could only hope she spoke the truth. He wouldn't be able to follow her on her mission. He lacked the skills, and limbs, necessary to scale walls, climb through windows, and sneak silently through the shadows. If he went with her, he'd only attract attention, and increase the likelihood of her getting caught in the act.

"I'll be waiting here for you when you get back," he said, taking a seat on the chair by her bed.

"I don't mind you waiting in my room for me to return," Lhasha told him, "but do you mind stepping out for a minute while I change clothes? Unless you want me to go out wearing this."

Hopping to his feet, Corin silently cursed himself for his stupidity. Of course Lhasha had no intention of leaving the building clad in the eye catching ensemble she had worn down to supper.

"I'll let you back in when I'm ready to go," the half-elf assured him as he marched back to his own room.

Twenty minutes later Lhasha knocked at the door separating their adjoining rooms. After a brief pause, she opened it and stepped through. She was clad head to toe in a black, form-fitting outfit. Her long, delicate fingers were covered by thin black gloves, and a wide belt hung with a variety of tools and pouches encircled her tiny waist.

"What do you think?" she asked coyly. "Like my work clothes?"

"Very . . . practical," Corin said at last, arching an eyebrow.

"Gond's hammer," Lhasha exclaimed, "I think that just may have been a joke! There's hope for you yet, Corin." With that she was gone, slipping out the window to her own room and gliding down the wall to the street two floors below. She disappeared into the gloom, becoming one with the shadows of the night.

CHAPTER SIX

As the young man waited for his superior to arrive, he began to wonder if it was all worth it. The life of a Harper was never easy. The road was hard, the demands relentless. Family and friends were often neglected or left behind in the course of doing one's duty. Death hounded a Harper's every step.

In Elversult, that life was particularly harsh. In addition to the usual difficulties, there were a wide variety of concerns peculiar to the area. Infiltrating the Purple Masks. Maintaining Yanseldara's rule of law in a city that was, until only recently, controlled entirely by criminals. Plus, Elversult had always been a flashpoint for the ongoing war between the Harpers and the Cult of the Dragon.

For this particular young Harper agent, all the other dangers paled in comparison to the anxiety he felt over the impending meeting with Vaerana Hawklyn, the leader of the Elversult Maces.

Just then the ranger burst into the room, her long legs never even breaking stride as she kicked the doors open and crossed the hardwood floor until she stood right beside the young agent, towering over him. It was almost as if the mere thought of Vaerana's name had conjured her out of thin air.

To call the woman responsible for the security of Elversult, as well as Lady Lord Yanseldara's personal protection intimidating was the grossest of understatements. It wasn't the gleaming armor she always wore, or the savage array of weapons belted on her waist and strapped across her chest. Her wild mane of honey blonde hair and the way her muscles flexed as she moved were imposing to say the least, but even these were not the cause of the sudden trembling in the young man. With Vaerana, the most frightening thing about her was something intangible—her blunt, straightforward, some would say rude, manner. She had a seemingly permanent scowl etched upon her face and hard, unblinking eyes that bore right through you.

"Well," she demanded sharply of the already nervous young man, "what do you want? I'm in a hurry."

Somehow the agent was able to speak without stuttering. He was, after all, a Harper. "I've brought news of the Cult of the Dragon."

"So spit it out already and quit wasting my time."

The young man was smart enough not to further annoy Vaerana by apologizing.

"There is a mage—Azlar is his name—who is rapidly growing in power and importance among the ranks of the dragon worshipers. He has just arrived in Elversult, accompanied by a platoon of elite guards."

The scowl on the ranger's face became even more angry, if that was possible.

"What's he here for?"

Shaking his head, the Harper agent replied, "We don't know. His mission has been shrouded in secrecy. All of our usual contacts in the cult have come up with nothing."

"What's the use in giving me a report if you don't know

anything?" she demanded. She didn't wait for an answer before continuing,. "If they're being that close-mouthed about what this wizard is up to, it must be something big. Very big. I don't like not knowing what those scaly Black Caps are up to. It's never good."

"Never," the spy agreed, instantly regretting his decision to open his mouth.

Vaerana fixed him with an angry glare. "Well, don't you think you better find out what's going on, instead of standing here chatting away the day with me?"

"Uh . . . yes. Of course. Right away."

And with that the ranger spun on the heel of her boot and stormed out of the room. The young man breathed a sigh of relief.

A full tenday had passed since Lhasha had formed her strange yet practical partnership with the taciturn soldier. Their relationship had already begun to settle into a familiar pattern. Every other night Lhasha would slip out to perform a burglary, returning after a few hours with a pouch full of coins. The rest of her evenings were spent dancing into the late hours while Corin relentlessly scrutinized the crowded tavern for non-existent enemies.

It didn't take many days for Lhasha to realize that Corin was always on duty. The warrior's vigilance never failed, it never flagged, it never let up. He was constantly on alert, every sense attuned to his surroundings, his thick muscles occasionally twitching in their perpetual readiness. On some level, Lhasha admired such dedication. But for the most part, she simply found it disturbing and unnatural.

Corin needed to relax, or he was going to explode. He had no outlet in his life, no way to ease the pressures of the world. That was probably what had driven him to waste his money and life on alcohol, but he didn't drink anymore. Not since she had hired him. Not even a glass of wine.

He didn't socialize either. Unlike Lhasha, he hadn't made friends with the staff. He barely even spoke to her. All her efforts to learn more about Corin, to turn the conversation to his past or his personal life before their business partnership, were met with cold silence.

Lhasha was certain that if she could just get him to open up a little bit their cold relationship would thaw. As it was, he was focused solely on his role as a soldier and bodyguard. When he wasn't hovering over Lhasha like a vulture over a fresh kill, he was in his room honing his already formidable martial skills with drills and practice. In Lhasha's mind, such obsession couldn't be healthy.

One night after supper, completely on a whim, she decided to do something about his one track mind. Somehow, she'd get him to open up. When the pulse quickening music of the halfling minstrels started, she resisted the urge to leap to her feet and dash out onto the dance floor.

The warrior gave her a look of mild surprise, but didn't say anything.

"I don't really feel like dancing tonight," she lied. "I'd rather just sit and talk, if that's all right with you.

The warrior shrugged indifferently.

"So, Corin," she said, "tell me something about yourself. Tell me your life's story."

"I don't feel like talking tonight."

She gave him a sour look. "You never feel like talking. To anybody. You might find if you didn't keep things so bottled up, you wouldn't be so miserable."

"I'm not miserable." His voice was dead, his words devoid of all emotion.

The half-elf shook her head. "You're not going to freeze me out this time, Corin," she insisted. "I think its time you let someone else share some of whatever burden you're carrying."

"My burden is my own business."

Inside, Lhasha smiled. Now she had him. "Actually, Corin, its my business as well. I can see it in your eyes, in the way you sit and stand, in the way you go about your duties as my bodyguard. Something is eating away at you, and that has a direct effect on me."

She paused to let her words sink in, and to give him a chance to respond. As she expected, he responded with silence.

"Corin," she insisted, "I have a right to know what's going on inside my bodyguard's head. You owe it to me to tell me about your past. About how you lost your hand."

The warrior glared at her. "I owe you nothing more than the protection of my blade."

"Then tell me as a friend, Corin." Lhasha had decided to lay all her cards on the table. She knew there was something worth saving in the grim warrior, a core of basic human decency hidden away beneath his bitterness and rage. She had seen glimpses of it, glimmers of promise. It wasn't in Lhasha's nature to turn her back on a person's suffering. She had learned that from Fendel.

But if she reached out to him, and tried to force him to open up what he wanted to keep hidden, she might just alienate him once and for all. She hoped it wouldn't come to that, but if she couldn't reach him tonight she might have to admit defeat and leave the angry man to his own self-destructive course.

"We've only known each other a tenday, but we've saved each other's lives. I think we've been through enough to consider ourselves friends. Tell me your story. It might even ease your pain."

The warrior laughed—a harsh, bitter sound. "You really think my pain so slight that you can talk it out of existence?"

"What can it hurt to try?" she insisted. "Do you think you're the only one who's ever suffered, Corin?" she added, her voice taking a harsher tone. Compassion wasn't the only way to make a connection.

"You know nothing of my suffering," the warrior shot back. "You couldn't even begin to understand."

"Try me."

"I was a soldier once, a warrior, a White Shield. I lost my hand in battle, and my life was over. There is no more to tell."

Lhasha had known drawing Corin out wasn't going to be easy, but his sanctimonious attitude was beginning to annoy her.

"When I hired you, I didn't realize you were a quitter, Corin. I lost both my parents when I was too young to even talk, but I managed to carry on. You don't see me wallowing in self pity."

The one-armed warrior sneered at her. "You know nothing about me, about what I've endured. You couldn't possibly understand my suffering."

"Then tell me," she demanded. "Explain it so I understand."

They locked defiant stares, then Corin dropped his eyes. His anger had given way to apathy. With a shrug of his shoulders he said, "Very well."

Corin collected his thoughts for a second then he spoke in a voice devoid of all emotion. "The battle that took my hand also claimed the life of many of my companions. Igland, the leader of our troop, was cut down in front of my very eyes. And the boy we were supposed to protect—a nobleman's heir—was seized by bandits and held for ransom.

"I lay in a bed for many tendays after the ambush, fighting for my life. My injury healed slowly, I became frail and weak. The blade that took my hand had poisoned me with foul magic. It was a month before I could even walk again. By that time the White Shields were no more. Leaderless, depleted in numbers and shamed by our failure to protect the boy, the surviving members of the White Shields had left the city, slinking away in disgrace one by one, but I chose to stay . . . Elversult is my home. I grew up here, my parents are buried here. How could I leave this place, despite all that had happened?"

Corin paused for a long moment, and when he resumed his voice was tight, his words tense with suppressed rage.

"At first I did not look for work, but spent my time praying to Lathander. They say he is the god of new beginnings and rebirth, and I prayed to him so that I could start my life over again.

"With each rising of the sun I made a pilgrimage to the Temple of the Dawnbringer, every day ascending the steep path that winds up the barren face of Temple Hill. I gave generously—virtually all I had—and prayed for many months to the Morninglord that I might be reborn and made whole again. But the clerics were powerless . . . their magic was no match for the foul necromancy of the dark blade that had marked me. The clerics did nothing for me, but they kept my coins."

Corin cast a hate filled glance out a nearby window, toward the bare hilltop that towered over all of Elversult. "Over the past year I found my money was better spent on bitter ale—at least it offered some temporary relief. But no matter how much I drank each night, the next morning I would awake again, stuck here in this city, beneath the shadow of that false Temple—a constant reminder of how the gods failed me, just as I failed to protect the nobleman's son. Perhaps that is justice."

"What happened to the boy?" Lhasha asked.

"He was returned, unharmed, after several months . . . though it might have been better for me if the bandits had just . . ."

Corin caught himself mid-sentence. "I bear no ill will to the boy," he said softly. "I am glad he is alive. I do not have to add the guilt of his blood to my burden."

He continued, his voice finally betraying his deep seated anger, rising into a shout. "But Fhazail—the pile of offal that was the boy's steward—I curse the bandits for not slitting his swollen neck!"

"Fhazail was ransomed with the young master, but he returned to Elversult with hate and revenge on his mind. He accused the White Shields of betraying the mission. Accused us of arranging the ambush. With the others gone, his finger pointed squarely at me, despite my injury. Of course he could not prove his lies, but the rumor spread . . . 'Corin Onehand cannot be trusted'!"

Corin pounded his stump into his left hand in anger, and then smashed it against the table. Noticing the startled glances of the other tavern patrons, the warrior lowered his voice before continuing.

"I trained myself to wield a sword again, but no mercenary company would hire me once Fhazail was done smearing my good name. Who will fight beside a man he does not trust? The Maces sent me away because of my wound . . . arrogant bastards wouldn't even give me a chance!

"I thought about ending my own life, but something stilled my hand as I held my rusty blade against my own throat. I heard the voice of Igland, my captain, calling to me from a great distance. As any good soldier, I heeded the call.

" 'Corin,' his voice said, 'the White Shields have been betrayed, and you must bring our killer to justice.' "

The warrior paused, trying to judge Lhasha's reaction to his story. The half-elf said nothing.

Corin resumed his tale. "Suddenly, it all became clear to me. There was a traitor on the mission, but it was not one of my fellow soldiers. Fhazail had arranged the ambush, and then turned the blame onto us."

"How do you know it was him?" Lhasha asked.

The warrior was silent for a long time. He had told the half-elf much, more than he meant to. Once the words started, it was almost as if they came unbidden, longing for release after being pent up for so long. Corin realized that he felt some connection to Lhasha. She treated him as an equal, rather than a cripple. She respected him for what he could do, instead of pitying him for what he couldn't, for that, he was grateful.

It was the rings that had given Fhazail away, of course. Those hideous rings that the vain steward always wore had exposed his lies. For some reason, Corin didn't want to mention the rings to Lhasha.

At the trial Fhazail was still wearing his precious rings, even after spending several months as a supposed prisoner of ruthless bandits. If Fhazail's story was true, the jewelry would have been taken from him. The brigands would have even gone so far as to cut the steward's fleshy digits off to steal his rings.

It was only after he had heard the voice of Igland that Corin had been able to remember this small but vital detail about the steward. The realization had come too late. By then, Fhazail had long since disappeared, and the chance for Corin to avenge his fallen comrades was gone.

Perhaps that was why he didn't tell Lhasha the truth. He was ashamed at his failure to recognize the proof of the steward's deception until it was too late. Or maybe he just felt he needed to keep something back, keep something hidden. He had bared his soul to Lhasha, left himself vulnerable. It was almost as if by keeping this one secret he could somehow convince himself that he had only told Lhasha as much as he wanted to, rather than what he needed to.

"I just know it was Fhazail," was the only explanation he offered his companion. "And so I spared my own life, in the slim hope that I might someday meet the traitor again and slit his throat.

"I was a protector, a guardian. My life had meaning. But when I lost my hand, my friends, and my profession, I lost everything. All that's left is revenge. The faint hope that I may someday draw my blade across Fhazail's throat. "

Lhasha shook her head sympathetically. "You have to let go of the past Corin. You have to move forward. If you don't, you truly are as dead as you claim."

"What is there for me to move on to?" he demanded angrily.

"Protecting me, for one thing," she replied.

Corin didn't reply, but stared pointedly at the table.

Suddenly Lhasha spoke up, her high voice rising to a squeal in her excitement. "I know! It's so simple, I don't know why I didn't think of it earlier—you need to move forward, to start a new life for yourself, to find a new purpose. You could become my apprentice!"

Without speaking, without even looking up from the table, Corin lifted his stump as if that explained everything.

"That's just an excuse," Lhasha chided. "I can pick a lock or a pocket with either hand, and you don't use your arms to move unnoticed through the shadows."

Now Corin did look up, fixing her with angry eyes.

"What makes you think I want to skulk through the night and rob people? Do I look like a thief?"

Caught off guard by the venom in his voice, the half-elf stammered out a reply. "I only meant . . . well, at least you'd be challenging yourself. You'd be learning some new skills, instead of lamenting what you had lost. Doing something besides wasting your life away in pathetic self-pity."

Corin didn't say anything, but merely sat in stoic silence—effectively ending their conversation. Faced with the impenetrable wall of stubborn quiet, Lhasha finally got up and left the warrior alone at the table. Corin noticed a score of eager young men were quick to swoop in and welcome the tavern's most popular partner back to the dance floor.

Corin watched the half-elf twirling to the music of the band. She spun wildly, as if trying to dance away her anger and frustration. Corin knew she had done all she could to reach him. Lhasha had offered her help, and he had rejected it. In fact, Corin realized, he had rejected her.

Several hours later, as they were each about to retire to their respective rooms, Corin awkwardly broke his silence.

"If you are still willing to teach me your trade, Lhasha, I would be willing to learn."

With a soft laugh and a warm smile she said, "Life is too short to carry grudges, Corin. Fendel taught me that. We can start tomorrow."

Fhazail's breath came in wheezing gasps. Sweat was running down his brow, dripping off his nose, chin, and even his flapping jowls as he trotted down the dark passage, his way lit only by the sputtering torch he held in his right hand. He wasn't used to such physical exertion. His muscles cried out in agony, threatening to knot up in cramps with every step. His heart thudded against the cage of his chest with the relentless violence of a barbarian berserker tossed into a cell at the Jailgates.

He didn't dare slow down. Fear kept him going. Not the fear of the shadows and creatures in the tunnel that scattered before the torchlight then closed in again in the darkness behind him, but fear of what lay at the end of the meeting. He was already late, and if he dared to stop the delay could have consequences far worse than agonizing cramps or an exploding heart.

As he continued to twist and wind his way through the labyrinth carved out beneath the Elversult streets, Fhazail cursed the unknown smugglers who had constructed the passages. The original builders had all died centuries ago, but as the network of tunnels grew and expanded the same meandering, irregular pattern had been adopted by the new builders. Some claimed the labyrinth was intentionally confusing as a way to thwart thieves and the Maces alike. Others just said an Elversult smuggler's mind was too twisted to even think in a straight line, let alone excavate that way.

At last, Fhazail could see a faint glow ahead. He doubled his lagging pace, and moments later he rounded a corner and found himself face to face with his appointment.

Or rather, face to chest. Fhazail's own gaze didn't even come up to the shoulders of the mighty orog who stood before him, filling up most of the tiny chamber they used for all their secret congregations.

"You're late," Graal snarled.

Fhazail's excuse stumbled out between gasps of air. "Not . . . my . . . fault. The directions . . . you gave . . ."

"Are you saying this is my fault?"

Fhazail shook his head.

"No . . . of course not. I'm . . . sorry."

In all the years he had worked for Graal, Fhazail had seen many men killed for less than the disrespect he had just shown. Of course, Fhazail knew he was too important to be killed without a very good reason. Ever since he delivered the information on the package the Cult of the Dragon had shipped into the city, he had become a favorite of Xiliath. Still, it was never wise to risk Graal's wrath. Not without a purpose.

"The fault was, of course, all mine," Fhazail said once he had caught his breath. "But your directions were complicated, and the tunnels are difficult to navigate. I lose all sense of direction in these passages."

Graal said nothing, and the silence made Fhazail nervous. He kept talking. "Maybe if I could get a map of the tunnels, so this wouldn't happen again—"

Graal barked out a harsh laugh. "A map? You bloated, simpering fool! There is no rhyme or reason to the smugglers' work! Half the passages are either dead ends, circle back to where they started, or lead directly into traps. Do you think the men who built these tunnels would have been stupid enough to make a map just so their enemies could find it?"

"Well, no . . . of course not, most mighty of warriors. I just meant a map of this area, the area where Xiliath operates. Or even just the areas under the supervision of the fearsome Graal."

Graal spat, not on the floor, but onto Fhazail's sweat-stained silk shirt. Fhazail knew better than to wipe it off. "I don't know which is worse, your pathetic attempts at flattery, or your stupidity. Why should Xiliath give a map of the tunnels he controls to someone as inconsequential as you?"

Fhazail knew he had his flaws, and he'd readily admit them. He was treacherous, he was weak, he was a coward. He was untrustworthy and willing to sell out his employer for a single chest of gold coin. Of course, Graal knew all this . . .they had worked together many times since Fhazail had first approached the orog to arrange the kidnapping of Lord Harlaran's heir.

Fhazail also had his strengths. He knew how to make the most of his situation, and he knew how to read people. He could exploit his position as one of Xiliath's favorites, and Graal's manner, more so than his words, gave away more than the orog realized.

"I don't think I'm as inconsequential as you would have me believe," Fhazail replied slyly, made suddenly bold by his assessment of the situation. As he spoke, the steward rubbed his oversized gold rings, drawing his courage from the reassuring feel of the thick bands of gold beneath his sweaty fingers. "After all, I am Xiliath's spy in Azlar's house—and Azlar is rising quickly through the ranks of the Cult of the Dragon. It was I, after all, who first told you about the package. Without me, Xiliath wouldn't have a clue what the cult was up to."

"Your tie to the cult mage makes you valuable, but not unexpendable," Graal threatened in a low voice, the tendons and sinews in the orog's mammoth shoulders knotting and unknotting in unconscious anticipation of coming violence. Fhazail could see the hilt of the enormous black blade strapped to Graal's back undulating with every flex of his muscles.

Graal's reply confirmed what Fhazail already knew . . . his worth to Xiliath was important. Otherwise Graal would have already chopped him down where he stood. Still, as Graal licked the two inch tusks protruding from his lower jaw, Fhazail knew the orog's fury was slowly working itself up to the point where even Xiliath's orders wouldn't save Fhazail from being sliced apart limb by limb.

Whenever Fhazail felt his stock was high, he liked to push the great beast . . . it was important to know where

Xiliath's right-hand man's limits were when it came time to negotiate fees. Fhazail also knew when to step back from the brink. The best way to avoid the orog's mounting wrath was to get the creature's mind focused back on his master's efforts to establish himself as a force in the Elversult underworld.

Fhazail's voice adopted its most servile tone.

"Of course I understand how lowly I truly am in Xiliath's plans," he said by way of apology. "Why have you summoned me here, Graal? I wait with eagerness to hear the service Xiliath demands of me at this time."

Graal stopped licking his lips, and much to Fhazail's relief the glaze of bloodlust in the orog's eyes was replaced by Graal's typical cunning glare. Fhazail knew his insolence had come very close to the limit this time. He filed the information away for future reference.

"The . . . package Azlar received. He has it in one of the Cult of the Dragon warehouses in the merchant's district. Attacking the mercenaries guarding the compound and the guards inside the warehouse would attract the attention of too many eyes. We don't want the Purple Masks to know of Xiliath yet, and Yanseldara or her attack dog Vaerana Hawklyn must not become wise to the cult's plan."

Fhazail nodded.

"Of course, O terrible Graal. I understand. The package must be moved somewhere less safe if Xiliath is to obtain it."

Graal grunted, acknowledging Fhazail's grasp of the situation.

"Azlar and his men need a scare put into them. Flush them out. Make the serpent worshipers slither out of their hidey hole like the worms they are."

"Well spoken, most eloquent Graal," Fhazail said with a bow. The corpulent steward had long ago learned that

Graal was much smarter than people realized. Most dismissed him as little more than an ignorant beast. Fhazail knew the orog liked to have his intelligence noticed.

Graal smiled at the compliment. At least, Fhazail thought he did. It was hard to tell with the tusks.

"Xiliath will leave the specifics up to you, steward. Find some way to make Azlar move the package." The orog's voice became even deeper than its usual growling baritone as he leaned in close to Fhazail, eclipsing the dim light from the torches on the wall. Fhazail could actually feel the words vibrating through the floor as Graal continued. "Make sure the Masks are not involved. They cannot learn about the package. And if Yanseldara gets even a hint of what is going on I will rip your fingers off and devour them one by one, rings and all."

Fhazail cringed beneath the hulking warrior, more for effect than out of any real fear. He nodded his understanding with a trembling chin. Satisfied that he had made his point, Graal stood up again and retreated a step.

"I already have the inklings of a plan," Fhazail said after quickly reevaluating where he stood, and deciding he was in a strong bargaining position. "However, it will take me a tenday or two to find an appropriate individual to carry out my plan. Of course, it will require something above my usual monthly fee."

Graal squinted until his already beady eyes were just pinhole slits beneath his heavy brow.

"How much?"

Fhazail swallowed once, his throat was suddenly dry. But he knew how far he could push the orog, or thought he did.

"Uh . . . double?"

Graal exploded into action, moving his massive bulk with unnatural speed. Roaring out curses in his guttural native tongue, he seized Fhazail under the armpits and hoisted him high into the air. The steward let out a shriek and went limp, certain the orog would smash his head against the floor, or tear his arms out of their sockets.

The orog only held him, keeping Fhazail's obese body suspended several feet above the tunnel floor.

"You do not know me as well as you think, Fhazail."

Graal released his grasp, and the merchant landed heavily on the ground, his legs unable to bear the weight of his own flesh after being dropped from several feet. Fortunately, Fhazail landed on his ample posterior, avoiding a twisted ankle or worse injury.

Graal stared down at him.

"I'll give you half."

Fhazail scrambled to his feet, an awkward, ungainly sight.

"Thank you, Graal . . . for your generosity and a valuable lesson," he said, bowing his head in acknowledgement.

The only reply was a grunt and a dismissive wave of Graal's massive paw. Taking the cue, Fhazail scuttled back the way he came. He would have bruises under his arms for a tenday from Graal's crushing grip, and tomorrow he'd be so stiff and sore from his hike through the tunnels that he'd barely be able to haul himself out of bed. The sweat stains on his silk shirt would be impossible to wash out. All for a bonus of half his normal fee. Half!

He'd been expecting at most a third. Fhazail smiled as he waddled through the tunnels.

CHAPTER SEVEN

G'day, Master Corin. Would Miss Lhasha appreciate you sneaking into her chambers like this?"

Corin, who had been fumbling with the lock to Lhasha's room, turned to face the speaker.

"Oh . . .Weedle," Corin said, recalling the halfling room steward's name at the last possible second. It had been nearly a month since he and Lhasha had first checked in to the Golden Staff, and even now Corin still sometimes forgot the names of the staff.

The warrior realized he had been caught in a compromising situation, and offered a quick explanation.

"Lhasha's out and I need to get into the room."

Weedle smiled impishly, a mischievous glint in his eyes as he arched his eyebrows.

"A surprise for Miss Lhasha, eh? In her room yet."

Corin coughed, slightly embarrassed at the portly little fellow's insinuation. "We're just friends."

Weedle shrugged

"None of my business, Master Corin. All I'm sayin' is Miss Lhasha's a fine looking lady, or so I've heard the patrons in the bar downstairs say.

A bit too tall and gangly for myself, of course. Anythin' over four feet tall's a bit much . . . ." Hastily he added, "No offense intended."

Corin shook his head to show he wasn't bothered in the least.

Weedle pulled a ring of keys from his belt. "Well it's no business of mine, but I've got a key for you here so you don't have to worry 'bout the lock no more."

"No," Corin protested. The whole point was to pick the lock and be waiting inside when Lhasha returned. He had to prove a point.

The halfling slowly put his keys back on his belt and gave Corin a sideways glance.

"Tall folk . . . never can figure you out. Well, if you need anything else, just let me know."

Nodding, Corin resumed his efforts on the lock, much more appreciative of the employees at the Golden Staff than when he had first rented the room in the early days of the Claws of the Cold. He was beginning to understand Lhasha's argument about being friendly toward the staff. If Weedle had caught him fumbling with the lock on a door the first night, he would surely have called for the inn's armed patrols to come and deal with the thief before hauling him off to the Jailgates, but the room steward liked Lhasha. He trusted her, and by association, he had even begun to like Corin somewhat. That was probably the only reason the Maces hadn't been called to haul Corin away.

However, Lhasha wasn't right about everything. In their month together, the warrior had been unable to convince his employer of the threat to her life, or of the necessity of having him keep guard while she slept. Despite his frequent efforts to change her opinion, despite the ever improving relationship between them, she still insisted he was being overly cautious and refused to listen to reason.

Corin suspected that their relationship was actually becoming a detriment to his job. He found himself listening to Lhasha when she spoke, he actually enjoyed her conversation. She was charming and often funny, and always in a good mood. More and more he was catching himself paying too much attention to her words, and not enough attention to their surroundings.

So far there had been no consequences, but Corin chided himself for the lapses. In spite of Lhasha's frequent urging to "take a break, relax" or "cut loose," he still believed in the basic White Shield tenets of ever vigilant, ever ready.

The only way to get through to his stubborn friend, Corin realized, was to demonstrate to Lhasha how dangerous her situation really was.

He withdrew a thin, stiff wire from his pocket. Lhasha had given him the pick shortly after she had begun teaching him how to open locks without a key.

"Every thief needs a lock-pick," she had insisted at the time. "It's as precious as a warrior's sword and shield. Always keep one handy—you never know when you might need it."

Using his one good hand, it took Corin several minutes of manipulating the pick before the lock to her room at last clicked open. Corin allowed himself a little smile.

Breaking and entering. In three short tendays he had come a long way from the man troubled even by the thought of working for a thief. Lhasha had taught him well. Corin had to admit she knew her profession. Learning how to pick locks, or move without a sound, or hide in the shadows, did seem to ease the bitter sting of Corin's memories. The half-elf had been right again.

But she wasn't right about this!

Having successfully negotiated the lock, Corin slipped into the room. He left it dark, and locked the door behind him. He settled into a chair to await Lhasha's return. She wouldn't listen to reason, so it was time for a practical demonstration of her own vulnerability, and if that meant giving her a good scare in the process, so be it.

Lhasha carefully studied the man from across the crowded tavern of the Fortunate Knight. He wasn't a Purple Mask, she was sure of that. The Masks prided themselves on being physically fit, a necessity for climbing into upper story windows. This man had to weigh at least three hundred pounds—he could barely climb the stairs, let alone a terrace. The tavern wasn't warm, but even from her hiding place in the shadows in the corner of the bar she could see his face was glistening with perspiration. No, he definitely wasn't a Mask, but she still had a bad feeling about the meeting.

Lhasha preferred to freelance, but on occasion she would do work for hire, if the price was right, and this price was very, very right. An unsigned note left at the front desk of the Wyvern's Pipe had been forwarded to Fendel by the proprietor. Knowing she needed money, Fendel had passed the message on to her. Very short, very mysterious—just a number, a time and a place. Lhasha didn't like mysteries, but the number on the page was too high to ignore.

If she'd told Corin what was going on, he'd have no doubt objected to the meeting. He objected to everything, even her clothes. "They attract too much attention. They make you stick out in the crowd." But of course, that was the whole point.

She told him she was going out on a job. It wasn't really like lying to him . . . it was for his own good. Corin took his job seriously. A little too seriously, sometimes. He wasn't even drinking anymore—not a drop since she'd hired him. These past few tendays he spent all his free time mastering the few thieves' tricks she'd taught him, or practicing with his sword, honing and refining his already impressive skill with the blade. His dedication bordered on mania. That was why she hadn't mentioned this rendezvous. No sense getting him worked up. Besides, she didn't need her hired muscle looking over her shoulder all the time; she had enough sense of her own to avoid walking into a trap.

Lhasha gave a quick scan of the rest of the bar before deciding it was safe to meet her prospective employer. She slipped out of her chair in the shadows—almost seeming to materialize from the darkness—and approached the fat man sitting at the table across the room.

The man glanced up, and wiped the sweat from his shiny forehead with a silk handkerchief. Now that she was closer, Lhasha could see that his entire wardrobe was silk . . . bright red, gold, and yellow, with a splash of orange for effect; plus some permanent sweat stains under his armpits and around his collar. He looked like some kind of bloated butterfly.

Lhasha herself had a similar outfit, and she briefly wondered if she looked as ridiculous in her silks as he did in his. No, she quickly decided. She didn't. On her it looked good.

Most of all, she noticed his rings, if that was even an applicable term. Little more than huge hunks of gold, encrusted with a variety of oversized, ill cut gemstones. Calling them gaudy would have been a compliment. Half a dozen bands of gleaming yellow, each completely devoid of any sense of style or taste, despite the obvious wealth that had been spent on the materials. Lhasha felt a brief touch of regret that so many beautiful gems had been condemned to an eternity encased in such ugly prisons of gold.

"Finally!" he said in an a voice as loud and overbearing as his dress and adornments. "I've been waiting a dragon's age."

A little taken aback by his lack of discretion, Lhasha apologized.

"I'm sorry . . . I didn't mean to keep you waiting."

The man waved his chubby hand in an imperial gesture of forgiveness, making the rings actually clunk against each other with a dull, heavy sound.

"No matter, you are here now. Fetch me some wine . . . if you have any that won't make a man of my station ill."

Lhasha couldn't help but smile a little at the mix-up as she took a seat.

"What are you doing?" the man protested, half rising from his chair. "How dare you presume to seat yourself at my table!"

Suddenly Lhasha wasn't smiling anymore. "Sit down and shut up, you blathering fool," she hissed. "I'm not the serving wench, I'm the person you're meeting!"

The man froze, half in his seat, half standing. "You? You're the best thief in Elversult?"

"I don't know if I'd go that far," Lhasha said modestly, "but I'm good. Very, very good. You were expecting someone else? A man perhaps?"

"No . . ." the man said slowly, lowering himself back into his seat. "Not a man, necessarily. Just someone more . . . imposing. You don't look like you're cut out for this kind of work."

"What kind of work do you think I do?" Lhasha asked suspiciously. "I'm not an assassin," she hastily added.

"No, of course not," the man said, shaking his head so vigorously the flesh on his cheeks and neck actually jiggled. His voice had changed from the imperious tone of a noble addressing a serf to the slick patter of a merchant trying to close a deal. "My inquiries around town weren't for an assassin, but for a thief. One of exceptional quality. One not working for the Purple Masks, or the Cult of the Dragon . . . not too many independent operators left in this town. My sources said to leave a message with the innkeeper at the Wyvern's Pipe. Imagine my chagrin when he told me you had recently checked out. But since you're here, I take it you got my message?"

Lhasha nodded. "It was passed on to me. You're offering an awful lot of money, probably enough to buy anything I could possibly steal. Something doesn't seem right about this."

The man gave her an oily smile that did nothing to reassure her.

"And yet you're here, despite your doubts. The sum must be to your liking."

"It's a good place to start the bargaining," Lhasha said.

The man shook his head, still grinning his repulsive smile.

"Oh no, my pretty little thief. The offer is non-negotiable. Take it or leave it. If there's one thing I know, it's how to read people. I can see you're already thinking of taking my offer."

Lhasha found his condescending attitude grating. Pompous and vain, he obviously felt himself above the unwashed commoners of the city. Lhasha wanted to get up and walk away, just tell him to take his offer and stuff it down his fat, swollen throat, but he was right . . . she was very close to accepting. It was more than she'd normally make in a month. More than enough to get Fendel started on Corin's prosthetic arm. She had to at least hear the odious man out.

"I'll admit you have my interest. What's the job?"

"Nothing too difficult. One of my competitors has recently brought a package into the city, something quite rare. Something you can't just buy. My industry is very competitive, and it is vital that I get the package for myself."

"What is it?"

He waggled a chubby finger under her nose.

"Tut-tut. You'll find out when you get there. It's in one of the warehouses over in the merchant's quarter. Heavily guarded, of course. I'll give you the exact location if you accept. Needless to say, the utmost discretion is required. That is why we came to you, and not the guild. Too many spies in the Purple Masks, no secret is safe with them."

"I don't like being kept in the dark," Lhasha said. "How large is this package? Will I even be able to carry it out if I find it?"

The fat man waved his hand dismissively, his horrible rings catching the light from the tavern's fire.

"I guarantee that won't be a concern."

Still, Lhasha hesitated. Her instincts were rarely wrong, and something about this job seemed off.

"As I said, I have a gift for reading people," the man said, "I sense you need something more. A sign of good faith, perhaps. Tell you what . . . I'll pay you half up front, the rest on delivery. Do we have a deal?" He extended a plump hand.

Lhasha considered the offer for several more seconds before clasping his hand in her own slender fingers.

"Deal."

Corin heard someone just outside the door. Lhasha was back earlier than he expected, he wasn't even in position. Moving as quickly as he could without giving himself away, he found a corner that would be well concealed in shadows when the door to the hall was opened. He'd wait until Lhasha was inside before springing out—hopefully a good scare would make her change her mind about a bodyguard at the foot of her bed.

The door was opened slowly, cautiously. Three silhouettes crept in, the last closing and locking the door behind them. The light from the hall had illuminated the intruders for a brief second before the door shut. Three men, their faces covered by violet cloths wrapped tight around their skulls. Purple Mask assassins.

Corin remained motionless, cursing himself for being unarmed. A stupid breach of protocol . . . a White Shield was trained to always carry a weapon, whether on duty or not.

Some of Lhasha's cavalier attitude must have rubbed off on him.

The men stood still, waiting for their eyes to adjust to the blackness of the room. Corin's only advantage was the fact that his eyes had already adjusted to the dark, it would take a couple minutes before his opponents would be able to pierce the dark well enough to see him in the deep shadows. He moved fast, hoping the gloom could compensate for his lack of a weapon.

He struck with lethal precision, bracing his stump against the back of one man's neck and wrapping his other arm around his target's forehead. One sharp pull and the man's neck broke with a barely audible crack of vertebrae.

As the body slumped to the floor, Corin yanked the short blade from the inert grasp of his first victim. The other two assassins struck out with their own daggers, zeroing in on Corin's location through the sounds of the kill. Their blows were uncannily accurate, knives slicing the air in a pattern designed to disembowel their unseen foe.

Corin had thrown himself clear, rolling in a backward somersault across Lhasha's bed and landing on his feet on the other side, placing the canopied mattress between himself and his attackers. The would be assassins paused, heads tilted at odd angles as they tried to sense Corin's new location.

The aggressive stance his opponents now assumed did not resemble men facing an unknown, unseen enemy. Somehow they knew where he was . . . they could feel him. Corin had heard stories of warriors who were able to do battle even in the dead of a moonless night, sensing their opponents only through sound and motion. Blind fighting, it was called. Obviously the stories were true.

Corin hefted the assassin's dagger, trying to get a feel for its weight and balance. He was used to handling a sword, and the tiny blade felt awkward in his hand. There was no sense of substance. It was too small to parry an incoming attack, too short to strike a killing blow without getting in very close, closer than Corin wanted to get.

He studied the shadowy forms of the men across the bed from him, focusing on the way they held their knives out in front of them, moving the blades in slow side to side circles. There was no hint of the awkwardness Corin felt while wielding the unfamiliar weapon.

Corin briefly considered calling for help, but decided against it. His enemies had a vague sense of where he was, and if he closed to engage them their sightless fighting ability would enable them to meet his attack. If he stayed silent and motionless, they still would have trouble locating him precisely. Calling for help would give his exact position away, and for all he knew the knives were balanced for throwing. So Corin kept quiet, and still.

If Corin waited too long, the Masks' own eyes would adjust enough for them to make him out in the darkness. It was time to act. He dropped flat to the floor behind the bed. Even as Corin's body struck the hardwood he heard the *thunk* of a dagger plunging into the wall above him. One of his foes had keyed in on Corin's movement, and with a flick of the wrist had launched a nearly fatal strike.

Corin used the momentum of his fall to roll under the bed in one smooth motion. An attacker dived across the top of the mattress and landed on the other side, throwing himself toward the sound of his foe in an effort to get in close enough to use his dagger. Corin's stump swept out from beneath the bed and knocked the Mask's feet out from under him. As the assassin hit the floor, Corin lashed out from his hiding spot with the knife, burying it deep in the man's side. He felt the blade penetrate the chest wall, slicing through the tough tissue between the ribs. Corin twisted the blade and drove it in farther. The muffled screams of the man told Corin he had punctured a lung, and the warm, sticky fluid spurting out from the wound meant he was sure to die soon.

From his spot beneath the bed, Corin saw the feet of the final assassin land on the floor just beyond the dying body of his companion. Drawn by the sound of his partner's death throes, the final man had leaped across the mattress to finish Corin off. Leaving the knife embedded to the hilt in the dying Mask's torso, Corin rolled out the other side of the mattress, toward the door. He popped to his feet, only to stumble over the body of the man with the broken neck and fall to one knee. His enemy was on him before he could recover.

A bolt of pain shot through the length of Corin's amputated arm as the assassin plunged the knife into his shoulder. Corin twisted away, dislodging the blade from the wound. He threw himself onto his back, bringing his feet up and kicking them out into the chest of his opponent before the killer could bring his blade to bear a second time.

The man stumbled back and crashed into the wall, but bounced off and leaped forward again. Corin rolled out of the way as the assassin's blade sank into the floorboards mere inches from his head, sending splinters flying. Before the Mask could recover and strike a second time, Corin scrambled to his feet and across the mattress, out of range.

Corin seized the hilt of the dagger embedded in the wall and wrenched it free, then turned to meet the expected charge, driving the blade forward to impale his foe, but his enemy wasn't there. The assassin stood in front of the door, his blade once again carving the tight little circles in the air before him.

"I can see you now. Your death is assured," he said in a harsh whisper.

Corin knew it wasn't an idle threat. Now that his enemy's eyes had adjusted, Corin was overmatched. If he tried to throw the knife the Mask would see it coming and easily step aside. In hand to hand combat Corin wouldn't stand a chance. Bleeding heavily from his wounded shoulder, he was already feeling woozy. He still wasn't even sure of the proper way to hold the dagger in his hand, whereas the man across from him was obviously an expert with the weapon.

"Tell me where Lhasha is and I'll try to make your death merciful and quick."

Corin hesitated. The next words he spoke would likely be his last, he didn't want to waste them.

Every warrior knows the margin between victory and defeat is no thicker than an archer's bowstring. The element of surprise, opponents whose eyes haven't yet adjusted to the darkness, a foe unfamiliar with the weapon he wields, such are the little things that can turn a battle. Even something as insignificant as the sound of a key at the door.

An assassin is always wary of discovery. In their profession they must be constantly aware of unexpected intrusions. Creaking floorboards, squeaking hinges, the click of a turning lock—these are the warning signs of discovery, and the assassin's attention is instinctively drawn to them.

The warrior's survival demands complete focus on the enemy before him. Every action of his foe must be accounted for and countered if the warrior is to survive.

As Lhasha turned the key to unlock her room the assassin's attention was drawn, for the briefest of moments, to the door. Corin's wasn't. He saw his enemy's distraction, and he took advantage. By the time assassin's gaze had shifted back to Corin it was too late to evade the knife hurtling through the air. The assassin realized the extent of his mistake as the blade buried itself in his throat; the last conscious thought he'd ever have.

CHAPTER EIGHT

Lhasha let out a short yelp of surprise as she pushed open the door to her chambers. The light from the hall clearly illuminated the figure of a man just inside the door as he clutched feebly at a dagger protruding from his neck. Another man lay dead at his feet. The far end of the room was thick with shadows, but with her ability to see in the infrared spectrum of light—a by-product of her elf heritage—she could make out the form of someone standing on the far side of the bed, clutching his arm. She nearly bolted, then noticed that the person still standing had only one hand.

"I told you you needed a bodyguard in your room," Corin said.

Lhasha was already over the initial shock. These weren't the first dead bodies she had seen, though she wasn't used to seeing them in her bedroom.

"Are you hurt?" she asked, her heat sensitive vision picking up a trail of warmth running down Corin's arm. "You're bleeding."

Corin shrugged.

"It's not too bad. I just need to keep my hand on it."

Lhasha stepped in and quickly closed the

door behind her. Fortunately most of the patrons were in the bar downstairs, so no one had responded to her little scream. With the door shut the room was plunged into near total darkness, and she was forced to rely on her innate ability to see the heat emanating from objects and creatures as she made her way to the oil lamp on the table. She struck the wick with her tinderbox and was momentarily blinded by the heat that sprang up from the lantern as her eyes made the switch back to viewing in the visible spectrum of light.

"There's another one behind the bed," Corin said by way of warning. "Pretty messy. You might not want to look."

Lhasha almost took a peek just to prove she wasn't squeamish, then reconsidered. The corpses in the doorway had more than filled her daily gore requirement. She patted the bed.

"Come here. Sit down and let me see your shoulder."

Corin came over slowly, keeping his good hand pressed firmly against the wound as he lowered himself into a sitting position on the mattress. Lhasha could see blood welling up from between his fingers. Physical confrontation was generally something she tried to avoid in her line of work, but she had managed to pick up a few medicinal skills from Fendel just in case.

"It's bad, Corin," she said matter-of-factly after taking a quick look. "I can tie it off for you, but we should get you to a healer."

She wrapped the wound several times, yanking the gauze tight before tying it off. Corin grunted softly and winced from the pain, but otherwise stayed silent.

"So are you going to tell me what happened, or leave me to guess?"

Corin's voice sounded groggy. The toll of the battle and the lost blood was showing.

"Not much to tell. I was in the room when they showed up. I knew they were here to kill you, so I killed them."

Lhasha gave him a curious look.

"What were you doing in my room?"

"It's a long story." Corin sighed wearily, then changed the subject. "We should leave right away. There could be more assassins coming."

"I doubt that," Lhasha replied, wiping the blood from Corin's wound off her hands with the edge of the already ruined bedspread. "I don't think they'd bother to send more than three of their crew to finish off little old me. Lucky thing they weren't expecting you."

Corin didn't reply right away, he seemed to be lost in thought—or letting his mind drift.

"When the assassins don't check in, the Masks will send someone to see why they didn't report. We'll have to move. Soon." His words were slow, and slightly slurred. Lhasha briefly wondered if he had been drinking again, but she couldn't smell any alcohol on him.

She thought he was done speaking, he had paused for a long time, but eventually he continued, though it seemed an effort to do so.

"And as soon as Weedle sees these bodies, he's going to get the Maces in here. They might have given up looking for the fugitives who started the riot in the Fair, but I still don't want to run into them. Too many questions we don't need."

He had a point.

"All right, let me pack a few essentials," Lhasha said. "We can go stay with Fendel, at least for tonight."

Corin rose and took an unsteady step toward the door.

"I'll . . . get my things. My . . . sword and . . . other stuff."

"No," Lhasha said firmly, as if speaking to a child, "I'll

get your things. You sit on that bed and don't move . . . you're bleeding bad enough as it is."

The fact that Corin didn't even argue merely confirmed how serious his injury was. His knees buckled and his body slumped back down, slouching forward as he sat on the edge of the mattress. He seemed about to topple over. Lhasha began to fear something more sinister than simple blood loss was slowing him down. The Mask assassins wouldn't be the first hired killers to coat their blades in poison.

It took Lhasha less than five minutes to get both Corin's and her own things together, but in that time Corin's complexion had paled to a sickly gray. He was sweating profusely, and shivering. His head was bowed forward, staring at the floor—he didn't even look up when she came back into the room.

There was no way for her to know what kind of poison was in Corin's system, but he didn't look like he'd survive the hour if she didn't get him some help. The situation was urgent, but Lhasha didn't panic. A few seconds thinking things out would be worth the lost time if it kept her from making a critical mistake.

Fendel could help, or at least get someone else to help, but she couldn't leave Corin here in the room while she went to fetch the gnome. The Maces might show up and arrest him. Or worse. It wouldn't be long until the Masks sent someone to investigate why their assassins hadn't checked in. She'd have to take Corin with her.

Hopefully he could still walk.

She tossed a handful of coins on the table to cover the cost of replacing the bloodstained bedding, wrapped an arm around Corin's waist, and pulled.

"C'mon Corin," she said with a grunt. "On your feet. Let's go for a walk."

Corin didn't respond at first, he was dead weight. She

couldn't even get him upright. After a few seconds he stood—very slowly.

"Keep moving, Corin," she said. "Let's go. Out the door."

Lhasha staggered beneath his mass, but thankfully Corin was still able to support much of his own weight. It was a struggle to get Corin down the stairs, but once she got him out onto the street, on the level ground, he was able to walk on his own.

The sky was just turning to dusk, and nobody paid much attention to the pair as they stumbled along. Most dismissed them as a drunk being carried home by this evening's chosen courtesan; those few who recognized the signs of poison knew better than to get involved in guild business. As they slowly made their way toward the Church of Gond, Lhasha kept up a litany of encouragement.

"Good, Corin. Another step. That's the way. Keep it going. One more. Again. You're doing fine."

Lhasha doubted if he even heard her. Corin's steps came in an unconscious rhythm . . . marching without thought or will. Lhasha guessed he had done his share of forced marches during his days as a White Shield—that was probably the only thing keeping him going now.

They were nearly two thirds of the way to Gond's church and Lhasha was starting to believe they'd actually make it. There was only a half dozen blocks to go. Then Corin tripped over a loose stone in the street. His weight shifted, and the full impact of his muscular frame came crashing down on Lhasha, dragging them both to the ground. Lhasha tried to absorb some of the blow as she hit the paving stones, but Corin's body slammed her to the street, knocking the wind from her lungs.

She gasped for air and tried to blink away the stars in her vision.

"Corin!" she coughed. "You have to get up."

There was no response from her burly companion. Lhasha pushed against his inert form, trying to roll him off so she could at least catch her breath, but his weight was too much for her to handle. She managed to slither out from beneath his body, and quickly felt for his breath. It was still there, but very faint and very, very slow.

She didn't want to leave him lying face down in the street, but she couldn't budge him. Abandoning him where he lay, Lhasha sprinted off toward Temple Hill.

Corin was oblivious to the outside world, but he had achieved a new level of consciousness, a hyper-sensitive awareness of his body's inner workings. Every system was shutting down, moving slower and slower. He couldn't fight the sensation. There was no need to fight it. He felt no pain, no anger, no sadness. Just fatigue, and soon even that would be gone. The blood was congealing in his veins, thickening until its flow became a mere crawl. After countless millions of beats throughout the course of his life his heart felt weary. It still struggled to pump the sticky, syrupy mass that was once his lifeblood, but the contractions were faint and irregular. The air felt like water in his lungs, thick with phlegm and fluid. His chest cavity rose and fell in ever diminishing increments until, finally, Corin's breathing stopped and he slipped into the cool depths of the embracing night. . . .

A blinding white light of unbearable agony shredded the dark, soothing veil. Fire surged through his body; blazing, burning, searing, purging. With a rush the blood erupted through his veins and his heart began a frantic pounding to keep up with the flow.

As the violence of the living world battered back the peace of the grave, a coughing fit wracked Corin's chest. His body convulsed and heaved until he hacked up a mass of gummy, sticky slime from his lungs. Air rushed in to fill the void, and Corin breathed again.

His inner consciousness vanished, pushed out by the overwhelming sensations of the exterior world. His body lay on the cold cobblestone street, his head resting in someone's lap. Small, delicate hands gently cradled him, and he could feel the brush of a silk sleeve against his cheek. He caught a whiff of expensive perfume.

He blinked open his eyes to reveal a face framed by the shadowy background of the early evening sky. A face etched with concern. A wrinkled, balding, face with a bulbous nose, oversized ears and a wispy gray beard. Fendel was standing over him.

"Welcome back," the gnome said, the worry being replaced by a smile. "We almost lost you. If Lhasha had got me here a couple minutes later you would have been beyond my skill to save."

Corin struggled to rise, but the gnome reached out a gnarled hand and pushed him back down.

"Lie still," a soft female voice said. It was Lhasha who was holding his head in her lap. "The poison's gone, but you've still lost a lot of blood. Let Fendel help you."

"I'm not sure how much I can do," the gnome said as he rubbed his hands together. "Like I said before, healing isn't Gond's specialty, but I can take away some of the sting."

The gnome began a soft chant, his hands and fingers forming elaborate patterns in the air. He reached down and placed his palm on Corin's wounded shoulder. This time there was no surge of fire, no agonizing purging of his essence. There was just a warmth, then a slight tingle, and then it was done.

Corin reached up with his left hand and gingerly felt his shoulder. No pain. He pressed harder, and still felt nothing. He pulled the bandage down and traced his finger over what remained of the wound. Just a slight scab, no worse than a child's scraped knee.

Fendel smiled broadly. "Didn't even leave a scar! Not bad for a two bit cleric, huh?"

Corin leaned forward and rose to his feet, leaning slightly on Lhasha as he stood up. Even the minor bumps and bruises from the battle seemed to be less painful now.

"I owe you my life, Fendel. If there's anything I can ever do to repay you . . ."

"Just look after my little Lhasha-love, that's all I ask."

Lhasha was up on her feet now, standing beside him.

"Don't worry, Fendel. Corin's doing a fine job of looking after me. He actually saved me from a squad of assassins earlier today."

"Purple Masks?" Fendel asked, frowning slightly.

Corin nodded

"Who else?" said Lhasha.

"This isn't good," Fendel muttered with a shake of his head. "Not good at all. We have to get you off the street while I think of what to do."

"Do you think you can walk?" Lhasha asked Corin.

"I'm fine," Corin replied as he scooped up the bag that held the few personal items Lhasha had grabbed from their rooms at the Golden Staff. She had just dropped the bag on the street beside Corin's unconscious body when she had ran off to get Fendel. Fortunately no one had stolen them in the ten minutes it had taken her to bring the gnome back to her injured friend. "In fact, I feel better than I have in a long, long time."

The half-elf gave him a skeptical look.

"Are you sure? In the last hour you've been attacked by trained assassins, stabbed in the shoulder, and nearly died from being poisoned."

"All in a day's work, Lhasha. All in a day's work."

CHAPTER NINE

Once they reached the House of Hands, Fendel used a key to open a door at the back of the wall surrounding the church grounds. If the gnome hadn't pointed it out, Corin wouldn't even have noticed the camouflaged entrance built into the stone.

"We want to attract as little attention as possible," Fendel explained. "The front might be under surveillance."

The secret door opened into the courtyard, still littered with the frames, canopies, riggings, and half finished structures of inventions being built in honor of the Wonderbringer.

"No one will bother us in my private workshop," Fendel assured them. "You'll be safe there, at least for tonight. It'll give us a chance to talk over Lhasha's . . . situation."

Fendel's workshop was in a much better state than the last time they'd seen it. The damaged tables had been repaired or replaced, as had the chairs. The reams of paper blueprints and plans still littered the scene, but Fendel had gathered them into neat little piles scattered over the furniture and floor of the room.

"I see you've cleaned up a bit," Lhasha said.

"The automatic farmer didn't work out, Lhasha-love. Too unstable. I've since decided to spend a few tendays focusing on simpler gadgets. Trying to get back into the High Artificer's good books, you know.

"Pull up a chair," the gnome continued. "I want to know exactly what happened."

Once they were all seated, Corin related his simple tale yet again.

"Three men broke into Lhasha's room. I knew they were there to kill her, so I killed them. Not much to tell. Nothing I couldn't handle."

Lhasha sniffed indignantly.

"You forgot to add that the poison they were using almost killed you. This is serious, Corin."

"I couldn't agree more," Fendel said in a grave voice. "I know people in this town. Important people. Connected people. People who know things. I thought I'd get a heads up before the Masks moved on Lhasha." The gnome paused and tugged thoughtfully on his scraggly beard. "I hadn't even heard that Lhasha was an active target, much less that they were sending someone out today. Somehow I'm out of the loop. I don't like being out of the loop. Things must be more serious than I thought."

"You mean I've got more of a reputation than you realized?" Lhasha asked with a slight smile.

"The world doesn't revolve around us, Lhasha-love," Fendel replied. "There are dark doings in Elversult these days. Always have been, I guess. Sometimes when the wheels of history get rolling, the little people like us are left to fend for themselves, or get crushed underneath.

"I was under the impression that my contacts had some influence with the Purple Masks. Since nothing had happened, I was actually beginning to think my contacts had managed to convince the Masks to forget all about you. Obviously that isn't the case.

"Events must have pushed the favors promised to an old gnome to the bottom of their list, and it was just good fortune that it took the Masks almost a full month to find you again. Now that three of their members are dead, I don't think there's any chance the Masks will agree to just forget about you."

"I dealt with them once already," Corin assured the gnome, "I'll deal with them again."

Fendel shook his head.

"No, Corin. You won't. They didn't expect you to be there this time, this wasn't a very well planned mission. The next time I guarantee you'll both be dead before you even know you're in danger."

Corin bristled. "I think you underestimate me, little man."

The gnome ignored the insult.

"It's not a slight against you Corin. You don't know what you're dealing with. I think you both need to leave town. Now. Take a trip to Teziir. Catch a ship up to Cormyr and lay low for a while, take a break from the burglary game. At least until my contacts in the thieves' guild let me know what's going on, and for Gond's sake, don't steal anything on the way."

"Wait, Corin," Lhasha said before her companion could continue the argument. "Fendel's always been there for me my whole life. He raised me from a baby. I've learned to trust his judgment. He knows this town better than anyone. If he thinks we should leave Elversult for a while, maybe we should."

Corin shrugged, momentarily taken aback by the ease with which Lhasha had consented to the gnome's suggestion. His own ideas were never accepted so readily. "I think you're both over reacting, but I go where Lhasha goes. My job is to keep you safe. It doesn't matter to me if its here or on the other side of Faerûn."

A look of relief crossed Fendel's grimy face.

"I'm glad you're being reasonable about this, Lhasha."

“We’ll leave tomorrow,” Lhasha assured him. Then added, “But I’ve got one last job to pull before I go.”

“But Lhasha-love—” the gnome began.

She held up a hand to cut him off.

“No lectures, Fendel. If I’m going to Cormyr to live in temporary retirement, I’ll need some money to tide me over. This job will pay more than enough to get me by.”

“If it’s money you need . . .”

Lhasha didn’t mean to laugh, but she couldn’t help it.

“Fendel,” she said once she’d caught her breath, “how are you going to get me any money? What you don’t spend on materials and supplies, you’ve donated to the Church.” In a softer voice she added, “And besides, I won’t accept charity from you. I can look after myself.”

Fendel didn’t say anything else, but by the look on is face it was obvious he disapproved.

“Relax,” she said, giving the gnome a kiss on his wrinkled forehead. “I’ll take Corin with me on this job, just in case. I’ve taught him a few tricks of the trade. He might as well put them to the test.”

The gnome gave heavy sigh, then threw up his hands in resignation.

“Well, if I can’t talk you out of it, the least I can do is make sure you have all the tools you need. Tell me about the job.”

Corin was always surprised at how dramatically the young half-elf’s demeanor changed as soon as she started talking shop. Usually her tone was light and playful, but she was dead serious when the conversation turned to business.

“It’s one of the warehouses in the Caravan district. Simple in and out. Don’t know the exact nature of the package, but I was specifically told carrying it out wouldn’t be a concern.”

“The Caravan warehouses, eh? I think I’ve got some

blueprints. Just give me a minute to find them."

While the gnome was rummaging about his workshop, Corin moved in closer to Lhasha.

"How can you steal something when you don't even know what it is?" he whispered.

Lhasha waved him off and curtly replied, "Don't concern yourself with the details, Corin. I don't try to tell you how to do your job, so don't you tell me how to do mine."

"Excuse me?" Corin said, still whispering—though his voice was strained with indignation. "You damn well *did* tell me how to do my job. You wouldn't let me stand guard in your room, remember?"

"That just proves my point," Lhasha answered without missing a beat. "We saw how things turned out when I interfered with your profession. The lesson is obvious: don't meddle with experts doing their job. When it comes to burglary, I'm the expert."

Maybe the lesson is that I'm always right and you're always wrong, Corin thought.

"This smells like a set-up. I won't let you walk into a trap." Corin said.

Fendel found what he was looking for and turned his attention back to his guests.

"I agree with your soldier friend," he said to Lhasha. Corin didn't know how much the gnome had overheard, but obviously his old ears were still sharp. "You hired Corin to protect you. If his instincts say something's not right, maybe you'd better listen."

"I've learned to trust my instincts," Corin added.

Instead of continuing the argument, Lhasha simply pulled out the small pouch tucked in her belt and dumped the contents. A handful of gems clattered onto the table—diamonds, rubies, amethysts, emeralds. One large stone bounced off the hard surface and skittered across the floor until it came to rest at the toe of Corin's boot. He bent down to pick up the multi-faceted stone, marveling at its size and hue. Corin didn't have the first clue of how to appraise precious stones, but even he could recognize the value of the gem in his hand.

Fendel, who Corin suspected was more familiar with the true worth of Lhasha's cache, was too stunned to even speak. All he could manage was a tiny whistle of amazement. Slowly he approached the table and picked up one of the glittering rocks.

"It looks genuine," he said after a few seconds of careful study.

"Of course it is," Lhasha said, slightly annoyed. "You know I could spot any fake even while blindfolded and drunk on Cormyrian wine. They're all real. If this job was a set-up, why would my contact have given me all this up front? Is luring me into a trap really worth this much money to the Purple Masks? To anyone?"

Neither Corin nor Fendel provided an answer.

"Besides," Lhasha added, "Corin will be with me."

"How much is all this worth?" Corin finally managed to ask.

"Enough to pay Fendel for whatever items he can give us," Lhasha said with a smile. "And I imagine we'll still have enough left over for a healthy down payment on your prosthetic arm."

Corin glanced briefly at his stump, then looked up at Lhasha again.

"We should use this to finance our trip to Cormyr. We need to buy supplies, we might need disguises, we might need to bribe some of the Teziir officials, we'll have to hire a ship to cross the Dragonmere . . ."

"We'll have enough," Lhasha assured him. "This is just a down payment. Once I deliver the package, we'll get the rest. More than enough to cover the trip to Cormyr. And believe me, we'll travel in style!"

After a few more seconds of marveling at the wealth on the table, Fendel at last turned his attention from the stones.

"We may not like this, Corin," he said to the soldier, "but we're not going to talk her out of it. So let's get down to the nuts and bolts and make sure this job is done right."

He carefully moved the gems aside, and unrolled a set of blueprints—building plans for a large warehouse. "This is pretty much your standard Caravan district warehouse," he explained. "You'll have to get past the city patrols assigned to watch the perimeter of the Caravan district. Shouldn't be too hard. Elversult doesn't pay its civil servants that well, and these guys don't have the pride and prestige that goes with being a Mace. Half the time they're asleep at their posts.

"But if this package is as important as your client seems to think, there'll be private mercenaries hired for extra security around the warehouse. Most likely they'll have guards watching the loading bays, and guards at all the exits. So you'll have to go in through the roof."

"That'll be a neat trick," Corin said. "What are we supposed to do? Scale the wall?"

"That won't be a problem," Lhasha assured him. "I can climb up there without even breaking a sweat."

"But if the warehouse is patrolled, you'll need me inside in case you run into any of the guards," Corin reminded her. "Maybe you can make the climb, but I can't. I doubt I could have made it even when I had two good hands."

"I've got that covered," Fendel said, a hint of excitement in his voice. "A new invention of mine."

"I hope it works better than that stupid farmer thing," Corin muttered as the gnome went over to a bench on the far side of his workshop and began to rummage through the clutter on top.

Fendel returned with a half dozen long metal poles. The poles were rectangular in shape, two fingers width on each side.

"The collapsible ladder," he said triumphantly.

Corin grunted.

"The last thing I want in a ladder is a tendency to collapse."

Fendel gave him a sour look.

"It won't collapse while you're on it. Guaranteed to hold the weight of an oversized ogre with a belly full of kobold stew."

Lhasha picked up one of the square poles. Watching her, Corin noticed that one end of each pole was hollow, the other slightly tapered.

"So how does it work?"

"Glad you asked, Lhasha, glad you asked." Fendel grabbed a pole in each hand. He slipped the tapered end of the first into the hollow end of the second and pushed. "Just slip them together like so," he said. "Keep adding another piece until they reach the top."

"That's a lot of pieces," Corin said. "We'd probably need a dozen or so."

Fendel shrugged.

"I've got plenty, and they're surprisingly light, but strong, very strong."

Corin hefted one of the four-foot lengths, surprised at how little weight there was. "Mithral?" he guessed.

"Partly," Fendel replied. "It's an alloy I like to work with. A little mithral, a bit of tempered steel, some iron, and a few other things thrown in. My own personal recipe."

Lhasha grabbed several of the pieces and snapped them together in the space of a few seconds.

"Good fit," she said. "I like it. Throw them in a backpack and you're ready to go."

"All right, I can see how they fit together," Corin

admitted. "But where's the ladder part? So far all we've got is a really long pole with squared off edges."

"Here's the beauty of it," the gnome said with obvious excitement in his voice. "See this mark?" he said, indicating a small circle imprinted on the base of each section. "Press here."

Corin hesitated, a little wary of what the gnome might have in store, but with Lhasha watching he wasn't about to refuse. Using his thumb, he applied firm pressure to the spot. The circle clicked inward, triggering a spring. Two sets of metal bars, popped out at perpendicular angles to the rod. Corin dropped his piece in surprise, letting it clatter to the floor.

Fendel let out a gleeful laugh, and picked the rod up again.

"See that? Spring loaded. You can stand on these, to use them as rungs to help you up and down the pole."

Corin picked the pole up to give it a second look. The small bars that extended out were attached to recessed hinges set into the main body of the rod. When folded down the bars lay almost flat against the pole. The area beneath where they folded down had been shaped and shaved away to allow the bars to lay flat against the pole in the recess, making them almost unnoticeable when they weren't extended.

Corin pushed on one of the bars, trying to bend the hinge. He grunted and strained, but couldn't budge it.

"I guarantee you won't be able to fold it back down," Fendel assured him. "Push the button again and they'll retract."

Corin did, and with a quick snap the bars folded back into place, recessed into their respective notches in the rod. Even though he knew they were there, Corin could barely see the thin line marking out the section that folded open.

"This craftsmanship is exquisite," Lhasha said admiringly. "I mean it, Fendel. Truly amazing work. You're the best." She gave him another kiss on the forehead. Corin wasn't certain, but he thought he caught the gnome blushing. It was hard to tell beneath the soot and grime that seemed to permanently cover his face.

"So," Lhasha continued, "this can get us onto the roof. Then what?"

Fendel jammed his finger down on the blueprint.

"All of these warehouses have a few ventilation chimneys in the roof. It helps cut down on smells and odors in the agricultural warehouses. If there's ever a fire, it gives the smoke somewhere to escape, so that it doesn't get trapped in the building and damage all the goods. Also helps keep them a little cooler in the summer."

"That's right," Corin said, nodding in agreement. "I remember one summer we were sent to guard a spice shipment at one of these warehouses. You could see little streams of light coming down during the day through those things." After a brief second he added, "But they had metal screens on them to keep the birds out."

"True," the gnome admitted. "The screen shouldn't be a problem. I can lend you a pair of metal shears that will slice through the mesh like thread. But a lot of the screens are reinforced by iron bars, to keep people like you out."

"So how do we get by those?" Lhasha asked on cue. "Don't keep us in suspense, Fendel. I know you've already thought this out."

"Another little invention of mine. I call it the Bar Spreader. Not the catchiest name, but it gets the point across."

Lhasha and Corin waited patiently while Fendel hunted through his collections of gadgets.

"Here we go," he said after a few minutes. "You just

attach these clamps onto adjacent bars, and start twisting with this handle. That turns the screw, and forces the clamps farther away from each other. Turn the handle enough times, and it'll bend the bars—no matter what they're made of."

Fendel gave Corin the quick once over, then added. "It wasn't designed for someone your size, my broad shouldered friend. The spreader will bend the bars enough for Lhasha to slip through, but you might have a tight squeeze."

"Maybe I should just go in alone," Lhasha said. "Corin can wait for me on the roof."

Corin flatly refused.

"I still think this is a trap. We only go if I'm with you every step of the way."

The gnome squinted one eye and tilted his head to the side, measuring the warrior's girth.

"You should fit, Corin—barely—but you won't be able to wear any armor."

"Just so long as I can bring my sword."

"Anything else you need to show us?" Lhasha asked.

"Sorry, Lhasha. This is kind of spur of the moment. I don't have much else. If I had a tenday to put something together . . ." After a brief pause, the gnome snapped his fingers. "Wait a minute! There is one more thing. Not an invention exactly, but it might come in useful."

From his belt the gnome pulled a large, oddly shaped earring carved from a solid chunk of grayish white stone.

"Jewelry?" Lhasha said, a little taken aback. "You know I love to make an impression, Fendel. But that thing. . . ."

"Not much for style," Fendel admitted. "But its not for parties. The earring is carved from a very rare kind of gemstone I, uh, stumbled across. Audimite, I call it."

"I still don't understand."

"Audimite has some rather unique properties." He handed the earring to Lhasha. "Go stand on the far side of the room, and clasp this to your ear. Corin and I will stay here."

Lhasha did as she was told.

Fendel put a hand on Corin's shoulder and pulled him down so that the gnome was able to bring his mouth close to the taller man's ear. The gnome leaned in so far that Corin could actually feel hot breath tickling the tiny hairs inside his ear. In a voice that was so faint it was almost imagined, Fendel whispered, "I think Lhasha's gaining weight."

From the other side of the room, Lhasha shouted out an indignant response."I'm in the best shape of my life, you blind old coot!"

"You heard that?" Corin exclaimed in disbelief. Even with the acute hearing of her elf heritage there was no way Lhasha should have been able to pick up Fendel's voice from that distance.

"Yeah I heard it, and I hear you, too. No need to shout."

"I wasn't shouting," Corin answered in a calm voice.

"You're still shouting," Lhasha countered. "You're so loud you're going to make my ears bleed!"

"Lhasha-love," Fendel said, still whispering. "The Audimite amplifies sounds. Take the earring off."

Lhasha did as she was told.

"How's this?" Fendel asked in a normal voice.

"Much better," she replied, rubbing her ear where the earring had been. "I thought Corin was going to blow my eardrums out."

"Yes, there are some dangers to using audimite, but if you need to eavesdrop from a safe distance, it can be pretty handy."

"Sorcery," Corin said. "Are you a cleric of Gond, or a wizard in disguise?"

"Oh, I assure you," Fendel said with a sly smile, "I'm a legitimate follower of the Wonderbringer. There's nothing in Gond's teachings that forbids us from working something of the magi's art into our creations. The High Artificer might not approve, but he rarely approves of anything I do anyway."

From the first time he'd seen Fendel's odd farming contraption, Corin had suspected something more than simple mechanical engineering in the gnome's work. For a brief second, Corin let his mind turn to thoughts of the metal hand Fendel had promised him. He had been skeptical about the possible results, but if the wizened inventor planned to infuse the creation with some type of magical enchantment. . . .

Lhasha brought the warrior's thoughts back to the here and now by quickly, and none too subtly, changing the topic from the role of wizardry in Fendel's craft. "The sooner we get started the better. Corin and I will go to the warehouse tonight."

"And then on to Cormyr," Fendel pointedly added.

With a sigh Lhasha consented."And then on to Cormyr. As soon as we get paid, of course."

CHAPTER TEN

Fendel was right about one thing, anyway. The Elversult guards assigned to patrol the perimeter of the Caravan district were asleep at their posts. Corin felt like kicking them as he and Lhasha walked past. Their disregard for duty sickened him.

Using the directions provided by the nameless employer from the Weeping Griffin, Lhasha led the way through the rows of warehouses that made up the Caravan district. A few were tiny, little more than storage sheds, but most were enormous buildings like the one they planned to break into. The warehouses were primarily owned by the various merchant guilds that operated in Elversult—individual merchants could then rent space from the guild to store their inventory. Some were still owned privately, by wealthy families or organizations rich enough and powerful enough to resist the pressure of the merchant guilds to sell their holdings.

From personal experience as a hired guard, Corin knew that most of the buildings held little that was of value to the common thief. Huge shipments of raw goods filled the warehouses; worthless to anyone but the guild artisans and craftsmen who would transform them into a finished product. If somebody stole the raw goods, the only buyers would be the same guild merchants who had imported the product in the first place. They wouldn't be likely to pay for the same goods twice.

To further protect against thieves, every shipment coming in to or going out of the guild controlled warehouses was meticulously inventoried and cataloged to verify a chain of ownership, making it virtually impossible to sell stolen goods in any measurable quantity. In the Caravan district forged documents, bribed customs officials, and counterfeit goods were the new tools of the crook. In Elversult's new culture of legitimate business, embezzlement was a much more efficient method of making a dishonest profit than simple robbery.

Theft was still a concern for some who operated warehouses within the district. Since Yanseldara had come to power, the smuggling trade in Elversult had fallen on hard times. Yet there was still enough illegal goods coming into the city to require significant storage facilities. Many of the privately owned warehouses were stocked with addictive spices, banned poisons, stolen gems or jewelry, slaves, and other contraband. The Purple Masks and the Cult of the Dragon had many operatives posing as humble merchants, operatives who preferred not to leave a detailed paper trail for Elversult officials to stumble across.

The underground activities of Elversult's criminal element were the only ones who really still needed to guard against burglars. They knew the city guards were useless, but they usually had no trouble coming up with their own mercenaries to watch over their inventory. Corin suspected the building Lhasha and he were breaking into was one of these illegal, and heavily guarded, warehouses.

"This is it," Lhasha whispered, setting the pack she had slung over her shoulder on the ground. "Keep watch while I pop Fendel's contraption together."

In the silence of the night the soft clicks, as Lhasha joined the individual sections of Fendel's collapsible ladder together, seemed conspicuously loud. Nobody came to investigate. In less than a minute she was done. She pressed the trigger on the bottom section, and the rungs popped out with a loud snap.

"Try to keep up," she said with a slight smile.

Corin watched her ascend for a few brief seconds and knew she'd be waiting on the roof long before he even neared the top of ladder. She didn't climb up, she glided. Every movement flowed into the next, each step up with a boot, each gloved hand reaching for the rung above—every action was part of a fluid, seamless whole.

Clad in what she referred to as her work outfit—all black, form fitting clothes that were a sharp contrast to her typical eye-catching ensembles—Lhasha quickly disappeared into the darkness that engulfed the top of the ladder. Corin knew she was still there, and still moving, but her graceful ascent allowed her to naturally blend into the soft shadows of the night.

After a moment's delay, Corin followed with more difficulty. In part, his progress was slowed by his handicap, but even more debilitating was his fear of heights. Despite his best efforts not to look down, Corin was well aware of the empty space yawning beneath him. With each step up, he had to make sure both feet were firmly planted on rungs of the same level before he dared to release the grip of his one good hand. Even with his amputated arm wrapped tightly around the metal pole, he felt as if he was on the verge of toppling over each time he let go of the ladder to reach for the next rung. The sensation of the ladder wobbling beneath his awkward, jerky movements did little to alleviate his fears.

By the time he finally reached the top, Lhasha had used the shears to cut through the wire mesh over the ventilation chimney, and had already attached the spreader to the iron bars that blocked the opening. Corin could hear the groaning of the bars as the metal became fatigued from the stress being applied by Fendel's invention.

Lhasha grunted softly with each turn of the screw, obviously it was hard, slow work. The air was still cool during these first few nights of the Sunsets, but Corin could see tiny beads of perspiration on Lhasha's forehead, the result of her efforts to try to bend the iron bars.

"Glad you made it," she said between breaths, noticing Corin standing above her. "Maybe you could give this contraption a try, while I collapse the ladder."

Corin nodded, still a little winded from the climb up. It hadn't been physically demanding, but he had been holding his breath virtually the whole way.

He turned his attention to the bar spreader. Lhasha had clamped it onto two of the bars as Fendel had shown them, now it was simply a matter of turning the handle. With only one hand, Corin couldn't get the same leverage as Lhasha, but his superior strength more than compensated for the mechanical disadvantage. By the time Lhasha had the collapsible ladder stowed away in her backpack again, Corin had bent the bars enough to open a hole several feet wide. The mortars holding the iron bars in place had begun to crack and disintegrate into dust as the bars warped and twisted. Corin gave a few more turns to the handle to weaken the stone foundations holding the bars in place, then yanked the entire mess—the spreader and the bars it was clamped to—out of the ventilation chimney, sending a small shower of dust onto the warehouse floor fifty feet below.

"That should do," Lhasha commented. With the bars removed, the chimney was easily wide enough for even Corin to slip through.

The chimney led them into the exposed rafters that crisscrossed the upper reaches of the warehouse, supporting the structure from inside. The floor below them was bustling with activity, even at this late hour—confirming Corin's suspicions about the illicit nature of the inventory stored there. Lamps and torches from the warehouse floor provided a flickering, half-illumination of the roof. Not enough to expose Corin and Lhasha, but enough to allow Corin to see the narrow beams they would have to crawl across. Unfortunately for Corin, the dim glow also emphasized how far a fall it was from his precarious perch.

"Why don't you wait here," Lhasha whispered. "I'll scout things out from up top."

"Don't do anything stupid," Corin warned, wrapping his arms and legs tightly around an intersection of the beams. "Remember why you brought me."

"I'll come back to get you before I head down to the floor," Lhasha promised.

She set off along one of the narrow beams, and again Corin could only marvel at the self-assured ease with which she maneuvered through the rafters.

Lhasha wasn't even aware of the thousands of intricate movements her muscles made to keep her perfectly balanced on the four inch wide wooden struts fifty feet above the warehouse floor. Every step was instinctive, every compensating motion unconscious.

She cast a quick glance over her shoulder at Corin, clinging to the beams like a drowning man to a piece of jetsam in a storming sea. Lhasha allowed herself a quick smile. She had seen him in action, she knew he wasn't clumsy or awkward. Put a sword in his hand and Corin moved with the grace of a dancer, but get him more than ten feet off the ground. . . .

Lhasha turned her attention to the floor below. Men were scurrying about, loading and unloading caravan wagons, moving boxes and crates from one side of the warehouse to the other. In a corner she noticed a group of men gathered together, standing idle. She scampered across the rafters until she was directly over them, then put on the earring Fendel had given her.

". . . think I'm going to go ask the foreman about it? Not for all the gold on the Dragon Coast," one of the workers said.

"You don't need to ask," another replied. "I'm telling you what I heard. There's someone in the stone room. That's why all the secrecy. Someone nobody's supposed to know about is hiding out in there."

"Some *thing,* you mean. I get a chill anytime I go near the place. It ain't natural," a third voice added.

The first voice laughed nervously.

"True enough. The supervisor didn't need to tell me the stone room is off limits. I won't go within ten yards of that corner of the warehouse anymore. No one will."

"Berg did."

The nervous laugh again.

"Yeah, Berg was always the stupid one. Had to go check it out for himself."

"And look what happened," the second voice said. "Berg hasn't been seen in a tenday. Whatever he found scared him so bad he ran off without even collecting his back wages."

"That's the official story, but we all know it's crap. If Berg was still alive, he'd have come back by now."

There was a long second of silence.

“I wish to Lathander that they had never delivered that package, whatever it is.”

Lhasha took the enchanted jewelry from her ear. From her vantage point, she could scan the entire layout of the warehouse. In a far corner she noticed that an area had been sectioned off from the main floor by a wall of stacked crates. Inside this area were several piles of barrels and boxes, and a small building built right inside the larger warehouse.

The tiny building couldn’t have been more than ten feet on a side, and less than ten feet tall. From the color of the roof and walls, Lhasha knew this had to be the stone room the men were talking about.

She crawled back to where Corin was still firmly anchored among the rafters. His good hand was holding on so tight, the knuckles were white.

“There’s a small area cordoned off in the back. There’s a tiny building in there made all of stone. I’ll bet my career earnings that our package is inside that building. Since the area’s blocked off, I can use Fendel’s ladder to climb down from the rafters on the far side of the barricade. Nobody will even know I’m here.”

“Sounds simple,” Corin said, keeping his eyes locked on Lhasha, and safely averted from the floor below.

“Maybe, but whatever’s in that room, the workers want no part of it. I heard them talking about one of them who went to investigate and never came back. The foreman probably caught him snooping around and took care of it,” she surmised. “I bet there’s more than a few bodies buried beneath the crates in this place.”

Corin nodded.

Lhasha continued, “Still, it might be a good idea to have you watching my back when I check this room out. That is, if you think you can handle crawling through the rafters to get there.”

Corin gave her a sour glare.

"I can handle it. You just lead the way."

"I'll go nice and slow," Lhasha said with a smile.

Much to Corin's relief, Lhasha set a very languid pace. It took them nearly ten minutes to reach the back of the warehouse. Once beyond the wall of crates separating the area surrounding the small stone building, Lhasha quickly snapped Fendel's ladder together piece by piece until it reached the floor.

"I'll go first," Corin said. "If there are any surprises down there, I want them to have to go through me. If a fight breaks out, just stay out of the way."

"I'm not completely incompetent," Lhasha protested.

"You brought me along to handle the guards," Corin explained, "and I'll have an easier time with them if I don't have to worry about keeping you safe during the battle." He cut off further discussion by adding, "Remember what you said earlier: don't argue with the expert."

Gingerly, Corin stepped off the rafter and onto Fendel's collapsible ladder.

"At least if you fall, you won't squish me on the way down," Lhasha teased.

"Not funny," Corin growled. "Wait up here till I give you the all clear."

With a deep breath, Corin began his agonizingly slow descent, carefully guarding against any possibility of a slip that would send him plunging to floor below.

CHAPTER ELEVEN

From a hidden corner a pair of malevolent eyes followed the warrior's progress. Coiled in the shadows between the boxes and crates the watcher studied him, and flicked its lips with a forked tongue. The watcher could hear his thoughts, and it knew there was another. A female, waiting up above. They were here to steal the package the watcher protected. That would not happen.

The man was nervous, the watcher sensed. He feared a trap. Yet still he came down. Foolish, like most humans.

The male reached the ground. *Look left, look right*, his thoughts said, *check for guards*. But he couldn't see the watcher lurking in the darkness.

The urge to leap out and strike was there, but the watcher would not yield to the temptation of the quick kill. It knew patience. It would wait for the other, then kill them both.

The warrior stood very still, then tilted his head, listening. The watcher remained as still as a statue, giving no clue to betray its presence.

At last the male waved a hand and called up in a whisper, "All clear, Lhasha."

The female quickly joined her companion on the floor. Her thoughts were free of the unease that plagued her companion; the watcher sensed this female was excited and curious. *I can't wait to see what this package is,* she thought. The watcher knew the female's curiosity would be her death.

It had been many days since the watcher's last meal—another overly curious human, a warehouse worker named Berg. Since then, none had dared come beyond the wall of crates. Even the rats and vermin avoided this area. And the watcher had been forbidden by the master to go out into the rest of the warehouse to hunt. Now the hunt had come to it. Two thieves caught in the act. Two meals for the taking. The small one looked tender and sweet, the large looked hearty and filling.

The watcher briefly considered unleashing a blast of magical fire to incinerate the intruders, but quickly passed up the idea. The fire could spread about the building. At the very least it would draw the attention of the workers—something the watcher was forbidden to do. Plus, cooked meat was tough and tasteless. The best food was fresh.

With a whisper of scales on scales, the watcher crept ever so slowly toward them, relishing the coming slaughter. The noise went unnoticed by the two intruders.

Slithering around a pile of bones and tough leather boots—the indigestible remains of the unfortunate Berg—the watcher moved to the edge of the shadows and waited. Its days were filled with numbing tedium. It had long ago grown bored with the assignment. Now it was curious to see what the thieves would do next. It would toy with them as it had toyed with Berg.

"How's it coming?" the male asked, as the female carefully scanned the area around the door. Her head dipped as she surveyed the floor, then tilted slowly back as her focus climbed the length of the door.

"These things take time, Corin. You don't want me setting off an alarm, do you?"

"An alarm?" the male asked.

"I don't see one yet," she admitted, "but if this package is worth the fee we've been paid, there has to be something besides nasty rumors and a wall of crates to keep those workers out."

"I was sure there'd be more guards," the male agreed. "Maybe they're inside, just waiting for us to open the door."

"Hold on, I'll check." The female finished her scan of the door, confident there were no trip wires or other devices to set off a warning. The watcher laughed silently. They were so cautious, so careful. Yet they were oblivious to the true threat, the creature that would feast on their flesh. Their doom hovered not twenty feet away, but their attention was on a harmless door.

The female leaned forward and carefully placed her ear against the door, listening for signs of life on the other side. Again, the watcher was still as stone.

"I don't hear anything. I think we're safe. Let me get my pick out," she added, standing up and turning to face her companion. "I'll start on the lock."

Then she froze.

"Corin," she whispered at last. "There's something in the shadows behind you. A snake, I think. A big one."

The watcher spat on the floor in disgust. The female could see her through the blackness, sensing the temperature of the watcher's cold blooded body against the slightly warmer background of the wooden crates.

"Don't move," the male whispered back. "I'll draw it out."

He did a slow pivot to face the watcher, and began to tap his foot on the floor in a soft, arrhythmic motion.

The watcher sneered. They thought it was an animal, an ignorant beast driven by instinct. They were fools.

The watcher began an incantation, its sibilant voice

weaving words of power in the air. A simple spell, yet effective. A magic shield to hide it from sight—even from the damnable heat sensitive vision of the female.

"Wait, Corin. It's gone now. It just sort of . . . disappeared."

The watcher began a second spell. A charm to put the thieves to sleep while it devoured their living bodies. It would gorge itself on their beating hearts, pumping and spurting blood from their still warm corpses until only swords, boots, and a small pile of bones remained.

"Sssleep," the watcher hissed as it finished the spell. The male drooped his head, the female shut her eyes, but only for a brief second. With a start they both snapped awake. They were strong. Stronger than the watcher first expected. Perhaps here was an adversary worthy of destroying—unlike that pathetic snoop Berg.

"Did you feel that?" the female asked. "For a second I was so tired I nearly passed out on my feet."

"Magic," the large one said, his voice louder than before. "There's more than just a snake hiding in those shadows."

"Wait, Corin. I see it again. In the corner. It's huge."

Casting the sleeping charm had nullified the watcher's protective spell of invisibility. The female thief could see it again, but the male still peered hopelessly into the darkness.

With another litany of arcane chanting, the watcher quickly cast a third spell—one to keep its opponents from communicating and coordinating their attacks.

The male tried to speak to his female companion, asking her to point him in the right direction. Only oppressive silence came from his lips. Desperation flashed in the warrior's eyes, and the watcher heard the words, *More sorcery. We're sitting ducks!* shoot through his mind. With a soundless scream, the male leaped to attack.

He launched himself into the shadows, scattering crates and boxes in a noiseless vacuum of carnage as he tried to flush his unseen opponent into the light. But he attacked without direction, and he was nowhere near his target. The female pointed to the watcher, and tried to call out, but her warning went unheard, and unheeded, swallowed up in the magical blanket of silence that engulfed them both.

Amused at the antics of its prey, the watcher at first did nothing as the male flailed away in his futile search, and the female tried in vain to attract his attention and point out their enemy. Soon the watcher grew bored, and slithered out from its hiding place to slay the intruders. The hunt was over, soon the feasting would begin.

The female let out a soundless shriek as the watcher closed in.

CHAPTER TWELVE

Corin had a bad feeling about this job. Right from the start, his instincts had been screaming that something was wrong. Coming down the ladder the feeling intensified. He brushed it aside. His fear of heights was probably just making him hypersensitive. But even when he reached the solid reassurance of the warehouse floor, the feeling persisted.

Someone was watching them, waiting for them. He took a quick peek left and right, but couldn't see anyone. The area around the stone room was dim and shrouded in shadows. The wall of crates blocked off much of the light from the lamps and torches of the main warehouse. Corin squinted into the darkness—a small army could be hiding in amongst the crates, and he might not even see them.

So instead he listened. It was almost impossible for a group of men to crouch in a hidey hole and stay completely motionless for any length of time. He listened for the sound of a faint cough, a sniffle, a shuffling of boots or the metallic chink of armor caused by a hand scratching a nose. He waited for nearly a minute, hearing nothing, and still he felt he was being watched, but there was nothing there. At last he motioned for his companion to come down.

"All clear, Lhasha."

Lhasha scampered down the ladder with an eager agility that made Corin cringe. He knew she was excited. She was dying to know what the mysterious package was. Corin just wanted to get it and get the hell out.

Lhasha flashed him a sly grin, trying to ease his tension. Corin ignored it, and kept scanning the shadows. C'mon, Lhasha, he thought. Let's get moving.

"How's it coming?" he asked, his voice betraying his impatience.

"These things take time, Corin," she answered. "You don't want me setting off an alarm, do you?"

"An alarm?" Was that why she was taking so long?

"I don't see one yet," Lhasha admitted. "But if this package is worth the fee we've been paid, there has to be something besides nasty rumors and a wall of crates to keep those workers out."

Corin couldn't agree more.

"I was sure there'd be more guards," he said. Then an idea struck him. "Maybe they're inside, just waiting for us to open the door."

"Hold on, I'll check." Corin momentarily diverted his attention away from the surrounding gloom to see Lhasha lean forward and place her ear against the door.

"I don't hear anything. I think we're safe."

"Let me get my pick out," she added, standing up and turning to face Corin. "I'll start on the lock."

Then she froze.

Corin knew something was wrong, he could see it in her eyes. His muscles tensed, the adrenaline began to flow, but he didn't move, not yet. Not until he knew what was going on. Sometimes sudden movement was the worst thing you could do.

"Corin," she whispered at last. "There's something in the shadows behind you. A snake, I think. A big one."

"Don't move," Corin replied. "I'll draw it out." His decision to stay still seemed like the right one, now. Corin knew how to deal with snakes, and a sudden reaction could trigger the serpent to strike. With deliberate slowness, he turned on his heel to face the darkness. He could make out only blackness, but he trusted Lhasha's elf ability to see in the dark. He began to tap his foot in a soft, irregular rhythm. Snakes sensed vibrations, it was how they hunted. With his tapping foot, Corin tried to mimic the actions of an injured animal twitching on the ground. It should lure the creature into the light.

"Wait, Corin. It's gone now. It just sort of . . . disappeared."

Puzzled, the warrior stopped his tapping. He didn't think Lhasha was the type to jump at shadows, but could she have imagined it? Or maybe the flickering flame of the distant torchlight was playing havoc with her eyes' ability to detect heat, making her see things that weren't really there.

He heard a faint, hissing whisper. It sounded almost like a word.

"Sssleep."

A sudden weariness washed over him and his head drooped. But he snapped it back up and fought off the sensation. Probably a reaction to some residual Mask poison still in his system.

"Did you feel that?" Lhasha asked. "For a second I was so tired I nearly passed out on my feet."

It wasn't the Mask poison, not if Lhasha felt it too. "Magic," Corin said, making no effort to silence himself now. They had already been discovered. "There's more than just a snake hiding in those shadows."

"Wait, Corin. I see it again. In the corner. It's huge."

Corin couldn't see anything. "Where is it?" he tried to ask, but his words made no sound. More sorcery, he thought, we're sitting ducks!

The White Shields knew how to deal with wizards. Hit them hard, hit them fast, and hit them often. A desperate, all-out assault could usually keep a mage from using his powers. The relentless attacks disrupted their concentration and prevented them from casting spells. How could Corin attack what he couldn't even see?

With a soundless scream of rage and frustration, Corin threw himself into the crates and engulfing shadows. He struck with his sword, he kicked out with his boots, his knees and elbows smashed into wooden boxes and barrels and sent them flying. A silent rampage of destruction, intended to drive his unseen foe out of hiding.

Then he saw it, slithering from the darkness and into the light—toward Lhasha. Its serpentine body was at least a dozen feet long, and covered with gleaming black scales. Its head was an unnatural hybrid of human and snakelike features.

The beast reared up from the ground, towering over the half-elf as she fumbled to draw her dagger. Its fanged head struck straight down at the tiny thief with lightning speed. Lhasha threw herself to the side and the beast's jaws clamped down on empty air, then Corin was between them.

Corin had heard tales of such creatures before, snakes with human heads. A naga, it was called, but as he faced his adversary, Corin couldn't have cared less what the monstrosity was called.

The beast hesitated before striking again, Corin could see the intelligence in its eyes. It was studying him, sizing up its foe before attacking. Corin was doing the same.

The naga's head swayed hypnotically from side to side as it evaluated him. Corin fought against his body's natural fascination with the soothing rhythm. He needed to stay alert. He couldn't allow the gentle swaying to lull him into a relaxed state.

The unnatural silence unnerved Corin. The familiar sounds of battle were absent, he felt as if he was fighting in a dream, as if things were not real. The silence distracted him, blurred his fighting instincts.

He needed to focus, to center his senses to compensate for the loss of sound, to keep himself sharp and aware in the noiseless vacuum, Corin keyed on the tiny visual details of the encounter.

The naga's eyes were yellow with narrow pupils of black. Its mouth was disproportionately large, like the unhinged jaw of a snake, and its fangs were long and sharp.

More importantly, the fangs were slightly curved—a good sign. Curved fangs were meant to grasp prey, to hold it and draw it into the mouth. Not like straight fangs. Straight fangs had only one purpose; to inject poison into a victim. Curved fangs, as fierce as they looked, were no more dangerous than a blade of the same size.

Corin was so intent on the creature's head that he almost didn't see the naga's tail lashing out at his legs. He skipped back, just out of range, then swung his sword high as the head swooped in for a quick second attack. The naga jerked its head back, narrowly avoiding the edge of Corin's blade. It retreated, and resumed the mesmerizing, snakelike swaying.

Cursing himself for being so careless, Corin faced his foe with a new respect for the danger of this encounter. He wasn't used to fighting monsters. Most of his career had been battles against other warriors. He knew to watch for the blades, the kicks, the head butts, but a tail was something unexpected, something new.

Carefully keeping the weaving head within the edges of his awareness, Corin turned his focus to the naga's tail. It tapered to a thin, barbed point. Drops of glistening moisture fell from the tip—poison! Corin noticed that while the head rocked from side to side, the poisonous tail moved with its own independent rhythm.

He wanted to attack, to take the offensive, but he wasn't sure how to approach. Attacking was all about pressing an opponent, forcing them to defend a series of thrusts and cuts that would throw them off balance and keep them from countering.

But how could he get this creature off balance? How would he even know when he had a tactical advantage?

As the naga's head swooped in from the side, Corin ducked underneath. From the other side the tail stabbed forward, but Corin was able to deflect the poisoned barb with the flat of his blade. He threw his shoulder into the elongated body of the beast, trying to drive it back, but the muscles of the creature twisted and curved their form around him, threatening to wrap him in their grip.

A slash from Corin's sword deflected harmlessly off the scaled underbelly of the creature—though it did cause the thing to recoil, giving Corin a chance to scamper away and reset himself for the next attack.

The naga shot forward again, still leading with the head. Corin slipped to the side, but this time he was watching for the tail. It whipped in belt high, and Corin calmly stepped back out of range and hacked at it with his sword as it swished past. He put the full force of his weight behind the blow, and was rewarded as the blade bit through the scales into the soft meat beneath, bringing up a small spurt of blood.

The creature slithered back quickly, stinging from the wound, trying to lure Corin into pursuing it, but Corin held his ground. He was beginning to understand the pattern of the creature's aggression. He knew how to avoid the attacks and retaliate with his own. If he took the offensive now, he'd have to begin a new strategy. Corin was content to fight a war of counter blows.

The naga hesitated, Corin could sense the bewilderment on its alien face. It was uncertain, hesitant. Like Corin, the naga could read the developing battle. It knew it needed new tactics to survive.

Corin braced himself for a different approach. The creature slithered forward, keeping its head low to the ground. It brought its tail in high, arching its back so the stinger could drop straight down on Corin from above. The warrior's blade arced through the air, a huge sweeping slash designed to intercept and sever the creature's tail.

There was nothing there. The attack had been a feint, a way to distract Corin while the creature darted past him toward Lhasha.

Corin expected to meet resistance with his wild swipe. When he caught only air he was left stumbling to the side. He took two steps to recover, and another to get his momentum heading back toward his opponent. Less than a second, all told. Far too long.

The naga was bearing down on Lhasha, who had heeded his earlier warning to stay out of the way by retreating toward the stone room when Corin had engaged the creature. Now she was trapped against the stone wall, unable to get away. She had her short blade drawn, but the way she held it told Corin she was inexperienced in combat.

The naga sensed Lhasha's vulnerability, and attacked with reckless abandon.

A quick head strike, two sudden lashes of the tail, another bite. Lhasha ducked and twisted and spun away to the side, but with no fear of counter blows the creature kept pressing forward.

Corin hacked down at the thing's back, leaving a deep, oozing gash on the scaly torso. Quick jabs from the naga's tail forced Corin back again as he parried the blows of the poisoned barbs, leaving Lhasha at the mercy of another round of attacks.

The half-elf stabbed her tiny blade into the naga's underbelly, the point pierced the skin and drew blood, but the naga was oblivious to her efforts. It slammed its writhing body into Lhasha, driving her back against the outer wall of the stone room, momentarily stunning her.

Before she could recover, before Corin could come to her aid, the naga stabbed its tail deep into her thigh. She opened her mouth in a scream Corin was glad he could not hear and dropped to the floor.

Corin was on the naga again, chopping and slicing at his enemy from behind. He rained short, quick blows onto the back of the creature's midsection. Most bounced harmlessly off the tough scales, but a few left deep wounds on the flesh beneath. With an undulating wave of rippling muscle, the creature's serpentine body snapped around like a whip. It caught Corin in the ribs and knocked him off his feet.

He thrashed his head desperately from side to side as he lay on the ground, the poisoned tail jabbing at him again and again, each time striking the ground mere inches from his face. Corin rolled out of range and scrambled to his feet, driving the creature back away from Lhasha with another series of attacks to its bleeding torso.

From the corner of his eye Corin stole a quick peek at the inured half-elf. She was leaning against the wall, the wound to her leg tied off to stanch the bleeding. Then she slumped to the floor, succumbing to the poison coursing through her veins.

Lhasha's collapse triggered something in Corin, a warrior's lifetime spent training in the arts of hand to hand combat snapped, leaving only a being blind with rage and intent on revenge. Corin hurled himself at the naga, heedless of his own safety.

For a brief moment Corin's defenses were down, leaving him wide open to any and all attacks from his foe. The naga was taken aback by the mindless ferocity of the sudden assault, the sudden shift from the tactical approach it had begun to expect. Retreating from the berserk warrior's wrath, it missed its chance to strike, and then Corin was on it.

He swung without thought, without strategy or technique. Primal fury fueled his blows. Stumbling forward in a blind madness he struck at the head, the tail, the body; overwhelming the creature with animalistic rage, hacking and chopping until his foe was nothing but a mass of bloody, quivering pulp beneath his relentless blade.

The magical silence ended at last, the spell spent. The thick, wet sounds of his blade butchering the naga's corpse touched the small part of Corin's mind that was still capable of rational thought. The sudden noise jarred him, brought him back to his senses. He dropped his gore-covered blade and ran to Lhasha.

He swept her up from the floor, her tiny frame all but weightless in his arms. She was breathing softly, but made no response when he called her name. He peeled back an eyelid, but her pupils had rolled back into her head.

He must take her to Fendel. The gnome had saved Corin from poison. He could save Lhasha, if he saw her in time, but it was a long, long way to the House of Hands.

Corin slung Lhasha's body over his right shoulder, holding her in place with the crook of the elbow on his amputated arm. With a speed born of desperate urgency he clawed his way up the collapsible ladder without a second thought, his fear of heights pushed from his consciousness by his concern for Lhasha.

Up in the rafters he draped Lhasha's inert form over the beams so she wouldn't fall off, then he began to pull the ladder up after him, stuffing the pieces into Lhasha's carrying pack as he disassembled them. He'd need the ladder to get down from the roof once they were outside the building.

He wasn't as fast as Lhasha at taking the ladder down. He hadn't practiced, as she had, and of course, his missing hand complicated matters even more. Each second he struggled was another second lost, another second the poison could spread through Lhasha's body.

With the ladder stashed inside, Corin quickly slipped Lhasha's carrying pack onto his back, then hauled her still unconscious form up onto his shoulder again. It was awkward crawling along the rafters with Lhasha draped across his back, but somehow Corin managed. He lifted her through the chimney vent, then pulled himself up after her.

On the roof he scrambled to reassemble the ladder, then used it to climb down to the streets of the Caravan district below, Lhasha still dangling from the now aching shoulder of his bad arm. At the bottom Corin gratefully shifted her weight to his left side, and set off at a running trot toward Gond's Church, leaving Fendel's collapsible ladder behind.

CHAPTER THIRTEEN

Corin's breath came in great gasps as he ran through the streets of Elversult. He prayed Lhasha still lived, but he couldn't spare the time it would take to stop and check. He was afraid of what he might find.

His legs burned from the strain of running while carrying the weight of his friend, but he ignored the pain. His left arm was wrapped around Lhasha's waist, bracing her. The stump of his right arm stuck way out to the side to help offset the extra weight slung over his shoulder. The uneven load caused him to hunch over and twist as he ran, and after only a few minutes he could already feel himself cramping up, but he didn't stop.

A soft voice inside his head drove him on. Lhasha's voice.

"Corin, let me down."

He was her protector, her guardian, her friend, and he hadn't been able to save her. The voice came again, he half imagined he heard it out loud.

"Corin, let me down."

Shaking his head to dispel the hallucinations, he doubled his efforts, but the accusation endured, it grew stronger with each repetition.

"Corin, let me down."

He wanted to throw his head back and scream apologies to the sky, drop to his knees and beg forgiveness for failing her, but instead he kept running, the relentless voice spurring him on, louder still.

"Corin, let me down."

And then, suddenly, the voice was a shout.

"Are you deaf? Corin, let me *down!*"

Corin was so stunned he actually dropped her. Lhasha landed with a loud grunt, scraping her chin along the pavement. She rolled over onto her back and glared up at him, massaging her side with one hand, and rubbing her chin with the other.

"First you crush my ribs, then you break my jaw."

"Sorry," Corin mumbled in reply, still too amazed to say anything else.

She smiled impishly up at him from the street. "You big lug, I'm just teasing you." She extended a hand for Corin to help her up.

Still trying to puzzle out the miracle of her unexpected recovery, the warrior grabbed both her tiny hands in one mighty paw and pulled.

"Whoa," she said, pressing a palm to her head once he hauled her to her feet. "Still a little woozy. Probably from all the blood rushing to my head while you carried me like a gunny sack."

"Sit down," Corin said quickly. "Rest a minute."

Lhasha waved him off as he came over to support her. "I'll be all right." She laughed weakly. "Some warrior I turned out to be, huh? One little stick in the leg and I pass out from shock."

"It wasn't shock. It was poison. From that thing's tail. The naga."

"Poison?" Lhasha glanced around. "Well, this doesn't look like the great beyond, so somehow I must have survived."

Corin had figured it out, now. "The venom wasn't fatal. That particular species probably devours their prey while it's still alive," he guessed. "The poison doesn't kill. It just keeps food from squirming during the meal."

"There's a pleasant image." Lhasha shivered, and wiped her still bleeding chin. "If its all the same to you, I could really use a drink right about now."

"There's a place just around the corner," Corin replied.

As always, the Weeping Griffin was virtually empty. Corin and Lhasha took a seat at one of the tables in the back. A hunchbacked serving wench limped over.

"Hadn't seen you in a while. Thought you were dead," she said to Corin, making no effort to hide the disdain in her voice. "Nothing's changed. Cash up front. What'll you have? The usual?"

Corin shook his head. "Nothing for me. Not anymore."

The waitress gave him a sour look. "This here's a business, see? No loiterin'! Yer keepin' me from me other customers!"

Lhasha took a quick glance around at the empty tables and chairs. "And which customers would those be?"

"I ain't takin' no lip form you, ye little tart!" the waitress snapped back. "Order somethin' or get out!"

Stunned at the harshness of their server, Lhasha stammered, "A . . . a glass of wine, please. Red."

The waitress stuck out her hand and held it there until Lhasha fished out a silver coin and placed it in her palm.

"Keep the change," she said, hoping to win the bitter woman over.

The waitress humphed once, cast a disapproving look at the both of them, and stomped off.

"We're lucky," Corin said after she left, "the friendly one's working tonight."

Lhasha smiled, then realized it wasn't a joke. She looked around in a slightly bemused state of mild revulsion.

"This place is a dump," she finally whispered. "Why would anyone ever come here?"

"It's cheap and nobody bothers you," Corin explained.

The waitress returned and slammed a goblet down on the table in front of Lhasha then limped off without a word.

The half-elf took a dubious sniff of the cup, then cautiously raised it up to her mouth. She paused, and wrinkled her nose in disgust. "Corin, there's a bug in my wine!"

"Just one?"

Lhasha set the goblet down and pushed it away without taking a sip. "Suddenly I don't think I need that drink anymore."

Corin shrugged, but otherwise had no comment.

Lhasha drummed her fingers on the table. "So what do we do next?" she wondered aloud.

Once she realized there wasn't going to be a reply from the other end of the table, the half-elf continued, talking the problem out loud to herself, more than anything.

"We didn't get the package, so we won't get paid," she said with a frown. "And we left Fendel's ladder and bar spreader behind. Those weren't cheap. Worst job I've ever done, bar none. I'll probably even have to give back the down payment when I go to rendezvous with the contact."

"He won't be there," Corin said simply. "We weren't supposed to survive."

"You still think this was all an elaborate set-up?" Lhasha asked incredulously. "That doesn't make any sense. If someone wanted me dead, why go to all this trouble?"

"This wasn't about you. You were expendable, a pawn. This was cult business."

Lhasha laughed. "Cult business? You missed your calling, Corin. With an imagination like that you should have been a bard, spinning stories for kings and emperors."

"But," she added after a moment's thought, "that snake thing—naga, you called it? It seems like the kind of creature that would be working for the Cult of the Dragon.

"And the cult is heavily involved in illegal smuggling," Lhasha continued, not even bothering to wait for Corin to jump into the conversation. "Everyone knows they secretly own several of the warehouses in the Caravan district. Plus, my contact said one of the reasons he hired me was my lack of cult affiliation."

She shook her head emphatically, rejecting her own arguments. "No, I'm still not convinced. Why even bother sending me in there if he expected me to fail?"

"He's trying to flush them out," Corin answered.

Lhasha nodded enthusiastically. "Of course. Forcing their hand, smoking them out. That's possible. Even a failed burglary could spook them. Make them move their precious package. Take it to a new location, maybe move it right out of the city.

"But who was he working for?" the half-elf mused. "And what about all the money he paid me up front?"

"The cult has lots of enemies. Powerful enemies."

"That's true," Lhasha admitted. "There's a lot of groups that would be willing to throw away a bag of gems if it meant causing trouble for the Cult of the Dragon." She chewed thoughtfully on her lip. "Yanseldara's been trying to drive the dragon worshipers out of her city once and for all. I hear she has Harper connections. The Harpers are working to bring down the cult."

"This isn't the Harpers' style."

"Yeah, you've got a point there. Fendel's run across them a few times, and from what he's told me the Harpers wouldn't send someone in to be an unsuspecting sacrifice. It goes against everything they stand for."

"The Masks?" Corin suggested.

"They've been warring with the cult for control of Elversult's underground for years," Lhasha conceded, "but I doubt the Purple Masks were involved. My contact made a point of telling me I was hired because I wasn't connected with the Masks, either. Given my current relationship with the local guild, the last thing they'd want is to give me a job."

After a moment, the half-elf reconsidered. "Unless they tried to kill two birds with one stone. Cause trouble for the cult by sending in a stubborn thief who refused to join their guild. Either I get the package and the cult suffers, or I get killed in the process. It's a win-win situation for the Masks."

Before Corin could register his opinion on her latest theory, Lhasha tossed it away herself.

"No, I just don't buy it. You didn't see this guy, Corin. No way he was working for the Masks."

"You sound confident."

"Believe me, I'm sure. I was dealing with the Masks long before I met you," Lhasha explained with a rueful smile. "I remember when they first started recruiting members. They knew they were in for a tough road. The cult controlled everything in Elversult back then—smuggling, slavery, assassinations, stolen goods. Any territory the Purple Masks moved into would have to be taken away from the Cult of the Dragon.

"They needed to drive the cult back bit by bit. It was all out war, Corin. Still is. The Masks knew the only way they'd stand a chance was if their members could beat the cult followers whenever their paths crossed. The

Masks wanted every advantage they could get.

"They insisted that all their members be in great physical shape. A small edge, but one they needed. It became part of the guild's culture; fitness is a basic Mask philosophy. You never see an overweight Purple Mask, it just doesn't happen. They don't let it happen. Its bad form. They consider it to be a sign of weak will and laziness. They'd never trust a fat man with something like this.

"But my contact—he had to weigh three hundred stone, easy."

Corin shrugged. "Not the Masks. Not the Harpers. So who?"

"Elversult's always attracted more than its share of the criminal element," Lhasha mused. "Could be a new organization, trying to make a name for themselves by going up against the cult. No way to know who, unless we find my contact again. Not much chance of that, I'll wager."

They sat in silence, neither one certain of their next step. Lhasha smiled as a mental image popped unbidden into her head. "I wish you could meet this guy," she said to Corin. "You'd get that pompous ass to spill his ample guts. You'd just wrap one of those fancy silk scarves around his neck, and squeeze until all those gaudy gold rings popped right off his fat little fingers. God, those things were hideous."

"What?" Corin seized Lhasha by the shoulder from across the table. "What did you just say?"

"S-Sorry," the half-elf said, taken aback by the sudden intensity in the warrior's eyes. "It just seemed like a funny thought to me, for a second. I didn't mean anything by it." She squirmed beneath the bruising force of the mighty hand gripping her shoulder.

Suddenly aware of what he was doing, Corin dropped

his hand and mumbled an apology. Lhasha rubbed her shoulder gingerly, trying to make sense of Corin's violent reaction. Across from her, the warrior clenched his fist and slammed it on the table, never taking his burning eyes off his amputated stump.

"Hey, its all right," Lhasha reassured him. "Nothing to get worked up over. Just a little bruise." In an effort to break the tension she jokingly added, "I'll just dock your pay."

Suddenly Corin stood up. "I can't work for you any longer," he declared.

"What? Hey, c'mon big guy. I was just kidding. I'm fine, really."

Corin shook his head. "You don't need me. You've got enough gold to get to Cormyr on your own. You can hire a small army of guards once those gems are sold."

Lhasha carefully studied her friend. He stood stiffly, almost at attention. What she had come to know as his professional stance. She knew he was serious.

"Corin, what's going on here?"

"I failed you. I knew this was a set-up. I should never have let you take this job. Then I led you right into the monster's grasp."

"Listen," she said urgently, "those things weren't your fault. You saved me from the Maces at the Fair. You saved me from the assassins in my room. And look at me, I'm still alive. I'm fine, just a little nick on the leg is all."

She stood up and took a step toward Corin, reaching out to put a hand on his shoulder. "You're not a failure."

He shrugged it off and stepped away. His eyes were hostile and threatening. "I didn't want to say this, but you leave me no choice. It's because of you that I'm leaving."

Lhasha recoiled as if she'd been slapped. "Wh . . . what are you talking about?"

Through clenched teeth Corin spat his words at her. "You've made this partnership impossible. You wouldn't listen to me on what inn to stay at. You wouldn't listen to me when I said this job was a trap."

"But Corin, that was just—"

He continued on as if he hadn't heard her. "I told you to stay back if there was any fighting, but you still managed to get yourself poisoned by the naga."

"I tried to—"

"You're irresponsible, reckless, and foolish. You don't think ahead. You're a menace. A threat to yourself and anyone around you. When you wind up dead, my reputation can't afford to take the blame."

"Your reputation?" Lhasha shot back angrily. "Until you met me you didn't have any reputation left! You were a drunk brawling in the streets, remember? I gave you a chance. I helped you get your reputation back!"

Corin sneered. "And what a grand reputation I have now—working for a second rate thief who dresses like a whore!"

Lhasha grabbed her drink and threw it at Corin. He didn't flinch, but the cup missed him by at least a foot and smashed against the back wall.

"Hey!" the waitress shrieked from across the tavern, "yer gonna pay fer that or I'm gettin' the Maces!"

"Here!" Lhasha shouted back, throwing a handful of coins on the table so hard they ricocheted off and scattered across the floor. "Now shut up, you withered old hag!"

Bottling up her rage, Lhasha turned back to Corin, who hadn't moved since his abrupt severing of their relationship. In a quiet voice she said, "Go see Fendel when you want your back wages. I'll be in Cormyr."

She spun on her heel and walked out, head held high. She kept her composure until she was safely beyond the door, then succumbed to emotion. Sobbing with anger and shaking with adrenaline from the confrontation she stumbled down the street, wiping bitter tears of betrayal from her eyes.

CHAPTER FOURTEEN

Over and over, Graal paced the length of the small subterranean meeting chamber. Four long, loping strides would bring him to one of the stone walls. He would punch the hard rock with his fist before changing direction and resuming the pattern.

Fhazail was late. It was bad enough the fat steward had sent word virtually demanding this meeting. Graal hated to be at anyone's beck and call. Then to keep him waiting . . .

The orog struggled to rein his fury in, lest he do something foolish and incur Xiliath's wrath.

This insult was just another in a long list justifying Graal's hatred for Fhazail. Add it to the appalling sight of yellow and orange silk shirts clinging to mounds of rolling fat, or the repugnant scent of perfumes and powders that embraced Fhazail like a desperate lover. It took days for Graal to purge their lavender stench from his nostrils.

It was more than just a physical revulsion that fueled Graal's hatred. Fhazail's attitude was galling to the orog. Graal inspired terror in lesser creatures, and he reveled in it. But in Fhazail's case there was no pleasure in the fear. Fhazail was brazenly craven, he kowtowed and groveled and whimpered and whined too easily. It was second nature to him. Fhazail felt no shame, no humiliation, no debasement when he cowered at one's feet, and Graal felt no power from intimidating such a fawning sycophant.

It even went deeper, Graal suspected. Graal could kill Fhazail on a whim, the steward knew that. Yet Graal sensed that somehow Fhazail was always in control of the situation. The corpulent coward always knew exactly how far he could go, and beneath his trembling exterior Graal suspected Fhazail was toying with him, laughing at him.

Despite the urge, Graal knew he mustn't kill Fhazail. Not yet. Xiliath was very specific about that. Fhazail was his master's most important spy within the Cult of the Dragon, the key to getting the package for Xiliath's own use. Once the package was delivered and Yanseldara's doom assured, Graal hoped, Fhazail's usefulness would be served. Then there would come a reckoning.

Graal heard wheezing coming from far down one of the darkened tunnels branching off from the small smuggler's den. Soon he could see flickering points of light tracing their way across the walls, floor, and ceiling of the rough hewn passage, the flame from the torch reflected and refracted by the garish gemstones set into Fhazail's audacious rings. The orog cared little for such baubles and trinkets. Wealth was only useful for the power it could buy. Fhazail was obsessed with such ostentatious displays. One more reason to lust after the steward's death.

Fhazail jogged into the room, his flab shaking and quivering with each labored stride. He gasped out an apology, but his words were all but lost in the roaring bloodlust that exploded in Graal's head at his sight. The orog struggled to suppress the rage, but the world became a vision of red.

Prostrating himself at Graal's mighty boots, Fhazail begged for his life. Words the enraged monster before him could no longer even understand. He was deaf to pleas, and devoid of mercy. Graal slowly raised his blade, savoring this long awaited moment.

A single word from his victim pierced the veil of his fury, halting his blade.

". . . Xiliath . . ."

The name momentarily stayed Graal's hand. The orog knew little of fear, yet he was ever conscious of his master's awesome wrath. He took a deep, growling breath and held it. His pounding heart, eager for the slaughter to come, began to slow. The fog of berserker fury receded.

"Repeat what you said," Graal snarled, "and I may let you live."

Without question or hesitation, Fhazail reiterated his pleas. "Forgive me, Graal, but I bring Xiliath news of the Dragon Cult's package." His begging sounded humble and sincere, his voice a near shriek filled with fear and terror.

Yet in the steward's eyes Graal could see something else. Fhazail knew he would not die tonight. He had pushed Graal to the very brink of a mindless wrath that would bring on swift and brutal death, but with a single word the steward had averted a bloody fate yet again.

"I don't know whether to kill you for demanding this meeting, or for making me wait," Graal threatened. But he knew it was an empty threat, and Fhazail knew it, too.

"When you hear my news you will understand," Fhazail explained. "The cult is moving the package, tonight. My plan worked."

"You never did explain your plan," Graal noted. "Xiliath might want to know where the gems he gave you went."

"I gave them to a thief," Fhazail said. "A down payment for the job. I hired her to break into the cult's warehouse. When Azlar heard about the attempted burglary, he panicked. He fears the package is not safe in Elversult. They are taking it out of the city tonight, as soon as it gets dark."

Graal raised his fist in anger, and Fhazail scuttled out of range. "Fool!" Graal spat at him. "The Masks cannot know anything of this! They have been infiltrated by Yanseldara's spies! If she learns of the package the plan is ruined!"

"Spare me, wrathful Graal!" Fhazail squealed, pitifully raising his pudgy hands over his head to shield the expected blow. "I have not betrayed Xiliath to the Masks! I found a young woman who was freelancing her talents. She has no connection to the guild."

"And what became of her?" Graal asked, slowly lowering his hand. "Is she dead?"

"Much to my surprise, she escaped with her life, though I doubt she had even a glimpse of the package. Somehow she killed the guardian. A naga. The door to the room where the package was kept was still locked. She knows nothing."

Graal scratched at his jutting lower jaw with his grimy, discolored nails. "One less snake-beast in the world to serve the dragon worshipers. Xiliath will be pleased at that. Continue your report."

Emboldened by the orog's reaction, Fhazail stood up and brushed the dust of the small cave's floor from his knees.

"Azlar wants to move the package to a cult stronghold hidden a few miles outside the city. Right now they are scrambling to clean up the mess in the warehouse. He wants to leave no trace of the cult's presence behind, nothing that might tip Yanseldara off to their plot. He ordered me to oversee the operation. I couldn't get away. That was why I was so late in coming here."

"And the workers? They are being silenced, I presume?"

Fhazail nodded. "Of course, most fearsome Graal. Azlar used his magic to alter their memories, for the most part. A few ran off in terror when the naga's body was discovered. They know better than to speak of what goes on in the warehouse, but I convinced Azlar of the need to send me out after them just in case they let slip a rumor of what they have seen. That's how I managed to get away to meet you."

"And when you find them?" Graal asked with a malevolent grin.

Fhazail shrugged. "I was given money to entice them to come back to the warehouse. If I can convince them to return, Azlar will erase their memories as well. If not, I will notify the cult assassins. They will deal with the workers and anyone they might have spoken to. I hope it does not come to that."

Graal laughed. "You are weak, Fhazail. I would not bother with the bribes, or the assassins. I would kill them myself."

The steward shrugged. "I lack your warrior's conviction." Then he added, "I must go back to my search for the workers soon. Azlar will grow suspicious if I do not return in a timely manner."

"Wait," Graal said as Fhazail turned to go. "I will report this news to Xiliath. I have no doubt he will act on it immediately. We cannot allow Azlar to bring his package to the cult stronghold. Your work in this matter is not done."

Swallowing hard, Fhazail asked, "What would you have me do, O mighty Graal?"

"I will take some of my men, and set an ambush for

the cultists. We will steal the package, and with any luck kill Azlar in the process. The loss of their prize and the death of such a promising mage from their ranks will leave the dragon worshipers reeling.

"You must lead them into the ambush, Fhazail. The usual place, just outside of town. I'm sure you remember."

"But . . . but how am I to make Azlar take that route?" Fhazail protested.

"Use your powers of persuasion, Fhazail. I'm sure you will be most convincing."

An all too familiar look popped into the steward's eyes. "Perhaps I could be more convincing if Xiliath provided me with inspiration of a monetary nature."

"No haggling," Graal warned in a low voice. "Now is not the time for your games."

Fhazail's head tilted ever so slightly as he gave the orog a brief, appraising glance. "Of course," he replied after assessing the situation. "Now is not the time for games. I will go at once."

CHAPTER FIFTEEN

To the casual glance, there was nothing remarkable about the warehouse. To someone hiding in the shadows, watching for the past several hours as deepest night fell, it was evident something important was taking place inside.

Corin had been watching the building since the early dusk. He had seen figures arrive in small groups of two or three every half hour, their forms hidden by dark, hooded cloaks. Elversult had a temperate coastal climate, it rarely fell below freezing even in the heart of winter. Now that they were in the first few days of the Sunsets, and spring was just a few tendays away, only foreigners from the southern desert lands found it necessary to bundle themselves up in such heavy garments. Foreigners, or those with something to hide.

A knock, a slight delay while passwords were exchanged, and the mysterious figures would be ushered in. Over a dozen so far, plus those that were already inside before Corin's vigil began.

In the ghastly light of their torches, Corin caught occasional flashes of armor and weapons peeking out from beneath the robes. Once he even caught a glimpse of an insignia—the unmistakable emblem of the Cult of the Dragon.

His instincts about the naga had been right, but Corin cared little about the cult, or their business here. He had come with only one purpose in mind.

Ever since the conversation with Lhasha at the Weeping Griffin, Corin had begun plotting his revenge. The half-elf's description left no doubt in Corin's mind about her contact's identity. Once, long ago, Fhazail had betrayed the White Shields, set them up and led them right into a trap. He had Corin's friends killed, played a part in taking his hand, and somehow managed to shift the blame onto the White Shields themselves. He had broken Corin's once proud spirit, and driven him into a nightmare of alcohol and despair.

Corin had always felt his meeting Lhasha had been pre-ordained. He sensed some greater force had brought them together. Lhasha had saved him, delivered him from his torment. She had dragged him out from beneath his burden, healed his spirit, and restored his honor and sense of purpose. He refused to believe it had all been mindless chance and random circumstance.

At first, Corin felt the gods had seen fit to bring them together to give him a second chance, a long overdue reward for the pilgrimages and contributions to Lathander's Church on Temple Hill. Now he understood the real reason behind their meeting. Inadvertently, Lhasha had brought Fhazail back into Corin's life. The gods had sent her as a courier, she had brought him a chance for revenge!

Or so he hoped. There was no real reason to believe Fhazail was working for the Dragon Cult, but Corin's instincts said it had to be. How else could Fhazail know about the mysterious package? Duplicity was a fundamental aspect of the steward's character and Corin was certain Fhazail would be trying to betray the cult as he'd betrayed the White Shields. The warrior could not even begin to fathom what treachery Fhazail plotted against the dragon worshipers, and he didn't care. He only cared about slicing open the steward's rolling belly.

So he went to the cult warehouse, and waited. Corin's only link to the man who had taken away everything he valued, his instincts had lead him there in pursuit of his prey, and he trusted his instincts.

If he was right, his vengeance was close at hand. Corin had watched a small army disappear into the warehouse over the past few hours, soon they would all come out. He needed to be ready. He might only get one chance to strike before the cultists took him down.

He shook his head, trying to gather his hatred into a lethal, focused rage. Despite his bitterness and anger about what Fhazail had done, Corin's mind kept returning to his fight with Lhasha.

His words had hurt her. They betrayed her trust in him. He had lied to her, and in his duplicity he saw something of Fhazail. The resemblance sickened him, but he had no other choice. Corin lusted after nothing but vengeance and he would willingly surrender his life to get it. But he wouldn't sacrifice Lhasha, he couldn't ask her to accept the risks of a suicide mission. Driving her away was the right decision—this mission was his and his alone. His brothers in arms deserved no less than to have their deaths avenged.

Despite his conviction, he could find no peace. A small voice inside his head—Lhasha's voice—urged him to give up his quest for retribution.

"This hate is of your old life," it whispered, "let it go. A new beginning awaits. Come with me to Cormyr and we can both be reborn."

Other voices answered, those of his fallen comrades. "You are a warrior!"

"You are a White Shield!"

"Remember the fallen!"

"The traitor must die!" The voice of their captain rose up from the anguished din. "Avenge our deaths!" Igland commanded. "In the name of the White Shields, Fhazail must pay!"

Loudest of all was Fhazail's own voice, reverberating through Corin's skull. "The White Shields were betrayed by one of their own!" it shrieked, just as Fhazail himself had done from the witness box at the inquest as he pointed the finger of blame and hurled accusations. "Corin One-Hand cannot be trusted!"

"Corin One-Hand is waiting for you, Fhazail," the warrior whispered to the night. "You can trust in that." Mercifully, the voices fell silent.

An hour later the cultists began to emerge. First came several runners, hurrying on ahead to scout a clear path through the all but deserted Elversult streets. They scurried through the darkness, a few returning minutes later to report that the route was free of prying eyes. Of course they didn't see Corin, who stayed motionless in the shadows across the street. Lhasha had taught him well.

A phalanx of warriors marched out next, their armor and swords no longer hidden beneath robes. Every second one carried a bright torch, the shadows surrounding them were banished by the light. Illuminated by the flickering fire, Corin could plainly see the mark of the Cult of the Dragon emblazoned on their breastplates.

Next came a tall man in wizard's robes. His head was bald, his face clean shaven. He looked too young to be a mage of any import, but the immediate, unquestioning responses of the soldiers as he gave them his orders told another story. From experience, Corin knew that those who made a living with the blade generally held magicians and sorcerers in disdain. Only a wizard of great power could command such respect from a whole company of warriors.

The mage quickly arranged the guards into a formation that was familiar to Corin. They built a protective wall around their leader, guarding him against physical attacks from any direction. The firelight reflected off the wizard's shaved skull, poking up from the near solid mass of shields, swords, and armor that surrounded him. Between their formation and the torches it would be impossible to get closer without being seen.

Finally two more figures emerged, quickly joining the young magic-user in the protection of the center of the company. One was completely covered in heavy robes. From the size, Corin suspected it to be a woman, though her face was veiled to protect her identity. She must be the mysterious package Lhasha had been sent after.

However, Corin registered all the information about her in a small, subliminal corner of his mind. On the conscious level, his full attention was focused on the figure guiding her out.

The sight of Fhazail, gingerly holding the woman's arm as if she were a lethal viper, filled Corin with a sense of vindication. If anything, the steward looked even fatter than before. His clothes looked more garish, and even from this distance Corin could plainly see that the steward still wore his hideous rings. The tawdry gemstones reflected tiny spots of flaming orange and red that danced across the helmets and armor of the guards surrounding him.

Corin resisted the urge to leap out and attack. He wanted vengeance, and he was willing to die for it—but only if it meant he could take Fhazail's life in the process. He wasn't about to waste his opportunity by launching himself against impossible odds.

If he had worn armor, Corin might have risked a brazen frontal assault. Protected by the heavy steel of full battle gear, he just possibly might have been able to withstand enough blows to reach Fhazail, and deal a fatal strike to the steward before succumbing to the combined blades of the guards surrounding his quarry.

Unfortunately, Corin was not wearing full battle gear. He wasn't even wearing so much as a thin mail shirt. After careful consideration, Corin had chosen to wear no armor at all on this night. It would have hampered his ability to lurk unseen, to pursue unheard. The cumbersome gear would have slowed his pursuit of a cowardly, fleeing opponent. And Corin knew he would have no need of armor to protect him from Fhazail.

Now he regretted the decision. With nothing to protect his vulnerable flesh from the attacks of his enemies, his hand was stayed. The wall of guards protecting the steward forced Corin to bide his time, and wait for a break in the shield wall.

In tight formation, the cultists moved out. The soldiers' boots struck the pavement in perfect unison, the result of many hours of intense drills and training as a unit. As he watched the guards march in perfect precision, Corin realized there was little chance of finding a weakness in their wall. He might not get a chance to strike Fhazail down after all, not tonight. Now that he had found his quarry, he would keep him in sight until he saw an opening. It might take days, maybe a tenday, but Corin had no intention of letting the steward escape his wrath.

As the armed platoon marched through Elversult, the runners shuttled back and forth, darting on ahead, then scampering back once they had verified that the street ahead was still clear.

Moving silently as Lhasha had taught him, and being careful to stay far enough back to remain cloaked in shadows, Corin followed the cultists through the deserted streets of the Elversult night.

Lhasha waited until Corin was a safe distance away before she emerged from her concealment, materializing from the dark of a nearby alley. It would be a simple matter to follow him without being noticed. He may have learned enough to keep out of the soldiers' unsuspecting eyes, but Lhasha herself was not so easily fooled.

She had been following him since shortly after their fight at the Weeping Griffin. At first she had been shocked by his actions, she had to admit he had caught her off guard. In their time together Corin had been anything but talkative, but Lhasha now knew that he was able to wield words almost as well as he handled a blade.

If he had simply screamed insults at her she would have seen through his ruse immediately. Corin was subtle, and dangerous. He first put her off balance by suddenly announcing the end of their partnership. He lured her into dropping her defenses by referring to his own weakness. Then, when she was vulnerable, he turned on her, striking at her own feelings of inadequacy by bringing up her failings in combat. In the end he had hit her in her most sensitive spots, insulting her skills as a burglar, belittling her chosen calling and her expression of her identity.

A masterful performance, she had to admit. However, he had underestimated her. She was no fool. It hadn't taken her long to realize the game he had played. At first she couldn't understand why he would do such a thing. It made no sense.

As she replayed the conversation in her head, the pieces fell into place. The key, she realized, was when he grabbed her shoulder. The violent reaction was out of character for him, at least since he had stopped drinking. Even in combat Corin attacked with precision, strategy, and purpose. She rarely saw him lose control. Something must have triggered it.

Suddenly it had all clicked. Her description of her anonymous contact had set him off. Corin obviously recognized the man. She remembered the venom in Corin's voice when he'd told her about the man who had destroyed him—the steward, Fhazail. She knew then that her contact and Fhazail were one and the same.

She also knew Corin was going to hunt Fhazail down and kill him, but Lhasha still didn't understand why he had tried to drive her away. Corin had to know she would help him however she could, despite her qualms about needless violence. Maybe his actions were out of respect to her, a way to keep her from becoming involved in something she might find distasteful. Or maybe the pain of the past was too personal to share, and the only way Corin felt he could end it would be to kill Fhazail by himself.

In either case, Lhasha would respect his desire to be left alone. But she wasn't about to let him go off without at least keeping an eye on him. If he got into trouble, she wanted to be there to help however she could. She had doubled back to the Weeping Griffin and waited. When he came out, she followed him, effortlessly blending into the silence and darkness of the night. He led her right to the cult warehouse.

At first she was surprised. She couldn't imagine why Corin would go back there. The last place she wanted to be was the site of such a recent, and horribly botched, job. She settled in to wait, certain it would all be made clear eventually.

When Fhazail emerged leading the cowled woman, Lhasha at last understood. How Corin knew his enemy was working with the Dragon Cult she couldn't even guess, in truth, it really wasn't important. Corin had found him, and soon he would try to kill him. That was all that mattered.

Lhasha feared her friend would leap out and attack the small army of guards. If he did, there was little she could do but stay hidden and watch him die. She vowed that if such a thing happened, she would take up the mantle of avenger, and follow Fhazail until she had a chance to sink a dagger into the soft, puffy white flesh between his ribs, in honor of the memory of her friend. She prayed it wouldn't come to that.

Fortunately, Corin showed restraint. He controlled his rage, and followed the group cautiously, and a little clumsily, at least by Lhasha's high standards. She knew he was waiting for his opportunity—one that might never come. Lhasha trailed in his wake, hoping he wouldn't succumb to anger or frustration and do anything rash.

CHAPTER SIXTEEN

With the runners watching the route ahead, the small knot of cult warriors made their way through Elversult's deserted midnight streets. Keeping to little-used thoroughfares, they marched from beneath the shadows of the warehouses in the Caravan District and wound their way through the city.

Corin quickly realized the cultists were taking their "package"—and Fhazail—into the forests just beyond the city's borders. There were no gates leading in or out of Elversult, no protective battlements encircled the city. Unlike a walled town, access was not restricted to the main roads. A reminder that Elversult was built by smugglers. It was virtually impossible to control the traffic of goods, or to prevent people from coming in or going out.

Within half an hour the armed group had reached the city's western limits. Although there were many paths through the groves that dotted the landscape around Elversult, the trees were not densely packed, and there were few if any wild animals and monsters for the first few miles outside the city. If the cult intended to travel quickly and without being seen, as Corin suspected, they wouldn't even bother taking the road—they'd cut right through the trees.

The soldiers changed formation, confirming Corin's hypothesis. Instead of the tight shield wall, they now marched several feet apart—a formation that allowed the war party to march through the forest in a relatively straight route and still maintain a formidable defensive perimeter. Between each man there was enough space to let the trunks of the thinly dispersed trees pass through the formation without having to break rank, and the men were still close enough to prevent anyone from slipping through their lines without being seen. Each soldier could clearly see the man on either side of him, making it impossible to pick them off one at a time without being noticed.

Corin knew he still didn't stand a chance of getting close to Fhazail, but he wasn't about to give up the hunt just because they had left the city. As the cultists moved through the trees, Corin became bolder, inching ever closer to the group, trusting the cover of the trees and the gloom of the forest night to keep him hidden, searching in vain for a break in their defenses and a chance to go after Fhazail.

He was so intent on his quarry that he never even heard the unknown assailant who rushed up and tripped him from behind. He hit the ground and his attacker leaped upon his back, a small hand threw itself across his mouth to stifle his grunt of surprise. Before he could gather himself and throw his undersized enemy from his back, soft lips pressed against his ear.

"Hold still. Stay quiet."

Lhasha. He froze at her words, and she removed her hand from his mouth, then rolled off his back and flattened herself on the ground beside him. She was so close he could smell the fragrant scent of the herbal mixture she used when rinsing her hair. Corin's head swirled with questions, but he knew better than to speak and reveal their location. Instead, he gently nudged Lhasha with his shoulder and gave her a quizzical look when she turned to face him.

With a nod of her head she pointed to the darkness ahead of them. The torches of the cult soldiers flickered and danced, constantly disappearing and reappearing as trees momentarily blocked Corin's line of sight. As the dispelling illumination of the fire marched on, the night closed in behind the group.

Just before it became impossible for Corin's eyes to pierce the darkness he saw a movement. Several figures materialized from the shadows that camouflaged them and fell into step behind the oblivious cultists.

The figures quickly vanished into the night with the receding torches, and complete darkness fell. Corin couldn't see his hand in front of him. Lhasha waited another ten seconds to be sure they were out of earshot then whispered, "I saw them with my night vision. You would've marched right into them."

Corin wanted to thank Lhasha for saving his life, he wanted to ask her what she was doing there, he wanted to tell her to go back to the city, but all of these were minor concerns. She was there now, and Corin knew she'd be staying.

"It's an ambush," he whispered instead. "They're surrounding the cultists. There must be a clearing nearby."

"How do you know?" Lhasha asked.

"That's where they'll hit. Attack from the cover of the trees while your enemy is out in the open. Come in from all sides and overwhelm them."

"Who are they?" Lhasha asked.

Corin didn't know, though he suspected they were working for Fhazail in one way or another. "It doesn't matter. When they strike, I'll have a chance to get at Fhazail."

"The fat one—that's Fhazail, isn't it? He was my contact back at Elversult, too." Corin nodded and Lhasha continued. "But you obviously must have figured that out already, or you wouldn't be here. Any chance I can talk you out of this?"

The warrior shook his head.

"Then at least let me help."

There was little chance he'd convince her to leave. In her own way, Lhasha was as stubborn as he was, and her elf vision would come in handy. "All right, but be careful."

"Always, Corin. What's the plan?"

"Lead me through the forest, watch for others hiding in the darkness. Get me close. When the ambush hits, it'll be utter chaos. I'll move in then and kill Fhazail. You stay out of sight in the trees."

"And after Fhazail, you'll just slip away from the battle and join me, right? We'll just leave the cult to its business and head back to Elversult, all right?"

Corin hesitated, and Lhasha pressed her point. "With Fhazail dead, there's no reason we can't stick with our original plan. Reform our partnership. Get enough money to pay for your arm. We can make a fresh start in Cormyr."

A fresh start. The words had a nice ring to them. Corin sighed, but his face wore the hint of a smile. "Agreed." The smile vanished, replaced by grim determination. "But not until Fhazail's dead."

They rose from the forest floor, and Lhasha led the way through the trees. It didn't take long until they had the cult troop in sight again. Just beyond them Corin could make out a large clearing. The army of cultists were already close enough to bathe it in light from their torches.

Corin and Lhasha hung back, making sure they didn't stumble into the ambush themselves, and they waited. They didn't have to wait long.

As soon as the last member of the cult war party set foot in the clearing, the air was filled with a volley of arrows. Most of them ricocheted harmlessly off the heavy armor of the cult guards, but a few went down with feathered shafts protruding from their torsos. The second wave of the ambush hit so fast the trapped soldiers barely had time to draw their weapons. The forest all around them erupted, and dozens of armed warriors burst from the trees, screaming their battle cries to the uncaring sky.

Corin leaped up and sprinted toward the battle, anxious not to miss his chance to slay the traitorous steward. Despite stumbling over countless unseen roots and fallen branches, he kept on his feet, driven by the promise of too long delayed revenge. Lhasha, not expecting him to react so suddenly and recklessly, scurried along behind trying to keep up.

Corin stopped when he reached the edge of the clearing to survey the field. He was impressed by what he saw. The cultists hadn't panicked beneath the unexpected onslaught of arrows. Several of the guards were down, the feathered shafts jutting out from their chests or stomachs. Most had survived unscathed, their heavy armor deflecting the deadly missiles. They had withstood the initial charge, and what could have been a slaughter had become an honest battle.

The cultists were still outnumbered by nearly four to one. They should have been quickly overrun, but somehow they were holding their own. It only took a second for Corin to understand why. Attacking the professional fighting unit of the cult soldiers was a rag-tag, mismatched crew of humans, dwarves, goblins, orcs, and kobolds.

Humans and dwarves were fine to fight beside, in Corin's opinion, the odd half-orc might even be tolerable but no warrior worth his salt wanted to have his army's fate resting on the shoulders of goblins, orcs, and kobolds. Tactical warfare was beyond their ability to grasp. Once the blood flowed, their base instincts took over—bloodlust, cowardice, and greed. They charged without reason or purpose, they broke morale and fled at the worst possible times and they'd even turn their attention from the battle to loot the bodies of the dead, both foe and friend. When they fought, it wasn't battle, but pure carnage. An organized, sustained effort could easily have routed the cult, but instead they had regrouped and were actually pressing their disorganized attackers back.

At first Corin thought the young wizard might have been using his magic to keep the cultists in the battle, but when he picked the tall mage's bald head out from the melee he realized the wizard had problems of his own. Two other mages, a bearded man in blue and a woman in red, were attacking him with spells from either side. Defending against the constant barrage kept the cult spellcaster from aiding his soldiers. Without the mage to help them, it was only a matter of time until the cultists would succumb to the vast numerical advantage of the attacking rabble.

Through it all, the mysterious veiled woman stood still as stone, arms hanging limply by her side, seemingly oblivious to the events around her. She had not moved since the ambush struck.

Corin's mind processed all this information in mere seconds, storing it away for future use. Instant analysis of a battle was second nature to the warrior, it happened automatically, leaving his conscious mind free to scan the clearing for signs of Fhazail. Despite his bulk, the steward had an amazing ability to avoid being noticed, like a roach scuttling beneath the floorboards of a room when you went to crush it with your boot, but at last Corin found him, cowering well clear of the battle on the far edge of the clearing. The mob who had launched the surprise attack didn't bother with him—proof enough for Corin that Fhazail had been aware of the ambush all along. The cultists, not yet aware of his treachery, still thought he was one of their own and left him alone as well. That suited Corin just fine. With nobody paying attention to Fhazail, nobody would be close enough to save him from his fate.

The shortest route to the steward was directly across the clearing, right through the heart of the battle.

"Stay here," he said over his shoulder to Lhasha, who had just now managed to catch up with him again. Corin leaped into the fray.

He made a mad rush perpendicular to the flow of battle, ignoring anyone who was not directly in his way. On either side would-be opponents swung at him, but without any armor to encumber his movement he was able to easily duck and dodge his way across the field of battle, avoiding the hurried swipes at his unprotected form.

Most of the combatants were too busy with the enemy in front of them to bother chasing him down once he was beyond the range of their blades, but halfway across the clearing a dwarf decapitated his opponent with a vicious swipe of his battle-axe. The helmed head of the unfortunate cultist bounced twice and rolled just in front of Corin's boot, nearly tripping him up and drawing the attention of the dwarf who had dealt the fatal blow. The stocky warrior turned to meet the charging Corin, hunkering down and bracing his feet wide in anticipation of the impact as he swung his axe in a wide arc parallel to the ground, looking to chop Corin in two at the belt.

Without breaking stride Corin dropped into a forward roll beneath the axe's path. The dwarf did a half turn to avoid getting bowled over by Corin's tumbling form, but he couldn't avoid the warrior's blade. As Corin somersaulted past he thrust his sword up under the dwarf's armpit, striking at the small space left vulnerable on even the best suits of armor. The blade easily bit through the inadequate mesh protecting the underside of the joint, running the enemy through. Corin's momentum brought him to his feet and he continued his sprint, scooping up the sword of a dead cultist to replace the one he had left buried to the hilt in the still twitching dwarf.

He was clear of the battle. Nothing stood between him and his prey. It was then that Fhazail saw him, bearing down with a clear path before him. Corin saw recognition in the steward's eyes, recognition and terror. Fhazail turned and took a few quick steps toward the woods, then pulled up short. Instinctively, Corin did the same.

It appeared as if an enormous living shadow had stepped forth from the forest, darkness incarnate. A creature clad all in black armor—from its heavy boots to its iron skullcap—grabbed Fhazail with one paw and yanked him into the cover of the forest behind it. The beast then raised its weapon to face Corin, the pulsating blade of the two-handed sword devouring all light that struck its blade. Graal.

Faced with the creature that had taken his hand, Corin felt hatred—but not the all consuming abhorrence he felt for a cowardly traitor like Fhazail. Here was an enemy, to be sure, but one Corin could understand, one who lived by the blade. Graal had killed Igland and maimed Corin, but it was done during battle, without duplicity or pretense. Graal had only done what any warrior would have done in the same position. What Corin himself would have done. The sight of Graal filled Corin with a lust for vengeance at the memory of their last battle, but he also felt a twinge of grudging respect. There was something else. A feeling Corin was unfamiliar with. As Graal began to slowly approach, Corin felt his knees buckle slightly. His palm felt clammy, he was unsure of his grasp on his weapon. The tip of his sword wavered, mimicking the slight trembling of Corin's own arm.

"You fear me, little man," the orog snarled. "I can smell it."

It was true, there was no sense wasting words denying it. Corin was afraid, and he hesitated.

Graal attacked with ruthless simplicity, his blade cleaving the air in an overhand chop. Corin made no attempt to block the sweeping blow, knowing it would only shatter his own weapon. Instead, he spun to the side. The great sword hewed the ground, leaving a deep gash in the earth. As his opponent's weapon sliced through the air mere inches from his face, Corin felt the dark hunger of the evil blade pulling at his very soul.

Before Corin could counter, Graal hacked at him again, forcing him to parry with his sword and deflect the attack to the side. The clash of swords rocked Corin back and sent numbing vibrations up his arm, nearly knocking his own sword from his hand.

His opponent fought seemingly without strategy or technique, but against this monster all Corin's warrior training, all his skill with a blade, were for naught. Graal struck with a relentless elemental fury, his strength and speed more than compensating for brutishly simple form. Corin was driven back in a stumbling retreat.

Spinning, diving, and rolling, Corin was able to stay mere inches ahead of his opponent's strikes. Corin was breathing heavily, he could feel himself wilting beneath the unremitting offensive. He was thankful again that he wore no armor. Encumbered by a metal suit, Corin would have been unable to evade the orog's blows, and he had little doubt that his enemy's dark blade would simply cleave through even the thickest plate. With each jump back, with every duck and dodge, Graal's blows came a little closer, each swing made Corin's retreat more desperate. He parried and blocked, deflecting the dark sword time and time again, yet every series of attacks brought the orog in tighter and closer, lessening Corin's ability to use his agility and quickness. Corin was powerless to mount any resistance to halt Graal's momentum, he was unable to keep the orog from pressing forward.

The orog howled a scream of rage and pain as Lhasha struck from behind, digging her dagger between the links of the monster's chain mail. Neither Corin nor the orog had noticed her stealthy approach.

The wound was deep, but not lethal. Graal spun around and swatted the half-elf away with the back of a paw, sending her sprawling across the battlefield.

Corin seized the opening and took the offensive. He lunged at his opponent's legs to keep him from setting his feet. He thrust and stabbed at the monster's torso, forcing it to lean back and keeping it off balance. Corin attacked with savage hacks and brutal slashes, chopping his blade down again and again, trying to deliver a blow solid enough to pierce the heavy, black chain mail protecting his opponent. Unused to being on the defensive, Graal gave ground, caught off guard by Corin's aggression and the speed of the unarmored warrior's pursuit.

The orog caught Corin's descending blade with his own and reversed the momentum, using his mass to throw the warrior back several feet and halt Corin's advance. The two faced each other again. Corin's fear was gone now, consumed by the exhilaration of physical combat. Graal pressed forward, but this time Corin was ready and he met the assault.

Attack. Defend. Attack. Defend. The familiar rhythm of battle began to develop, but Corin could still sense he was overmatched. He needed to use his agility and his quickness to offset the orog's size and strength, but he couldn't keep the orog off him. Defend. Attack. Defend. Defend. Inch by inch Graal closed the distance between them, gaining ground faster than Corin could fall back, making it harder and harder for Corin to take the initiative. Soon he would be in full retreat again.

From the corner of his eye he saw Lhasha rise to her feet. She wiped away the blood from her mouth and snatched her dagger up from where it had fallen on the ground. She circled around behind the orog, looking to stab him in the back again.

Graal saw her, too, and quickly stepped back, trying to keep both Lhasha and Corin in front of him. Corin tried to rush the orog, but Graal met the charge and Corin had to break off his attack to protect his vulnerable, exposed flesh from the orog's savage blade.

Graal wasn't given the chance to press the advantage. Lhasha was still circling, staying wide and trying to get behind Graal. The orog had to advance slowly, cautiously, always keeping her in his sights. Corin regained his footing, and Graal's chance was gone.

Corin had underestimated the half-elf. Lhasha hadn't been able to stand against the charge of the naga in the warehouse, but even Corin had struggled with his tactics against the snake. But in a battle against an outnumbered soldier, one like Graal, she understood the key to victory. As long as she stayed wide and kept trying to circle behind their opponent, the orog was hamstrung. He couldn't drive Corin back with mindless fury, unless he wanted to taste the bite of her blade in his back again, and if Graal turned his focus to Lhasha, Corin would jump at the opening.

The three of them circled in an awkward dance of feints and aborted maneuvers, oblivious of the main battle that raged less than fifty feet away. Corin would press forward, but each time the orog had the strength to drive him back and blunt his attack. Graal would advance on Corin, but Lhasha would move in behind and the orog would have to retreat until he had both his opponents in his view once again.

They were at a stand-off, and Fhazail was nowhere to be seen.

CHAPTER SEVENTEEN

Azlar understood the instant the first arrow whizzed by his ear. The young wizard was highly intelligent, and he knew the game of treachery all too well. His rapid advance through the Cult of the Dragon had been as much a product of his political acumen as his magical prowess. The mage cursed himself as he ducked behind the shields of the two guards who rushed over to protect him, angry that he hadn't figured it out earlier.

"We know there is a traitor among us," Fhazail had whispered in his ear earlier that night at the warehouse. "It could be anyone. Undoubtedly there will be an ambush waiting for us soon after we leave the city."

"That is why we have the guards," Azlar replied. "Only an insane fool would attack a squadron of Dragon elite escorting a mage with my power."

Fhazail merely nodded in the direction of the workers busily chopping the naga's corpse into pieces small enough to stow inside barrels of flour. "Does that look like the work of someone sane?"

"Very well," Azlar conceded, "what do you suggest?"

“Merely an alternate route, O wondrous wizard. If we take an unexpected path through the forest, our enemies will be caught unawares. We will miss their ambush completely.”

“And you know of such a route?”

“But of course, most magnificent mage” the fawning steward replied.

Azlar had foolishly taken Fhazail’s path—right into a trap. The fat man would die for this.

The barrage of arrows stopped, and with a yell a horde of goblins, orcs, and kobolds burst from the surrounding thicket. Azlar snapped his head from side to side, but amazingly Fhazail was nowhere to be found. The mage stood up to his full height, determined to blast Fhazail into tiny pieces for his treachery. Even as he ran through a mental list of the spells he could use to obliterate the corpulent infiltrator he heard a familiar incantation.

He threw himself to the ground and scampered away on all fours from the soldiers who had been guarding him. A second later the air was split by the sizzle of electricity, and a lightning bolt shot in from either side, striking the guards, fusing their armor and frying the helpless men inside.

Azlar began an incantation of his own, oblivious to the sound of sizzling skin inside melted metal and the smell of cooking flesh wafting up from the nearby corpses. A shimmering shield of magical power materialized around his form. His defenses in place, he turned his attention to his enemies.

On the left was a white-haired mage clad in a deep blue cowl, to his right a middle-aged female wearing bright red robes. The male unleashed a shower of glowing orbs that rained down on Azlar, only to be absorbed harmlessly in the nimbus of energy surrounding the young spellcaster. From his right a column of fire erupted from the hands of the sorceress in red, but protected by his spell, Azlar felt only the faintest hint of heat as the inferno struck him.

He began another spell while his enemies scrambled to raise their own defenses. The air around the female flickered and blurred, and suddenly there was not one but four red robed sorceresses opposing him, each one completely identical in appearance and actions.

Azlar sneered in contempt. The red mage's defense was a minor casting, a spell designed to confuse an opponent, to keep them guessing as to which figure was the mage, and which were merely harmless mirror images. The spell was barely worthy of Azlar's powers, it would only buy the woman a few more seconds of life.

Her partner was not so lucky. His hands and arms wove frantic patterns in the air, words of arcane power spilled from his mouth, but he was too slow. A blast from Azlar's hand encased the rival mage in a tomb of ice, freezing his spell on cold, dead lips.

Each of the sorceress's reflections began going through the identical actions as she prepared another casting. The shimmering shield around Azlar flickered then winked out of existence, dispelled by his opponent. A bolt of flame appeared in Azlar's fist. He hurled his spell at the four red robed women in front of him, choosing his target at random. The flaming arrow struck unerringly, completely engulfing the target in fire. It was the wrong target. The reflected image winked out of existence, but Azlar's real enemy was unharmed.

She returned his volley with an arrow of her own. It conjured into existence in mid-air and streaked toward Azlar. He casually stepped to the side. The missile struck the ground, splashing acid in a small circle around the impact point, scorching and searing the grass of the clearing with its corrosive juices.

From Azlar's fingertips a swarm of glowing projectiles arced toward another of the red robed figures. A simple spell, quick and deadly, but only if unleashed on an actual creature. Another reflection vanished under the attack, leaving only two—one of which was the real enemy.

The sorceress hesitated. Azlar knew her arsenal of magic was nearly depleted, while he had many spells left. A thin green ray shot from his hand, and this time he found the right target. The woman tried to scream, but her cry was cut off as she disintegrated into a small pile of dust. Azlar turned his eyes to the clearing, determined to find Fhazail.

He was oblivious to the tide of the battle. He scanned the edges of the fray, certain the steward would be lingering on the farthest reaches of the violence, and then he saw the man's unmistakable round form, cowering on the edge of the trees. Azlar conjured an enormous spider's web between the trees, ensnaring Fhazail in a mass of sticky, virtually unbreakable strands.

With the traitor safely trapped by his spell, Azlar's attention focused on the field of conflict. Dead goblins, orcs, and kobolds littered the earth, but there were still many, many more pressing forward. Azlar's men were slowly being drowned beneath wave after wave of attackers.

Azlar began a spell of mass destruction, one that would kill both friend and foe alike. A desperate move, but one that was necessary to protect the package from falling into enemy hands. He stopped abruptly and broke off in mid-casting, allowing the gathering magic to fizzle uselessly away. A cruel smile crossed his lips as inspiration struck.

He cast another spell, one different than what he had originally planned. Azlar reached out with his mind and seized hold of Fhazail's psyche, crushing the steward's will with his own, using his magic to mentally dominate the still hopelessly ensnared man.

"Fhazail," the mage whispered. "Look over here, Fhazail. At the package. Look closely. Watch her, and don't blink."

Compelled by Azlar's sorcery, Fhazail's head turned until he stared intently at the still cloaked woman.

Azlar briefly touched the simple gold ring on his right hand. The package took a small step forward, responding to the magical enchantment of the ring. The wizard focused his mind, and the figure slowly reached up and removed her veiled hood.

Corin saw the eyes of his enemy go wide as Graal reacted to something behind Corin. The warrior resisted the urge to turn and look, thinking it was some orog trick designed to distract him and leave him vulnerable. He tensed for the expected assault from his enemy, but instead of leaping to attack, Graal turned and fled into the trees. Corin didn't even try to follow. The move was so unexpected, he could do nothing but stand there stunned in bewilderment.

"What . . . what just happened?" Lhasha asked, as confused as Corin.

Corin shook his head. "I have no idea." He glanced into the trees where Fhazail had been hiding, and saw the steward had been imprisoned in some kind of cocoon. No, not a cocoon. A web. Corin moved slowly toward his enemy, sword drawn, eyes searching the forest for a new, unseen opponent.

He wanted the satisfaction of killing Fhazail himself, he wasn't going to leave him to be devoured by some giant spider. Corin wasn't about to rush in and end up becoming a meal himself. His senses were finely attuned to his immediate surroundings, but he could still hear the sounds of battle from the far side of the clearing. From the curses of the orcs, the yelps of the goblins, and the whining barks of the kobolds Corin could tell that the cultists now had the upper hand.

From the shadows that still partially concealed Fhazail, making him little more than an obese silhouette, there was nothing. At the very least he had expected Fhazail to say something, to react to his menacing approach with pleas for mercy or cries for aid. The steward said nothing. He didn't even move.

"Fhazail," Corin called out. "I'm coming for you, Fhazail." And still, he could elicit no reaction.

He moved a step closer, and realized something was wrong. Very wrong.

Squinting through the shadows Corin could just make out Fhazail's face, his features frozen in a grotesque mask of horror. His coloration wasn't right. He was ashen, had an unnatural pallor, and there was something else.

From just over his shoulder he heard Lhasha warn, "They're heading this way."

He pulled his attention from Fhazail and turned in the direction she pointed. The ambushers were being routed. Goblins and kobolds fled in panicked terror, the cultists in close pursuit. The human cultists hewed them down from behind, stabbing them in the back as they tried to run, pursuing their foes like dogs on the hunt. Some of the orcs and goblins still held their ground, but the tide of battle was surging toward them, sweeping across the clearing like a wave breaking over the sand.

Behind the combatants Corin could just make out the figure of the young mage, but the barrage of magic one normally expected from a wizard in battle was absent.

The young man merely stood in place, his fist raised high above his head.

Stranger still, a woman in robes was walking the battlefield, systematically approaching the pockets of orcs and humans who still held their ground against the cult soldiers' rapid advance. Wherever she walked, their ranks broke and men fled in terror—or stood completely stiff and motionless, as if paralyzed by fear.

Her back was to Corin and Lhasha, but even through the night's gloom Corin was sure she was the one he had seen with Fhazail and the young wizard when they emerged from the warehouse—the infamous "package." Her hood was down now, her head uncovered. Through the darkness Corin could just make out her wild, unkempt tresses swaying in the wind. Only, there was no wind tonight, and her hair didn't so much sway as . . . wriggle.

"Gods save us," Lhasha whispered as the woman began to turn in their direction.

Protected by the power of his ring, Azlar alone could look upon what no creature, man or beast, should ever see—the face of the medusa. For a moment he was held prisoner by the vision. Though a monster, the medusa had the elegant features of a stunning noblewoman. Her skin was pale and flawless, her lips full and red. Her aristocratic beauty was marred only by the mass of writhing snakes atop her head and her empty, vacant eyes depicted a reflection of her magically enslaved mind.

Azlar shook off the bedazzling effects of the charmed medusa's unexpected appearance, and looked out across the battlefield. Already half a dozen enemies had been turned to stone—the inevitable consequence of gazing on the medusa's features. A few cultist statues dotted the field as well, casualties caught unaware by their master's sudden unleashing of his secret weapon.

Raising the hand with the ring above his head to focus his powers, Azlar mentally commanded the medusa to march into the battle. He took care to focus his new toy's deadly countenance on their attackers, trying to avoid excessive casualties among his own men. Enemies smart enough or lucky enough to shut their eyes as the medusa approached were spared the horror of being turned to stone, but with their self-imposed blindness they were quickly cut down by Azlar's soldiers or slain by countless bites from the venomous serpents of the medusa's hair.

"Don't look!" Lhasha screamed.

Corin clenched his eyes tight. With his vision gone, the sound of the quickly approaching battle became very loud. In seconds, the fleeing horde would run right over them, and with their eyes shut they wouldn't even be able to see it coming.

"Corin!" Lhasha called out, trying to be heard above the cacophony of the panicked soldiers approaching. "Don't open your eyes! One look at that thing's face and you'll turn to stone!"

"Get to the woods!" Corin yelled to her, eyes still pressed firmly shut. "Get away as far and as fast as you can! Don't look back!"

"You too!" Lhasha hollered back. "Get out of here! I'll meet you back at the Weeping Griffin."

Corin took a hesitant step over the uneven ground, trying to gauge his sense of direction without opening his eyes, and then a stampede of unseen assailants bowled him over. From the rank smell and high pitched yelping,

Corin knew they were kobolds. They tumbled to the ground with him, but instead of hacking him to pieces, Corin heard them scramble to their feet and continue their mad rush to escape the battlefield.

Corin lay still. The kobolds had just run him down, their pursuers couldn't be far behind. The heavy clumping of the cultists' mailed boots thundered around his head and prone body, but he didn't try to roll out of the way, he didn't even flinch. He gave no hint at all that he was still conscious or alive, nothing to attract the attention of a passing soldier.

The heavy footsteps were past him. He could hear them, galloping off after the fleeing kobolds. The battle swept over him as he lay on the ground. He heard the clash of metal, the splinter of bone, the grunts of soldiers wielding their weapons, and the wails of the injured and dying. For a few brief seconds he was in the eye of the storm, and then the melee moved on as the cultists pressed their enemies ever farther back.

Corin wondered about Lhasha, but he couldn't risk attracting attention to himself by calling out. He didn't dare open his eyes to search for her. All he could do was pray she would make it back to the Weeping Griffin. Keeping his eyes pressed tight, he began to crawl along the ground, heading in a direction he hoped led to the safety of the forest.

CHAPTER EIGHTEEN

Graal almost let the one-armed man have Fhazail. It would have been a quick end to the orog's problems, and a perfect end to the evening. The cultists were hopelessly outnumbered, Graal's troops would soon overwhelm them and take the package for their master. With the package all but delivered into Xiliath's hands, the steward's usefulness was over. The one-armed man could have him.

Xiliath might not approve. The orog's master was ruthless and cruel, but unlike Graal he was also careful, he planned ahead. The orog had no idea what strategies Xiliath might use to consolidate his power in Elversult's underworld. His master might still have need of Fhazail. If he learned the orog had done nothing to help. . . .

So Graal had intervened, stepping forth from the darkness to defend the despicable coward from the one-armed soldier's sword. He saw a flicker of recognition in his enemies eyes, and Graal's dark blade pulsed hungrily in his hands. It had tasted this man's flesh before.

His mind flashed back, through hundreds of men, women, and children he had slain and maimed over the years. Precious few of his opponents had survived long enough to leave an impression on the orog's mind, but this one he knew. A White Shield.

The memory of their storm-tossed battle on the Trader Road fuelled Graal's bloodlust, and his semi-sentient blade throbbed with arcane power, responding with a bloodlust of its own. The White Shield trembled before the orog's wrath.

"You fear me little man," Graal snarled, "I can smell it."

The fear made the man cautious, reluctant to attack. Graal had no such qualms. He struck with wild, untamed ferocity, overwhelming his tiny one-armed opponent.

Then the cripple's bitch stabbed him in the back. He swatted her away, but the moment was lost. The White Shield seized the advantage and drove him back—a worthy opponent.

Worthy, but still inferior. Graal slowed the man's assault. He used his massive bulk to take away his opponent's momentum and regain the advantage, but not before the female was up again. Graal couldn't advance, he couldn't simply bury his enemy beneath a flurry of psychotic blows, lest he expose himself to another bite from the female's blade.

The orog wasn't used to being thwarted in battle. He kept the soldier at bay, but he needed to even the odds. Graal glanced over the White Shield's shoulder, seeking followers of his own that he could afford to draw away from the battle.

What he saw shocked him.

His army was in ruins. A few of his best warriors held their ground, but the fodder had turned and fled, the dragon worshipers butchering them from behind like the miserable curs they were. Sheer numbers still favored his army, but their morale had broken, the tide of battle had turned.

It took only a moment for Graal to understand. He saw Azlar, the cult wizard, in the middle of the clearing surrounded by three of his guards. The wizard's fist was thrust straight up into the air.

Then Graal saw the package. Or rather, the back of her. Azlar had unleashed the medusa on Graal's troops, they scattered before her like dust. In her wake he saw only statues and corpses bloated by the poison of her venomous tresses.

Oblivious to the White Shield and the female, Graal cast his eyes to the earth and sprinted into the cover of the trees.

The forest was alive with the sounds of Xiliath's escaping forces. They fled without thought or reason, heading in any direction that led away from the clearing. The sounds of the cult soldiers hunting them down could also be heard.

A goblin stumbled past the orog, completely unaware of the looming presence of his general. Graal silenced the goblin's terror filled shrieks with a single swipe of his paw, clawing out its throat.

A second later a pursuing cult soldier appeared from among the trees. Graal brought his sword to bear on his opponent, chopping down on his shoulder. The blade sliced through armor, flesh, and bone, biting deep into the human's torso. The cultist keeled over in a shower of spurting blood.

Graal was no blood-crazed fool, he was not above fleeing when a battle was lost. But even the prospect of facing the medusa was preferable to having to report his failure to Xiliath. "Do not come back without the package," Xiliath had warned him. "The package, and the ring that controls it." Graal had little doubt that the ring was on Azlar's finger.

Moving with surprising stealth for a creature his size,

Graal worked his way along the edge of the clearing, staying just far enough in the trees to remain out of sight. He kept his eyes on the ground, and away from the battlefield. If he could make his way to the trees behind Azlar, in the direction opposite the fighting, he should be safe from the medusa's gaze. The wizard would hesitate to turn the creature's gaze back toward himself. The ring would protect Azlar, but Graal was counting on the mage wishing to preserve the two soldiers guarding him from the horrible fate of becoming a living statue.

Graal paused, and sneaked a quick peek out into the clearing. He had judged correctly, he was behind Azlar and his two bodyguards. The orog hesitated a second, aware of the consequences if he misjudged the wizard's reluctance to turn the medusa in his own direction, but Graal was also aware of the consequences of failing Xiliath.

He burst from the trees with a roar, his blade already carving swaths through the air. The guards reacted quickly, stepping between Azlar and the charging enemy.

Two long strides brought Graal into range, his blade tore through the pitiful shield of the first guard, tore through his arm, tore halfway through his chest.

The second guard got in a hurried shot, but the blow was rushed and off balance. It deflected off the heavy black chain of Graal's armor without even drawing blood. The orog wrenched his blade free from the first soldier, leaving a gaping, gruesome wound in the corpse. He caught the second blow from the remaining guard with his sword, shattering his opponent's blade with a flash of dark magic.

The orog stabbed forward, running the sword through the soldier's stomach until it protruded from the other side. The mage, confident in the abilities of his bodyguards to dispatch a single foe, wasn't even looking in

Graal's direction. He gazed out over the battlefield, seeking the few remaining members of Azlar's army that still fought desperately against a foe they could never withstand.

With a casual calm, Graal slid his sword from the impaled soldier and let the body sag to the ground. The man, too stupid to even know he was dead, clutched at his stomach in a feeble attempt to staunch the blood and organs spilling out of the cavernous wound.

Azlar turned at the sound of the man's groan, suddenly realizing he was in danger. Graal could not afford the luxury of savoring his foe's final agony—the medusa, at the mental command of Azlar, was already turning in their direction. Graal slashed the blade once, cleanly severing the upraised hand of the wizard.

Azlar screamed in agony, but Graal barely noticed. He was too busy following the flight of the wizard's hand. Carried by the momentum of Graal's sweeping blow it sailed a dozen feet through the air and bounced once on the ground.

Following the path of the limb brought the medusa into the farthest edge of Graal's peripheral vision. The orog saw her collapse to the ground as the spell of the ring was shattered, leaving her mind momentarily as weak as that of a newborn, but she would not remain in such a state for more than a few brief seconds.

Ignoring the weeping wizard, Graal lunged for the bloody hand, dropping his weapon in his haste. In his mind's eye he could already see the medusa slowly rising to her feet, her mane of snakes thrashing madly in rage. Free of the enthralling enchantment of the ring, she would do anything in her power to keep another from using it to enslave her.

The orog dropped to his knees, pulling at the ring with his massive, but surprisingly agile, paws. He clawed at the circle of gold, trying to wrench it free of the pale finger, but the gore-smeared hand was slick, Graal couldn't get a firm enough grip on the ring to pull it over the knuckle of the severed hand.

Behind him he heard the angry hissing of dozens of serpents, and menacingly soft footsteps approaching.

"Dare you face me now?" the medusa shrieked, though whether at him or Azlar the orog couldn't say. He kept his eyes firmly on the ground, kept his back to the creature. She was not far from him now. He could guard against gazing at her face, but not her hair of lethal vipers.

Graal snapped the finger at the knuckle and a helmet of white bone popped up through the already graying skin. He twisted the mangled digit and tore half of it off, allowing him to slide the ring free.

He thrust it on one of his own meaty fingers. The magic of the ring expanded the circle to slip over the gnarled joint of his knuckle, then contracted it to a snug, almost painful fit. Graal spun around, still on his knees. The medusa was virtually on top of him.

He stared up in wonder at the face of the medusa, kneeling in seeming supplication and reverence at the power contained in her countenance. Only the magic of the ring kept his limbs from petrifying as he sat spellbound by the vision. For Graal, the porcelain skin and delicate female features of the monster held little appeal, yet like Azlar he too thought her truly beautiful as he gazed upon her face.

For Graal, it was not the physical that captivated him, but the malevolent arrogance reflected in her gaze, the understanding of her own awesome, destructive capabilities shone in her eyes. There was something else as well. Despite the ring on Graal's finger, the medusa's eyes were clear and sharp—she was still of her own mind.

"Do you fear me yet, ignorant beast?" she sneered at him. "Well you still should." The serpents on her head lashed out.

The orog threw himself onto his back, scuttling away like a crab across the gore stained earth. The medusa watched him with contempt, then began a slow, deliberate pursuit.

"Though you are not made stone, do not think your fate will not be horrible," she whispered, sauntering after the hastily retreating Graal, relishing his seeming helplessness. "I shall devour your flesh and strip your bones."

The orog had been bedazzled by the prospect of gazing upon the face of death itself—a most uncharacteristic mistake. He had been absorbed in the moment. But the moment was over now. Still on his back, Graal softly caressed the ring, his fingers gliding over the warm gold for but an instant.

The medusa's head jerked back and her eyes momentarily clouded over.

"I am not the stupid animal you think," Graal said to her, relishing the fear of dawning realization in her eyes. "My mind is strong enough for this."

He rubbed the ring again and focused his will. The creature threw her head back, the serpents of her hair went limp. Inside his mind, Graal heard the sound of her anguished psyche screaming. Her body was silent.

"Return, my pet," Graal said. "Return and destroy the cultists."

The serpents began to writhe in a sleepy rhythm, and the medusa returned to the battle. The orog cast a quick look around for Azlar, but the wizard was gone, vanished into the forest. He had taken his hand with him. No matter. His death would have been nothing more than an added bonus.

With the package on their side now, ultimate victory

came quickly for Graal's troops. The orog's skill at controlling the creature was not as honed as Azlar's, however, so several of his own men were inadvertently struck down by the medusa's curse. Graal shrugged indifferently at the casualties. If Xiliath felt compassionate, he might have them restored to their former, living state. If not, they would make fine additions to his master's trophy room.

Replace your hood, Graal silently ordered once the last cultist had been dispatched. *Pull down your veil. Your work is done. For now.*

The medusa did as she was ordered. Graal pulled a curled horn from his belt, and blew a long, howling blast. It was a signal to his fleeing troops that the battle was theirs. The deserters would return in due time to join their comrades in the looting of the dead—though if they knew how Xiliath dealt with cowards they would not be so eager.

As his followers trickled back, the orog surveyed the carnage of the clearing. Bodies littered the field, along with roughly two dozen statues. A few of these had been smashed into rubble by vengeful enemies or accidental blows during the battle, leaving no chance of restoring the unfortunate soul trapped within.

The corpses could be stripped and left behind, but the statues and the rubble had to be collected and taken to Xiliath's hideout. There could be no clues that might give the Elversult authorities any inkling of what had truly happened there.

At a word from Graal, the carts the troops had dragged with them from Xiliath's base in Elversult were wheeled out from the trees and into the clearing.

"Search the woods for more statues," Graal ordered. "And load these onto the carts. The pieces, too. Leave nothing behind."

Fascinated, Graal studied the face of each statue as it was piled onto one of the wagons. A small, almost child-sized figure was placed on board. "Hello, my pretty one," Graal whispered to the statue.

"Can you hear me, I wonder?" he asked, leaning in close to fully appreciate the stone-etched horror in the half-elf's face. From the female's pose it appeared as if she had stumbled, probably while running with her eyes closed. Instinctively, she had reacted to the fall by opening her eyes at the worst possible time. It was a miracle she hadn't shattered from her inevitable fall to the ground after being petrified.

"Where is your friend?" Graal muttered, hoping to find a one-armed statue among the collection. The search proved fruitless, and he frowned in disappointment. But when several of his men emerged from the forest carrying an unmistakably obese statue of Fhazail, all Graal could do was tilt back his head and howl with joyous laughter.

CHAPTER NINETEEN

"Still waiting fer yer friend?" the surly waitress at the Weeping Griffin asked Corin again, her voice so shrill it made his teeth grate. She had been asking him every fifteen minutes or so, obviously anxious to have him either order or leave. But the look in Corin's eyes must have been preventing her from telling him flatly to get out.

Corin didn't even bother replying anymore. His glare spoke volumes enough.

"I don't think she's comin,' " the waitress said with a nasty laugh. "She musta stood ye up!"

"She'll be here," Corin said softly, his voice filled with menace.

The hunchbacked serving wench wisely beat a hasty, limping retreat. As she scurried off she shouted back over her shoulder, "Tell yer friend she can't be breakin' anymore o' me glasses!"

In vain, Corin searched the virtually empty interior of the seedy tavern for any sign of Lhasha, hoping she might have come in while he was distracted by the waitress. But she wasn't there. Corin had been waiting a long time.

He considered going back to search the woods around the clearing, but what if she showed up while he was out looking for her? He also considered going to see Fendel—maybe the gnome had some fantastic invention to help locate Lhasha. But again, Corin was afraid of Lhasha arriving while he was gone, then leaving to go search for him. Once such a vicious circle began, it might take days before they caught up with each other.

Drumming the fingers of his only hand on the table, he tried to analyze the situation logically, to survey it as he would survey a battle. It was possible Lhasha had mistakenly gone somewhere else to meet up with him. Possible, but highly unlikely. He dismissed that option.

It was also possible she was lost in the woods, confused by the darkness and the unfamiliar surroundings. Her elf eyes would let her see through the night, but Corin knew the range of her heat-sensitive vision was not very far—twenty yards at most. She wouldn't walk into an open pit, but she still might not be able to figure out her exact location with such limited sight.

If she was lost, it would be pointless for Corin to go looking for her. He'd have no idea where to even begin. Dawn was only a couple of hours away now. With the rising sun, Lhasha would find her way back to Elversult and the Weeping Griffin soon enough.

Of course, there was one other possibility. One that Corin refused to even consider. Not yet, anyway. He'd give her a few more hours to find her way back with the rising sun before he'd give up on her.

The door to the streets outside opened, a rare occurrence at the Weeping Griffin. Most of the regulars were already there. Corin looked quickly, hopefully, to the door, but instead of Lhasha's petite form, three men bundled up in robes entered. Knowing patrons came to this tavern for privacy and a chance to be left alone with their problems, Corin didn't pay any more attention to the group.

He was staring intently at his stump, still debating what to do about Lhasha when one of the robed men sat down at his table. Corin glanced up sharply and realized the other two had crept up behind him. On either side he felt the tip of a dagger pressing against his ribs.

"Don't call out, speak only when necessary to answer my questions. Keep your voice low," the seated man whispered, "and you just may get out of this conversation alive."

Corin's eyes flitted over the few people scattered about the bar, looking for some help. The other patrons stared pointedly at their drinks. The waitress, obviously sensing trouble was brewing, had disappeared behind the bar. Unfortunately, Corin knew the last thing on her mind would be alerting the authorities. At the Weeping Griffin, everyone's business was strictly their own.

Giving a nod to show he understood the hooded man's instructions, Corin turned his attention to his uninvited guest. Up close, Corin could see beneath the shadows of the man's cowl. He recognized the young face and shaved head of the cult wizard, and a chill ran down his spine.

"My name is Azlar," the man said. "And I have a proposal for you, Corin One-Hand. One that you might be very interested in hearing."

Corin nodded again, and the knives against his sides eased up their pressure slightly.

"Do you know who I work for?" the mage asked.

"I'm not stupid," was the warrior's short reply.

"No, of course not. Then you also know that we possess great power and influence. Not just in Elversult, but all across Faerûn. I am here to offer you a chance to join us."

"Why me?"

"The Cult of the Dragon has many powerful allies, but we are always looking for more to aid in our cause," Azlar explained. "You have proven your worth on the battlefield, and in dispatching my . . . guardian . . . in the warehouse."

Despite the blades pressed to his ribs, Corin was in no mood to be tactful.

His instincts told him that the mage's visit to the Weeping Griffin was a bad sign for Lhasha, and the thought of the half-elf suffering because of his own quest for revenge against Fhazail filled him with a reckless, frustrated rage.

"I don't see myself worshiping dead lizards," he spat out. "Find some other convert to brainwash into your twisted faith."

Azlar reacted to the warrior's vehemence with a rational calm. "Not all who serve us do so out of religious duty. There are . . . other considerations."

Corin snorted in contempt. "Money, power, slaves. Do you think I would sell my soul so cheap?"

The mage lifted his arm and rested it on the table, then pulled his sleeve back. His hand was pale and discolored, one finger had been horribly mutilated. A jagged scar encircled his wrist.

"Torture?" the warrior sneered. "I will not be broken so easily."

"Not torture," the wizard replied, "but healing. Earlier this evening, my hand, the one you see before you, was severed by the foul orog's dark blade. As yours was, long ago."

Corin looked again, more closely this time. "You're lying," he whispered, unable to take his eyes off the spellcaster's hand. "Even the priests of Lathander couldn't heal me."

"The Cult of the Dragon has magic more powerful and ancient than the Dawnbringer's pathetic little houses of worship. Join us and such a miracle could be yours. You know I speak the truth."

Corin did know it. More than his instincts, more than just wanting to believe. He knew it was true. In Azlar's scars he could see the pain, suffering, and loss of his own severed limb. Both men had been marked by Graal's sword, they shared a kinship, but Azlar's hand had been restored.

"See," Azlar said as the fingers flexed and curled. "It works as well as ever. We could do the same for you, Corin One-Hand. Though in your case a magically created limb would have to be a suitable replacement, since the original is long since lost."

Unaware he was even doing it, Corin began to rub his stump.

"Of course the procedure is immensely painful. Pure agony in your case, I suspect. But I'm sure you would agree that fleeting pain is a trifling price to pay."

Fendel had offered him a prosthetic arm, a hand made of metal. Largely on that promise, Corin had formed his initial partnership with Lhasha. Now Azlar was offering a limb of real, living flesh.

"How . . ." was all he could say, cautiously reaching out with trembling fingers toward the mage's restored hand. The gray palm was cold to Corin's touch.

"In our studies, we have learned much about necromancy and the restoration of animation to bodies and flesh—human as well as dragon."

Azlar's words, meant to reassure and tempt the warrior, had the completely opposite effect. Corin recoiled in revulsion from the undead flesh, shivering at the unnatural feel of it beneath his caress.

"Keep your zombie hand, wizard. I would rather stay crippled than become such a thing." In the back of his mind Corin half expected to feel the cold steel slide between his ribs as punishment for his insult.

Instead, Azlar quickly withdrew his hand, hiding it from view beneath the long, draping sleeve of his robe.

"Do not dismiss my offer yet," the wizard cautioned,

showing no sign that he was angered by Corin's reaction. "There is more on the table."

The warrior said nothing. He had no desire to play Azlar's game anymore.

Sensing his potential recruit's reluctance, Azlar continued the conversation without waiting for the one-armed man's reply.

"There is an old saying: The enemy of my enemy is my friend. We share a common hatred, Corin of the White Shields. We have both been betrayed by the steward Fhazail."

The name caused Corin to stiffen momentarily, but otherwise he made no response.

The cult mage misjudged the warrior's reaction. "You are surprised I know of your history, perhaps? Rest assured, Corin, I know much about you. My divinations are powerful. Join with us, and I can lead you to Fhazail. I can lead you to your vengeance."

"My vengeance is over. Fhazail is nothing but a statue. I saw him myself. He is trapped for eternity in a stone prison."

"He was turned to stone," Azlar admitted. "I orchestrated it myself. But you are foolish if you believe such a condition is not reversible. Before I could deal more permanently with the traitor I was forced to flee the battle. I suspect Fhazail has been taken from the field by his allies. They might restore him to his previous abundantly fleshy state.

"Fhazail has a knack for surviving such potentially lethal situations. Surely, Corin One-Hand, you can not sit idly by if there is even a chance Fhazail will emerge from his latest scheme of betrayal unscathed. You must seek justice for what he did to you and your fellow soldiers."

For two years Corin had nursed his vengeance, even at his life's lowest ebb it was always there, a flickering ember in the depths of his soul. He fueled it with alcohol and bitter vows cursing the injustice of the world, and when Lhasha brought the steward back into Corin's life the ember ignited an all consuming inferno in his mind.

Corin had nearly thrown everything away in his quest for revenge. His rebuilt career and reputation, his partnership with Lhasha, even his own life—all of it sacrificed for one last shot at Fhazail!

But in the hours waiting for Lhasha to return, that fire had been quenched. The hate had filled a void, feeding on itself in the vacuum that was Corin's life. However, his life was no longer a vacuum. His actions had consequences that reached beyond his own existence. Only now could the warrior understand how much his misguided hunger for "justice" had truly cost him, and what it may have cost Lhasha.

"Fhazail is not my concern anymore," Corin said in a somber voice. "You'll not lure me into your scaly fold so easily, dragon worshiper."

The young wizard sat back, stroking his chin thoughtfully. "Perhaps I have misjudged you. I see now that your concern is no longer for your own needs, but for the well being of another."

The warrior kept silent.

"My knowledge of you extends beyond your history with Fhazail," Azlar pressed. "I know of the thief, and of your . . . relationship."

Corin ignored the insinuations of Azlar's lascivious smile. "Quit playing games, mage. If you know something about Lhasha, then tell me."

Azlar gave a sympathetic sigh, artificial and forced. "When our package was taken, there were several casualties of her power. Many of my own soldiers were victimized as you must have seen. I regret to tell you your friend shared their fate."

"No!" Corin shouted, then quickly dropped his voice as he felt an increase in the pressure of the daggers against his ribs. "No. How would you know what happened to Lhasha?"

"Do not speak without thinking, fool! Did I not say my divinations were powerful? After the battle our attackers gathered up all the unfortunate victims of the package."

"The medusa, you mean. Why not call it what it is?"

Corin never saw the blow, but he felt it. A fist buried itself into his kidney, doubling him over in his chair, his head banged against the table. "Speak the name of the package again," Azlar whispered harshly, "and the next pain you feel will be from the daggers."

The wizard didn't wait for Corin to recover, but he kept on talking. "One of the statues was of a young lady. Your pretty thief, Corin One-Hand, but do not despair. There is still a chance she may yet be saved."

Trying to shake off the effects of the savage, unexpected punch Corin couldn't reply right away. If Azlar spoke the truth, the Dragon Cult might be his only chance to find and save Lhasha, but the cult wasn't known for its generosity. Any hope they offered him would be tempered with serious consequences. Dealing with demons was never wise.

Still, he didn't have many other options. "What . . ." he gasped, "what do I have to do?"

"Very good, Corin," Azlar said. "I'm glad you are not so stubborn that you refuse to see reason. Many people are blind to their own best interests when they hear the words Cult of the Dragon. You will learn that we are not unreasonable. We merely want you to perform a simple task for us. And in the process, you may be able to save your little friend."

"One job? And then we're done?"

"One job, and you need never deal with the Dragon Cult again. A fair deal for you, I think. A bargain, even."

Despite the assurances, Corin still had his suspicions, but he left them unspoken.

"The horde that attacked us are working for someone named Xiliath. This individual has been operating a small underground crime syndicate in Elversult for the past year. We know something of Xiliath's operations, but we know very little about the leader himself. Xiliath always deals through middle men and underlings. Rest assured, if we knew his true identity, or where to find him, the cult would have disposed of this upstart long ago.

"However, we do know that Xiliath runs his minor empire from the safety of the smugglers' caves carved out beneath the city streets. I'm sure you've heard rumors of their existence?"

Corin nodded. Every citizen of Elversult knew something of the legendary smugglers' tunnels, a vast network of passages and caverns carved out beneath the city long ago by those who wished to traffic goods away from prying eyes. According to legend, over the centuries the tunnels became so infested with traps, monsters, and other dangers that even the smugglers themselves were no longer able to safely operate from them. Well over a hundred years ago, the labyrinth had been abandoned by the very smugglers who had created it.

Despite the almost universal knowledge of their existence, the citizens of Elversult knew almost nothing of the tunnels beyond the bards' tales and ancient myths. The exits to the main streets were well hidden, and the rumors of deadly traps and horrific monsters left behind when the smugglers deserted their underground bases were enough to dissuade most people from seeking them out. Those few adventurous souls who did set off in search of the legendary caverns beneath the city never returned.

"As you must know," Azlar continued, "the maze of tunnels has never been fully explored, and sending our men in to flush Xiliath out was never worth the risk or the bother. In the past, the Cult of the Dragon regarded Xiliath as nothing more than a minor annoyance; far less troublesome to our cause than the Purple Masks, or Yanseldara's she-bitch Vaerana Hawklyn and her Harper allies.

"But with the theft of our package, Xiliath has become much more than just a minor nuisance. The time has come to destroy his operations, if not the man himself."

"How does this concern me?"

"Through means that do not concern you I have obtained a map of the tunnels. Specifically the section that makes up Xiliath's lair. We will use this map when we move on his underground stronghold. However, given Fhazail's recent treachery, I am reluctant to risk my men until I know the map is genuine."

From his robes Azlar produced a rolled scroll. "Here is a copy of our map. You will infiltrate Xiliath's base and verify the map's accuracy for me."

"How does my scouting help Lhasha?" Corin asked, slowly unrolling the map. According to legend the tunnel system beneath Elversult was vast, but the complexity of the document before him was staggering, and, from what he could tell, this was only a small section of the entire network.

"As I said earlier, Xiliath's men collected all the statues from the ambush and brought them back to their leader's stronghold, including your Lhasha. If you look on the map you'll see a particularly large cavern in the heart of Xiliath's tunnels. This area has only one entrance, no doubt heavily guarded. The smugglers who built the tunnels used it as a storage room for valuable merchandise. Here, Xiliath keeps those things he considers valuable—like the package, and her victims."

"So he's taken Lhasha there?"

"Undoubtedly," the wizard responded. "If you can use this map to reach her, and bring her out, then obviously its worth will be proven."

"Even if I do find her, what good will it do?" Corin asked. "I can't carry her out on my shoulders, not if she's . . ." His voice trailed off, unable to voice her horrible fate.

From beneath the voluminous folds of the mage's robes a small vial appeared on the table. "This will restore your friend to her natural state. Simply pour it over her stone form. Be warned: There is enough for a single use, and no more. Do not waste it."

With his good hand Corin picked up the vial and carefully examined it. It would take a pretty firm blow to shatter the thick, solid glass of the heavy container. The stopper was wedged tightly into the neck, with no chance of it coming loose accidentally. Through the opaque distortion of the vial, Corin could make out a syrupy, brightly colored liquid inside.

"It's a suicide mission," he said, still studying the potion. "There'll be guards and traps all over the place. Restoring Lhasha might set off some type of alarm, and getting out will be twice as hard as getting in."

Azlar shrugged. "That is not my problem. This is the chance I'm offering to you."

Corin thought it over for a few minutes. He knew Azlar wasn't telling him everything. It was obvious the mage held something back, but Corin doubted he'd get anything more out of the wizard.

"It's a deal. I'll do it for Lhasha."

"Don't wait too long," Azlar warned. "We are loathe to leave the package in Xiliath's hands for any length of time. If you have not returned in a couple days, I will have to assume you have failed, and the cult will take other steps."

"I'll go tonight. I just need to get some supplies."

"Be careful who you speak of this to," the wizard cautioned. "If news of the package reaches the authorities, Xiliath will likely destroy all the evidence. I'm sure I need not explain the consequences of using the potion on a pile of rubble."

The image of Lhasha's shattered form rose unbidden to Corin's mind, and he grimaced as if in pain. Azlar, misinterpreting his gesture, waved his hand, and his goons withdrew their knives and stepped away, still keeping a cautious eye on the one-armed warrior.

Corin slowly pushed his seat back and rose to his feet. "Where will I find you once I'm done?"

"You will not find me. We shall never speak again. If you succeed, I will know."

With nothing more to discuss, Corin left, casting a contemptuous glance back at the hunchbacked waitress cowering behind the bar, watching him go.

Azlar waited until Corin had left before rising himself. Instantly his bodyguards were beside him, ready to give their lives to protect the cult's latest rising star. Azlar didn't even acknowledge them. He was thinking about the one-armed warrior.

Of course, he didn't expect Corin to succeed. The map he had given the one-armed man was incomplete. It showed only the most heavily used and well-guarded passages controlled by Xiliath. Azlar's own map, the true copy, contained several less secure routes into Xiliath's stronghold as well as weaknesses in his defenses. The sheer size of the tunnel system made it impossible for Xiliath to guard every access point to his lair. The very thing that had kept him safe from discovery this past year now made him vulnerable to attack.

When Corin descended into the underground labyrinth, he would quickly be spotted by Xiliath's guards. The alarm would be raised, and the warrior would find himself facing the greater part of Xiliath's army.

This was fine as far as Azlar was concerned. Corin was nothing more than a distraction, a way to draw the attention of the main part of Xiliath's forces. While he bumbled foolishly into certain death, Azlar and his men would launch a surprise attack of their own through a different passage. By the time Xiliath's troops realized their mistake, Azlar would already be safely back on the city's surface with the package.

But the one-armed man was strong. He had destroyed the naga in the warehouse. Azlar couldn't underestimate him. If he somehow managed, against all odds, to escape with his life the cult would need to take steps to insure his silence. Permanent steps.

However, that was a matter not yet worthy of serious consideration. Recovering the package took precedence. Satisfied with his plan, the wizard spun on his heel and marched out the door, his guards following closely in his wake.

It was nearly ten minutes after he'd left before the waitress dared to come out from her hiding place.

CHAPTER TWENTY

"Are you here for the worship services?" the priest of Gond asked.

"No, not really. I need to see Fendel." Corin had tried to find the secret door in the back of the temple grounds that the gnome had brought them through last time, but his search had proved fruitless.

"I'm sorry, but Fendel is extremely busy right now. He toils in his workshop in the service of the Wonderbringer. Perhaps one of our other artificers can help you?"

"It has to be Fendel. It's very important."

The priest who had greeted him at the door to the House of Hands gave him the once over, as if mere visual inspection could give him some inkling as to Corin's purpose. Obviously, he didn't like what he saw.

"I'm sorry, but Fendel hates to be interrupted when he is performing Gond's will. Perhaps if you came back in a few days."

Corin was reluctant to explain his situation to the priest in any sort of detail. He still didn't trust religious institutions on general principle, and any mention of the Dragon Cult would probably send the underling running to the High Artificer. Ultimately it would get back to

Yanseldara. For Lhasha's sake he couldn't let that happen, but he needed to see the gnome. He couldn't do this without help.

"Please," he implored. "It's about Lhasha."

The mention of the name of Fendel's ward affected a sudden transformation in the attitude of the priest. "Is Lhasha in trouble?" he asked, the concern evident on his sooty face.

"I'm afraid I can't say. Please, take me to Fendel."

"Of course," the priest replied, without even a hint of his former reluctance. "Follow me."

Soon they stood before the familiar door of the gnome's workshop. The priest knocked several times, banging his fist emphatically against the wood.

"Go away!" came the voice from inside.

"Fendel," the priest called out. "There's someone here to see you!"

"Then go away and take him with you!"

"It's about Lhasha," Corin called out.

A second later the door opened. Fendel used one grubby hand to usher Corin in, while the other shooed his fellow priest away. With the heel of his boot he kicked the door closed behind them.

As usual, Fendel's workshop was a collage of indecipherable blueprints and unidentifiable, half-finished projects. This time Corin cared little for the intriguing inventions scattered about.

"Where have you been?" Fendel chastised, shaking Corin's elbow in exasperation. His tone was that of a parent addressing a young, willful child. "I heard about your little misadventure in the warehouse—leaving my ladder behind like some kind of calling card! Completely unprofessional.

"Is that why didn't you come back here yesterday morning? Thought I'd be mad, or something? Or was Lhasha just too embarrassed by the gaff to look me in the eye?"

Suddenly the gnome stopped his tirade. "Wait a minute—where is Lhasha? What happened?"

"They took her," Corin said flatly. "I'm going to get her back."

"Who took her?" Fendel demanded, clenching his grip on Corin's elbow.

"Someone named Xiliath. At least, someone working for Xiliath." The warrior shook his elbow free from the gnome's grip. "I'm going to get her back."

"Xiliath," the gnome muttered, rubbing his dirty, scraggly beard. "I've heard that name before." He turned his eyes to Corin, his gaze piercing. "You better tell me what happened. Everything."

"I don't have time for stories," Corin said through slightly clenched teeth. His failure to protect Lhasha had been eating away at him since the meeting with the cult wizard, and Corin was loathe to share his humiliation with the gnome. "I just need some supplies. I'll have to pay you on credit."

"Don't be stupid," the gnome spat, "I'm not charging you for anything. Not for this. But if you really want my help in getting Lhasha back, you'll tell me everything that happened. Solving problems is what I do best."

Realizing the gnome was right, Corin swallowed his pride and related the entire shameful tale: his inability to sense the set-up at the cult warehouse, his selfish efforts to find Fhazail and exact his vengeance, his cowardly flight from the ambush by Xiliath's army in the clearing, the conversation with Azlar at the Weeping Griffin. He even told Fendel about the medusa. Corin held nothing back in his confession. Once the words started, they gushed forth in a litany of his faults, a fountain of guilt and remorse spilling out at the feet of his small, wrinkled confessor.

When he was done, the gnome said nothing. He just stared at the floor for a long, long time.

"I'm sorry I couldn't protect her," Corin whispered, his voice choking slightly. "There is no excuse, but I will get her back!"

Fendel waved a sooty hand dismissively. "Don't drown in self-contempt, Corin. I hardly see anything you have to be ashamed of." The gnome cut Corin's protests off by adding, "It's all water under the bridge, anyway. We have to focus on what comes next, not what's been done."

The warrior nodded. Move forward. A lesson he had learned in his time with the White Shields, one he had unfortunately forgotten with the loss of his hand. Regret was a crutch for the weak. The strong learned from their mistakes, they didn't wallow in them. This was not the time for apologies, it was the time for redemption.

"Fendel," he said, his voice assuming its usual steadfast timbre, "give me whatever you can. Equipment, advice—everything. I *will* get Lhasha back."

"Give me a minute," the gnome responded, still tugging at his beard. "Let me piece this all together." He began to whisper, half to himself and half for Corin's benefit.

"The Cult of the Dragon. Xiliath. What do they have in common? A charmed medusa. But why smuggle a medusa into Elversult?"

The gnome looked up at Corin, his eyes alight with sudden understanding. "Yanseldara. They're going to kill her. Whoever controls the medusa has the perfect assassin. Just place her in the crowds lining the street during the parades of the Greengrass festival. One look and the Lady Lord of Elversult is nothing but a pile of stone, Vaerana, too. In the chaos and terror of the medusa's discovery, it wouldn't be hard to overturn their carriage, and smash them both to bits."

Corin didn't doubt the veracity of the gnome's conclusions. In fact, he didn't really care. All he wanted was to get Lhasha back. "Are you going to tell the High Artificer?" he asked, a hint of concern in his voice.

"No. He'd go straight to the Moonstorm House and report this to Vaerana. The cult and Xiliath will both be watching our city's leader very closely. Even a hint that their secret is out and they'll disappear for a few months until the search for them dies down. . . ." The gnome's voice trailed off

"And they'll take Lhasha with them," Corin finished.

"If they don't simply destroy all the evidence," Fendel added ominously.

The gnome's dire warning conjured a grim pause in the conversation. Fendel dispelled the heavy silence with a clap of his dirty hands.

"No dwelling on what ifs. Let's get down to business, Corin. Show me that potion the wizard gave you."

Without bothering to ask why, Corin produced the vial and placed it in the gnome's hands. Fendel jiggled the container, studying the way the contents rolled and rippled inside the glass.

"Looks genuine," he admitted, "but I'll need to do a few tests to be sure." He set the bottle down. "Let's see that map."

After a few minutes of careful study of the intricate layout of the tunnels beneath Elversult's surface, Fendel raised his head. "This is another set up. They want you to fail. If you try to get into Xiliath's lair through the smugglers' tunnels on this map you're as good as dead."

Corin had suspected as much. The Cult of the Dragon wanted their package back, and the warrior knew the lizard worshipers would consider him very expendable. Likely they wanted him to draw attention away from their own efforts to infiltrate Xiliath's hideout. But he didn't tell any of this to Fendel. There was no point.

"Going down into the smugglers' tunnels is virtually a suicide mission," Fendel continued. "But I may have a solution. Here, I'll show you."

Leaving Corin's map spread out across his workbench, Fendel rummaged around his workshop before returning with several scroll tubes. He proceeded to remove the documents inside and unroll them. "Hmmm. . . . Not this one. Hang on . . . nope. Ah . . . here it is."

He laid his own version of the map out on the table, side by side with Azlar's. To Corin's curious glance, they appeared almost identical—a dizzying picture of meandering routes crossing over, under, and through each other.

"How did you get this?" the warrior asked in amazement, staring at what appeared to be two copies of the entire legendary smugglers' system.

"I wasn't always in the service of the Wonderbringer," the gnome answered. "The tunnels were an easy way to move about the city without being seen, and a good place to hide out. I spent enough time down there in my day, I decided I might as well map them out to pass the time."

"You were a thief," Corin said as the realization slowly dawned. "A burglar. Like Lhasha."

"Who do you think got her into the business?" the gnome replied, slightly amused by Corin's reaction. "I'm surprised Lhasha never mentioned it, but I guess you aren't one for small talk."

True enough, Corin thought.

"Of course, things were different back then," the gnome continued. "Elversult was a savage, violent city before Yanseldara took over. Didn't have to worry about the Maces, but there was always another thief around the corner looking to slit your throat and take what you worked so hard to steal."

"But you said traveling the tunnels was a suicide mission," Corin pointed out, bringing the gnome back to the topic at hand. "How did you survive them?"

"I didn't go through the tunnels, I went under them."

Seeing Corin's confusion, the gnome clarified. "Everyone knows about the tunnels beneath the city. What most people don't know is that there is another network of passages below the original smugglers' tunnels—the sub-tunnels, if you will."

Corin was skeptical, but the gnome continued his explanation.

"It was only a matter of time, really. The smugglers came to realize that avoiding the Elversult authorities was easy, but avoiding each other was much tougher. The tunnels were full of guards, traps, monsters—you name it. And everyone wanted a piece of everyone else's action.

"So some of the more resourceful smugglers decided they'd build themselves another set of passages they could use to move quickly and safely between important areas, like Xiliath's storage cavern on your map. And of course, they were careful to make sure very few people would ever know of the new passages' existence. You could say they're the smugglers' tunnels of the smugglers' tunnels. But that's quite a mouthful, so I just call them the sub-tunnels."

"You've been in these sub-tunnels?" Corin asked, the excitement obvious in his voice.

Fendel nodded.

"Then you can tell me how to use them to find Lhasha!"

"Tell you? I'll show you. Did you really think I'd just sit here while Lhasha's in trouble?"

"This isn't a quest for an inventor or a thief," Corin said, remembering what had happened with Lhasha and the naga. "You'll just be in my way."

“Don’t underestimate me.” Fendel’s voice was hard as iron. The prospect of a job to be done had brought about a sudden metamorphosis in his usual jovial mood. As Corin had seen with Lhasha, the gnome’s disposition became serious and cold when it was time for business.

“I’m much more than just a thief, as you’ve already guessed from my inventions. I doubt my magic is a match for the young cult wizard, but I know my fair share of incantations. Anyway, you’ll need all the help you can get. The sub-tunnels might give you safe passage to Xiliath’s treasure room, but finding the way into them won’t be easy, even for me. And there’s bound to be guards in the treasure cavern when you get there. Alone, you’ll never even get close enough to Lhasha to use that potion. Together we might actually stand a small chance of getting her out alive.”

It was pointless to argue. Corin knew how stubborn Lhasha could be; now he understood where she got it from. Fendel also spoke the truth. With a mage by his side—even a minor spellcaster—his odds of success were much higher.

Corin shrugged. “So be it. We’ll go together.”

Fendel gave a curt nod then turned his attention back to the map.

“Look here,” the gnome said, pointing a gnarled finger at a point on the page. “If I remember right, we can get into the sub-tunnels through a secret door somewhere around here. If the cult’s info on Xiliath is accurate, the sub-tunnels should then take us straight under his treasure room.”

Corin took a closer look and saw the route as the gnome traced it with his gnarled finger—a straight line running beneath the larger network of caves, right through the heart of the area Azlar had marked on his own map as Xiliath’s lair.

"The sub-tunnels are well hidden," Fendel continued. "If we're lucky, even Xiliath himself might not know about them. No guards, no alarms. In and out in a matter of minutes, and no one the wiser."

"As soon as night falls, we'll go in," Fendel added. "That'll give me some time to get my things together, make sure this potion from the cult can really do what they claim, and memorize a few spells. Plus, it'll give you a chance to rest. When was the last time you slept? I've seen liches who looked more alive than you."

"I got some rest a couple nights ago. A few hours. Before Lhasha and I went to the warehouse." Two straight days without sleep. Corin had gone much longer on forced marches with the White Shields. That night he and Lhasha broke into the warehouse seemed a long, long way from where he was now.

The gnome nodded. "It shows. If you don't get some rest you won't be much use when we go after Lhasha."

Everything Fendel said was true, arguing would only waste time and energy. For Lhasha's sake, Corin consented to his orders. "I'll lie down. But I doubt I can sleep."

Fendel rummaged around his workshop again, and produced a crystal flask of clear liquid. "Take a swig of this. It'll knock you out. One gulp, no more. I don't want you waking up a tenday from now."

Corin took the bottle from Fendel's hand and popped the stopper out.

"Better lie down first," Fendel warned. "It works fast."

Heeding the gnome's advice, the soldier went into the small bedroom attached to the back of Fendel's workshop and stretched out on the bed in the corner. His feet dangled off the end of the tiny mattress, but at least it was comfortable. He could hear Fendel rummaging around in the workshop.

"Now, where did I stash my spellbooks?" the gnome muttered as the door separating the bedroom and the workshop slowly closed, drawn shut by the springs Fendel had installed on its hinges.

Corin took a sniff of the liquid. Odorless. He raised the flask to his lips. One long drink, two coughing gasps of surprise as the liquid burned down his throat, a three-count while he waited for the potion to take effect—and Corin knew no more.

CHAPTER TWENTY-ONE

By the light streaming through the window when he awoke, Corin knew it was early evening. He had slept for nearly twelve hours, but he wasn't stiff or sore at all. Fendel's elixir had left him feeling refreshed and rejuvenated, and even the cuts and bruises from his fight with Graal had all but vanished. He got to his feet and went back into the workshop to find Fendel.

The gnome glanced over from his workbench to the stirring warrior.

"Feeling better?" He didn't bother to wait for the answer he already knew. "I have something for you."

Clasped in his wrinkled, grimy hands was a gleaming metal arm. The light from the setting sun glinted off the fingers and the wrist. The gnome walked over and held it out toward Corin, as if making an offering at the feet of an emperor.

"But Lhasha just gave you the down payment a couple days ago," Corin said, slightly confused.

"The idea of building a working prosthetic kind of tweaked my imagination," the gnome explained with a rueful smile. "And I knew Lhasha would eventually come up with the gold for the rest. So the day after I first met you I went out and purchased the materials. I've been refining and tinkering with it the past month—things are always pretty slow around here during the Claw of Winter anyway. I think it's finally ready."

"I . . . you know I can't pay you. Not yet, at least," Corin said.

"This isn't charity, Corin. Getting Lhasha back isn't going to be easy. Every advantage helps. Besides, I know you'll pay me back. If we survive.

"Here," the gnome concluded, handing the artificial limb to the speechless warrior, "try it on."

With his left hand, Corin raised the prosthetic for a closer look. "It's light," he said, hefting its weight.

"But sturdy," Fendel assured him. "The alloy is one of my own making. Harder than mithral. Maybe even stronger than adamantine."

Corin examined the finely crafted limb in more detail. It was about the same distance from Corin's elbow to where the tips of his fingers would have been. The base was hollowed out and contained a complicated leather strap to secure the piece over the small stump of forearm protruding from his elbow.

The hand had five distinct digits. The thumb was even opposable. The knuckles were made of a fine mesh, while the rest was made of solid metal. The wrist contained an odd hinge that allowed the hand to twist, bend, and rotate on the end of the metal arm.

"How do I keep it from just flopping around?" Corin asked curiously.

"Don't worry, I've thought of that," the gnome replied. "Just put it on and see how it works."

Corin slid his forearm into the base, lashed the strap around his elbow and pulled it tight. He felt a warm tingle shoot from the end of his stump and up right through his shoulder, and the hand sprang to life. The metal fingers began to clutch, clench, and twist. The hand writhed in circles on the end of its wrist. Corin recoiled in surprise.

"It's all right," Fendel assured him, "that's supposed to happen. Give it a few seconds to adjust to you."

Heeding the gnome's instructions, Corin stood still while the alien appendage slowly ceased its spastic motions. With a hint of trepidation in his voice, Corin asked, "What next?"

"Try making a fist."

"How?" Corin was unfamiliar with even the most mundane of magics, and Fendel's invention was obviously an artifact of tremendous enchantments.

"Just make a fist. Like you used to. Clench the other hand, too, if that helps."

Corin did, clenching his left hand into a tight ball while staring at the right. In unison, the metal fingers curled in, and the thumb overlapped them. Corin uncurled his left hand, and the prosthetic did the same. Then he tried clenching a fist with just his artificial hand. To his amazement, it worked.

"Praise the Wonderbringer," he gasped.

"Try picking something up," Fendel urged.

The warrior walked over to a hammer on one of the workbenches. Instinctively, his left hand started forward, but he pulled it back. He extended his right arm, concentrating on opening the fingers. They responded to his mental commands and wrapped themselves around the handle. He raised the tool up, and brought it down on a slightly protruding nail, pounding it back into place. The wrist moved with a natural, fluid motion as he swung the hammer. He didn't even have to think about it.

"Well, what do you think?"

There was no reply from Corin, though not because of his usual taciturn nature. He was truly speechless.

"Not as good as the real thing, I'll admit. You can't feel anything with it—I never could figure out how to incorporate a tactile component. And it'll take a long time before you have any sense of how hard you're squeezing something. I wouldn't shake anyone's hand for a while."

Gripping a tool was one thing, but Corin needed to know if his new arm would stand up to a true test. He set the hammer back on the table and pulled his sword from its scabbard. He took a few slow, arcing swings; the most basic of moves. The arm moved clumsily, awkwardly—far too cumbersome to effectively strike an opponent.

Frowning, Corin tried a simple parry and thrust combination. The wrist failed to turn properly, and the sword sliced the air at a completely ineffective angle.

"Don't think about it so much," the gnome advised. "Just relax. Don't try to steer it—let the limb think for itself."

Think for itself? Corin began to wonder how powerful Fendel's magic really was. Could the metal appendage actually be sentient?

While he was considering the ramifications of his new limb's potential intelligence, Corin's mind had ceased to focus on the mechanics of his stroke. The sword sliced through the air with a sharp swish. The wrist pivoted and the arm reversed its momentum, carving a path back against the original stroke. A difficult move, executed with near flawless precision.

Corin continued his exercises, running through the traditional positions and movements of his warrior training. Instead of trying to control the sword, he watched it, allowing the limb to move on its own, free from the fetters of his conscious mind.

"Gods," he muttered in awe as the weapon became a flickering, flashing reflection of light whirling through the air, battling a horde of imaginary foes. "It's a better soldier than I am!"

"I highly doubt that," Fendel replied. "It's just drawing on your own talent. If I tried to use it, I'd likely slice off the tip of my nose. It may not seem like it, but you do control the hand. The trick is to control it at a subliminal level."

With a simple, casual thought Corin caused the arm to cease its display of swordsmanship. The warrior built up a picture of an opponent in front of him—an amalgamation of all the nameless, anonymous foes he had fought and defeated countless times in his years as a White Shield. He engaged his imaginary opponent with a series of standard attack and defense combinations. A sweep at the knees, a reverse cut at the belt, a simple cross block, and a quick counter.

The arm responded, but its movements were sluggish. Corin tried to disengage his mind and attacked again. The sword became a blur of movement, a savage, overpowering attack, but not the moves Corin intended, or expected. He grimaced. If the arm insisted on executing moves he wasn't anticipating, he'd eventually leave himself vulnerable.

He tried again and again. Searching for the balance between conscious action and instinctive reaction. For a brief second, it was there. The sword flowed with the grace and lethal beauty of a true White Shield, executing an array of strikes, blocks, and counter-strikes that would render most opponents defenseless for the final blow.

When Corin drove home the final thrust to impale his phantom foe, the blow went awry. Lethal, probably, but not a clean kill. He swore in frustration and hurled his sword to the ground.

"What good is an arm if it wields a sword like an undisciplined rookie recruit? I'd be better off using my left hand!"

The gnome scowled at Corin as he bent to pick up the blade. "Keep practicing," he spat, jamming the hilt back into the cold fingers of the metal arm. Then, in a softer voice he added, "Just trust your instincts."

Corin bowed his head in embarrassment at his outburst. Only a fool thought he could use a weapon without many, many hours of practice.

"Fendel," he said intently, "your creation is truly amazing. Eventually, I'm sure it will be of great use to me, but I don't have the time to master it right now. We have to go after Lhasha."

"Keep at it," the gnome said, reaching up to give Corin a pat on the shoulder. "I don't want to leave until dark, anyway. Xiliath probably has eyes on every street corner, and we can't risk him seeing us go into the tunnels. You've still got a few hours."

Nodding, Corin resumed his drills, though he expected it to be an exercise in futility. Still, it was something to occupy the time, to keep his mind from conjuring up images of statues tipping over and smashing into broken rubble.

"I've still got some more preparations of my own to make," Fendel told him. "I thought I'd left this kind of thing behind when I joined the House of Hands, so it's taking me longer to get my things together."

As the wrinkled little man again disappeared through the door leading to his private storeroom, Corin heard him mutter, "Now, where are those spell components? I was sure I had some sulfur around here somewhere."

The twin blades twirled and danced in intricate patterns, the swish of their strikes crisp and true as they carved the air around Corin. The warrior swung the weapons with the controlled fury of the legendary berserkers of the Cold Lands. The speed and savagery of his blows sent ripples of wind wafting across the sheen of sweat that coated his bare torso.

Two hours ago he had struggled to manage the alien attachment tied to his amputated stump. Now he wielded a pair of swords with the artistry of a master, both his arms—one of warm flesh, the other of cold metal—acting in perfect unison.

It had taken Corin almost an hour just to achieve a level of basic proficiency with his new limb. Since that time his skill had progressed in phenomenal leaps and bounds. Further evidence of Fendel's talent as both an inventor and a spellcaster. In one short evening the gnome's creation had allowed Corin's ability as a warrior to far surpass the level it had taken him years to achieve on his own. The fury of the dual weapons magnified his assaults exponentially, making him a match for any warrior on the Dragon Coast—possibly even the mighty orog Graal.

Corin was so intent on his exercises that he hadn't even heard Fendel return. He reacted to the unexpected sound of the gnome's greeting behind him by spinning around and dropping into a defensive fighting crouch, the right sword poised to launch a quick thrust, the left ready to deflect an incoming blade. He relaxed when he realized it was only his host.

"I see you've gotten the hang of your new arm," Fendel said, a hint of pride in his voice as he laughed at his own bad pun. "And I see you found yourself another weapon, too."

"I noticed it on one of the benches. I didn't think you'd mind."

"Of course not, of course not. I used to carry that blade by my side whenever I went out on a job," the gnome said wistfully. "It's got some minor magic forged into its design. It glows whenever an enemy's nearby."

Corin flipped the sword in the air and caught it by the blade, offering the hilt to Fendel. "I was just practicing. You can have it back."

The gnome shook his head. "No, it's probably better if you keep it. It'll be far more useful in your hand than in my clumsy grasp. I'm not much good with a blade, to be honest."

A curt nod of acknowledgment was Corin's only reply. This was not the time for gushing speeches of thanks or rambling monologues of gratitude, though Fendel deserved both in great measure—for the sword, for the arm, for everything. Words could come later; right now only actions mattered. Corin was hungry for battle. His warrior's mind was focused solely on the task at hand: rescuing Lhasha at any cost and mercilessly hewing down any who would stand in his way.

"I've got a few things together already," the gnome explained, seeming to completely understand Corin's understated reaction. "Come into the back, and I'll show you."

They passed through the rear door of the large workroom and into the small, cluttered storeroom built onto the back of Fendel's workshop home. Corin wasn't surprised to see a small workbench in the center of the room, covered with a variety of items.

"I think I've got everything we might need," the gnome said by way of explanation. "Just a few last minute items to load up, and we're off."

Gods, Corin thought, surveying the array of equipment and items covering nearly every square inch of the table, *we'll need an army to carry everything!* But he knew Fendel was full of surprises, so he kept his reservations to himself.

"Rope," the gnome said. "Fifty feet. You can never have too much rope." He stuffed the coil of thickly braided hemp into a small bag on the table.

Corin suspected he was checking each item off on his own personal mental list, rather than speaking for the benefit of his larger companion.

"Stakes," Fendel continued. "Good for propping open doors or wedging them shut. Very handy." A half dozen six-inch metal spikes were added into the bag.

"A couple lanterns. I can see in the dark, but you can't." To Corin's amazement, the two large, hooded oil lamps were jammed into the bag as well. The rope alone should have bulged out the sides of the sack, but it still looked empty. Magical containers of almost limitless capacity were not unheard of, but Corin had never actually seen one before.

"A few flasks of oil, a couple spare wicks, my lucky tinderbox." As he named each item, Fendel dumped them all into the wondrous bag. If the situation wasn't so serious, Corin would have chuckled at the ludicrous sight of Fendel jamming item after item into the bag that couldn't possibly hold more.

"A couple sledge hammers, a ladder, a crowbar, a couple lock picks, a grappling hook. A couple walking sticks for probing the walls and floor ahead, in case there's traps." The gnome held up a pair of oversized spectacles. "My special goggles, just in case we run into that snakey-haired friend of yours."

Corin realized his mouth was hanging open. He snapped it shut and wondered what they would do with all of this stuff.

"What do they do?" Corin asked curiously as the glasses disappeared into the bag.

"Very handy," Fendel assured him. "I wish I had a pair for each of us, but one set will have to suffice. It's a little something I whipped up while you were sleeping. The lenses will protect against the power of the medusa's gaze, I hope. Can you think of anything else we might need?"

"The potion. The one to restore Lhasha."

The gnome patted a hard leather case at his hip. "Safe and sound right here. You could hit this with a mace and the bottle inside wouldn't break.

"Anything else, my heavily muscled friend? Do you need some armor? I might have a few bits and pieces lying around that would fit."

Corin shook his head, remembering how easily and fluid his movements had been during his recent training session—and recalling his last encounter with Graal. Armor would only slow him down and limit his ability to attack quickly and evade the blows of an opponent. It would also make it almost impossible to sneak silently past any guards if the opportunity arose.

Corin now trusted more in his ability to avoid an enemy's eyes and blades, than in the protection offered by a suit of armor.

Taking a deep breath, Fendel muttered, "Then it's time to go."

CHAPTER TWENTY-TWO

Only a few blocks away from the House of Hands, just at the base of the bare, windswept tor that dominated Elversult's skyline, sat a small inn. The Pilgrims' Progress was a popular resting spot and one-night stopover for those who had business with either of the temples at the summit of Temple Hill.

Fendel led Corin around to the stables at the back. While the warrior kept his rather intimidating form concealed in the nearby shadows, the gnome approached the stable doors. He spoke a few whispered words to the groomsman charged with the care of the mounts housed in the building, and Corin heard the faint clink of coins changing hands. Fendel motioned for Corin to follow him inside.

The gnome took him to an empty stall at the back and brushed away the hay with his boot to reveal a small trapdoor in the floor. A heavy padlock kept the door secured in place. Corin watched with admiration as Fendel worked the lock with his nimble fingers, and a few seconds later the way was open.

From the magical bag at his side, Fendel produced the two lanterns Corin had seen earlier. "Close the door," he whispered to the warrior, igniting the lamps.

Corin's eyes had adjusted to the darkness, so the blazing illumination caused him to wince in pain and surprise.

"Sorry," Fendel apologized as he reduced the light source to a faint sliver by turning the heavy metal shield that covered the lamp.

"I used to traverse this section of the smugglers' tunnels quite frequently in my working days," the gnome said as he handed one of the lamps to Corin. He adjusted the second one before lighting it.

"We have a ways to go to reach the entrance to the sub-tunnel system, but this passage is empty. Or, at least, it was the last time I was down here."

A nod from Corin showed he understood, and Fendel set off. The warrior followed close behind, his left hand holding up the lamp so that its beam lit the way ahead. He couldn't feel Fendel's sword in the grasp of his metallic right hand, but he knew it was there, drawn and ready.

The air inside the tunnel was stale and frigid, only a few degrees above freezing—noticeably cooler than the mild Elversult nights in the first tenday of the Sunsets. Guided only by Fendel's sense of direction and his memory of his old haunts, the pair wound their way through the twisting tunnels. Fendel's map was stashed safely in his magical pack, but the absence of any kind of landmark or reference points in the tunnels would have made it all but useless, Corin realized.

They passed by countless archways and branching passages, but Fendel never hesitated. Sometimes he veered left, sometimes right. For the most part, he continued on straight ahead. It didn't take long before Corin was completely lost. If the gnome was off course, they might never find their way back.

After nearly twenty minutes, the gnome pulled up

short. Corin, who had been trailing a few steps behind, tensed himself and began to scan the gloom beyond the range of his lantern's glow for signs of trouble. He saw nothing but half-imagined specters conjured by the play of light and shadow over the rough-hewn surface of the tunnel walls.

"This is it," Fendel announced, setting his lantern on the damp floor. He began to run his fingers lightly over the irregular rock face of the right wall.

Corin's eyes scanned the stone facade, but he couldn't make out any visible signs of a door. He briefly wondered not only how Fendel had been able to find the door tonight, but how he had ever located it in the first place.

"I don't see any traps," Fendel said after several long moments of careful inspection. "Let's see if I can find the trigger."

Corin set down his lantern and drew his second sword. Until this point they had been in an unclaimed, unused section of the Elversult tunnels. Beyond the secret door was a route leading to the heart of Xiliath's lair. If Lhasha's mysterious captor knew about the sub-tunnel leading to his treasure cavern, the least they could expect would be a few guards along the way.

The gnome's hand came to rest on a small, unremarkable outcropping of rock.

"Ready?" he whispered. Corin nodded, and Fendel pulled down on the trigger.

Soundlessly, the door swung in toward them. A dark, open mouth loomed before the two. Even the light from their torches couldn't pierce the wall of blackness that blocked the tunnel's entrance.

"Someone cast a spell here. This darkness wasn't here last time I used this tunnel. Of course, that was a long, long time ago. I think I can counteract the spell, at least temporarily." He didn't need to say what they were both thinking. Someone had cast a darkness spell, that meant someone knew about the tunnel.

Taking a step forward to shield Fendel while he prepared his incantation, Corin braced himself for an attack. By itself, the murkiness—magical though it was—wasn't an effective deterrent to thieves or invaders. It was a mere diversion, masking a more sinister threat. Corin was ready for whatever would confront them when the gnome dispelled the shadows.

He could hear the mumbled words of Fendel's incantation and the rustle of his clothing as the gnome performed the complicated gestures and intricate actions required to weave his magic. Suddenly, the darkness was gone. The entrance to the secret passage was bathed in light. Not the feeble light from their shielded lamps, but the bright glow of a clear afternoon.

With the entrance clearly visible, the reason for the magical darkness became evident as well. A step beyond the archway was a yawning pit. Corpses and skeletons were impaled on enormous spikes lining the bottom.

"Looks like nobody's used this passage for a while," he concluded, sheathing the sword in his left hand and picking up his lantern.

"Or maybe something just comes along and cleans the bodies up," Fendel countered, "bones and all."

From his magical sack, Fendel pulled out the long ladder he had somehow stuffed inside earlier that evening. The pit was only a standing leap across, but the deadly spikes below made the prospect of jumping unappealing.

Fortunately, the ladder was long enough to easily reach the other side. Without looking down, Corin slowly made his way across the makeshift bridge spanning the small pit. He moved from rung to rung with agonizing precision, keeping his mind focused on the far side and the potential for an ambush as he crossed.

He reached the opposite edge without incident. Nothing rushed out at him, no creatures or guards waylaid his progress. A second later, Fendel skipped casually across the ladder, moving with the same unconscious grace and carefree ease Corin had earlier admired in the gnome's half-elf protégé during their assault on the cult warehouse.

"Traps, but no guards," Fendel said once he had stuffed the ladder back into his enchanted sack. "It's possible Xiliath knows about this tunnel but hasn't shared his secret with anyone else. If he's ever cornered, or betrayed by his own people, he'll always have one last escape route he knows won't be blocked."

Again, Corin agreed with Fendel's assessment. Maybe luck was with them. If Xiliath hadn't even told his guards about the passage, it might be possible to sneak in and out without ever being noticed.

"Here," Fendel said, producing one of the walking sticks from his bag and handing it to Corin. The sturdy staff was about four feet long, several inches around, and made of a light, gnarled wood. Sturdy, yet fairly light. Many of the older citizens of Elversult used such things, leaning on them to help support their feeble joints as they wandered the streets of the fair.

"Don't take a step until you've used this to prod the way ahead of you for danger. Like this." The gnome removed a second staff from his bag and gave a visual demonstration, striking the end firmly against the ground before advancing cautiously forward.

Corin nodded and sheathed his sword. He now clasped the wooden pole in his left hand, and the lantern in his right. Fendel's spell had illuminated the first few yards of the secret tunnel, but the rest of the way was still unlit. However, the magical darkness that had blocked even the beams of their lanterns had been centered over the deadly trap and didn't extend the entire length of the passage.

Their progress was slow and tedious, the methodical search for traps a frustrating but necessary activity as they crept along the gradually sloping passage. After ten minutes they had made little headway—at this point the passage had leveled out, leaving them well below the network of the original smugglers' tunnels. Already, Corin could feel his impatience and frustration mounting.

Half an hour later, the necessity of their tedious pace was suddenly and graphically demonstrated. The pressure of the end of the gnome's staff on the floor unleashed a volley of darts from hidden slits in the walls. The projectiles fired from either side and embedded themselves in the opposite wall only an arm's length ahead of Corin and Fendel.

Neither said a word, but they exchanged a quick glance to assure each other they were both unharmed. Fendel thumped the end of his staff on the floor again, but yielded no effect this time. The trap had been loaded only for a single round.

One look at the corroding, crumbling wall around the protruding darts and Corin understood why a second wave of missiles would have seemed unnecessary to the trap's architect. The darts had been dipped in acid.

The sub-tunnel narrowed, forcing them to walk single file. Corin took the lead—despite the traps, he was still worried about running into a guard, and he wanted to be between the gnome and any potential foes. Passing his lantern to Fendel, he drew his sword with his metal arm. His other hand was wrapped firmly around the wooden staff.

Corin pressed the pace, driven by a growing sense of urgency. At the rate they were going, it would be dawn before they ever got close to Xiliath's trophy room. He rapped his staff in quick, staccato bursts against the floor, occasionally giving a few raps to the roof above or the walls on the side. Fendel trailed a step behind, a lantern in each hand to light the way, his own staff stashed safely in the bag.

The faint whiff of sulfur brought Corin up short. The warrior heard the clatter of Fendel dropping the lamps, then the gnome yanked Corin backward by his belt, pulling him off balance. As Corin toppled back the staff fell from his hand. His metallic limb kept a firm grasp on his sword, however.

The floor erupted in a wall of fire where Corin had been standing a moment before, incinerating the wooden pole and igniting the oil spilling out from the lanterns. Scrambling back from the heat, Corin and Fendel could only watch as the hall ahead of them flared up in a roaring inferno.

The flames lasted for less than a minute before sputtering out, casting the tunnel into utter darkness. Corin heard Fendel's chant, and a second later the way before them was lit by the now glowing end of Fendel's pole. In the magical light, Corin could see the melted metal casings of their lanterns.

"Sorry," Corin said, his voice loud in the cramped passage, "I should have been more careful."

"Maybe," Fendel answered slowly, "but I think that was no ordinary trap. Probably a warding glyph."

Corin nodded. Any guilt he felt about the near disaster he had caused quickly vanished. Warding glyphs were powerful magic. Fendel surely didn't expect a simple soldier to avoid them. Corin suppressed a shudder as he realized how close he had come to a grisly death.

"I better take the lead," the gnome advised. "If there are any more wards I might be able to spot them."

They continued on. With the gnome in the lead the

pace was much slower than the one Corin had set. Fendel held the glowing end of his staff out far in front of him, still using it to tap and prod the way ahead while his keen eyes sought out the telltale signs of magical protections.

Despite his best efforts they stumbled right into the heart of the third trap. Neither Corin nor his gnome guide noticed the tiny symbols engraved on the rock wall as they passed, but they both heard the whoosh of air as the enchantment was sprung.

A cloud of billowing, noxious vapors materialized around them, its appearance so sudden they didn't even have time to hold their breath. Corin dropped to his knees. He could feel the fumes burning his eyes and exposed skin. In the corner of his tear-filled vision he saw that Fendel had collapsed unconscious, succumbing to the poisonous fog almost immediately.

The brackish mist crawled down Corin's throat and seared his lungs, but Corin hardly noticed as he struggled to keep from blacking out. He reached out with his left hand and seized Fendel's ankle, gagging and choking on the fumes as he dragged both himself and Fendel down the tunnel, back the way they had come.

In the thick haze, he couldn't even seen three feet ahead. He had no idea how far the cloud extended back down the tunnel. Realizing his vision was useless anyway, Corin clenched his eyes against the acrid smoke and continued to pull himself along. He felt his skin blistering from the corrosive cloud. His chest heaved as it tried to expel the contaminated air filling his lungs. Corin fought against the urge, knowing even the poisonous air in his lungs was far safer than the thickening fog that enveloped him now.

Two minutes later—limbs shaking, muscles crying out for air—Corin could hold out no longer. The trapped air in his lungs vomited forth in a stinging spew, and his rebellious body took a long, deep breath. Instead of the agony of more poison slithering down his throat, Corin tasted only the cool, damp air of the tunnel.

With great gasps he swallowed the dank air, flooding his burning lungs and feeding his starving muscles with stale oxygen. He rolled onto his side, opened his eyes, and glanced back over his shoulder. Fendel's glowing staff still lay on the ground behind them—he could just make out the pinpoint of its light through the brown cloud. Corin had managed to drag himself and Fendel only a short distance beyond the edge of the deadly fog, but the magic that had conjured the mist kept it tightly concentrated, and there were no signs that the vapors would spread any farther.

Hopefully it wasn't too late. Like Corin, Fendel's exposed skin was red, raw, and festering with sores. The warrior checked his smaller companion for some sign of breath and was relieved to find a steady rhythm of air coming in and out. He rolled the gnome onto his stomach and began to pound him on the back. After a few quick strikes the gnome wretched, hacking up long strings of black, sticky phlegm before going into a prolonged coughing fit. The warrior waited patiently for the fit to pass, grateful his guide was still alive.

"Are you all right?" Corin asked once Fendel had regained his composure. His voice was hoarse and rasping, his throat ragged and swollen from the effects of the gas.

"I'll . . . I'll be all right," the gnome answered, rubbing his own throat.

Corin rose to his feet and helped the wrinkled little man stand up as well.

"So, how do we get by this?" The billowing cloud showed no signs of dissipating.

"I can handle it," Fendel assured him. "Just give me a moment to catch my breath."

The gnome cleared his throat, wincing at the pain as he did so. He spat out another glob of the dark phlegm, then spoke in the arcane, indecipherable language of spellcasters.

As the magic gathered, Corin first felt, then heard, the rushing wind. It grew from a whispering zephyr to a roaring crescendo in mere seconds, the currents so strong they nearly ripped the clothes from Corin's back as they whipped through the tunnel.

Corin's ears popped continuously with the changing pressure in the tunnel as the force of the tempest rose, tearing great holes in the cloud, rending the fabric of the mist like the garments of a grieving mourner. The wall of fog disintegrated into mere wisps and puffs before being swept away altogether. As suddenly as it had risen, the storm broke.

The gnome stood with his hands braced on his hips, his hair tousled and tangled from the winds, his face breaking into a broad grin as the last vestiges of his spell dissolved away.

He caught Corin's eye and gave the warrior a grin.

"I love that spell," he said before going over and retrieving his glowing staff.

The injuries of both men were minor—a few quick healing spells from Fendel and their skin was restored to a healthy, pink-hued glow. They continued on.

"If my calculations are correct," the gnome said after another twenty minutes of cautious, trap-free advancement, "we're almost there. I suspect there'll be another surprise before we get to the end, though."

Corin's grip on his twin swords tightened. Traps were well and good, but the warrior knew the best protection was a living, thinking guardian—whether man or beast.

If they were close to their goal, his instincts said, the last hurdle would have to be something he could fight. Trusting his instincts, Corin squinted into the shadows ahead, searching out the foe he knew was awaiting them.

They heard the guardian long before they saw it.

It began with what sounded like conversation, dozens of voices speaking simultaneously, their nonsensical chatter overlapping and merging into a single, incoherent whole. The incomprehensible din quickly rose to a deafening cacophony, reverberating throughout the narrow tunnel.

The very thoughts in Corin's mind were pushed out of his skull by the babbling chaos. The noise grew louder as the creature approached, but Corin was incapable of cogent action. He stood slack jawed, arms dangling at his sides, staring mindlessly into the abyss from which the creature would emerge.

"Corin!" someone nearby shouted, but the name held no urgency for the enthralled warrior, its meaning swallowed up by the pandemonium emanating from the darkness.

The beast emerged from the shadows, an oozing, amorphous slime of eyes and teeth enmeshed in a squirming jelly of mushy, formless flesh. It crept across the cavern floor by extending gooey pseudopods and sticky tendrils from its amoeboid body, then pulling the rest of its gelatinous form forward. Hundreds of eyes twisted and swayed atop stalks protruding from the viscous puddle. Within the shapeless, quivering mass of runny flesh countless maws of tiny razors gnashed and wailed, producing the horrible commotion overpowering Corin's senses.

Corin's body took a reflexive step back. Even in his dulled and deadened state it recoiled from the repulsive, advancing specimen.

"Corin!" he heard again, yet he remained oblivious. The sharp pain of a hard slap to his cheek snapped him from his stupor. He shook his head to clear the confusion from his mind and gave a nod to Fendel to let the gnome know the stinging blow had brought him back to his senses.

"Fall back," the gnome shouted above the clamoring uproar. "Let me take care of this!"

Corin hesitated. If combat was imminent, he should face their adversary, not the little gnome. Then he took another look at the gibbering, babbling mass of mucous-like matter. He imagined a host of the slimy protrusions snaking out toward him if he got in close enough to use his swords, engulfing his legs, wrapping around his arms, dragging him helplessly to the ground. He shuddered as his mind summoned the unbidden image of his own body immobilized by the gummy tentacles while the mass of mouths and eyes enveloped his form and devoured him alive.

He grunted at his lack of mental discipline, as he snapped out of his reverie. Attacking the horror would be a foolish proposition, he realized. How could he possibly engage it in combat? It had no arms or legs, no obvious vital organs. Slicing the thing in half might actually create a pair of independent beings, forcing him to deal with not one but two alien, unfamiliar opponents. Recognizing his own talents were useless in this situation, the soldier assented to Fendel's order and retreated—leaving the wizened mage to his own devices.

Fendel's hastily cast incantation conjured a wheel of burning flame, its diameter nearly as tall as the gnome himself. The wheel stood upright on the surface of the tunnel floor. With a mere point of his finger, Fendel started the wheel rolling toward the hideous entity.

A tentacle of dripping slime shot out from the thing's

center and wrapped itself around the blazing wheel. The gooey substance of the tentacle instantly melted into bubbling liquid. The stench of searing sludge assailed Corin's nostrils, making him retch.

The chaotic babble rose to the pitch of a scream and the creature's form raised itself up into an oozing pillar, dozens of mouths spewing spittle and bile at the burning wheel rolling relentlessly forward. Wherever the spray struck the rock, it exploded in a burst of flashing, white-hot light, nearly blinding Corin.

But the spray from the many mouths couldn't quench the magical flames of Fendel's burning wheel. The monster slid backward, tendrils and pseudopods groping behind it in an effort to escape the heat. The thing was slow, much slower than the gnome's fiery juggernaut.

The wheel rolled over the center of the creature's mass, its viscous body beginning to seethe and boil from the heat. The gibbering babble became shrieking screams as the creature was consumed by the fire. Fendel's concentration never wavered. He rolled the wheel back and forth across the dying monstrosity until the only sound left was the crackle of the flames and the soft, wet explosions of popping bubbles from its cooking flesh.

"I suspect the way from here on in will be clear," Fendel observed calmly, plugging his nose to keep out the foul stink of the steaming corpse.

Plugging his nose against the smell, Corin could only hope the gnome was right.

CHAPTER TWENTY-THREE

"This is it," Fendel said, running his hands over the ceiling a few feet from the stone wall blocking their path. "We'll be coming in through the floor near the south wall, if memory serves."

If Corin didn't know better he would have assumed they had somehow gotten lost and run into a dead end, but by now he had learned to trust the gnome's sense of direction.

He didn't know how Fendel had been able to guide him so easily through the sub-tunnels without even looking at a map, or how the gnome had unerringly chosen the right path at every fork and branch. Maybe magic unlocked the small man's long-forgotten memories of his old hideout, or maybe Fendel had spent so much time down there he had never really forgotten the layout. To Corin, the explanation was unimportant. The only thing that mattered was that Fendel had delivered on his promise: He had brought them through the labyrinth to Xiliath's treasure room.

"Assuming that lizard-worshiping wizard's information is accurate, there're bound to be a few guards up above," Fendel cautioned. "But they won't be watching for us to come in this way. They'll be watching the main entrance to the north. If we act fast, maybe we can take them out before they set off any alarms."

"Do you have any spells that would do the trick?"

"No. Most of my spells are designed to protect, or hinder. I never got the knack of those quick-killing incantations. I can maybe slow them down, but I can't keep them from setting off an alarm."

"Leave the guards to me then," Corin said. "You just find Lhasha and use that potion to set her right."

"Fair enough," the gnome replied, pulling out the iron stakes and a heavy hammer he'd stashed in his magical bag earlier that evening. "But before I look for Lhasha, I'll have to wedge this trapdoor open. If it shuts behind us, I don't think we'll be able to open it from the other side. It won't do Lhasha any good if we rescue her and don't have a way out."

In less trying circumstances, Corin would have grinned at the methodical, organized, and ever practical functioning of Fendel's mind. As it was, he was simply grateful he had agreed to let the gnome come along. Already the little man's cautious preparation and forethought had saved his life countless times.

"Are you ready to do your thing?" the gnome asked.

Corin nodded.

Fendel flipped the trigger, and the trapdoor above their heads swung open with a groan.

With a boost from his larger companion, the gnome quickly scrambled up through the hole above them, and a second later Corin had pulled himself up and through it as well.

The cavern was huge, easily large enough to fit any of the buildings from the warehouse district inside. Set into the wall at regular intervals were burning torches, casting a dim glow about the entire room. The west side of the cavern was filled with wooden crates and barrels—like the Cult of the Dragon, much of Xiliath's operation was financed by smuggling contraband into the city. In the southwest corner were racks of weapons and stacks of armor. A cache large enough to equip a small army. In the southeast corner was the hooded, motionless figure of the medusa.

As the wizard had promised, the cave was full of statues—victims of the medusa's gaze. Forty, maybe fifty in all, were scattered about the room. In the dim light it was impossible to get an exact count—and impossible to pick Lhasha out from the bunch. Corin realized their chance of a quick in-and-out mission was very remote.

The only entrance to the great cavern, besides Fendel's secret door, was a wide arch in the north wall, guarded by four heavily armed soldiers. But instead of facing out into the approaching hall, as Corin had hoped, they were all looking back into the room, their attention drawn by the incriminating moan of the secret door's long neglected hinges.

Corin's battle cry rang through the chamber as he leaped through the door and charged across the cavern to attack, hoping all four of his opponents would enter the fray. Three of the soldiers did rush to meet Corin, but the fourth turned and disappeared through the arch and into the network of tunnels beyond. Within minutes, Corin knew, the lone guard would return with a platoon of troops to bolster the room's defenders.

One of the men running toward Corin easily outdistanced his two companions, and met the metal-armed warrior in the very center of the cavern. His fleetness of foot was rewarded with the honor of being the first to fall before Corin's twin blades.

The metal arm dealt the first blow, a lightning quick thrust to the midsection. The sword was true to the mark, gouging a deep wound in the guard's side. That alone might have been enough to finish him, but even as the first blade was inflicting potentially lethal damage, the second slashed at the guard's thigh. The edge of Fendel's enchanted sword, which Corin now wielded in his left hand, cut to the bone, severing the man's artery.

Corin went into a spin to keep his momentum moving forward as he wrenched the blades free and brought them both to bear again. The soldier collapsed. Beneath him, one of Corin's swords hacked at the dying man's chest as he fell, the other carving a ragged gash across his throat to insure only a corpse would hit the floor.

The other two men came into range and engaged Corin simultaneously. He easily fended off their initial thrusts, the twin blades allowing him to deflect their coordinated attacks. He turned the dual fury of his swords on the man to his left, using one weapon to open up the guard's defenses, allowing the other blade to strike unimpeded.

The merciless slaughter of his mates broke the third guard's morale. He dropped his sword and tried to run, but Corin hacked him down before he had taken three steps, the point of Fendel's sword slipping between the rings of his mail shirt with the screech of metal on metal. Stabbing an unarmed foe in the back didn't bother Corin in the least. The White Shields believed in an honorable code of conduct, but only a fool extended his chivalry to the battlefield. Any enemy stupid enough to turn his back on an armed foe deserved to die.

During the brief but bloody battle, Corin had caught the heavy sounds of Fendel's hammer, pounding stakes in place to make sure the trapdoor stayed open. He glanced back at his companion to see the gnome had finished securing their escape route and was now darting about the room, moving from statue to statue, seeking out his young ward's petrified body among the stone silhouettes barely visible in the shadows of the torchlight.

Corin joined in the search. With reinforcements already on the way, their only hope was to find Lhasha and get out before the second wave of Xiliath's army reached the room. However, like Fendel, he could do little but run haphazardly from stone figure to stone figure, changing course only when he got close enough to recognize a particular statue was too tall or too wide to be Lhasha.

A deep, growling voice echoed from the roof and walls of the cavern, pulling Corin up short.

"We meet again, White Shield!"

Graal stood in the archway of the main entrance, halfway across the room. He was flanked by four guards on either side. Immediately to his left was an ancient man in a gray robe, his white beard hanging down to his belt as he leaned heavily upon a staff to support his age-withered bones. Even from across the room, Corin could see a brightly glowing ring on the old mage's hand.

Corin knew he was overmatched, without even accounting for the mage's magic. His new-found skill with two weapons was no match for the overwhelming numbers ready to oppose him. From the hallway behind Graal he could hear the footsteps of many more soldiers approaching. Victory was impossible, but maybe he could buy Fendel some time, or at least keep the gnome from being noticed.

"Do you have the courage to face me alone," Corin taunted the towering orog, "or do you need your lackeys by your side to defeat me?"

The orog replied with a roar of laughter. "Why would I be stupid enough to duel you one on one when I have an entire army at my disposal?" He turned to the old wizard at his side. "Unleash the medusa. Turn this fool to stone."

Graal pointed a huge paw toward Fendel, who was trying to creep away into the shadows on the far side of the room while he still searched for Lhasha. "Don't forget the other one."

The wizard raised a trembling fist into the air, the glowing ring intensifying in brightness. The medusa responded by taking a slow step forward. Her hood remained in place. Corin put his head down and barged across the room toward the orog and his soldiers.

If the warrior's time was at hand, it would end on the point of a sword, falling in battle the way a White Shield was supposed to die, not trapped in some hellish limbo of eternal stone.

The force of the sudden explosion from the east wall knocked Graal's men to the ground, including the frail wizard—the old man's staff was sent careening across the cavern floor. Even the orog's giant frame was sent reeling backward by the devastating concussion that rocked the cavern.

Corin was hurled through the air by the blast. He hit the ground and rolled several times until he smashed into the side of one of the crates piled up against the west wall, knocking the wind from his lungs. Small clumps of earth and pebbles hailed down on him, and a cloud of dirt and dust choked his lungs and stung his eyes.

Dazed, he rolled onto his side and looked back toward the far wall at Fendel, assuming the gnome had cast some earth-shattering spell. But the gnome was nowhere to be seen. He too had been blown clear by the unexpected detonation. Despite himself, Corin glanced over to the medusa. She lay crumpled on the floor, her face still shrouded by her hood and veil, her enslaved mind incapable of giving her body the order to rise to its feet without the volition of the stooped old mage who wore the ring.

On the east side of the room, standing in the rubble of what once had been a square chunk of solid stone wall, was Azlar. The wizard's arms were fully extended at the level of his shoulders, his palms facing outward and his fingers splayed. A green glow enveloped his hands as the last remnants of his powerful spell shimmered and flickered before winking out.

A platoon of armed cultists poured into the cavern through the breach, looking to overwhelm their still-stunned foes. Six of them formed a protective circle around the young wizard commanding them.

"The ring!" Azlar shouted to the rest of his troops. "Bring me the ring! Snap the old man's bony finger off if necessary, just bring it to me now!"

As the cultists approached, the ancient sorcerer struggled to rise, then fell back to the floor as his weakened bones failed him and his eyes rolled back into his skull. Though the mage's body was old and frail, his magic was powerful. A spell discharged from the tip of the aged wizard's staff, triggered by the old man's collapse. A ring of blue fire sprang up around his unconscious form, engulfing the first two cultists who tried to touch him. They died screaming in agony, blue smoke wafting up from their charred corpses.

Graal was there, already recovered from the concussive shock of Azlar's entrance. A single sweep of his black blade disemboweled one unfortunate cultist. Another was decapitated by the return stroke of the orog's blade. Graal struck with precise fury, chopping two more cultists down before the others stumbled back, fleeing before his wrath.

By the time Corin rose to his own feet Graal's position had been augmented by the arrival of the second wave of Xiliath's reinforcements. They circled the old mage, his motionless body still on the ground. Because of the shield of blue flame surrounding him, no one was able to check if he still lived.

As if drawn by the arrival of Xiliath's reinforcements, a second wave of cultists swarmed in through Azlar's magically wrought entrance. For a brief second, the two armies faced each other in silence. And then all the Nine Hells broke loose as they launched themselves at each other's throats.

Corin wasn't exactly surprised by the arrival of the cultists. Azlar's plan was very much like the one Fendel had proposed—come in through an unexpected route and catch the guards unprepared. Instead of using the long forgotten sub-tunnels, Azlar had simply used his magic to blast a completely new route through the earth. And instead of a single gnome inventor, Azlar was accompanied by forty or fifty fanatically loyal Cult of the Dragon soldiers.

Corin had suspected all along that Azlar was somehow using him as bait, and the manner of the wizard's timely entrance merely confirmed his suspicions. Azlar had expected Corin to try and blunder his way in through the main entrance, approaching through the tunnels to the north. If he had come that way, Corin knew, he would have been spotted long before reaching the heart of Xiliath's lair, drawing the attention of Xiliath's troops away from the treasure room itself.

All of this passed through Corin's head on an intuitive level. The information was cataloged and analyzed instantaneously—then filed away as useless in the current situation. As usual, the whys and hows of the situation mattered little to Corin—it was only the here and now he cared about.

All around Corin armed men were engaged in brutal hand-to-hand combat, but for the time being, the cultists and Xiliath's men were focused on each other. Conscious of possible broken bones and other injuries, Corin rose gingerly to his feet and stood alone in the center of the melee like a calm eye amidst a raging storm. His head moved quickly from side to side, seeking out Fendel. At last he found him. The gnome was crumpled on the fringes of the battle. Injured by the blast, Fendel writhed in pain. Fortunately, like Corin, he was being ignored for the moment.

Corin raced across the battlefield, ready to slash down any foe foolish enough to get in the way of his reckless charge to the old gnome's aid. But the soldiers of both sides were far too concerned with the enemies bearing directly down on them to take notice of a single man running past on the fringes of their peripheral vision, and he reached Fendel's side without opposition.

"Here!" Fendel shouted as Corin dropped to a knee beside him, trying to be heard over the thunder of battle and the blast still ringing in his ears. "Take this." He stuffed the hard leather case containing the potion to reverse the medusa's curse into Corin's belt. "Find Lhasha!"

"What about you?" Corin yelled back.

"Can't walk," the gnome said with a shake of his head, clutching his leg just below his knee. "Broken, maybe. I'll only slow you down. You go. I'll stay here and try to cover you."

There was no sense arguing. After a quick check to make sure the bottle was secure, Corin waded back into the fray, determined to find Lhasha at any cost.

CHAPTER TWENTY-FOUR

When he burst through the wall of Xiliath's treasure room, Azlar was momentarily surprised to find several guards in the chamber. He had expected the one-handed man's suicide mission to draw their attention away from this room. If he had looked closely, Azlar would have noticed a familiar form crumpled against the crates near the far wall, but the young wizard's attention was drawn elsewhere.

He noticed a white-haired mage lying on the floor, a glowing ring pulsating on his finger.

"The ring! Bring me the ring! Snap the old man's bony finger off if necessary, just bring it to me now!" He recognized the blue flame that sprung up in a protective circle around Xiliath's wizard, but he didn't bother to warn his men about the possible consequences.

Azlar watched with detached interest as the first of his men was incinerated by the spell surrounding the old wizard. However, his nonchalant attitude changed to one of eager fascination as an enormous figure entered the fray.

A giant orog in black armor rushed to the fallen mage's defense. In one great leap the beast crossed the distance between itself and the incapacitated wizard, chopping down the cult soldiers who were standing over the stricken form. It hacked away indiscriminately with its black blade, sending Azlar's men scurrying away like frightened children.

Azlar recognized the creature that had taken his hand at the ambush in the clearing—the beast known as Graal. Seeing the beast in battle, the cult wizard's thoughts were not those of revenge. The monster was magnificent in his ferocity.

Friend and foe alike fell before Graal's assault, feeding the creature's ravaging blade, fuelling his killing lust. Blood spurted up from the severed limbs and gushing wounds of those around the orog as bodies fell, adding to the ever growing pile of grisly corpses at Graal's feet. Gore covered the monster from head to toe, turning his black armor crimson. The thing licked a splatter of warm blood from his chin, his long, bestial tongue running languidly over his tusks.

Yet even amidst Graal's unbridled orgy of death, Azlar noticed that the creature was careful not to harm the old wizard at his feet. If the old mage died, the medusa would break free and turn her devastating powers on everyone within the chamber. The beast understood the potential consequences. He was intelligent, and he could be a useful ally—if brought under proper control.

Azlar motioned for the troops he had initially held back in reserve to enter the battle. As they rushed by him, the cult mage began an incantation—a spell to dominate the orog, to cage his wild fury and bring him under Azlar's control.

Unseen claws extended out from Azlar's mind, grasped at the orog's essence, trying to steal his identity, his sense of self, his very will to act. The beast shook his great head, tusks snapping at the invisible enemy trying to get inside his mind. The orog threw his head back and bellowed his howling defiance to the stony roof, thrusting the invader out.

Azlar's eyes widened as he realized the armored monster had resisted his spell. Graal's yellow eyes focused on him and a low growl escaped his throat. Azlar's knees momentarily buckled. The monster began a march toward him. All thoughts of taking the orog alive vanished from Azlar's head.

With a single barked command Azlar's personal bodyguard, a half dozen of the cult's best warriors arrayed in a protective circle around the young mage, moved forward to destroy the threat.

They surrounded their opponent, striking from all sides. The beast took clumsy swings at them, first one opponent, then another, spinning and twisting in a vain attempt to guard against all six of the attackers at once. The guards easily avoided the hurried blows, dancing out of range then slipping back in as the creature turned toward another foe and left himself vulnerable. Little by little, the six men surrounding the orog picked away, relentless as gnats. The orog's arms and legs began to bleed from countless cuts and wounds, and his thick, fur became matted with the sticky liquid.

With a desperate, animal fury the beast swung wildly, throwing himself off balance. Much to Azlar's relief, Graal tripped over his own feet and collapsed.

Instantly, the gnats were on their fallen foe. Sheer numbers overwhelmed the creature, beating him down with a barrage of blows to the body and head. Graal's armor reverberated with the song of battle as the weapons rained down. Blades rang off his mail shirt, and edged weapons meant to cleave his skull clanged off his iron helm.

To Azlar's amazement, the creature shrugged off the blows and rose to his knees. From the half-prone stance the orog slashed at the forest of legs around him with short, powerful strokes, slicing sinew, muscle, cartilage, and bone, leaving one of Azlar's men with nothing but a stump below mid-thigh.

The orog's dark sword glowed with a black light, and Azlar heard the unmistakable hum of necromancy. The young wizard felt the power of the black sword's magic as the blade in Graal's talons drank from the stolen life-force of the dying cultists.

Before Azlar's horrified eyes the most serious of his enemy's wounds closed over, healing instantly. Bolstered by the influx of new life, the orog heaved himself to his feet, knocking the circle of attackers off balance. Before Azlar's guards could recover from their foe's unexpected surge, a second cultist had fallen, his chest torn open diagonally from his shoulder to the opposite hip by a single, swift stroke of the sinister weapon. More of Graal's wounds spontaneously closed, and the orog stood a little straighter.

Realizing his warriors were overmatched, Azlar began a spell of mass destruction, one that would destroy both the relentless animal of war and his own guards.

The spell was cast in a matter of seconds, but even in that short time the orog had slain another of Azlar's men, leaving only three of the original six cultists standing. A carefully placed ball of fire erupted around the four figures still engaged in the melee, engulfing the combatants. Azlar recoiled from the blaze of his own spell, shielding his face from the heat. The inferno lasted only a second and was gone. The young mage looked up to see the charred remains of his loyal bodyguards smoldering on the cavern floor. The orog was still standing.

The beast's flesh was blistered from the heat, his coarse, dark mane was singed in places and burned clean off in others. But the orog was relatively unharmed. He grinned at Azlar, a malevolent smile full of sharpened yellow teeth and fierce, pointed tusks.

The young mage hurled another spell at the creature, a bolt of electrical energy strong enough to fell an umberhulk. The lightning struck the orog full in the chest and rocked the monster back a half step, but instead of tearing a hole through Graal's torso, the bolt was absorbed and dispersed by the monster's black ringed armor, again inflicting only minimal damage.

With a chuckle resembling a snarling growl, the orog advanced on Azlar again.

The raging battle between Xiliath's troops and the cultists was both a blessing and a curse in Corin's eyes. The chaos and confusion allowed him to move freely about the battlefield as he searched for Lhasha, but the violence of the confrontation was taking a heavy toll on the statues in the cavern. Wild, off-balance swings by soldiers broke limbs or shattered stony features. Warriors from both sides darted back and forth between the petrified bodies, using them for cover and concealment, sometimes toppling them over through careless disregard or sheer malice. Already several of the medusa's unfortunate victims were now nothing more than piles of rubble, forever beyond hope of salvation.

From the corner of his eye, Corin caught a glimpse of a small group of Xiliath's guards moving in to cut him off. As he turned to face the advancing threat, the guards collapsed in coughing, choking heaps, overwhelmed by the green cloud of noxious fumes that had materialized in their path.

Fendel. Corin quickly glanced over his shoulder at the old gnome, tilting his head in unspoken thanks for the magical aid. Fendel was too busy conjuring another spell to notice the gesture.

Turning back to the carnage, Corin saw two cultists momentarily bar his path, but their weapons slipped from their suddenly clumsy grasps—another spell from Fendel. Unexpectedly unarmed, they offered no resistance as the one-armed warrior chopped them down without even breaking stride.

Corin felt a sudden chill in the air descending from above and peeked up to the high ceiling. A dark cloud formed near the cavern's roof—black as the harbingers of the fierce storms that pounded the Dragon Coast throughout the Claw of Winter. Fendel was preparing to unleash a tempest within the room.

A fleeting feeling of panic seized Corin's chest—would the fury of the storm destroy more statues? But the feeling quickly passed. Fendel would never do anything to endanger Lhasha. Best to let the wizard worry about his spells, Corin realized. He had to stay focused on the task at hand. Lhasha was somewhere in the cavern, one of the countless forms still unidentifiable in the shrouding shadows of the dim torches. He could feel it. He knew it.

A stone form glimpsed from the corner of his eye brought him up short. Not the lithe, almost childlike statue of his half-elf friend, but an enormous, circular mound of rock. The statue was so squat and round it almost resembled a boulder. Corin knew only one man in Elversult with that shape.

Xiliath must have felt it best to leave the treacherous steward in his petrified state until the plans with the medusa were done. It wasn't hard to imagine Fhazail's double-crossing of the cultist becoming a triple-crossing of Xiliath's own schemes. Or perhaps there was another explanation, another reason why the corpulent steward had not yet been restored.

The statue was less than twenty feet from where Corin was standing, half hidden behind a small stack of crates.

It would only take a minute for Corin to dash over, move the crates aside and smash the statue to bits, destroying Fhazail forever, as punishment for his betrayal of the White Shields on the Trader Road. But every second Corin spent avenging his dead companions was a second lost in his quest to save Lhasha—precious time in which the half-elf's statue could be inadvertently destroyed by the ravages of war.

Corin's lust for revenge had already cost Lhasha far too much. Pushing all thoughts of Fhazail from his head, Corin resumed his search for his friend.

A loud clap of thunder from the roof announced the completion of the gnome's latest spell. A blizzard of blinding snow and huge chunks of ice, hard as frozen rock, battered the beleaguered soldiers in the center of the chamber. A surprised chorus of alarmed shouts rose up above the cacophony of battle, momentarily drawing Corin's attention away from his search and to the battlefield. Soldiers on both sides were pelted with snow and ice. They slipped and fell in the slush, scrambling to avoid the weapons of their enemies while trying to dodge the fist-sized hail that pummeled them from the cavern ceiling. Many of them didn't get up again.

The lethal blizzard proved only a momentary distraction to Corin. He was far enough from its center to avoid the worst of the storm. If anything, the spell would keep the armies occupied and less likely to focus their attention on him.

After an eternity of several minutes, Corin's perseverant searching was rewarded.

Most of the statues were standing, frozen in midstride as they fled the medusa's gaze. But Lhasha's form was lying on the ground, her arms thrust out as if to brace a fall. By some amazing fluke, Corin surmised, she must have caught the medusa's eye while tumbling to the ground.

The miraculous fact that she hadn't shattered upon striking the ground was lost on Corin as he fumbled to open the case in his belt. His prosthetic arm, combined with the magic of Fendel's forged blade, provided no handicap in combat. But his metal hand lacked the precision and dexterity to perform fine, exacting movements. He struggled with the case for several long, frustrating seconds before managing to pop the latch. Using his good hand he grasped the thick glass bottle and yanked the stopper out with his teeth.

He raised the bottle to her lips, then paused. Obviously Lhasha couldn't drink the potion in her current state. He glanced back toward Fendel, hoping for guidance, but the gnome was too focused on his spells to notice Corin crouched over Lhasha's prone form.

Realizing there was only really one possibility, Corin carefully poured the contents over the statue, trying to distribute it as evenly as possible. The liquid beaded as it struck the half-elf's face and body. It trickled along the ridges in Lhasha's petrified features and the creases in her petrified clothes. Then the droplets began to move with a life of their own, slipping and sliding over the rock, moving faster and faster until they became a shimmering glow racing over every inch of Lhasha's stone body.

The shimmer became a shroud of blinding light, wrapping itself around Lhasha. It flared a deep violet, then flickered to blue, red, and finally pink, the brightness and intensity of each color increasing until Corin was forced to momentarily avert his gaze, squeezing his eyes shut against the glare.

"Wh . . . Where am I? What happened? C-Corin? Is that you?"

The warrior opened his eyes and looked down at the confused half-elf with a reassuring smile. "Yes, Lhasha," he said, extending his left hand to help her up. "It's me."

Graal rushed the young wizard, his huge weapon descending in a two-handed chop intended to split the mage from skull to pelvis, but the mage slipped aside, and the blow caught only air. Graal kicked out a boot, catching the thin man under the chin and crumpling him to the floor.

The orog wasted no time gloating over his dazed opponent but stabbed down, looking to run his sword right through his foe, pinning him to the ground. Graal's kick had less effect than he imagined, and the nimble mage still had enough of his senses left to roll out of the way. Graal's sword struck only the stone floor of the cavern—driving itself several inches into the rock.

It took Graal several seconds to work his blade free, and in that time the bald wizard had found his feet again. The man was quick and wiry, Graal had to give him that. Still, there was little fear of the mage even attempting to engage Graal in a physical confrontation.

As he pulled his dark sword free of the cavern floor, Graal heard the sounds of an incantation. Trusting his magical armor to protect him from the brunt of the spell, Graal held his ground and turned to face the wizard—only to see Azlar vanish before his eyes.

Graal's senses were keen. He had the eyes and ears of a predator. He could hear hurried footsteps, and he caught a glimmer of distorted light fleeing from him—a warping of the air itself. The mage was still around, he was just invisible. The orog turned his huge head from side to side, trying in vain to pick up any more telltale signs that would reveal the mage's location.

He heard the faint swish of rustling robes at his back, and Graal wheeled but saw nothing. Heavy breathing to his left; a half-imagined shadow flickered in the torchlight. Graal took his shot, hoping to land a lucky blow—but his blade met with no resistance.

He paused and listened again, trying to pick out another sound or glimmering distortion that would pinpoint his enemy's location. Nothing. The wizard was nowhere nearby. He must have retreated into the covering confusion of the melee in the center of the cavern.

Graal stared out over the battlefield, surveying the carnage. Someone had unleashed a storm of hail and ice on the combatants, but even over the blizzard's fury the orog could clearly hear the thunderous clash of metal on metal as the opposing soldiers hacked mercilessly at each other. The armies were evenly matched, for the moment. But an invisible wizard roaming the battlefield at will would quickly turn the tide against Xiliath's men. Within the chaos of the battle and the blizzard, there was virtually no chance of detecting the subtle flickers of light or faint sounds that would betray Azlar's location.

A quick glance at Xiliath's own wizard dispelled any hope Graal had of receiving aid from the old mage. He still lay crumpled and unconscious on the ground, though his body had begun to convulse. Graal looked over in the direction of the charmed medusa. Her hooded form was undergoing a similar series of seizures as her mind fought to break free of the bonds imprisoning her. Recovering the ring and using it to dominate the medusa was impossible—the blue shield still surrounding the old wizard kept even Graal from approaching. But with the ring wearer virtually comatose, the magic enslaving the medusa was growing ever weaker. Soon, Graal realized, she would gain her freedom.

Graal was no coward and no fool. An invisible wizard and an angry medusa were more than he cared to face. If Xiliath himself were to appear on the scene things would only get worse. Even Graal shuddered at the thought of his master's rage being unleashed on the battle.

With occasional glances back to make sure he wasn't being followed, Graal escaped out the newly formed tunnel in the east wall of his master's treasure room. The orog knew Xiliath had undoubtedly already sealed up all the other routes back to the surface, and only the unfamiliar section of the smugglers' labyrinth beyond the cultists' passage offered any chance of ever reaching the surface again.

He set off with long, loping strides, leaving his men to deal with the consequences of the cultists, the soon-to-be-released medusa, and the imminent arrival of Xiliath.

CHAPTER TWENTY-FIVE

Lhasha took Corin's extended hand and struggled to her feet.

"Are you all right? You look like you can barely stand."

Leaning on her sturdy companion for support, Lhasha gave a slight nod, her head bowed to the floor. "I'll be fine. Just give me a few seconds. I feel a little woozy."

"Understandable, given what you've been through."

The half-elf glanced up, casting a mildly curious peek in Corin's direction. The only response she had expected was the one-armed man's typical stoic silence or a single gruff word acknowledging her condition. His sympathetic comment caught her off guard.

"I hate to rush you, but Fendel's waiting for us," Corin continued, his voice firm but lacking the sharp edge it usually carried. "I know you're a bit out of sorts, but we're in the middle of a war zone right now. We have to get moving. I'll carry you, if you don't feel up to walking."

The shock of hearing a whole paragraph emerging spontaneously from Corin's mouth nearly knocked Lhasha off her already unsteady feet. There was something different about her usually taciturn companion. Different, but good. Despite the battle raging behind him, despite the concern in his features and the urgency in his voice, he seemed relaxed. At peace with the world—and himself.

And then she noticed the prosthetic attached to Corin's right arm. The flawless silver surface seemed to sparkle and glow in the flickering light of the cavern. The gleaming metal was pure and pristine, as the lines and proportions flowed seamlessly along the contours, a work of true genius and artistic beauty. Fendel had really outdone himself.

"Your arm," she said reverently, overwhelmed by her emotions. She was so proud of Fendel she felt like crying and so happy for Corin she felt like laughing. With a trembling finger she reached out to touch it.

Corin was oblivious to her state. He might not have even heard her soft whisper of amazement. He simply scooped her up like a sack of potatoes, threw her over his shoulder, and set off at a canter back toward where Fendel waited for them. No explanation, no apology. Her friend may have changed, Lhasha realized, but he still preferred actions over words.

Lhasha was too drained from her ordeal to even object. With each pounding step Corin took, her body was jarred and shaken. She welcomed the feeling, relishing the physical reality of it. It helped exorcise the terrifying images that threatened to push their way into her newly restored consciousness—surreal memories and dreamlike recollections of a hellish nether existence, neither alive nor dead, but trapped in some horrible stony limbo.

As Corin carried her across the unfamiliar cavern the memories faded, buried so deep they would never rise to the surface again, but Lhasha knew they'd always be there.

The world spun as Corin flipped her off his shoulder and cradled her in his arms before setting her down on the ground beside Fendel.

"Something's wrong," he said to the gnome.

"Nothing's wrong," Lhasha protested, scrambling to her feet. "I just needed a few seconds to gather myself, is all. I'm fine. Really."

"The same can be said of me now, as well," Fendel added, standing up beside her. "A little healing magic, and I'm as good as new," he explained in response as Corin gazed at the torn, bloodstained leg of his breeches. "Gonna have to get some new pantaloons, though."

Any more words from the gnome were cut off by a suffocating hug from Lhasha. Fendel returned the gesture with as much force as his old joints could muster. A sharp cough from Corin caused them to break their fond embrace.

"Can you save the reunion for later?" the warrior asked pointedly, nodding in the direction of the still raging battle.

Fendel nodded. "Of course, of course. This rescue mission won't be much use if we don't all get out of here alive. It won't be long until one side or the other pays some attention to us, and our work isn't done yet."

"Lead the way," Lhasha said, clapping her hands in nervous anticipation. "I have no idea how you got in, but I'm eager to see how we're getting out."

"Just hold on a second, Lhasha," Fendel cautioned, holding up a gnarled hand to quiet her. In his other hand he held the strange glasses he had shown Corin earlier. "We may have a problem with the package. You two better keep your heads down. Look at the floor until I tell you it's safe. We don't want any more unfortunate accidents."

Slipping the protective lenses onto the bridge of his nose, the gnome craned his neck to survey the battle. "Where in Gond's name did that medusa go?" he grumbled.

"She was right over there in that corner just a minute ago."

Lhasha shivered at the mention of the creature's name. "Who cares? Let's just get out of here before we run into her." Like Corin, she was taking Fendel's instructions to the letter and staring intently at the ground.

"We can't just leave her behind to fall into the hands of whoever wins this battle," Fendel explained. "As long as she's still in Elversult, Yanseldara's life is in danger. The Lady Lord has many enemies, and a charmed medusa is the perfect assassin. We have to deal with this problem now, one way or another."

"Who cares about Yanseldara?" Lhasha made no effort to hide her exasperation. "She can look after herself. Let Vaerana and her Harper friends take care of her. The medusa's their problem now!"

The gnome gave Lhasha a stern glare of disapproval, his eyes distorted and buggy through the thick glasses. "I thought I raised you better than that," was all he said.

Ashamed, Lhasha replied in a chastened voice, "You did. I didn't mean that. I'm just . . . scared."

Fendel gave the half-elf a reassuring pat on her cheek and turned his attention back to his search of the room. "Uh-oh," he muttered. "Things could get messy. Don't look up," Fendel ordered. "The medusa's broken free. By the Wonderbringer's smock, she'll kill them all. That would not be any great loss."

After a moment's consideration, the gnome added, "Get to the surface, both of you. I'll follow as soon as I can."

"What are you going to do?" Lhasha demanded, her gaze firmly on the ground.

"I've got a few spells ready to take care of our snakey-haired friend. I didn't want to kill her, but there's not much choice anymore."

"No," the half-elf said with a shake of her head, still staring at the floor. "We're not leaving without you."

"Don't be foolish," Fendel scoffed. "There's nothing you can do here, not with that beast making everyone into statues left and right. My glasses will keep me safe."

"From the medusa," Corin pointed out, "but not from Graal or Azlar."

"Believe it or not," Fendel said after taking a moment to scan the battlefield, "but I can't see that oversized orc or the bare-scalped mage anywhere. Maybe they ran off when the medusa broke free. I suggest you do the same."

"We can't," Corin said flatly. "The door to the sub-tunnel is closed. It must have been blown shut when Azlar came blasting through that wall. I wouldn't even know how to open it. You're the only one who can lead us back to the surface."

The gnome cursed in his native tongue. "All right, you're right. This is what we'll do. Stay close to me, and keep your eyes down. Watch my heels.

"I'll lead you across the cavern to that passage the cultists blasted to get in here. It must lead back into the main tunnel system somewhere. There might be a few guards, but it shouldn't be anything you can't handle. Most of their forces would have been brought into the battle already, so I doubt they've kept much back in reserve.

"Wait for me where the passage meets up with the original smugglers' tunnels. It should be easy to recognize the place. I think I can lead us out safely."

Corin grunted to show he understood and would follow, the gnome's instructions.

"I still don't like leaving you behind," Lhasha objected.

"There's no choice, really, but don't worry, Lhasha. I'll only be a minute or two until I catch up with you."

"It really is the best plan," Corin added.

With a sigh, Lhasha consented.

Their progress across the cavern was painfully slow. Lhasha followed behind the gnome, staring only at her mentor's heels. Corin trailed Lhasha, his eyes never leaving her leather boots. Their route wound in a wide semicircle as their leader tried to avoid the constantly shifting fringes of the melee.

Fendel described the scene as they went, trying to reassure his virtually blind followers despite the horrifying sounds of the gruesome battle only a short distance away. "There's a ton of statues out there, but nobody seems to care. The soldiers aren't running away. These have to be the hard-core followers, the real fanatics of each group. They're still at each other's throats. It's like they don't even know there's a medusa heading right for them, leaving a petrified forest behind her.

"Nobody's noticed us yet," the gnome continued. "And we're almost there. I think we're going to make it."

Suddenly the gnome pulled up short. "Gond's Flaming Forge," he whispered. The sounds emanating from the battlefield suddenly changed from fierce battle calls and war cries to terrified screams and shrieks.

"The medusa's dead!" Fendel yelled, breaking into a run. "Don't look back, don't stop! Just get to that blasted exit as fast as you can!"

Azlar watched the orog flee out into the smugglers' tunnels. The young wizard knew he could hunt that beast down later at his leisure and attempt to capture him alive when the odds were more favorable. For the time being, however, he had more pressing matters to attend.

The old mage on the floor was as good as dead, though he was still untouchable because of the blue magical shield encircling his body. Azlar shrugged. He would merely wait until the spell burned itself out and get the ring later. With the retreat of Graal, Xiliath's military leader, the outcome of the battle had become inevitable.

Cloaked in his powerful spell of invisibility, the wizard roamed the battlefield at will. Jets of flame fanned out from his fingers, incinerating one of Xiliath's guards. Bolts of lightning erupted from his fists, striking his nearest foe, then arcing from the frying corpse to the unfortunate man beside the first victim. The lightning continued jumping down the line from target to target, leaving smoldering husks in its wake as it continued its deadly chain. Half a dozen of Xiliath's men were electrocuted by the spell, but Azlar didn't even notice. He had already moved on, forgetting in the heat of the moment that he was no longer shielded by his spell.

He hurled glowing orbs of pure energy into the fray, stunning some of Xiliath's soldiers so they could be easily hacked down by the cultists. Others were melted by burning acid or caught in deadly clouds of poisonous gas. A few of his own men went down as well, screaming as they died from the effects of Azlar's magic—expendable sacrifices in the greater cause.

In a matter of minutes, the wizard had wrought utter havoc on his enemies. Their casualties would have broken the morale of lesser soldiers. Grudgingly, Azlar had to admit that Xiliath's men were at least the equals of his own troops, though the cultists now had a distinct numerical superiority.

Azlar was toying with his foes now. He followed the progress of one soldier through the melee, preparing to unleash a spell that would bring about a gruesome, horrible death on the hapless man.

The mage carefully tracked the fighter as he sprinted across the cavern floor, making his way toward an unsuspecting foe. Azlar raised his still hands in the air and began the incantation to seal the man's fate, but when the intended victim suddenly turned to stone, Azlar's concentration was broken.

Casually, Azlar turned to the corner where the medusa had fallen. The creature was up now, her deadly face unveiled for all to see. Her serpentine tresses writhed in furious outrage, striking and snapping at the air in their desperate hunger for vengeance.

Azlar had taken precautions before this expedition to recover his stolen package. He had cast a spell before setting out. He had nothing to fear from the medusa's gaze. His men, however, were not immune to the effects, and neither was the army opposing them.

Statues began to crop up among the soldiers with alarming speed, and the common threat to both sides quickly became obvious. But neither force panicked—they were too well trained, too fanatical in their loyalty to their respective masters. Until the order to retreat was given, these warriors would remain at each other's throats, their relentless hatred matched only by their armed counterparts on the other side.

Azlar made no attempt to halt the medusa's progress. He didn't want to risk damaging her with a spell, and for all he cared she could turn every other living thing in the room to stone. All he had to do was stay beyond the reach of the vipers on her head, and he had nothing to fear. Once Xiliath's old mage finally died or the spell protecting him wore off, Azlar would take the ring and regain control of the assassin he had worked so hard to acquire and smuggle into the city.

Until that time, he thought, he would stay still and quiet, protected from sight by his invisibility, and watch his creature at work. Except he could now see his hands. His invisibility was gone, and Azlar had to find cover. Azlar let his eyes drift, taking in the details of the chamber he had failed to notice before. The huge cache of weapons in the southwest corner. The chunks of ice and snow scattered about the room, melting remnants of a spell cast over the melee earlier in the battle. And in the far corner of the room, unguarded and almost unnoticeable, a secret door in the floor.

Had Azlar known about this entrance before, he would not have wasted his energies tunneling through the earth to reach this chamber. Curious, the mage approached the secret door. It was closed, but Azlar could see no handle or chain. Obviously it could only be opened from beneath. There was something else. A faint sound from under the earth, a dull roar coming from beneath the heavy door. The sound was getting closer. Azlar took several cautious steps back.

The door flew open, nearly bursting from its hinges as the monster exploded up from the sub-tunnel below, erupting through the cavern floor to hover high above the soldiers still waging war on each other. Azlar fell to the ground, numb with terror at the apparition before him.

For a second the intruder loomed above the battlefield in all its terrible glory, a creature of pure evil, a legendary denizen of the fabled Underdark, the sphere of many eyes, the great eye tyrant—a beholder.

Its gigantic, spherical body pulsed with power and all-consuming rage, levitating high above the chamber floor. The numerous eyestalks atop its head flailed about, looking in a dozen directions at once. The great central eye darted from side to side, taking in the entire scene. Azlar realized the awful truth. Xiliath had come.

Without a warning, without a word, Xiliath, unleashed his wrath on the battle. A magical fear descended on the combatants, creating terror among friend and foe alike. The steadfast discipline of the two armies, their unshakable morale, broke like a dam before the flood as a wave of panic washed over the assembled troops. Soldiers from both sides threw down their weapons and ran screaming from the cavern, completely oblivious to anything other than the unimaginable levitating horror that had emerged from beneath the cavern floor.

As the men scattered like insects under an angry boot, the eyestalks atop Xiliath's body unleashed their rays of destruction, choosing targets without any regard to allegiance or loyalty. Those struck by the rays rarely survived. Some collapsed into a comatose sleep, trampled under the feet of the fleeing mob. Others were hurled through the air by unseen forces and smashed against the cavern walls, their limbs twisted and shattered. A few were transformed to stone, adding to the medusa's own collection of statues. Many died instantly, their hearts bursting inside their armored chests when touched by the deadly bolts. Most were simply obliterated, reduced to tiny piles of ash before they could even scream.

Azlar cowered back into the shadows of the chamber walls, no longer able to hide behind his magical invisibility. Xiliath turned his attention to the medusa, who was too involved in her own rampage of destruction to have noticed Xiliath's entrance.

Xiliath focused a single eyestalk on the medusa's form, and Azlar saw her body stiffen. She spun around, clutching at her serpentine locks with her hands, oblivious to the snakes' agonized writhing as they snapped and bit at her hands. Protected by his own incantations, Azlar was able to stare directly into her tortured eyes. He recognized what he saw. A battle of wills was being waged inside the medusa's skull. Xiliath was trying to dominate her mind with the power of his magical eye.

"No!" she screamed, snapping her head back as if it had been struck. The glazed look receded from her eyes, leaving only a blazing anger. "Not again! I will not be your slave anymore!"

"Xiliath!" she screamed, the identity of the fearsome monster as obvious to her as it had been to Azlar mere moments before. "You shall pay for my suffering!"

The beholder's unflinching central eye met the gaze of the snake-haired woman. Xiliath stared directly into those flashing eyes that meant a stony fate worse than death for most mortal creatures, and to Azlar's amazement, nothing happened.

A look of surprise and then understanding flickered across the medusa's beautiful features. Her serpentine locks hissed in anger, but she refused to flee. She bent down and scooped up a long spear from where one of the panicked soldiers had dropped it on the floor. With surprising strength, she hurled the weapon across the cavern at the hovering sphere.

The weapon bounced harmlessly off Xiliath's leathery hide.

From the cover of the shadows, Azlar watched as the beholder slowly advanced on the medusa. Again and again, she took up weapons from the floor and threw them at the monster, trying vainly to halt his methodical, relentless advance. Her desperate throws were hurried and wild, most far from their mark. Those that struck Xiliath's hide bounced harmlessly away. A single shaft punctured the large central eye of the beast, sinking deep into the pale flesh of the orb. The beholder merely shook the weapon free and let it fall to the ground below, seemingly oblivious to the effects.

Finally, the medusa's courage broke. She turned to run, but a beam from one of the eyestalks atop Xiliath's head struck her between the shoulder blades, slamming her to the floor. A second beam engulfed her, and the writhing snakes atop the medusa's head began to smolder and burn, their agonized, hissing screams drowned out by the sizzle and pop of the snakes' own boiling blood.

Somehow, the medusa clambered to her feet, but Xiliath was right on top of her now. She dropped to her knees, the steaming blood of the snakes on her head dripping down to cover her face with dark, crimson streaks. Cowering before the beholder, the medusa clasped her hands together, begging for mercy. A single thin ray arced down from above, striking the medusa flush in the chest.

Azlar was unable to pull himself away from the scene, captivated by the terrible power of the eye tyrant's mere presence, fascinated by the vicious slaughter Xiliath had unleashed. The medusa's shriek cut through the air, piercing Azlar's eardrums. She dissolved in an explosion of light that seared Azlar's eyes—though the wizard still refused to look away.

Then the medusa was gone. Where she stood was only a smoking crater and a small pile of dust.

The graphic reality of the medusa's death snapped Azlar back to his senses. The wizard knew he had to escape the chamber. Xiliath would spare no one—even his own men would perish for having learned the secret of his true identity. Most of the panicked soldiers ran in confused circles around the room, their terror so great they were unable to even form cogent thoughts of escape. The beholder ignored these for the time being, Azlar noticed. The monster was focused on those still sane enough to try to flee the cavern.

Several of the terror-stricken soldiers disappeared through the passage Azlar himself had torn into the treasure vault's wall, seeking an escape through the ancient smugglers' tunnels. The mage knew few, if any, would ever see the surface. Those who avoided the countless traps still active from the long-vanished underground criminal empire would become victims of the gruesome monsters that had taken over the tunnels when the smugglers had left.

Xiliath turned to focus another barrage of death on the medusa, and Azlar allowed a tiny seed of hope to be cultivated in his mind. The door to the secret entrance Xiliath had used to enter the chamber was still open. The tunnel beneath, Azlar knew, would eventually lead him to the surface.

The young mage emerged from his hiding place in the shadows and sprinted across the chamber toward the door. Just as he reached his escape route a beam from one of Xiliath's eyestalks slammed the door to the sub-tunnel shut. The door locked with an audible click, trapping Azlar within the cavern.

The wizard spun to face the creature now bearing down on him. Another beam from one of Xiliath's small eyes struck Azlar, and the wizard felt his limbs grow heavy and ponderous. He tried to turn and run, but every movement was agonizingly slow and labored. His feet felt too heavy for his legs.

He glanced back to see the beholder floating toward him, an evil chuckle rumbling out from the gaping row of teeth at the bottom of Xiliath's spherical body. The beast did not move exceptionally fast, but Azlar knew his own magically hampered movements prevented any hope of escape through flight.

In desperation, Azlar began to cast a spell to save himself, the incantation taking far longer than normal. The arcane words came in a sluggish drawl, the somatic gestures were performed in a deliberate, measured pantomime of true spellcasting. Yet such was Azlar's power that the spell still managed to function. A shield of flame encircled him. It was similar to the one Xiliath's now-deceased mage had cast, though Azlar's protective fire was red, not blue.

From Xiliath's central eye a cone of energy rippled the air, engulfing Azlar and instantly snuffing out his protective shell, leaving him completely defenseless.

Azlar's shrieks echoed throughout the cavern as Xiliath bit deep into his shoulder and tore away a chunk of flesh. The screams became muffled as the beholder's maw descended to engulf the wizard's head and torso. Xiliath's jaws bit down, severing Azlar's body in two just below his ribs, and the voice of the Dragon Cult's rising star was stilled forever.

CHAPTER TWENTY-SIX

Fendel moved surprisingly fast for such a small, wrinkled gnome. Lhasha easily matched his pace, her lithe form bounding over the stones in soft, light steps, but Corin fell steadily behind. In part, he was burdened by the swords he carried in each hand. There was something else. He wasn't used to fleeing a battle. It went against all his training, everything he had ever practiced, everything he stood for as a White Shield and a warrior. Part of him resisted his own efforts to escape.

In the short time it took the group to cross the room and reach the arch of the cultists' passage, the warrior was already several paces behind his companions. As Corin entered the magically formed tunnel, soldiers darted past him on either side. He slashed out with his weapons without even thinking, his instincts for killing taking over. He hewed one man down with a single, fatal blow to the back and crippled the other with a hack to the leg, hamstringing the man.

It was only after his opponents fell to the floor that Corin realized they weren't attacking him. They weren't even armed. They had been fleeing the battle, running from whatever it was that had put Fendel to flight.

He passed or was passed by many more fleeing cultists as he ran, and he even noticed a few soldiers he suspected were Xiliath's own men running in terror from the unknown horror back in the treasure chamber. Corin no longer swung his swords at the defenseless men, though the pair of naked blades were still clenched in his grasp. The panic of the other soldiers had finally helped the White Shield realize that the time for killing was over. Escape and survival were his only goals now.

Several hundred yards into the well-lit, perfectly symmetrical tunnel Azlar's magic had formed, Fendel came to a stop, wheezing and bending over to brace his hands on his knees as he struggled to catch a second wind. Lhasha pulled up beside him, her own breath coming in quick, short gasps. A few seconds later, Corin stumbled to a stop just a few feet away, nearly collapsing from the strain of their extended sprint.

Fendel motioned with his hand, urging the other two to clear a path from the center of the passage. Panting, the trio pressed themselves up against a wall, trying to stay out of the way of the small groups of terrified soldiers still streaming past every few seconds. The panicked cultists, intent only on escaping the terror of the main cavern, paid no heed to the three figures huddled off to the side of the passage.

The gnome, despite his age, was the first to recover enough to speak. "We should be safe here. For a while."

From back down the passage the chilling screams of those trapped in the main cavern could still be heard.

"What . . . the Abyss . . . happened?" Corin managed between gulps of air.

"Beholder. Big one. Came up through the trapdoor in the floor and started killing everything in the room. Even turned the medusa into a pile of dust."

"Xiliath?" Corin asked.

Fendel nodded. "That'd be my guess. Probably been hiding out in these tunnels for the last few years, working through front men to keep his existence a secret. We have to get out of here so we can warn the authorities. They won't want him floating around loose under the streets."

"Wait a minute!" Lhasha protested, more than slightly annoyed. "How come you wanted to take care of the medusa yourself, but you're willing to dump the beholder off on someone else? Don't tell me you've got some kind of double standard working here."

"Don't scold me like a child," Fendel replied, without any real malice in his voice. "My actions made perfect sense, if you think about it. A medusa can hide in a crowd. With her hood up, she looks like any ordinary citizen. If I didn't do something about her when I had the chance, the Maces would never have found her until after Yanseldara had been turned into a statue. By then it would have been too late.

"But a beholder won't be sneaking up on anyone. As soon as the city guard finds out what Xiliath really is, they'll have patrols scouring the tunnels to hunt him down."

"Won't the patrols just get slaughtered?" Lhasha countered, a hint of accusation in her words.

"Not if they're properly prepared," Corin interjected, coming to Fendel's defense. "Get a squadron of well-trained soldiers, arm them with crossbows and other ranged weapons, throw in a few battle mages to cast protective magics over them, and the patrol will be able to deal with just about anything. Even an eye tyrant."

Lhasha chewed thoughtfully on her lip for a few seconds. "I guess it makes sense," she reluctantly admitted. Then, after a few seconds she added, "I'm sorry Fendel. I don't know what came over me. I just . . . I didn't mean to snap at you."

The old gnome leaned over and gave her a long, reassuring hug. "Think nothing of it, Lhasha. Anyone who's been through what you have is entitled to be a little out of sorts."

"Besides," he added, giving her a grin and tweaking her small nose to try to cheer her up. "I'll be the first to admit I was running scared. With my glasses to keep me from turning to stone, I knew I could face the medusa. But a beholder's a little more than I can handle. When I saw that thing hovering over the battle, I just wanted to get out before one of those eyes turned in our direction." He concluded with a laugh. "I just got you back, Lhasha. I wasn't about to risk losing you again."

With a shake of her head and a warm smile Lhasha replied, "Oh, Fendel! Always looking out for your poor little girl." She returned his hug with one of her own.

Corin shifted uncomfortably at the sentimental display between Lhasha and her mentor. "We still need to get out of here," he noted, trying to shift the conversation back to their immediate situation. "Hugs won't get us back to the surface."

"Of course, of course," the gnome said hastily, gently pushing Lhasha away. Lhasha gave Corin a sour glare, her eyes chastising him for the embarrassment he had caused the old gnome with his tactless comment. Corin ignored her angry stare.

"Sooner or later," Fendel said, moving on to the topic Corin had not-so-subtly suggested, "this passage has to link up with the original tunnel system. We won't be able to get into the sub-tunnels from up here. I only knew about the one way in. All the other doors connecting to the network below are one way, just like the one back in Xiliath's vault. You can come up from below, but not down from above. We'll have to find our way to the surface through the smugglers' main tunnels."

"You told me traveling those tunnels was suicide," Corin reminded him.

"Virtually suicide," Fendel clarified. "But it's not like we really have a choice, is it?"

From his bag Fendel produced the staff he had used when he and Corin had come through the sub-tunnel. The end still glimmered with a magical glow.

"Lhasha and I will check for traps—you guard our backs. Even if the cultists or Xiliath's men don't decide to try to chase us down, there might be other predators in these caverns tracking us."

They set off, and it didn't take long until Fendel was proved right yet again. "Here," Fendel said, "you can see where the wizard started blasting his own path through the earth."

They had come to a **T** intersection. Unlike the perfectly symmetrical passage they were currently in, both of the branches before them were irregular and uneven, the walls and floor roughly hewn from the surrounding rock.

"So which way do you think the cultists came in from?" Lhasha asked, trying to peer down each direction for some clue.

"I couldn't even begin to guess," Fendel admitted, "but it doesn't really matter. Both ways will lead us back to the surface. Eventually."

"Left," Corin said with sudden certainty.

"How do you know?" Lhasha demanded.

"Just a gut feeling."

With a shrug, Fendel said "Then left it is. Lhasha, stay close and take your time looking for those traps. We've had enough nasty surprises for one night."

Their progress was, if possible, even slower than the pace Fendel and Corin had set through the sub-tunnel. This time, however, Corin wasn't bothered by their overly cautious advance. Lhasha was back with him, for one thing. And he now had some firsthand experience with the potential dangers awaiting the reckless traveler beneath Elversult's streets.

As if to reaffirm Corin's newfound concern for safety, the sounds of far-distant screams could be heard periodically—cultists falling victim to the horrors of the smugglers' labyrinth as they blundered through the tunnels, trying to find their way back to the surface.

The trio encountered numerous side passages and branches on their slow journey. Fendel never hesitated in his choices, though to Corin there seemed to be no rhyme or reason to his decisions. The one-armed warrior could only hope the gnome's sense of direction wasn't as disoriented as his own. Maybe Fendel was drawing on long-buried memories to lead them out. Or maybe he was just guessing.

For his own part, Corin kept casting glances back over his shoulder. He could feel creatures watching them, malevolent eyes in the darkness. The faint whisper of scuttling feet just beyond the illuminated range of Fendel's staff was so frequent Corin had ceased to even notice it.

Whatever was following them, stalking them, was scared enough to keep its distance—for now. However, not all the creatures in the darkness knew such restraint. The bloodcurdling screams of dying soldiers and the feral sounds of monsters feasting on fresh meat could occasionally be heard emanating from far-off corridors. Corin knew few, if any, of those who had escaped Xiliath's wrath would ever see the surface.

Every so often Lhasha or Fendel would hold up a hand in warning, and they would all stop. The two thieves would confer briefly over the trap that had been discovered. If the snare was simple, such as a trip wire, they would disarm it. With some of the devices they used Fendel's walking stick to set them off from a safe distance. For larger traps, such as hidden pits, they would come back and explain to Corin the proper path to take to avoid the danger.

These were the worst for the warrior. He did his best to follow precisely in the exact footsteps of his smaller companions, carefully avoiding stepping on the areas they had identified as pressure triggers, though he could see no distinguishing features on the uneven floor as he crossed.

At these times—his weight awkwardly balanced, his eyes focused on his feet, everything about him vulnerable—Corin could feel the unseen eyes surrounding them move in closer, waiting eagerly for the single misstep that would set off the trap and give the hidden predators their chance to strike. Corin was careful to insure that chance never came.

But Tymora cares little for care or caution.

"There's another trap just ahead," Lhasha explained to her burly friend after yet another lengthy consultation with Fendel. "A real nasty one. A crusher, Fendel thinks. We're pretty sure we've got it figured out, though. Fendel's going first. Once he gets safely to the other side, he'll give us the all clear and I'll lead you across. Until then, we'll wait here. That way, if anything happens to Fendel . . ." She couldn't finish.

Corin nodded to show he understood, though the name "crusher" meant nothing to him, other than conjuring up a series of gruesome mental images of mangled limbs and bodies. The warrior sheathed the sword in his left hand so he could hold the glowing staff Fendel offered him.

"Hang on to this for a minute. I won't need it, and I don't want to leave you here in the dark while I go across."

"Good luck," Corin whispered.

The gnome soon disappeared into the shadows, vanishing as soon as he was beyond the range of the glowing pole. "Is he all right?" Corin asked anxiously after several seconds of agonizing silence.

With the advantage of her heat-sensitive vision, Lhasha could still see Fendel's form in the blackness. "He's just taking his time. He wants to be sure he doesn't hit a trigger. Even one wrong step could be fatal."

They could do nothing but stand and wait. Corin didn't know which was worse: the helpless feeling of sitting idly by while the gnome risked his life to find them a safe route, or the anticipatory dread that came with the knowledge that he, too, would have to cross the trapped area.

A sharp whistle from the blackness signaled that it was time for Lhasha and Corin to cross.

"All right, follow me," Lhasha urged. "Stay close—step only where I step. *Exactly* where I step."

The instructions were the same at every trap they had crossed so far, yet for some reason Lhasha's voice seemed more urgent this time. The pit of Corin's stomach rumbled ominously.

The warrior's fate was in Lhasha's hands now. Or rather, her feet and her eyes. Corin simply had to trust that the half-elf had watched and memorized every careful step Fendel had taken through the trigger area, and he had to assume Lhasha could duplicate that path without error.

Only several months ago, putting his own life so completely into someone else's care would have been unthinkable. If there was anyone he was willing to trust, it was Lhasha.

Ahead of him, the half-elf paused momentarily, uncertain of her next move. Corin glanced back over his shoulder, his attention drawn by the sound of something rushing at them out of the darkness. He didn't dare move his boots from their spot, but he did pivot on the balls of his feet to face the noise, and flexed his knees to brace against a surprise attack from the shadows.

The illumination from the staff's tip couldn't fully pierce the black veil behind them. Whatever was charging at them would remain unseen until the last possible second. Behind him, Corin heard the soft rustle of Lhasha's silks as she continued her path, so intently focused on choosing the safe route that she hadn't noticed Corin was no longer at her hip until they were separated by several yards.

Only then did she turn around to see what was holding up her companion. Even as she was about to ask what was wrong, the creature from the darkness exploded into view.

It was a man, nothing more. One of the soldiers from the battle, bleeding from his many wounds, his eyes glowing with crazy fire. His face was frozen in a rictus of insane fear, his eyes nothing but pupils, dilated to their full size by the man's reckless charge through the pitch-black tunnels.

He didn't even seem to notice Corin, didn't react at all to Lhasha's shouted warnings to stop. He came straight forward, stumbling along, arms flailing wildly as he scrambled to escape whatever unseen demons he imagined still pursued him.

He barreled right into Corin, knocking the warrior off balance, causing the one-armed man to lose his footing. The crazed soldier tripped over Corin's knee, and was sent sprawling across the floor—triggering the trap.

Even Corin's untrained ears could make out the unmistakable sound of gears grinding and high tension steel springs releasing. Corin's reflexes and instinct for survival were the only thing that saved him. He dived forward at the sound, tucked into a ball, and rolled out of harm's way—back down the part of the tunnel they had already come from.

From behind him he heard a booming crash, the sound of thunder or an earthquake. He hopped to his feet and spun around to see the consequences of the trap.

The crusher was aptly named. Two huge chunks of granite had slammed together, sealing the cavern and instantly pulverizing anything that happened to be caught in between the tons of solid rock. A trickle of blood seeped out from the barely visible seam where the two colossal blocks of stone met, and a single foot of the crazed runner jutted out from the side Corin was on, twitching for a brief second before going still and limp.

Lhasha was nowhere to be seen. Corin ran up to the stones, yelling out her name. "Lhasha! Lhasha! Are you all right!"

"I'm all right," she called back, much to his relief. "I'm on the other side. Fendel's here, too. Are you hurt?" Her voice was somewhat muffled by the wall of granite between them.

"No!" Corin yelled back. "I jumped clear. Is there any way to open these things up again?"

For nearly a minute there was no reply—Corin assumed Lhasha and Fendel were examining and discussing the mechanics of the trap, trying to figure out a way to re-open the tunnel.

"Corin?" Fendel called out finally. "There doesn't seem to be any way to move these rocks. Looks like this trap was a one-shot deal."

The gnome paused, giving the warrior a chance to reply, but Corin didn't speak. There wasn't anything to say, really. Fendel filled in the silence soon enough, anyway.

"Do you have some light? You're not stuck back there alone in the dark, are you?"

"No," Corin yelled back. "I've still got your fancy glowing stick here in my hand. I can see all right."

"Good, good," the gnome sounded relieved. "Hang on to that pole. There's things in the dark you don't even want me to tell you about." The gnome took a second to think before continuing. "Just stay where you are. Don't move. The tunnel we're in branches off just ahead, I think one of them might eventually lead us back to you."

There was no point in arguing with the gnome's advice. The granite blocks were impassable, and Corin knew the odds of him finding his own way out were next to nil. Corin suspected that Fendel had an uncanny ability to maintain his sense of direction and perspective, even while trapped in an underground maze.

"It could take us a while to find you," Lhasha called out. "We don't want to set off another trap on the way. Just hang tight and we'll get you in due time. All right, Corin?"

"I'll be here waiting," he replied. A second later he added, "You two be careful."

Either they had already set off and hadn't heard him, or they didn't see any point in wasting time answering back. Whatever the case, Corin's only reply was the echo of his own voice bouncing off the tunnel walls.

He stood Fendel's staff in the crook formed by the tunnel wall and one of the granite stones now blocking his path. The warm glow of the gnome's magic gave Corin enough light to make out his immediate surroundings, but little else.

Ever vigilant for the sounds of an unseen enemy

approaching through the gloom, Corin settled himself down, sitting with his back against one of the granite slabs. Sooner or later, Fendel and Lhasha would find him. There was nothing to do but wait.

CHAPTER TWENTY-SEVEN

Corin was used to waiting. During his time as a White Shield, he had spent more than his share of dark nights guarding caravans or standing watch over an encampment. He was used to doing nothing but sitting and staring, eyes focused only on the impenetrable darkness.

There were tricks a soldier could use to pass the hours on a long watch, ways to relieve the monotony of duty. Corin's favorite was counting heartbeats. It had the advantage of helping him keep track of time as it passed. Sixty beats a minute. Ten minutes passed, twenty. Thirty.

Of course, time was always relative, and in these particular circumstances it was essentially meaningless. It might take Lhasha and Fendel an hour to find an alternate route back to where Corin waited. Or four hours. Or anywhere in between. They would get there when they got there, and tracking every minute wouldn't speed things up.

Still, counting heartbeats gave him something to do, a way to stave off the boredom. At four thousand beats, something happened.

Or rather, something stopped happening. Upon first escaping from the beholder and entering the smugglers' tunnels, Corin had been struck by the oppressive silence, marked only by the far-off sounds of the battle in the vault and punctuated by the occasional distant scream of one who fell victim to the perils of the labyrinth.

But eventually, Corin's ears had begun to pick up faint, half-imagined noises coming from the darkness. The scuttle of beetles scattering before the light, never seen but always there. The scampering of tiny, clawed feet. Rats, subterranean lizards, and other predators were fleeing before the strange intruders in their realm of eternal night.

Once noticed, these ambient sounds were instinctively dismissed, pushed to a subconscious level of awareness within Corin's mind. Suddenly, the sounds stopped, vanishing completely as the unseen creatures in the shadows froze or scurried away to safety through the narrow cracks and fissures in the stone. Corin finally understood what true silence was.

The malevolent eyes that Corin had felt hounding his every step were gone, too. Gripping his swords tightly, Corin rose silently to his feet, moving out from the granite wall behind him. He was unsure what to expect, but he wanted to have room to maneuver.

The silence was soon broken by the sound of someone approaching. The noise was still far off but unmistakable. Deep rasping breaths. Heavy, methodical footsteps. The sharp chink of metal rings sliding across each other with every stride of the armored individual advancing.

No glimmer of light betrayed the progress of the one approaching. The being could see in the dark, Corin realized. Like a half-elf, or gnome, or orog.

When Graal finally emerged, stepping boldly into the light of Fendel's glowing staff, Corin wasn't surprised, and neither was his opponent.

"And so my hunt is over," Graal growled. "We have unfinished business, White Shield."

Corin said nothing, but held his ground.

Graal hesitated. "You no longer fear me." His voice was somewhere between disbelief and mockery.

Corin made no reply. He owed this beast no explanations. The arm gave him a chance—slim though it was—of besting the orog in combat, nothing more, but the mere chance was enough.

The night he lost his hand, Corin's very soul had been rent asunder, his spirit shattered into a million fragments. Alcohol washed away much of his broken self—the fires of hate and revenge consumed even more. Pieces of what he had once been were lost beneath the earth, buried with the bodies of his dead comrades. The fragile bits that remained had been swept away by the hollow winds of a bleak and pointless existence, until there was nothing left but a shell of a once-proud warrior.

But in the past month Corin had been reborn, rising from the ashes of his own destruction. The alcohol was gone, the hateful fires of revenge were quelled. The void left by the corpses in his past had been filled by his friendship with Lhasha. There was purpose in his existence. His life had meaning and value once again.

Corin knew he might die in the dark tunnel, but he would die with the knowledge that his life had not been wasted or given in vain. Lhasha had been saved, and if the price of her salvation was an end to Corin's mortal existence, that was a sacrifice the warrior was prepared to accept.

Misinterpreting the silver-limbed warrior's stoic silence as speechless fear, the orog laughed. "I will enjoy taking your other arm this time, White Shield."

Corin let his enemy come to him, let the beast come well into the light to negate any possible advantage Graal might have in the shadowy tunnel.

The orog rushed forward, trying to gain a strategic

advantage by using his momentum to drive the smaller man back and pin him against the wall. Corin stepped up into the charge, and they met with a clash of blades that rang throughout the caverns.

Corin dodged to the side, using one blade to intercept and deflect Graal's attack while the other thrust forward, looking to catch the orog on its point and use the great beast's own weight and momentum to drive the blade home.

Graal twisted away and leaped nimbly back, showing amazing agility for a creature of his size and bulk. The sword ricocheted off the dark ringed mail covering Graal's torso. The orog was unharmed, but his advance had been blunted.

Corin followed up with a series of quick stabs and cuts at his foe's chest, forcing the orog to sidestep and spin away from the blows, turning Graal so that his back was to the wall Corin had been against only moments before.

Corin's blades flickered in and out, each swinging on a different trajectory and striking from a different angle. He went after his enemy's legs now, looking to slice open the few inches of unprotected flesh below the hem of the black, iron kilt and above the orog's heavy leather boots.

Graal stumbled back, momentarily overwhelmed by the unfamiliar dual-bladed attack. The creature parried desperately with his own heavy weapon, somehow managing to smack down each strike with the flat of the dark blade. He was unable to keep Corin off him, unable to drive the undersized warrior back or slow his furious assault.

The orog's retreat stopped only when the beast's back touched the hard stone of the granite blocks behind him. Graal pushed off from the wall, using it for leverage as he swung his knee up, catching the Corin in the gut and doubling him over. Corin dropped to the ground and rolled away, springing to his feet.

Graal had not pressed his advantage. The orog was hesitant, Corin realized. Uncertain. The knowledge fuelled Corin's confidence.

The two combatants circled slowly, each trying to work the other into a position of disadvantage against the walls. One would advance, and the other would momentarily retreat. But just as quickly, the tide would then shift, and the aggressor would be forced back, dancing away from the counterthrusts of his foe.

With each round of give and take the warriors inflicted small wounds on each other. Dozens of small nicks and cuts on Corin's arms and body—an inevitable result of any battle—began to bleed. In and of themselves, none of the wounds was fatal, but they gradually sapped Corin's strength, slowing him down. Even as Corin became more fatigued he could feel his opponent getting stronger, the dark necromancy of Graal's foul blade drawing sustenance from Corin's wounds.

The longer the battle raged, Corin realized, the greater his opponent's advantage would become. If he couldn't finish the orog off soon, he would surely die in the darkness of the smugglers' tunnels. The one-armed warrior launched a reckless, all-out assault against his foe, determined to bring a quick end to the confrontation—one way or another.

The sword in Corin's left hand arced down, a desperate blow designed to kill, or at least throw his already stumbling opponent off balance. The orog parried, the edge of his enormous black sword catching the flat of Corin's own blade at an angle more precise than a jeweler cutting a diamond—and Corin's sword shattered.

The shock of the vibration ran down the length of the weapon, through the blade and into Corin's hand. His hand tingled, his fingers became numb. The useless hilt slipped from his grasp and clattered on the floor to lie beside the shards and slivers of tempered steel littering the ground.

The orog seized the moment and brought his own blade in hard, aiming for Corin's unprotected left side. Corin had to reach across his body with the weapon held in his metallic right arm to parry the blow, but he didn't have the leverage to fully turn the course of Graal's fierce attack.

Corin partially deflected the orog's dark blade. It bit into Corin's hip, buckling the one-armed man's leg and dropping him to a knee. A second blow came in from overhead, a wicked two-handed chop straight down. Unable to brace for the force of the attack, Corin threw his own blade up in desperation, parallel to the ground and perpendicular to the course of Graal's weapon.

Graal's sword was halted in mid-arc but the strength of the orog's blow slapped Corin's remaining sword out of his metal hand to clatter on the ground. Without pausing, the orog raised his blade for the killing blow and brought it down again on his weaponless opponent. Corin threw his right arm up over his face in a vain effort to protect himself.

The dark blade sliced down in a mere blur, powered by the fury of the orog's bloodlust. Yet for Corin, all was still. The black sword hung motionless in the air. The White Shield could see the individual etchings on the surface of the foul weapon, shimmering with an obsidian glow. The deadly arc of Graal's weapon would lop off his prosthetic arm. The blade would continue unabated, slicing through Corin's shoulder and diagonally across his torso—a sure kill.

But to Corin's awareness, time had stopped. Frozen in the moment with the dark blade hovering inches above him, the warrior's mind flashed back to a night three years ago—the night of Igland's death, the night the White Shields were betrayed, the night Corin lost his hand.

The surrounding light and shadows of the cavern dissolved into the black of a storm-filled night. The far-off cries of doomed men in distant corridors and the faint scuffling of the unseen denizens of the tunnels became the sounds of his fellow White Shields battling Graal's companions. The warm blood soaking Corin's clothes and covering his face became the cold, viscous mud of the Trader Road mixing with the pelting raindrops of the raging tempest above. Corin felt his knees sink into the ground beneath him, as if it were soft earth rather than unyielding stone.

His world had come full circle, back to where he was two years ago. Helpless once again beneath the savagery of Graal's dismembering blade.

But this time something was different. He could no longer hear the screams of his comrades dying around him. There was only silence, and knowledge came to Corin.

His companions were alive.

Unlike Igland, Lhasha and Fendel would survive this night—even if Corin did not.

The storm vanished, replaced by the surroundings of the smugglers' tunnels once again. The sinister blade still hung frozen above the gleaming silver of Corin's prosthetic arm, poised to continue on its lethal path.

This time Corin was unafraid.

The eternal moment was over, and Graal's blade came down upon Corin's arm. The forged metal of the enchanted blade struck the metal alloy of the prosthetic—and Graal's blade erupted! Corin was blinded by an explosion of darkness, disintegrating into a shadowy cloud of dust that covered both men like a venomous mist. Each jet black piece of Graal's evil sword now oozed swirling magical vapors. The smoky tendrils swam toward each other in a gathering tornado of power that had been unleashed from the broken blade. The tornado whirled in a frenzy until Corin could no longer follow the motion with his eyes. Then nothing.

The following explosion hurled Corin back, slamming his body hard against the floor. The spot where Graal had delivered what should have been a death blow was now a smoking crater. Huge chunks of irregular stone littered the corridor, torn loose from the walls and floor by the concussive force.

Corin struggled slowly to his feet, only partially aware that his prosthetic was undamaged by the blow. The dark cloud of dust from Graal's blade made it difficult for Corin to see and almost impossible to breathe. His ears still rang with the echo of the catastrophic explosion reverberating throughout the labyrinth.

Graal lay on the floor near the epicenter of the blast, his body jammed up against the stones of the crusher trap. A crack in the rock and a bloody smear marked the spot where the orog's massive form had been slammed against the granite blocks. Graal lay motionless, the hilt of his now vaporized blade still clutched in one mighty paw, blood trickling from his lip like drool.

A sprinkle of dust and pebbles from the ceiling above wafted down on the orog's unconscious form, drawing Corin's attention upward. The explosion had ripped the tunnel roof apart above the sight of the blast. Huge cracks snaked their way along the ceiling, spreading outward like a spider web woven into the rock.

Too injured and weak to stand, Corin began to crawl back down the tunnel, away from the unstable ceiling. Small bits of debris rained down on the back of his head, and when he glanced up he noticed the entire structure quivering as if it would collapse at any moment. As he inched ever closer toward safety, Corin couldn't help casting continual glances back over his shoulder at Graal.

The orog still lay on the ground, though his body was twitching slightly now.

From head to toe, Corin was coated in the noxious cloud of black dust expelled when Graal's blade had exploded. He breathed it in through his lungs, it seeped in through his pores. He felt it congealing in his blood, and leeching into his bones. Poison, disease, death—the taint of pure evil—swallowing him whole.

He tried to will himself forward, but his body refused to answer. With his last ounce of strength, he rolled onto his side to look back down the tunnel at Graal once more.

The orog struggled to his knees. The beast shook his mighty head and dropped the now useless hilt of his once-fearsome blade to the floor. Graal's head moved slowly from side to side as he scanned the rubble until his gaze came to rest on Corin's prone form lying nearly fifty feet away.

The orog let out a roar that Corin's still deafened ears couldn't hear and took a single step toward his helpless foe.

Corin watched an avalanche of rock and earth bury Graal as the tunnel caved in above his head. Corin's ears popped as the air around the two was driven down the narrow corridor, instantly displaced by tons of stone. A cloud of dust and dirt billowed up from the spot of the cave-in. It crawled across the floor, enveloping Corin.

Corin knew no more.

Lhasha and Fendel found him later, spread unconscious not twenty feet from where the ceiling had inexplicably collapsed, covered in a sticky mess of dirt, dust, and blood.

CHAPTER TWENTY-EIGHT

Fendel resisted the urge to glance back as the door to the bedroom built onto the back of his workshop closed behind him. He knew the scene well enough already.

Corin rested fitfully beneath the blankets bundled tightly around his shivering body. His head rocked constantly from side to side, the beads of perspiration on his brow reflecting the single candle burning at the side of his sick bed. Occasional spasms caused his arms to twitch and his legs to thrash, kicking the covers onto the floor.

Each time this happened, Lhasha would silently pick the tangled sheets up from the bed, and gently tuck them around Corin's body. Otherwise, the half-elf kept a silent vigil at his bedside, slumped forward in a chair by the bed, her elbows on her knees and her head resting in her hands as she fought to stay awake so she could watch over Corin.

Fendel knew she was exhausted. He was too. Neither of them had rested since they had found the unconscious man in the tunnels only yards clear of where the tunnel had collapsed.

Somehow they had managed to get Corin's unconscious form back to Gond's temple. But any faint hopes either Fendel or Lhasha might have harbored for their friend's quick salvation had been dashed immediately by the High Artificer. He had placed his hands on Corin's brow, then withdrawn them hastily, his nose crinkling in revulsion.

"The stench of death is on him, a curse so evil it burns at my touch," Elversult's ranking cleric of Gond had declared. "I am truly sorry, but I do not have the power to free him from its grasp."

With that, Lhasha had collapsed into the chair Fendel had brought into the room. She shed no tears, said no words. There was no point in crying or speaking. She was beaten, devastated. With no hope, she merely sat down to be with her friend when he finally succumbed, trying simply to make his last hours as comfortable as possible.

That was how Fendel left her. He gave her no explanation as he slipped away. There was no point in giving her false hope. He doubted she would even notice his absence, for the time being. There was one other place the gnome could go for help, an authority higher than the Artificer. Someone who might, just possibly, have the power to save Corin. But the gnome had no idea if she would even deign to hear the plea of a simple cleric of Gond.

Fendel weaved his way through the streets of Elversult, the early morning sun casting the shadow of Temple Hill across the sprawling city. The Churches of Lathander and Waukeen reflected the light of the dawn, shining like radiant beacons atop the mount.

The gnome turned his back on them and continued on his way. There was no help to be found there. The House of Coins was nothing more than a shrine to a dead god. They had no power to save Corin.

The Tower of the Morn seemingly offered some promise, but Corin's bitter experiences in the past with Lathander's church merely confirmed what the gnome would have suspected anyway. The Dawnbringer's priests were healers, but they had little experience with the foul, sinister magic that had infected the one-armed man.

Fendel knew there were those who had fought against such dark sorcery for generations, those who had spent centuries defending Faerûn against necromancy and similar evils.

The Harpers. They alone might be able to offer some remedy for Corin's affliction.

"You better make this quick," Vaerana Hawklyn snarled. "Just because I agreed to see you doesn't mean I'm in a good mood."

"Surely you weren't still sleeping?" Fendel replied, his tone mocking.

"I haven't slept a wink in nearly two days!" She seemed generally offended by the suggestion. "Something big is going down with the Cult of the Dragon, and our agents haven't been able to find out a thing! I don't have time to sit and chat with old friends who'd rather spend their days tinkering with foolish gadgets than serving the cause of justice. We haven't all retired, you know."

"This isn't a social call," Fendel snapped back. The brash ranger always brought out the worst in him—just one of the reasons he had left the life of a Harper behind, deciding instead to retreat to the peaceful confines of Gond's church and raise a young, orphaned half-elf. "This concerns the Cult of the Dragon."

Suddenly, he had Vaerana's full attention. "Well, don't keep me in suspense," she said, her voice slightly more civil than before.

Fendel hesitated, then took a deep breath. "You won't believe this . . ." He recounted the events of the past few days in detail—the Cult of the Dragon plot, the death of Azlar and the medusa, the existence of Xiliath the beholder.

The leader of the Elversult Maces didn't say anything, but the look on her face was one of obvious skepticism and disbelief.

"I wasn't working alone," the gnome explained. "I had some help. Lhasha, for one."

"That orphaned half-breed?" the ranger laughed. "She had a hand in this?"

Fendel cast Vaerana a sour look. "There's more to Lhasha than meets the eye. And she had a friend with her. Corin."

"The one-armed thug who nearly caused a riot in the Fair," Vaerana said. Seeing the surprise on Fendel's face, she added, "Did you really think I didn't know about that? I knew he'd gone to see you, and I figured you'd straighten him out. That's the only reason he wasn't arrested."

"Well . . . thanks, I guess."

"Don't say I didn't do you any favors," Vaerana replied before adding thoughtfully, "It's a good thing all our enemies hate each other at least as much as they hate us. Half the time I think that if the Harpers disappeared for a few years, everyone we're fighting against would just wipe each other out. Then we could *all* have the luxury of retiring to pursue our hobbies."

Fendel ignored the verbal jab. "You still need to deal with Xiliath," he reminded the Lady Protector of Elversult. "His power base is gone, but the eye tyrant's still floating around in those tunnels somewhere."

"I'll get some patrols together to go hunt the beholder down. Or at least drive him out of Elversult," Vaerana assured him. "I appreciate everything you've done Fendel. It's too bad your Harper pin's collecting dust somewhere in a drawer. You really knew how to play the game."

The gnome blushed slightly at the compliment. Any praise from the ever-demanding Vaerana Hawklyn was high praise indeed. But he still hadn't come to the real reason for his visit.

Noticing the wrinkled man had made no move to leave, Vaerana sighed. "Something else, gnome?"

"The Purple Masks. They've got a death sentence out on Lhasha. I know you've got Harpers high enough up in the guild to get it rescinded."

"We're not about to risk years of working our agents into positions of power just to protect one poor orphan girl!" Vaerana protested. "Sometimes sacrifices have to be made for the greater good."

"C'mon, Vaerana. Be reasonable. Don't you owe her something after all this?"

The ranger considered his words for a few seconds before nodding. "All right, you win. The Harpers are always good to those who serve the cause—whether willingly or not."

"There's something else. The one-armed warrior, Corin. He's hurt. Or sick. He's wasting away. I doubt he'll live until tomorrow."

"So get one of your Gond buddies to help him. That's what you clerics do, isn't it?"

"This isn't some ordinary wound. It's . . . I don't know what it is, but even the High Artificer can't help him."

"What makes you think the Harpers can help?" Seeing the look Fendel gave her, Vaerana relented. "Fine. I'll see what we can do. But I'm not making any promises."

Lhasha was still sitting in the chair by Corin's bedside. Her muscles were so stiff and sore, she had given up trying to find a comfortable position. So she sat motionless, helplessly waiting for her friend to die.

Fendel had left several hours ago and had not returned. The half-elf imagined he was praying to Gond for guidance, or possibly respecting her privacy in the final hours she would share with Corin.

The end was close now. Lhasha could see his condition rapidly deteriorating. His body no longer lay still but thrashed about in the throes of violent and unrelenting seizures. His head snapped from side to side with such force that acrid beads of perspiration flew from his fevered brow. Between clenched teeth he muttered and groaned incessantly, nonsensical babbling frequently punctuated by wracking coughing fits.

Despite Corin's suffering and her own discomfort, Lhasha found it a struggle to keep her eyes open. She had long since given up on her efforts to keep the covers over her friend's shivering body; as soon as she put them on, he would kick them off. She was too tired to continue the pointless effort of bending down to retrieve them. Her exhaustion was fighting a pitched battle against her concern for her friend, and at long last her exhaustion was winning. Lhasha felt her eyelids closing, but she could do nothing to resist.

She was awakened from her fitful doze by the feel of a cold blade pressed against her throat. The unseen assassin leaned in close to whisper in her ear. Lhasha tensed in her chair, her eyes scanning the room for Fendel. The gnome was still nowhere to be found.

"The Purple Masks hold your life in their hands now, half-elf," the voice hissed. Lhasha braced for the expected sensation of the razor-sharp blade slicing across her throat, but the assassin's blade never moved.

"You have dealt a serious blow to the Dragon Cult," her assailant continued. "By exposing the eye tyrant, a potential rival of the guild is no longer a threat. The

Masks are grateful for your aid, whether intentional or not. For that, we shall let you live."

Lhasha's breath came out in a rush. She hadn't even been aware she was holding it. The knife was still jammed against her throat.

"Don't make the mistake of thinking we have gone soft," the voice warned. "Your life is spared, but you are out of the burglary business. Retired. Permanently. Perform even one job in Elversult and your life is forfeit once again."

The blade was pressed harder against her throat, drawing a single drop of blood.

"Do you understand, my pretty little ex-thief?"

She nodded with a barely perceptible tilt of her head, afraid of giving a more visible response lest her own movements drive the cold steel deeper into her skin.

"Count to ten before turning around," the voice warned. "Speak of this to no one."

The knife blade was gone. Lhasha was not so stupid as to jump up and try to catch a glimpse of the unknown messenger. She stayed motionless in the chair, counting slowly to ten before rising to her feet and walking over to lock the door.

Her heart was pounding, her hand shaking as she fumbled with the latch. Every fiber tingled with nervous adrenaline; she was conscious of even the slightest sound. Even so, she didn't notice the two robed figures—one man, and one woman—who materialized magically behind her, stepping into the room through a shimmering door in the very fabric of space itself.

The female waved a hand, and Lhasha collapsed to the floor instantly, snoring softly.

The male stepped over to the bed, and began to examine Corin. "We can do nothing about his missing limb. The wound is too old. The curse has settled in too deeply."

"But can we save him?" the female asked.

Her companion nodded, and they each drew a small powder case from their belts. The male's case was bright red, like the fine particles inside. The female's was a dark green. They sprinkled the dust over Corin's writhing form, chanting softly as they did so.

When Lhasha came to, the intruders were gone. She wasn't even aware they had been there at all. She ran to Corin's bedside to make sure he was all right. For the first time since they brought him to the workshop, Corin was sleeping peacefully.

CHAPTER TWENTY-NINE

Fendel paused at the door of the Glowing Staff's tavern, his eyes seeking out his friends. He saw them sitting at a table in the corner, his eye caught by the bright turquoise of Lhasha's blouse, and the aquamarine sash thrown over her shoulder. Corin was dressed far more conservatively, wearing a simple gray woolen shirt. In the warrior's left hand he held a quill, and a parchment was spread out before him.

Sitting across from Lhasha and Corin was a young man. A sword was propped up against the side of his chair. Fendel stepped in through the door but didn't approach right away. He had no wish to interrupt. After a few minutes, the man rose to his feet and left, giving the gnome a nod as he went by.

"Fendel," Lhasha exclaimed, finally noticing the old gnome standing by the door and waving him over. "Come have a seat!"

The old gnome sauntered over and sat down with a smile.

Corin lifted his cup to his lips with his metal hand and drained the contents. "Just water," he explained, noticing the gnome watching him with interest.

"It's not that," Fendel laughed, slightly

embarrassed at being caught staring. "I was just impressed with how well you've learned to use your prosthetic."

Corin nodded. "It's been nearly two months," he said, then paused and glanced down at the floor. A second later he continued without looking up, his voice hesitant and uncertain. "I have to tell you something, Fendel. Something I should have said a long time ago."

The warrior's voice was soft, almost uncertain as he continued. "You've done a great thing for me, Fendel. This arm . . . you have no idea how much it means to me. What you've done for me. I just . . ."

Corin trailed off in embarrassment. "I'm not much for words, Fendel."

The kindly gnome interrupted softly. "I understand, Corin. You don't have to say anything."

"No. That's not good enough," Corin said, shaking his head while still staring at the floor. "It needs to be said. I just wish I knew how to say it better."

He glanced up, staring intently into Fendel's eyes. With his good hand he reached out and took a firm grip on the gnome's arm, giving it a heartfelt squeeze.

"Thank you, Fendel. Truly. Thank you."

The gnome nodded and patted the soldier on his burly shoulder. "You're welcome."

For a brief moment, just before Corin released his grip on the gnome's arm, Fendel actually saw the warrior smile.

To dispel the awkward silence that followed, Fendel changed topics. "So business is good, I take it? The newly resurrected White Shield Company is doing well?"

Lhasha flashed her mentor a wide grin. "I'm making more money guarding people's valuables than I ever did stealing them!"

"We're expanding again," Corin added, his voice

returning to its usual self-assured timbre. "We're hiring two more recruits. That makes over a dozen, now."

"That young fellow you just interviewed one of your prospects?" the gnome asked.

Corin shrugged noncommittally, but Lhasha burst in before he could speak. "He's got my vote!" She fanned herself with her hand for effect. "Did you see his gorgeous eyes?"

Her business partner grunted. "Takes more than pretty looks to make a good guard."

Lhasha patted his arm. "I know that. But it doesn't hurt if they're pleasing to the eye. What about that girl from Waterdeep you hired?"

"She's a mercenary with five years' experience," Corin protested.

"And legs up to her eyebrows," Lhasha countered with a laugh. "I've seen the way she looks at you, Corin. You should take her, uh . . . under your wing."

Fendel pushed his chair away and stood up, chuckling to himself. "I see you're busy right now. Stop by my workshop later today if you have some free time. You're always welcome at the House of Hands. That goes for you too, Corin."

"Oh, don't go yet," Lhasha pleaded. "Sit down and have a drink. We're rich enough to take a few minutes off for our friends."

"No, I should get going," Fendel explained. "I need to pick up some supplies for the church. We've got a big project in the works, truly awe inspiring. I'll show you the blueprints when you stop by. I just wanted to see how things were going."

"Better than I ever dreamed," Lhasha assured him. "It's amazing how much business we're bringing in! My reputation as Elversult's most successful thief is drawing clients so fast we can't keep up with the demand."

Corin snorted. "You don't suppose the referrals have anything to do with my old White Shield reputation and connections?"

"Don't be foolish," Lhasha chided. "Everyone knows that if you want to keep your valuables safe from thieves, you have to hire a thief to guard them. Know thy enemy, know thy self."

"I don't think that's how the saying was intended," Corin replied.

The gnome shook his head and, with a wave, left the pair to their squabble. He knew the real explanation behind the phenomenally quick success of the reborn White Shields. It wasn't Lhasha's reputation as a thief or Corin's connections from his White Shield days.

When Fendel had learned of their plans to start up a mercenary outfit, he had called in the last of his favors with his old friends. A few key referrals from some rather influential figures on the Elversult political scene—recommending the reborn White Shield Company for discreet, professional protection—was all it had taken to get the gears turning.

Once the word was out, the prospective clients had beaten a path to Corin and Lhasha's door. Or rather, they had beaten a path to the Glowing Staff, where the White Shields were currently operating. Obviously, any mercenary group endorsed by the Lady Constable of Elversult herself was going to do all right.

FORGOTTEN REALMS®

DRIZZT RETURNS

For the first time since *The Silent Blade*, Wulfgar and Drizzt cross paths again–but has Wulfgar's long road to redemption brought him too far from his past to ever really go home? Before either the barbarian or the dark elf can answer that question, there's a hammer to recover, a hammer that's been stolen away on a pirate ship that sails the Sea of Swords.

Sea of Swords

The latest novel by *New York Times* bestselling author

R.A. Salvatore

October 2001

And now available in paperback!

Servant of the Shard

R.A. Salvatore

The evil drow Jarlaxle and the cunning assassin Artemis Entreri come to grips with the devilish power of the Crystal Shard . . . and neither will be the same again.

July 2001